Disney

TREASURE ISLAND

STARRING
MICKEY MOUSE

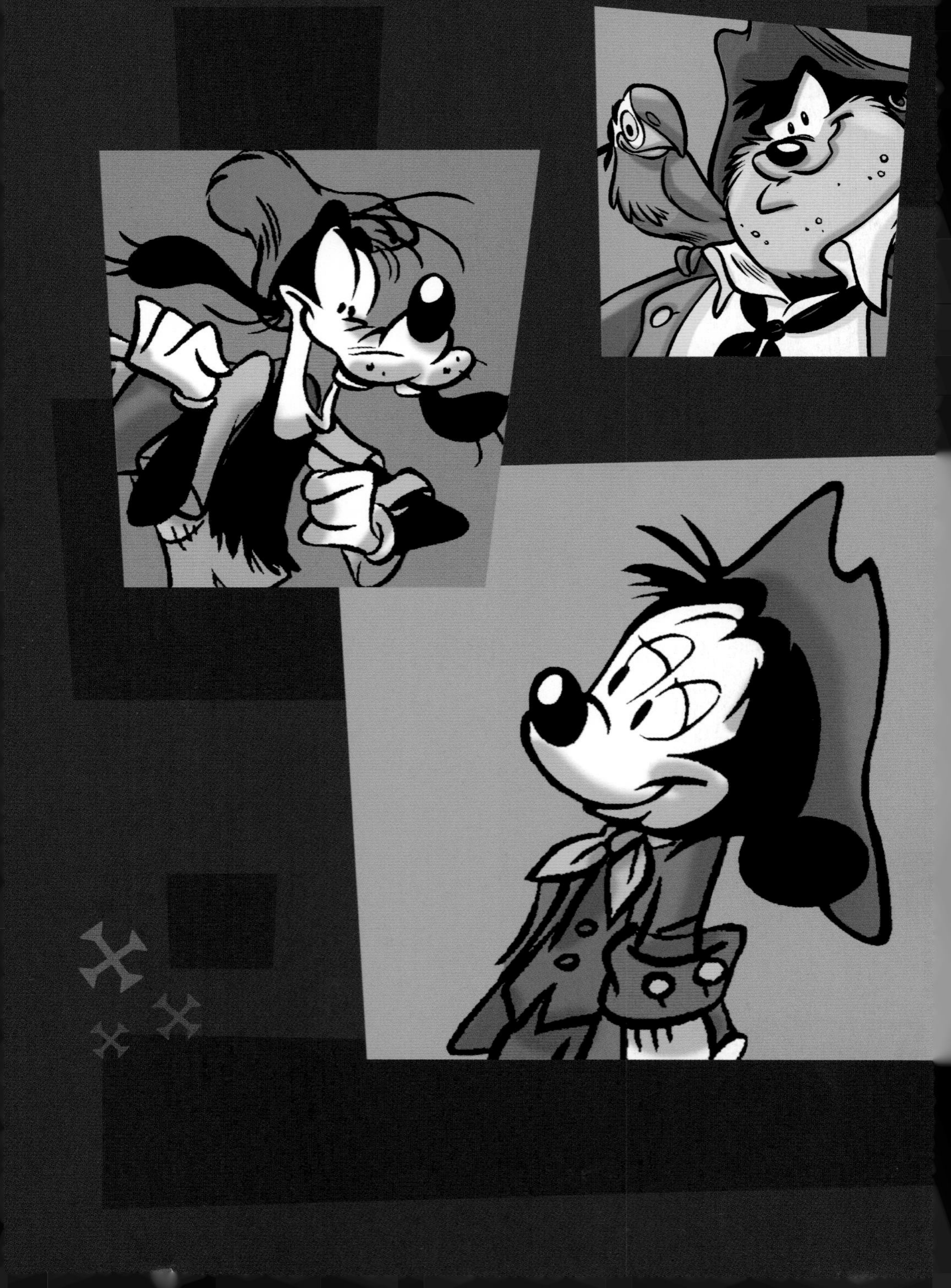

DISNEY

TREASURE ISLAND

STARRING
MICKEY MOUSE

Script by .... **TERESA RADICE**

Art by .... **STEFANO TURCONI**

English Translation by .... **ERIN BRADY**

Lettering by .... **RICHARD STARKINGS**
and **COMICRAFT'S JIMMY BETANCOURT**

Based on the classic novel by
ROBERT LOUIS STEVENSON

DARK HORSE BOOKS

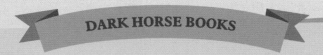

DARK HORSE BOOKS

President and Publisher . . . . MIKE RICHARDSON

Collection Editor . . . . FREDDYE MILLER

Collection Assistant Editor . . . . JUDY KHUU

English Translation Copy Editor . . . . ANNIE GULLION

Designer . . . . CINDY CACEREZ-SPRAGUE

Digital Art Technician . . . . SAMANTHA HUMMER

Special thanks to Sanjay Dharawat, Konner Knudsen,
and Justin Knipper at Dark Horse Comics.

NEIL HANKERSON Executive Vice President • TOM WEDDLE Chief Financial Officer • RANDY
STRADLEY Vice President of Publishing • NICK McWHORTER Chief Business Development Officer •
MATT PARKINSON Vice President of Marketing • DALE LaFOUNTAIN Vice President of Information
Technology • CARA NIECE Vice President of Production and Scheduling • MARK BERNARDI Vice
President of Book Trade and Digital Sales • KEN LIZZI General Counsel • DAVE MARSHALL Editor in
Chief • DAVEY ESTRADA Editorial Director • CHRIS WARNER Senior Books Editor • CARY GRAZZINI
Director of Specialty Projects • LIA RIBACCHI Art Director • VANESSA TODD-HOLMES Director of
Print Purchasing • MATT DRYER Director of Digital Art and Prepress • MICHAEL GOMBOS Director of
International Publishing and Licensing • KARI YADRO Director of Custom Programs

DISNEY PUBLISHING WORLDWIDE GLOBAL MAGAZINES, COMICS AND PARTWORKS

PUBLISHER Lynn Waggoner • EDITORIAL TEAM Bianca Coletti (Director, Magazines), Guido Frazzini (Director,
Comics), Carlotta Quattrocolo (Executive Editor), Stefano Ambrosio (Executive Editor, New IP), Camilla Vedove (Senior
Manager, Editorial Development), Behnoosh Khalili (Senior Editor), Julie Dorris (Senior Editor), Mina Riazi (Assistant
Editor), Jonathan Manning (Assistant Editor) • DESIGN Enrico Soave (Senior Designer) • ART Ken Shue (VP, Global
Art), Manny Mederos (Senior Illustration Manager, Comics and Magazines), Roberto Santillo (Creative Director), Marco
Ghiglione (Creative Manager), Stefano Attardi (Computer Art Designer) • PORTFOLIO MANAGEMENT Olivia Ciancarelli
(Director) • BUSINESS & MARKETING Mariantonietta Galla (Marketing Manager), Virpi Korhonen (Editorial Manager)

Published by Dark Horse Books
A division of Dark Horse Comics, Inc.
10956 SE Main Street
Milwaukie, OR 97222

DarkHorse.com
To find a comics shop in your area,
visit comicshoplocator.com

First edition: October 2018
ISBN 978-1-50671-158-4

Digital edition
ISBN 978-1-50671-160-7

1 3 5 7 9 10 8 6 4 2
Printed in China

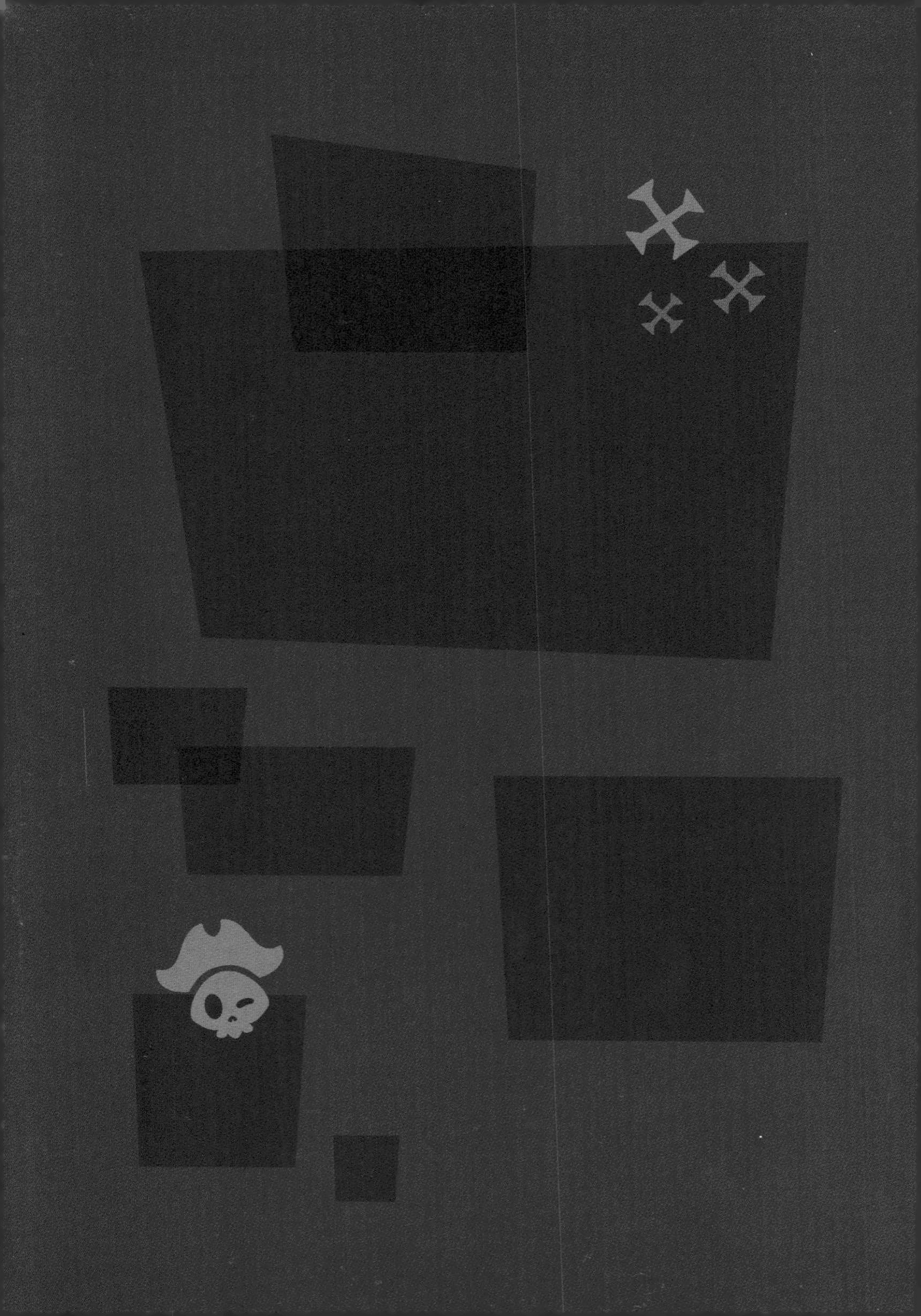

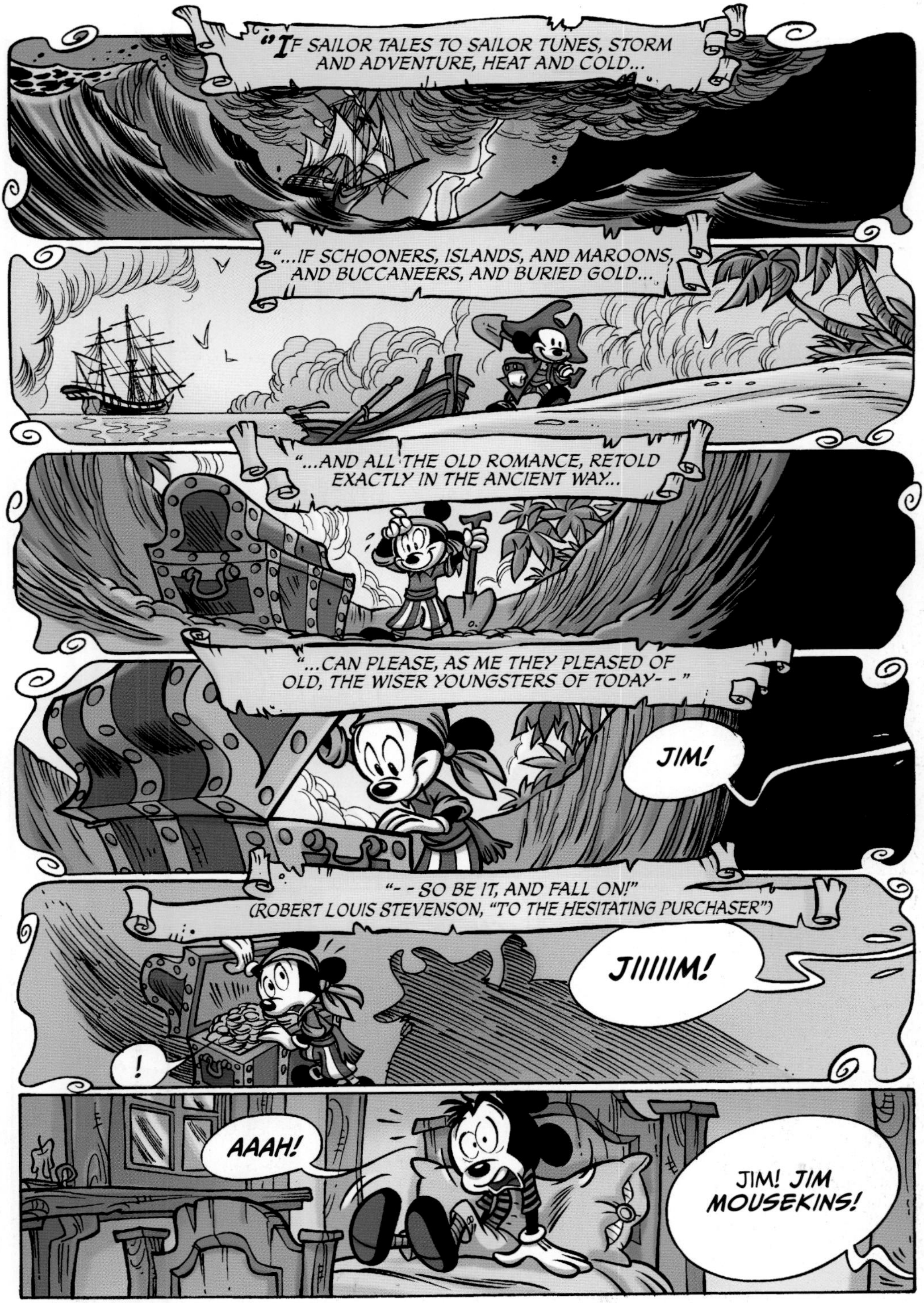
"IF SAILOR TALES TO SAILOR TUNES, STORM AND ADVENTURE, HEAT AND COLD...
"...IF SCHOONERS, ISLANDS, AND MAROONS, AND BUCCANEERS, AND BURIED GOLD...
"...AND ALL THE OLD ROMANCE, RETOLD EXACTLY IN THE ANCIENT WAY...
"...CAN PLEASE, AS ME THEY PLEASED OF OLD, THE WISER YOUNGSTERS OF TODAY- - "
JIM!
"- - SO BE IT, AND FALL ON!" (ROBERT LOUIS STEVENSON, "TO THE HESITATING PURCHASER")
JIIIIIM!
!
AAAH!
JIM! JIM MOUSEKINS!

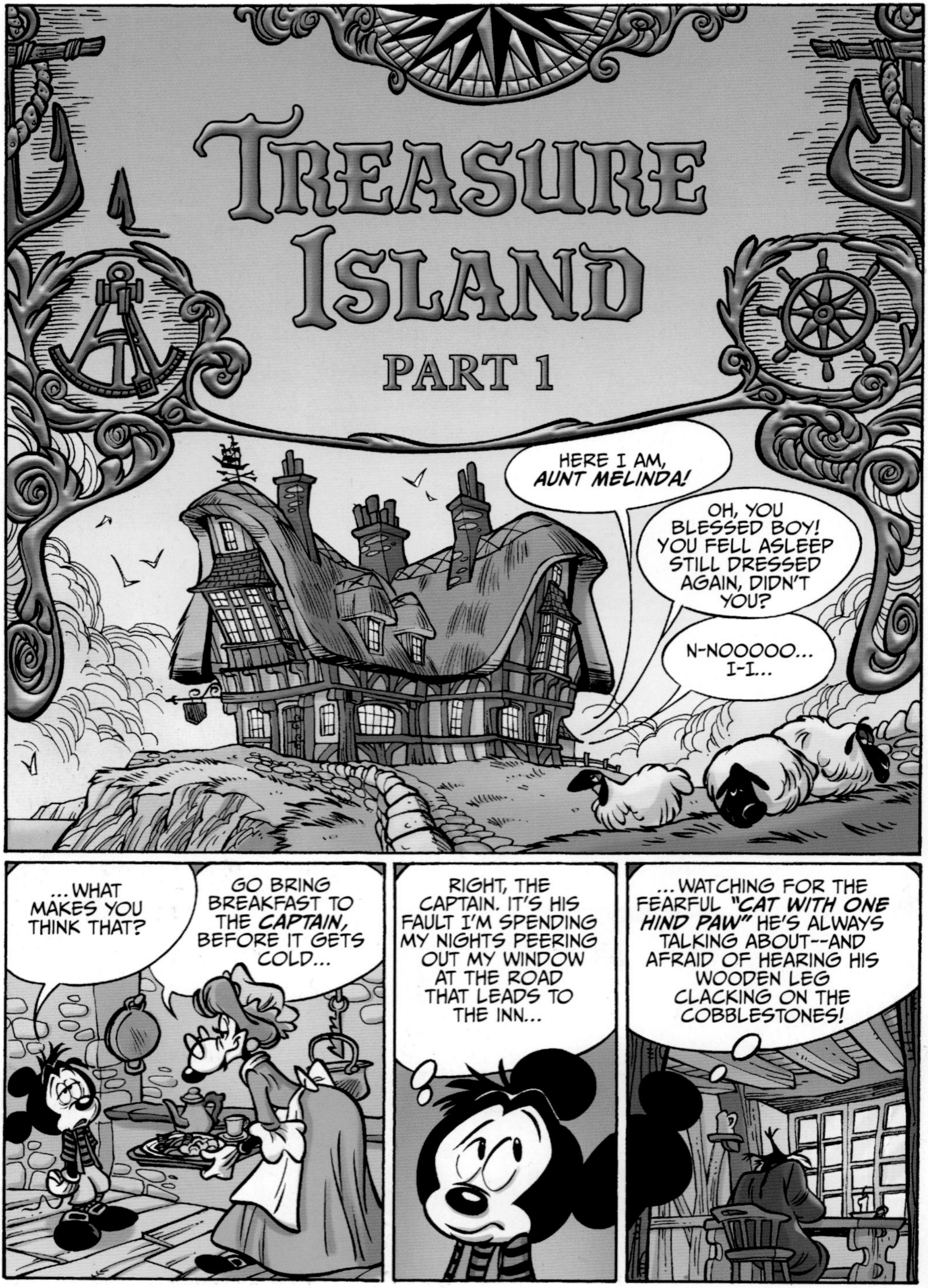
TREASURE ISLAND
PART 1
HERE I AM, AUNT MELINDA!
OH, YOU BLESSED BOY! YOU FELL ASLEEP STILL DRESSED AGAIN, DIDN'T YOU?
N-NOOOOO... I-I...
...WHAT MAKES YOU THINK THAT?
GO BRING BREAKFAST TO THE CAPTAIN, BEFORE IT GETS COLD...
RIGHT, THE CAPTAIN. IT'S HIS FAULT I'M SPENDING MY NIGHTS PEERING OUT MY WINDOW AT THE ROAD THAT LEADS TO THE INN...
...WATCHING FOR THE FEARFUL "CAT WITH ONE HIND PAW" HE'S ALWAYS TALKING ABOUT--AND AFRAID OF HEARING HIS WOODEN LEG CLACKING ON THE COBBLESTONES!

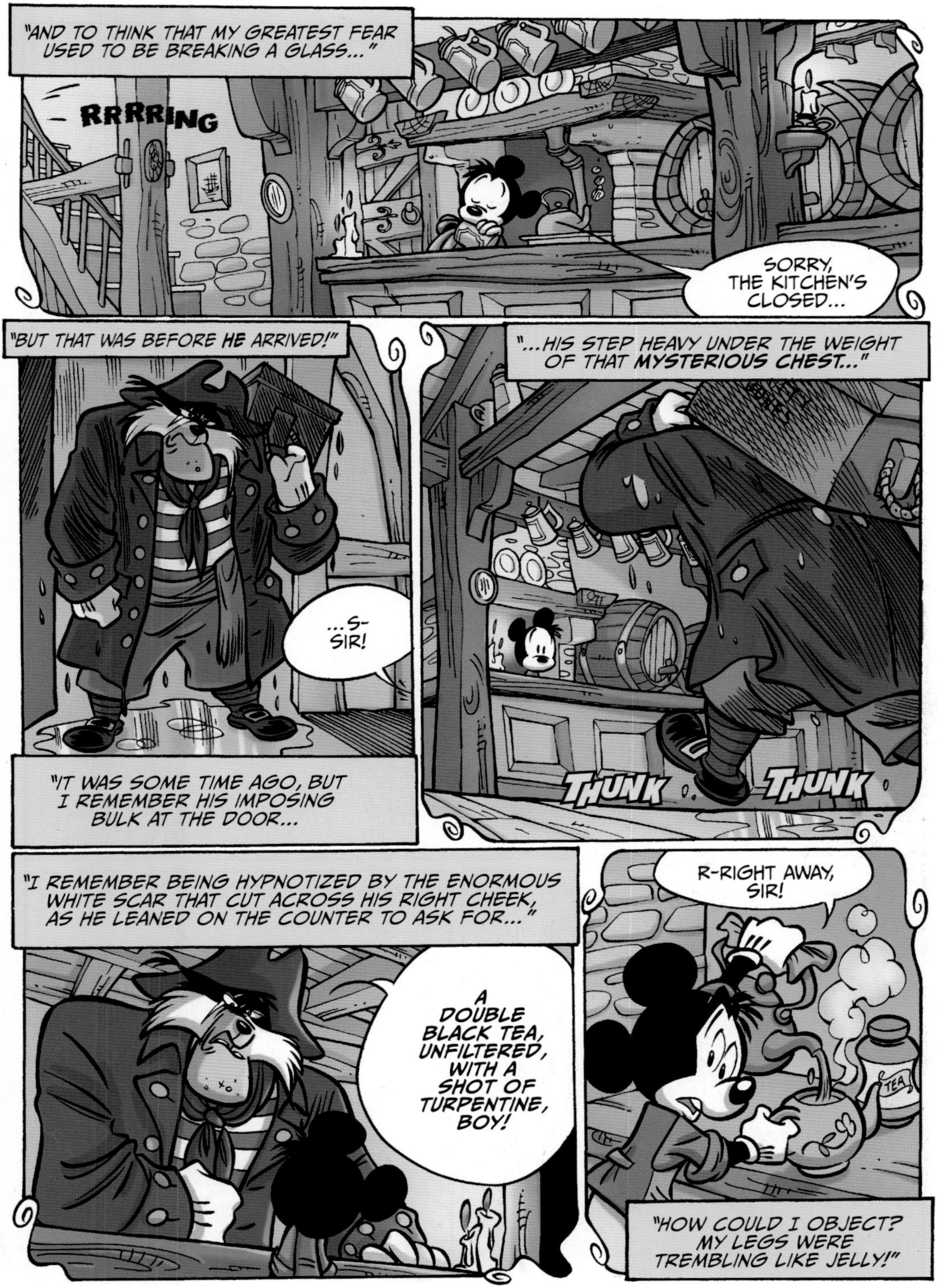
"AND TO THINK THAT MY GREATEST FEAR USED TO BE BREAKING A GLASS..."
RRRRING
SORRY, THE KITCHEN'S CLOSED...
"BUT THAT WAS BEFORE HE ARRIVED!"
...S-SIR!
"IT WAS SOME TIME AGO, BUT I REMEMBER HIS IMPOSING BULK AT THE DOOR...
"...HIS STEP HEAVY UNDER THE WEIGHT OF THAT MYSTERIOUS CHEST..."
THUNK
THUNK
"I REMEMBER BEING HYPNOTIZED BY THE ENORMOUS WHITE SCAR THAT CUT ACROSS HIS RIGHT CHEEK, AS HE LEANED ON THE COUNTER TO ASK FOR..."
A DOUBLE BLACK TEA, UNFILTERED, WITH A SHOT OF TURPENTINE, BOY!
R-RIGHT AWAY, SIR!
TEA
"HOW COULD I OBJECT? MY LEGS WERE TREMBLING LIKE JELLY!"

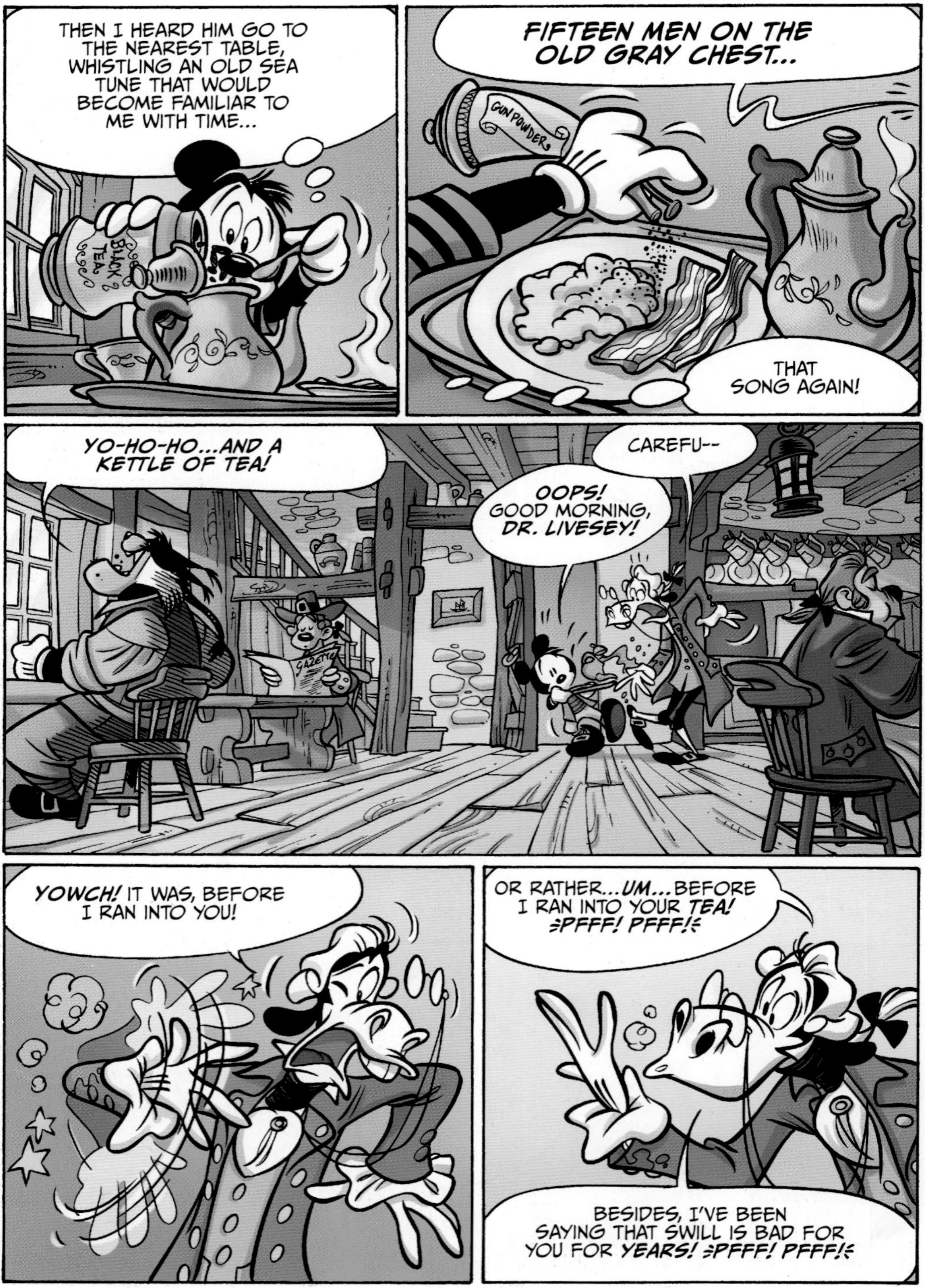
THEN I HEARD HIM GO TO THE NEAREST TABLE, WHISTLING AN OLD SEA TUNE THAT WOULD BECOME FAMILIAR TO ME WITH TIME...
BLACK TEA
FIFTEEN MEN ON THE OLD GRAY CHEST...
GUNPOWDER
THAT SONG AGAIN!
YO-HO-HO...AND A KETTLE OF TEA!
CAREFU--
OOPS! GOOD MORNING, DR. LIVESEY!
GAZETTE
YOWCH! IT WAS, BEFORE I RAN INTO YOU!
OR RATHER...UM...BEFORE I RAN INTO YOUR TEA! PFFF! PFFF!
BESIDES, I'VE BEEN SAYING THAT SWILL IS BAD FOR YOU FOR YEARS! PFFF! PFFF!

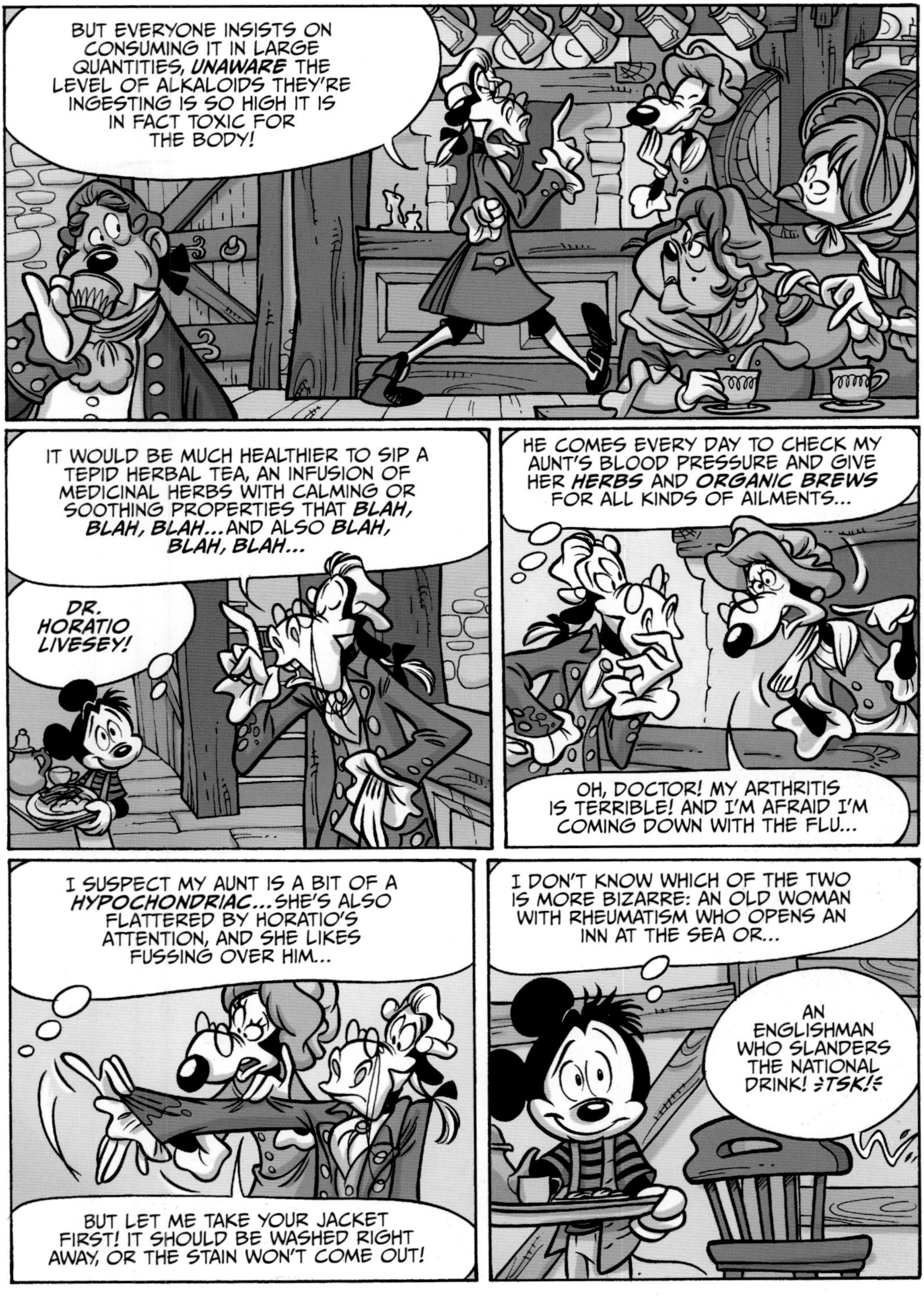
BUT EVERYONE INSISTS ON CONSUMING IT IN LARGE QUANTITIES, *UNAWARE* THE LEVEL OF ALKALOIDS THEY'RE INGESTING IS SO HIGH IT IS IN FACT TOXIC FOR THE BODY!
IT WOULD BE MUCH HEALTHIER TO SIP A TEPID HERBAL TEA, AN INFUSION OF MEDICINAL HERBS WITH CALMING OR SOOTHING PROPERTIES THAT *BLAH, BLAH, BLAH...* AND ALSO *BLAH, BLAH, BLAH...*
DR. HORATIO LIVESEY!
HE COMES EVERY DAY TO CHECK MY AUNT'S BLOOD PRESSURE AND GIVE HER *HERBS* AND *ORGANIC BREWS* FOR ALL KINDS OF AILMENTS...
OH, DOCTOR! MY ARTHRITIS IS TERRIBLE! AND I'M AFRAID I'M COMING DOWN WITH THE FLU...
I SUSPECT MY AUNT IS A BIT OF A *HYPOCHONDRIAC...* SHE'S ALSO FLATTERED BY HORATIO'S ATTENTION, AND SHE LIKES FUSSING OVER HIM...
BUT LET ME TAKE YOUR JACKET FIRST! IT SHOULD BE WASHED RIGHT AWAY, OR THE STAIN WON'T COME OUT!
I DON'T KNOW WHICH OF THE TWO IS MORE BIZARRE: AN OLD WOMAN WITH RHEUMATISM WHO OPENS AN INN AT THE SEA OR...
AN ENGLISHMAN WHO SLANDERS THE NATIONAL DRINK! *TSK!*

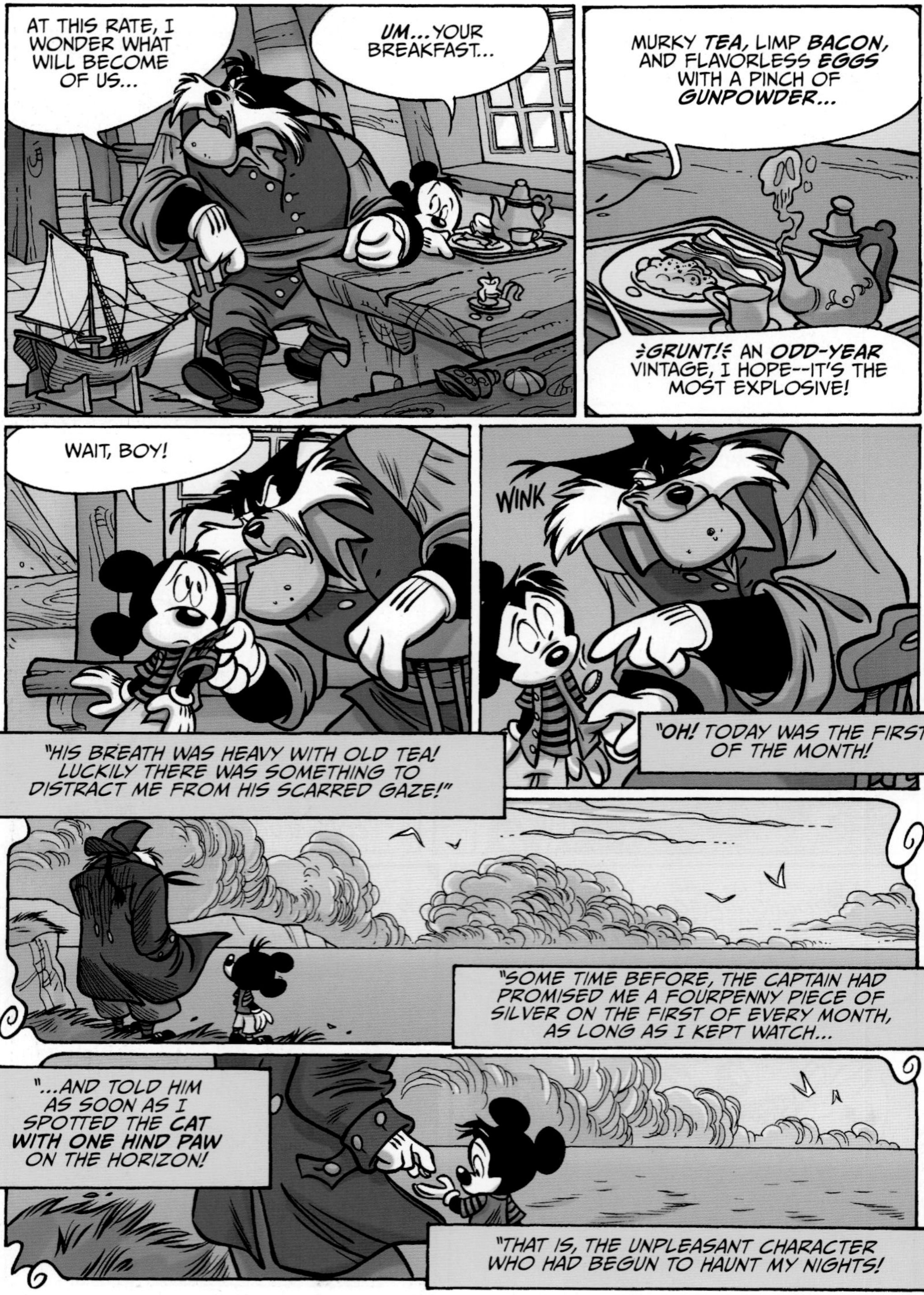
AT THIS RATE, I WONDER WHAT WILL BECOME OF US...
UM... YOUR BREAKFAST...
MURKY TEA, LIMP BACON, AND FLAVORLESS EGGS WITH A PINCH OF GUNPOWDER...
⁑GRUNT!⁑ AN ODD-YEAR VINTAGE, I HOPE--IT'S THE MOST EXPLOSIVE!
WAIT, BOY!
"HIS BREATH WAS HEAVY WITH OLD TEA! LUCKILY THERE WAS SOMETHING TO DISTRACT ME FROM HIS SCARRED GAZE!"
WINK
"OH! TODAY WAS THE FIRST OF THE MONTH!
"SOME TIME BEFORE, THE CAPTAIN HAD PROMISED ME A FOURPENNY PIECE OF SILVER ON THE FIRST OF EVERY MONTH, AS LONG AS I KEPT WATCH...
"...AND TOLD HIM AS SOON AS I SPOTTED THE CAT WITH ONE HIND PAW ON THE HORIZON!
"THAT IS, THE UNPLEASANT CHARACTER WHO HAD BEGUN TO HAUNT MY NIGHTS!

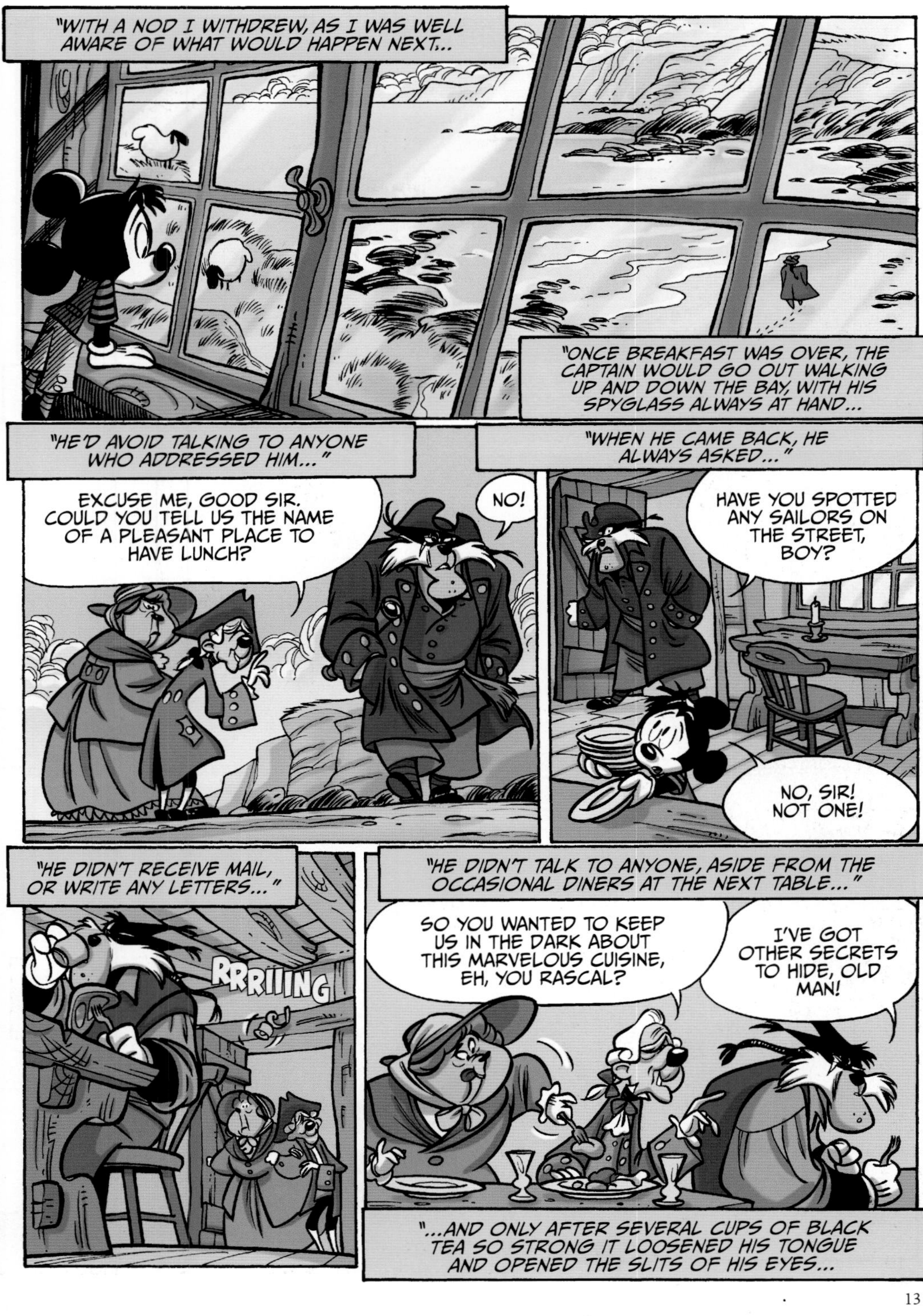
"WITH A NOD I WITHDREW, AS I WAS WELL AWARE OF WHAT WOULD HAPPEN NEXT...
"ONCE BREAKFAST WAS OVER, THE CAPTAIN WOULD GO OUT WALKING UP AND DOWN THE BAY, WITH HIS SPYGLASS ALWAYS AT HAND...
"HE'D AVOID TALKING TO ANYONE WHO ADDRESSED HIM..."
EXCUSE ME, GOOD SIR. COULD YOU TELL US THE NAME OF A PLEASANT PLACE TO HAVE LUNCH?
NO!
"WHEN HE CAME BACK, HE ALWAYS ASKED..."
HAVE YOU SPOTTED ANY SAILORS ON THE STREET, BOY?
NO, SIR! NOT ONE!
"HE DIDN'T RECEIVE MAIL, OR WRITE ANY LETTERS..."
RRRIIING
"HE DIDN'T TALK TO ANYONE, ASIDE FROM THE OCCASIONAL DINERS AT THE NEXT TABLE..."
SO YOU WANTED TO KEEP US IN THE DARK ABOUT THIS MARVELOUS CUISINE, EH, YOU RASCAL?
I'VE GOT OTHER SECRETS TO HIDE, OLD MAN!
"...AND ONLY AFTER SEVERAL CUPS OF BLACK TEA SO STRONG IT LOOSENED HIS TONGUE AND OPENED THE SLITS OF HIS EYES...

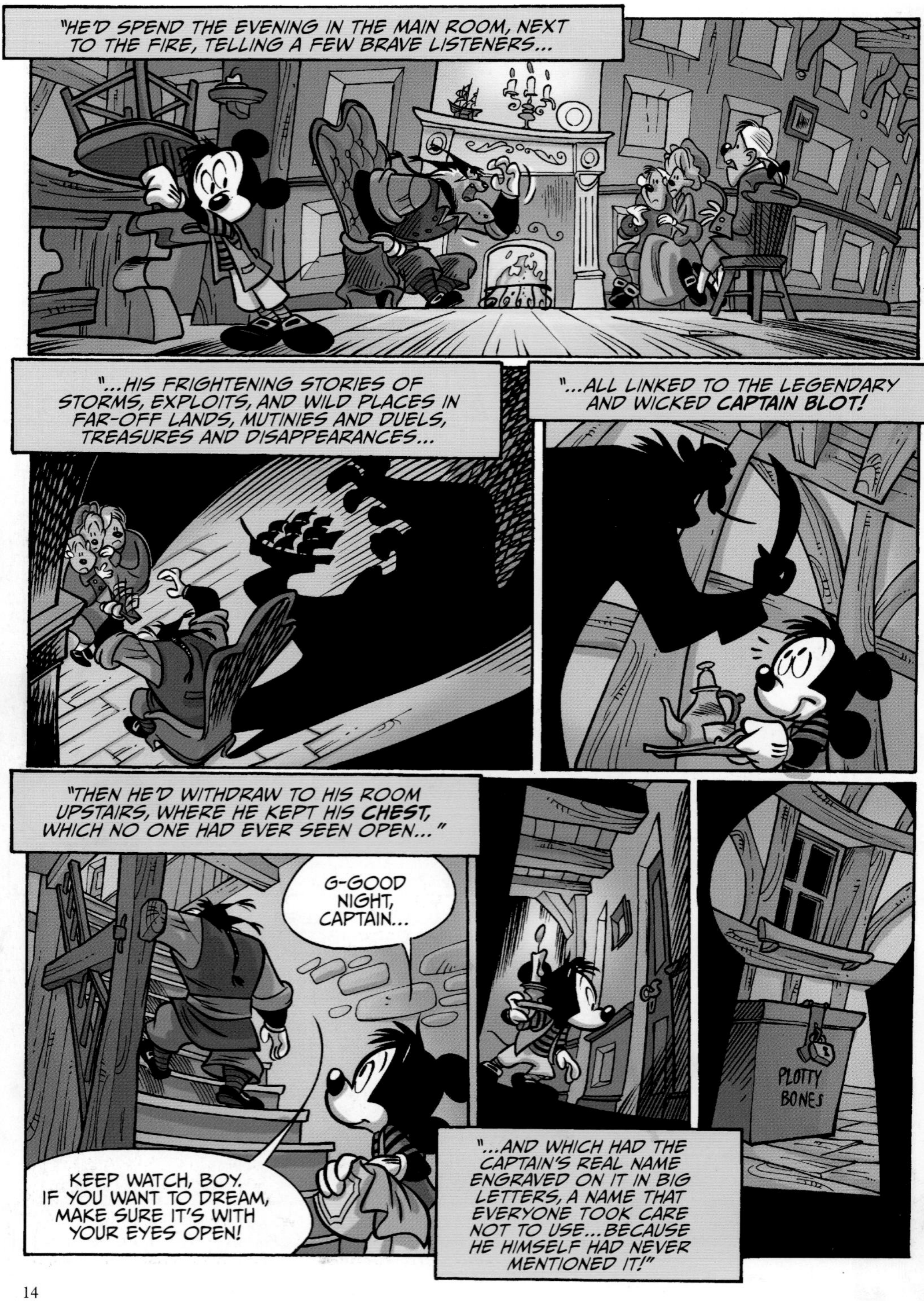
"HE'D SPEND THE EVENING IN THE MAIN ROOM, NEXT TO THE FIRE, TELLING A FEW BRAVE LISTENERS...
"...HIS FRIGHTENING STORIES OF STORMS, EXPLOITS, AND WILD PLACES IN FAR-OFF LANDS, MUTINIES AND DUELS, TREASURES AND DISAPPEARANCES...
"...ALL LINKED TO THE LEGENDARY AND WICKED CAPTAIN BLOT!
"THEN HE'D WITHDRAW TO HIS ROOM UPSTAIRS, WHERE HE KEPT HIS CHEST, WHICH NO ONE HAD EVER SEEN OPEN..."
G-GOOD NIGHT, CAPTAIN...
KEEP WATCH, BOY. IF YOU WANT TO DREAM, MAKE SURE IT'S WITH YOUR EYES OPEN!
PLOTTY BONES
"...AND WHICH HAD THE CAPTAIN'S REAL NAME ENGRAVED ON IT IN BIG LETTERS, A NAME THAT EVERYONE TOOK CARE NOT TO USE...BECAUSE HE HIMSELF HAD NEVER MENTIONED IT!"

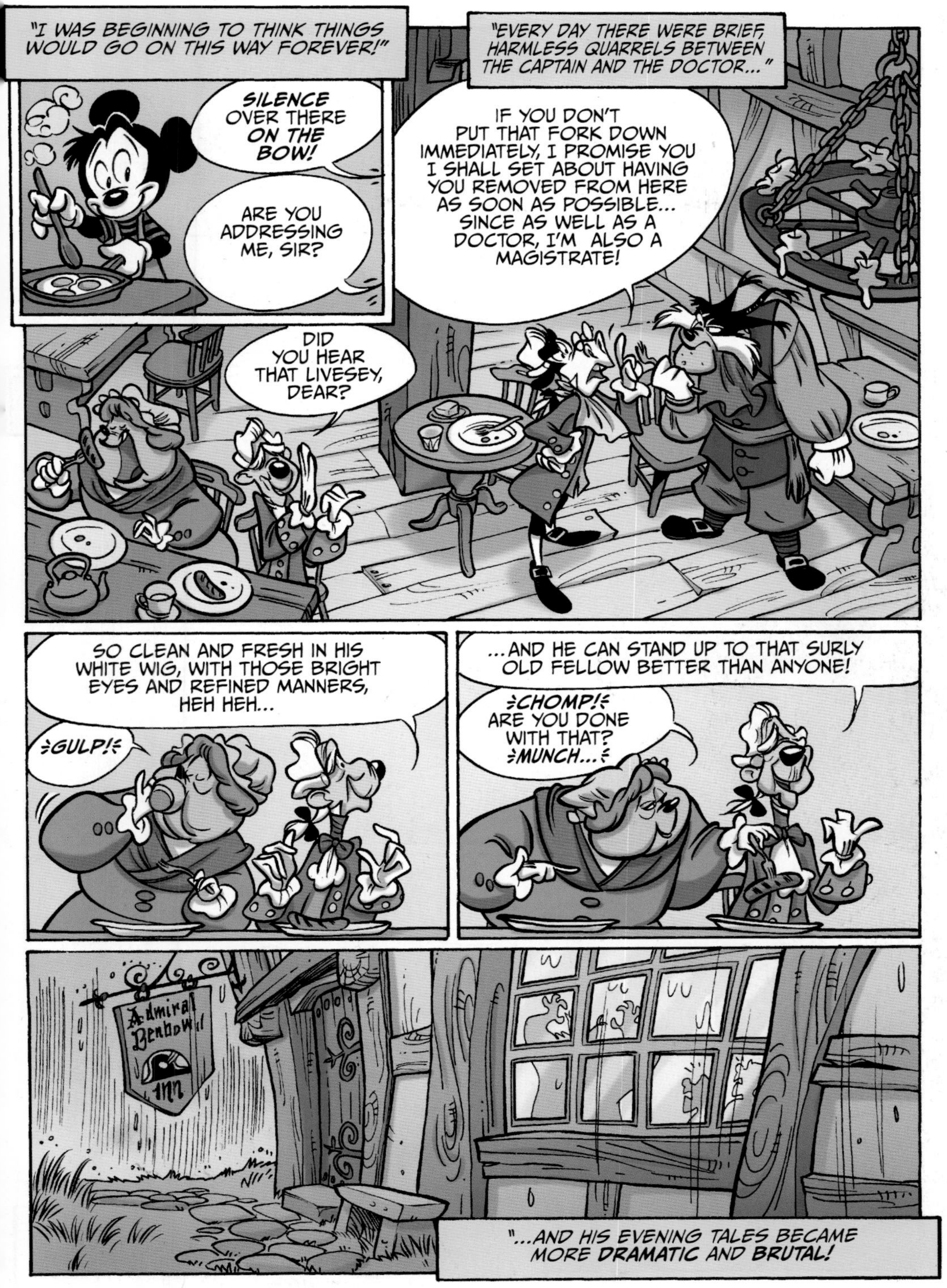
"I WAS BEGINNING TO THINK THINGS WOULD GO ON THIS WAY FOREVER!"
SILENCE OVER THERE ON THE BOW!
ARE YOU ADDRESSING ME, SIR?
"EVERY DAY THERE WERE BRIEF, HARMLESS QUARRELS BETWEEN THE CAPTAIN AND THE DOCTOR..."
IF YOU DON'T PUT THAT FORK DOWN IMMEDIATELY, I PROMISE YOU I SHALL SET ABOUT HAVING YOU REMOVED FROM HERE AS SOON AS POSSIBLE... SINCE AS WELL AS A DOCTOR, I'M ALSO A MAGISTRATE!
DID YOU HEAR THAT LIVESEY, DEAR?
SO CLEAN AND FRESH IN HIS WHITE WIG, WITH THOSE BRIGHT EYES AND REFINED MANNERS, HEH HEH...
GULP!
...AND HE CAN STAND UP TO THAT SURLY OLD FELLOW BETTER THAN ANYONE!
CHOMP! ARE YOU DONE WITH THAT? MUNCH...
Admiral Benbow Inn
"...AND HIS EVENING TALES BECAME MORE DRAMATIC AND BRUTAL!

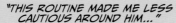

"THIS ROUTINE MADE ME LESS CAUTIOUS AROUND HIM..."

...AND I HIT HIM MERCILESSLY, LIKE THIS!

PLOTCH

BUT HE WAS A TOUGH NUT! HE GOT BACK UP BRANDISHING HIS SABER, SO I...

"I WAS BEGINNING TO WONDER WHETHER HIS STORIES WERE EXAGGERATED OR EVEN MADE UP...

"LIKE WHEN THE CAPTAIN CONFIDED TO ME THAT HE HAD BEEN NONE OTHER THAN..."

...OLD BLOT'S *FIRST MATE* ON THE *WALRUS*!

A-ARE YOU SERIOUS?

YEAH...

LISTEN CLOSELY, BOY: I KNOW SECRETS THAT SOME WILL SOON TRY TO TAKE FROM ME BY FORCE...

"...AND BLAH, BLAH, BLAH! I WAS STARTING TO THINK THAT PLOTTY BONES, KNOWN AS 'THE CAPTAIN,' WAS NOTHING MORE THAN AN OLD WINDBAG...

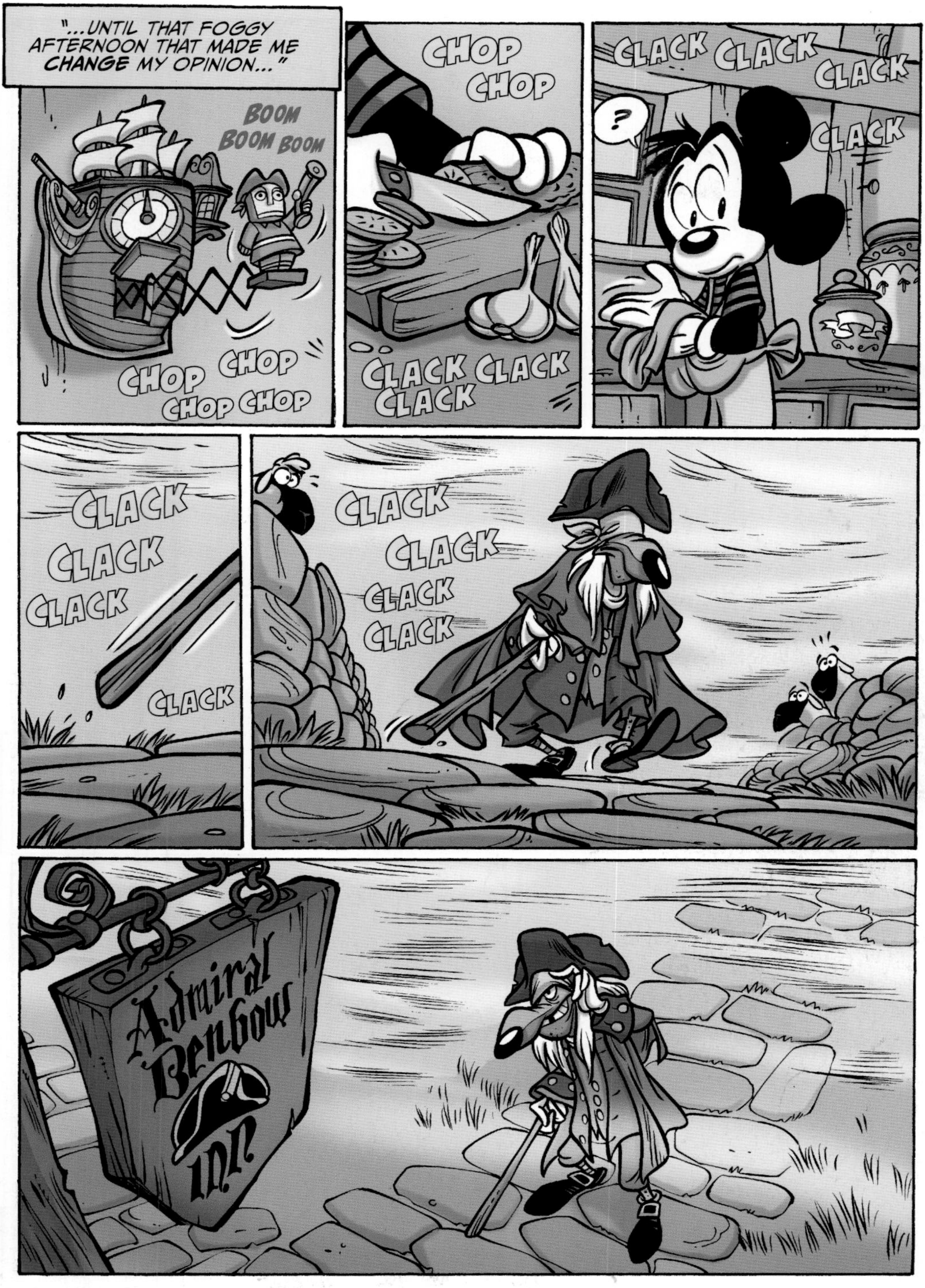
"...UNTIL THAT FOGGY AFTERNOON THAT MADE ME CHANGE MY OPINION..."
BOOM BOOM BOOM
CHOP CHOP CHOP CHOP
CHOP CHOP
CLACK CLACK CLACK
CLACK CLACK CLACK
?
CLACK CLACK CLACK CLACK
CLACK CLACK CLACK CLACK
CLACK CLACK CLACK CLACK
Admiral Benbow INN

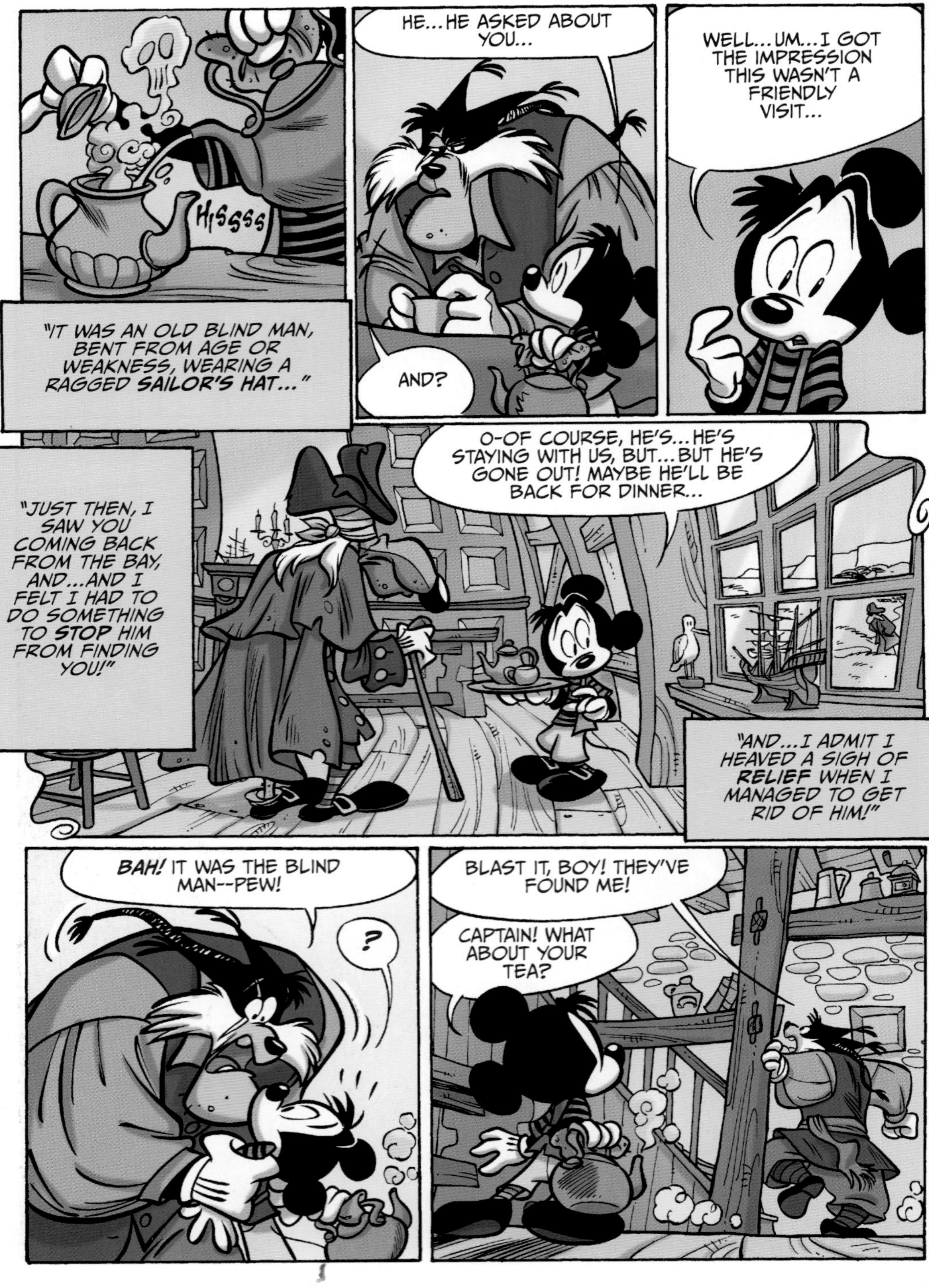
HISSSS
"IT WAS AN OLD BLIND MAN, BENT FROM AGE OR WEAKNESS, WEARING A RAGGED SAILOR'S HAT..."
HE...HE ASKED ABOUT YOU...
AND?
WELL...UM...I GOT THE IMPRESSION THIS WASN'T A FRIENDLY VISIT...
"JUST THEN, I SAW YOU COMING BACK FROM THE BAY, AND...AND I FELT I HAD TO DO SOMETHING TO STOP HIM FROM FINDING YOU!"
O-OF COURSE, HE'S...HE'S STAYING WITH US, BUT...BUT HE'S GONE OUT! MAYBE HE'LL BE BACK FOR DINNER...
"AND...I ADMIT I HEAVED A SIGH OF RELIEF WHEN I MANAGED TO GET RID OF HIM!"
BAH! IT WAS THE BLIND MAN--PEW!
?
BLAST IT, BOY! THEY'VE FOUND ME!
CAPTAIN! WHAT ABOUT YOUR TEA?

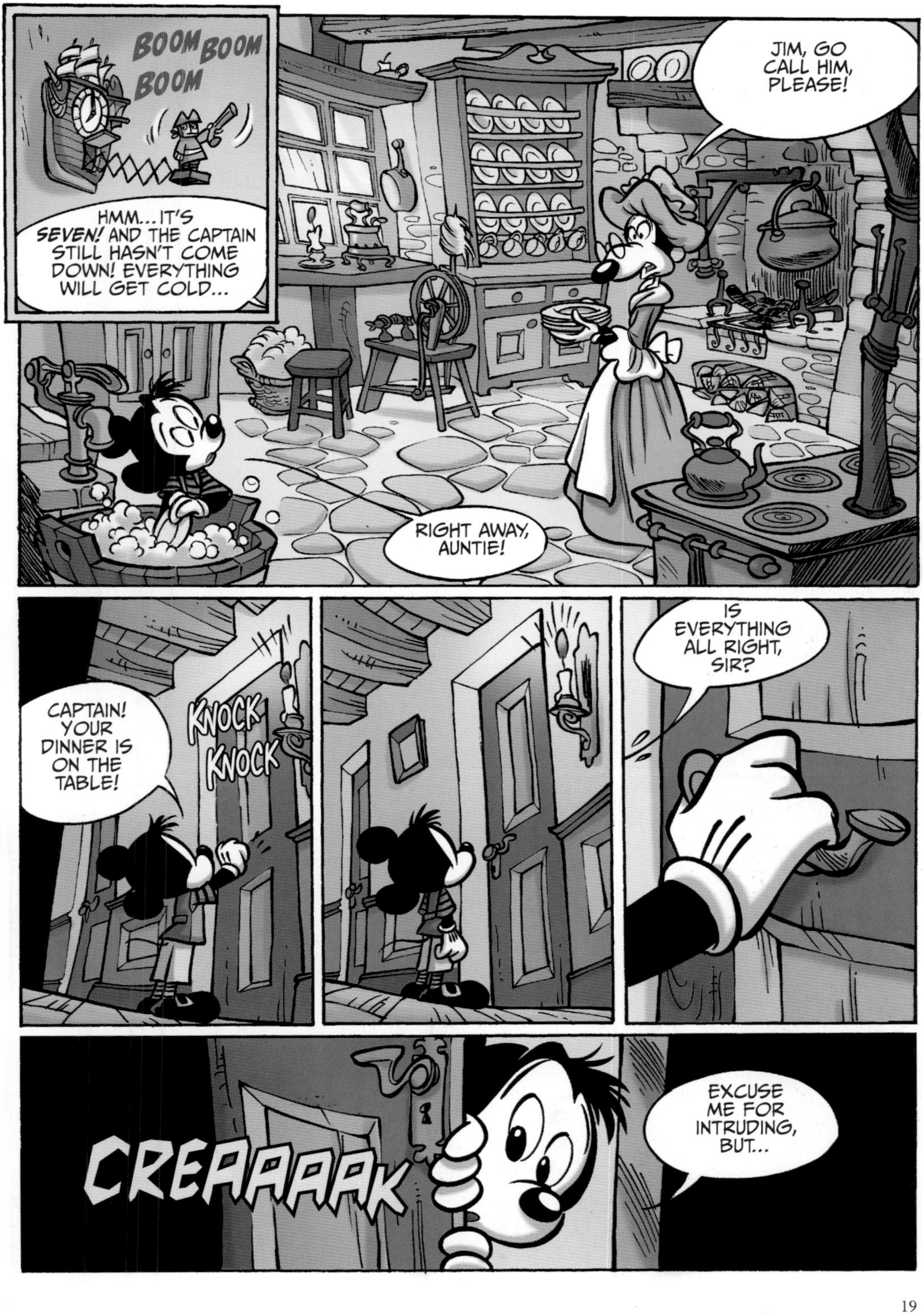
BOOM BOOM
BOOM
HMM... IT'S SEVEN! AND THE CAPTAIN STILL HASN'T COME DOWN! EVERYTHING WILL GET COLD...
JIM, GO CALL HIM, PLEASE!
RIGHT AWAY, AUNTIE!
CAPTAIN! YOUR DINNER IS ON THE TABLE!
KNOCK
KNOCK
IS EVERYTHING ALL RIGHT, SIR?
CREAAAAK
EXCUSE ME FOR INTRUDING, BUT...

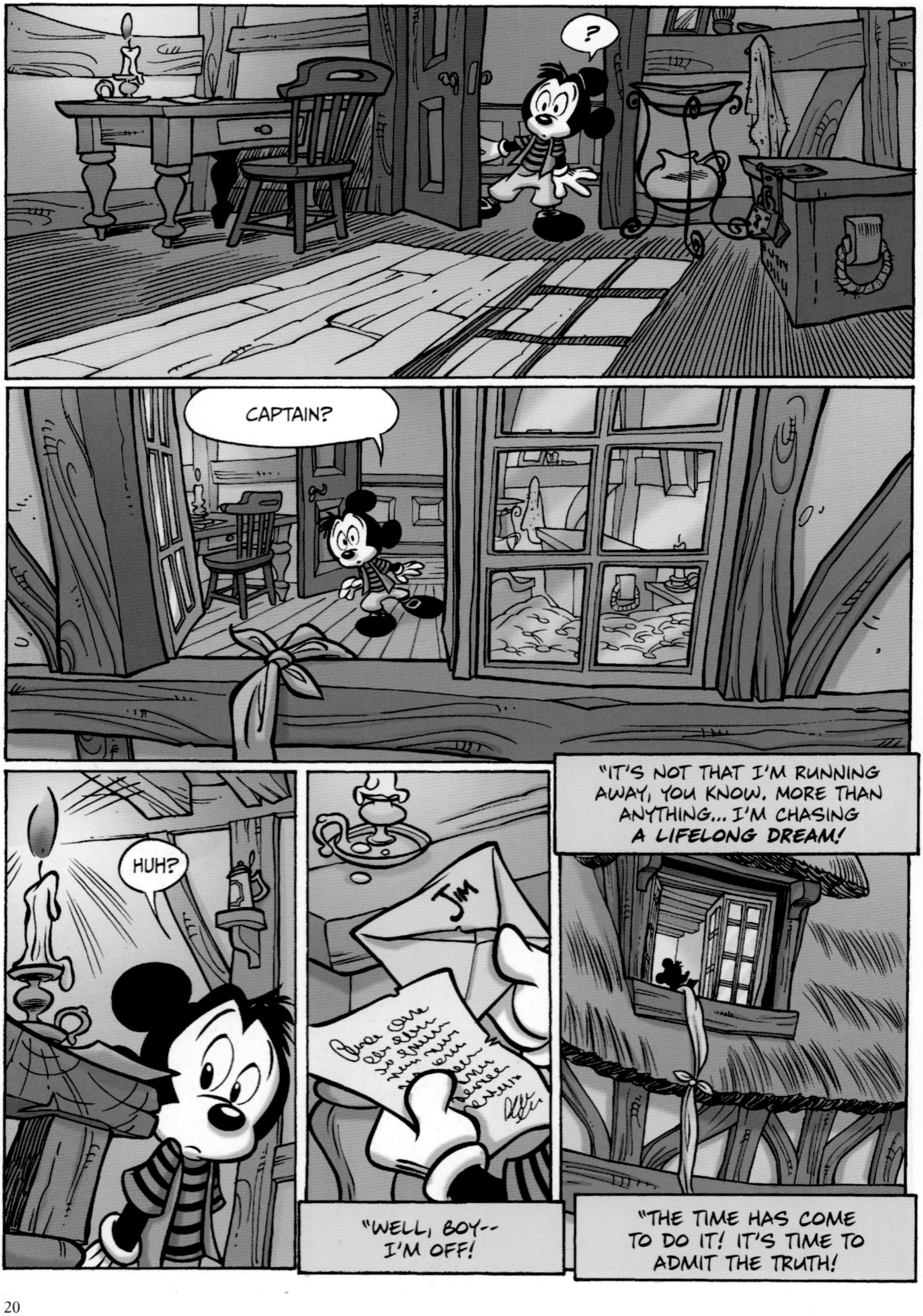
?
CAPTAIN?
HUH?
JIM
"WELL, BOY--
I'M OFF!
"IT'S NOT THAT I'M RUNNING AWAY, YOU KNOW. MORE THAN ANYTHING... I'M CHASING A LIFELONG DREAM!
"THE TIME HAS COME TO DO IT! IT'S TIME TO ADMIT THE TRUTH!

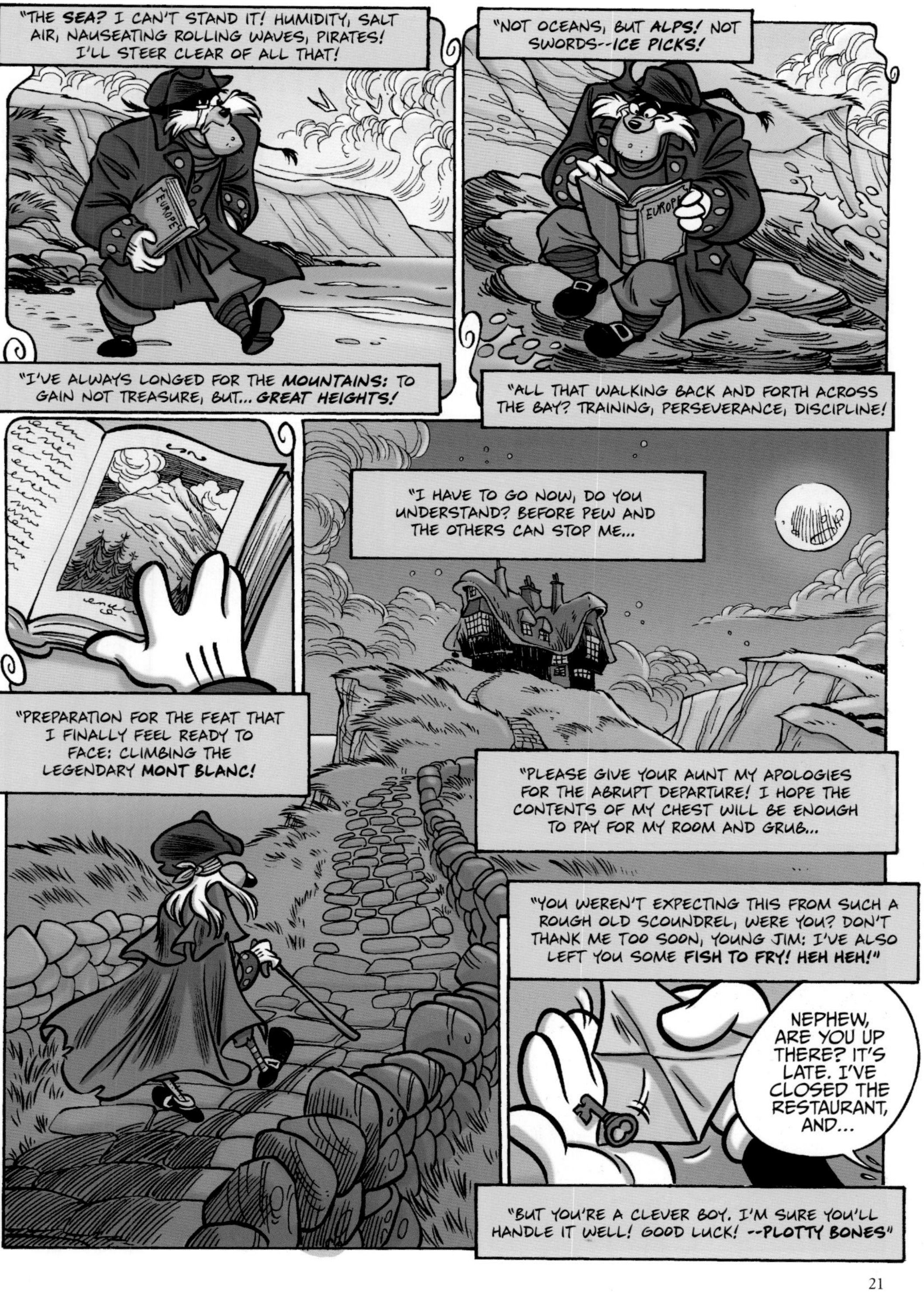
"THE SEA? I CAN'T STAND IT! HUMIDITY, SALT AIR, NAUSEATING ROLLING WAVES, PIRATES! I'LL STEER CLEAR OF ALL THAT!
EUROPE
"I'VE ALWAYS LONGED FOR THE MOUNTAINS: TO GAIN NOT TREASURE, BUT... GREAT HEIGHTS!
"NOT OCEANS, BUT ALPS! NOT SWORDS--ICE PICKS!
EUROPE
"ALL THAT WALKING BACK AND FORTH ACROSS THE BAY? TRAINING, PERSEVERANCE, DISCIPLINE!
"PREPARATION FOR THE FEAT THAT I FINALLY FEEL READY TO FACE: CLIMBING THE LEGENDARY MONT BLANC!
"I HAVE TO GO NOW, DO YOU UNDERSTAND? BEFORE PEW AND THE OTHERS CAN STOP ME...
"PLEASE GIVE YOUR AUNT MY APOLOGIES FOR THE ABRUPT DEPARTURE! I HOPE THE CONTENTS OF MY CHEST WILL BE ENOUGH TO PAY FOR MY ROOM AND GRUB...
"YOU WEREN'T EXPECTING THIS FROM SUCH A ROUGH OLD SCOUNDREL, WERE YOU? DON'T THANK ME TOO SOON, YOUNG JIM: I'VE ALSO LEFT YOU SOME FISH TO FRY! HEH HEH!"
NEPHEW, ARE YOU UP THERE? IT'S LATE. I'VE CLOSED THE RESTAURANT, AND...
"BUT YOU'RE A CLEVER BOY. I'M SURE YOU'LL HANDLE IT WELL! GOOD LUCK! --PLOTTY BONES"

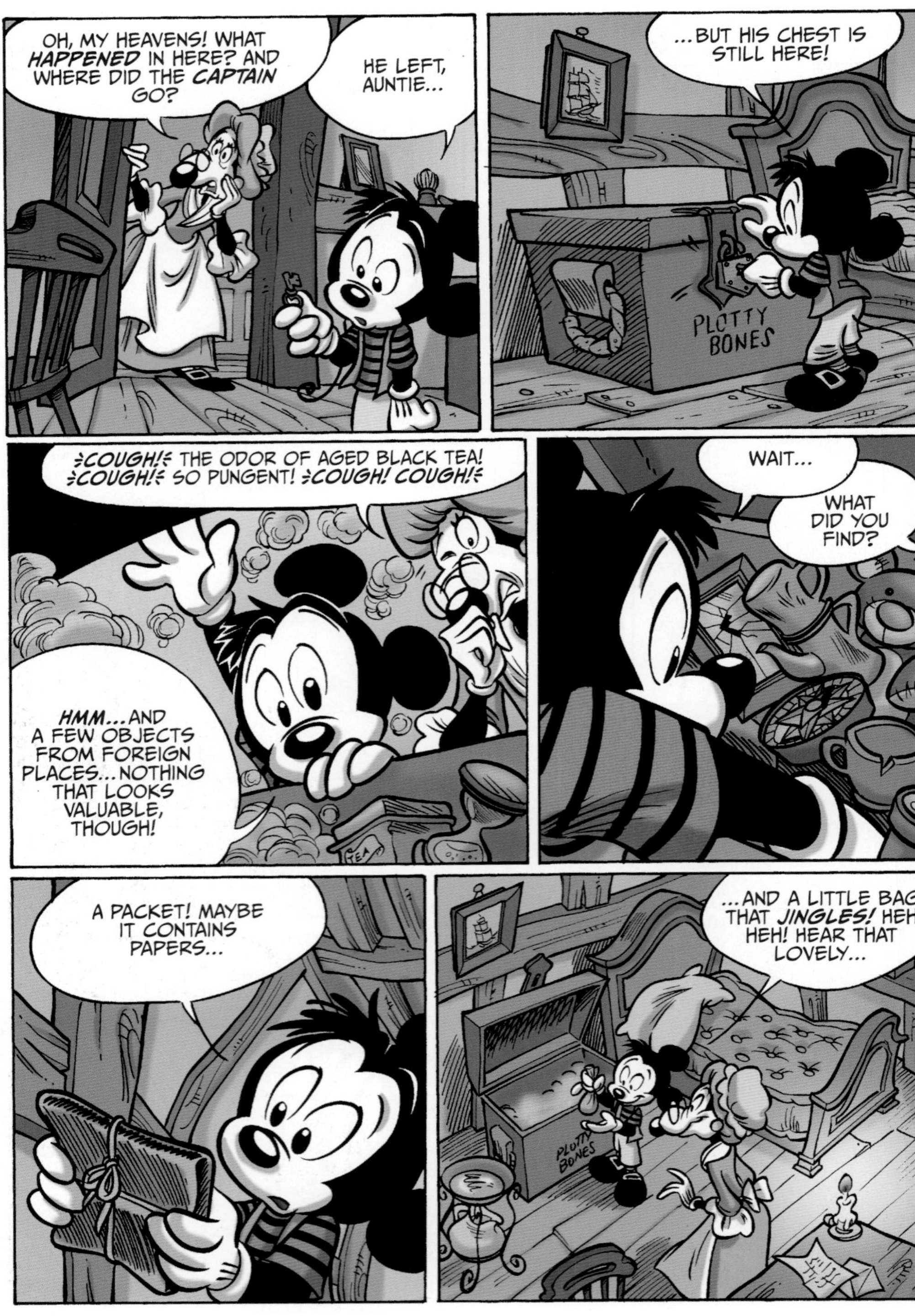
OH, MY HEAVENS! WHAT HAPPENED IN HERE? AND WHERE DID THE CAPTAIN GO?
HE LEFT, AUNTIE...
...BUT HIS CHEST IS STILL HERE!
PLOTTY BONES
COUGH! THE ODOR OF AGED BLACK TEA! COUGH! SO PUNGENT! COUGH! COUGH!
HMM...AND A FEW OBJECTS FROM FOREIGN PLACES...NOTHING THAT LOOKS VALUABLE, THOUGH!
TEA
WAIT...
WHAT DID YOU FIND?
A PACKET! MAYBE IT CONTAINS PAPERS...
...AND A LITTLE BAG THAT JINGLES! HEH HEH! HEAR THAT LOVELY...
PLOTTY BONES

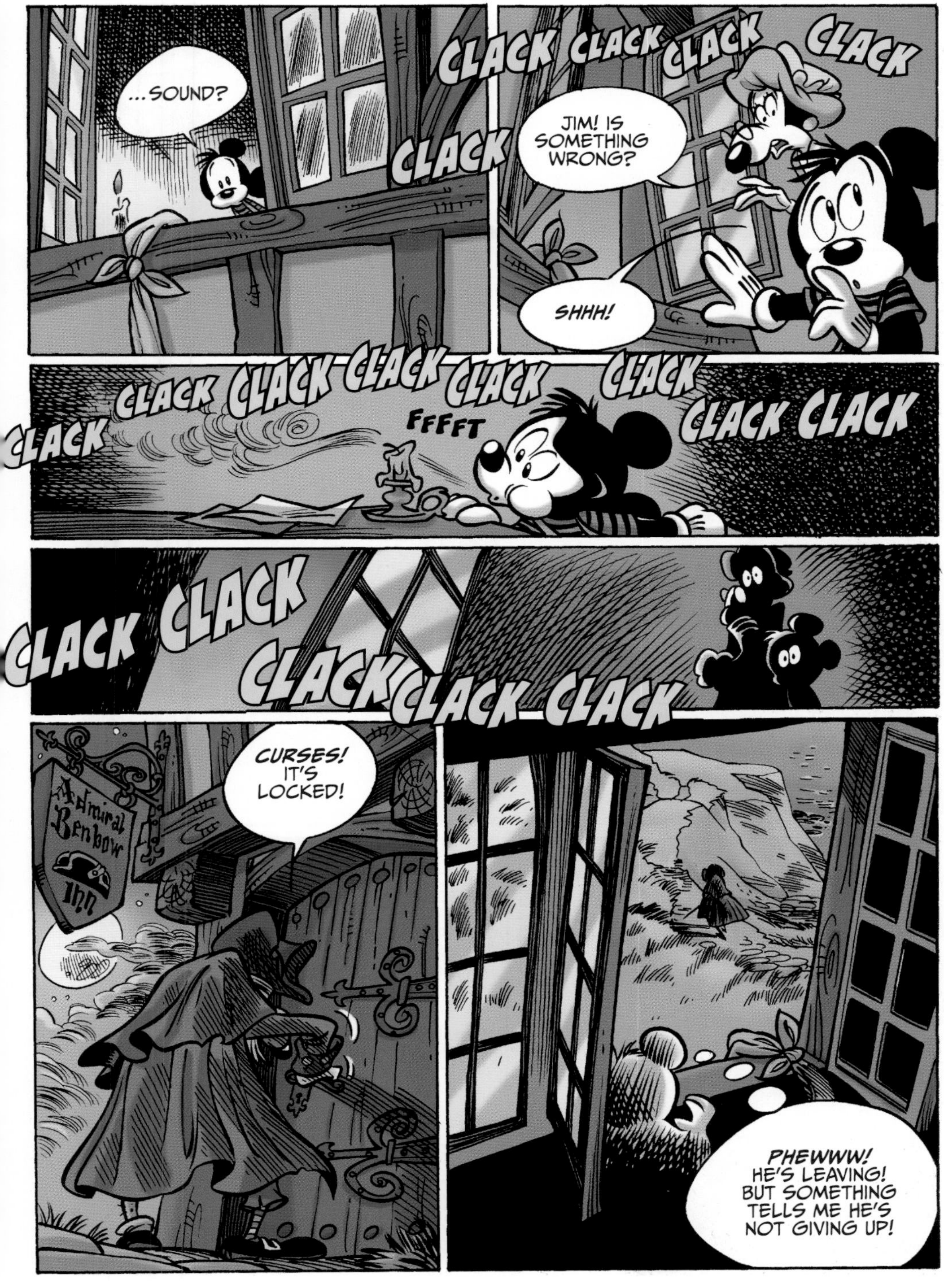

...SOUND?
CLACK CLACK CLACK CLACK
CLACK
JIM! IS SOMETHING WRONG?
SHHH!
CLACK CLACK CLACK CLACK CLACK CLACK
FFFFT
CLACK CLACK
CLACK CLACK
CLACK CLACK CLACK CLACK
Admiral Benbow Inn
CURSES! IT'S LOCKED!
PHEWWW! HE'S LEAVING! BUT SOMETHING TELLS ME HE'S NOT GIVING UP!

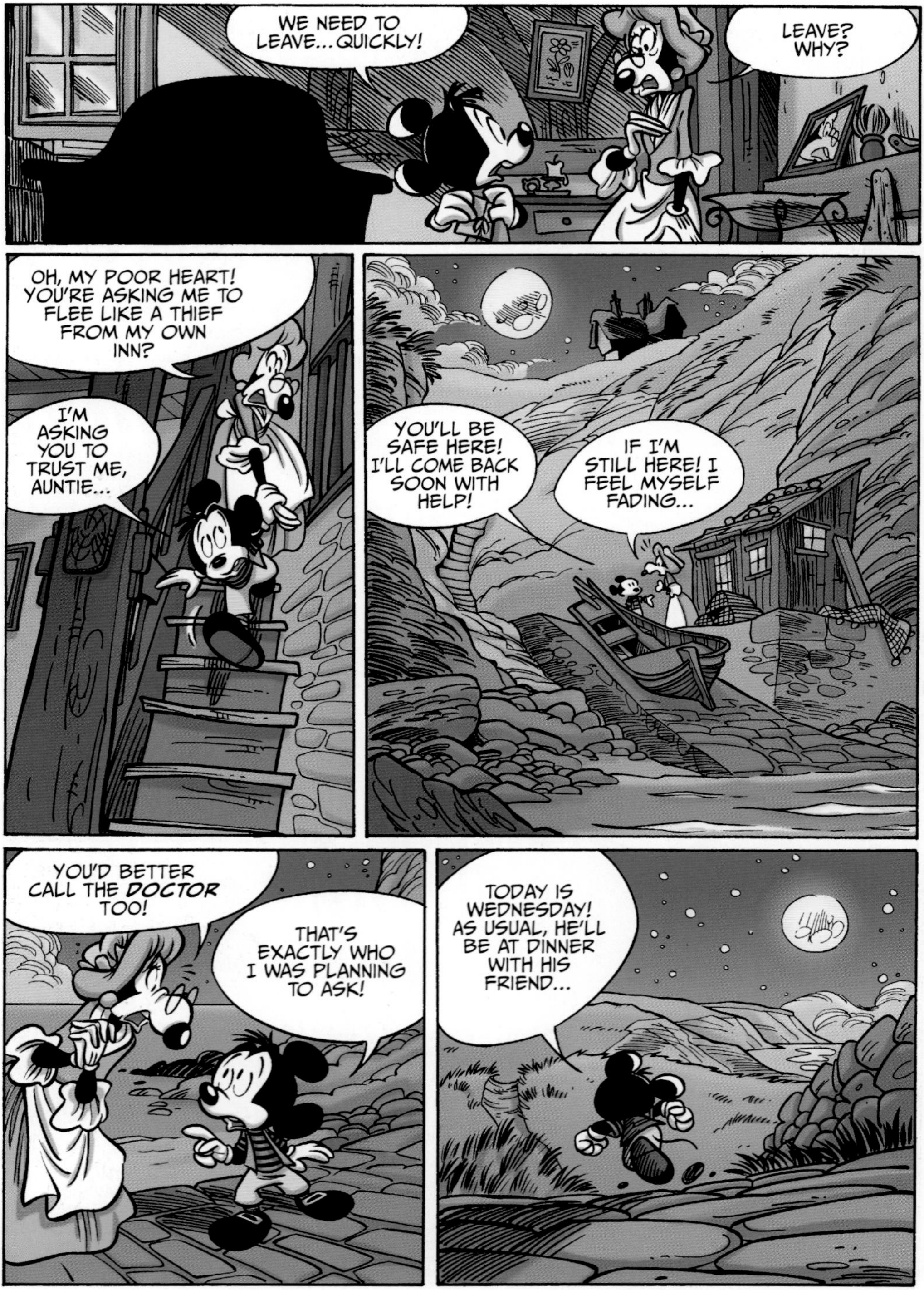
WE NEED TO LEAVE... QUICKLY!
LEAVE? WHY?
OH, MY POOR HEART! YOU'RE ASKING ME TO FLEE LIKE A THIEF FROM MY OWN INN?
I'M ASKING YOU TO TRUST ME, AUNTIE...
YOU'LL BE SAFE HERE! I'LL COME BACK SOON WITH HELP!
IF I'M STILL HERE! I FEEL MYSELF FADING...
YOU'D BETTER CALL THE *DOCTOR* TOO!
THAT'S EXACTLY WHO I WAS PLANNING TO ASK!
TODAY IS WEDNESDAY! AS USUAL, HE'LL BE AT DINNER WITH HIS FRIEND...

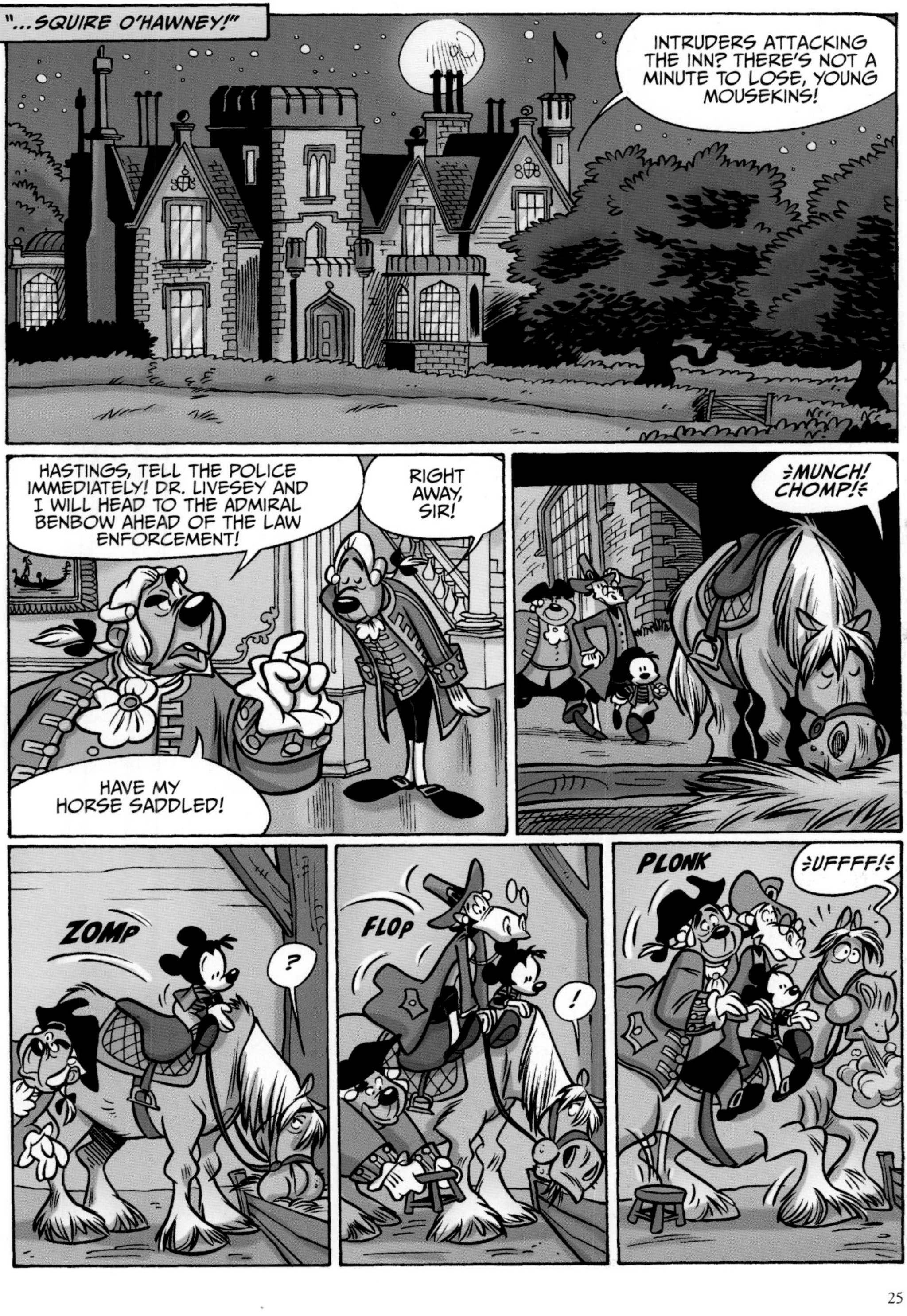
"...SQUIRE O'HAWNEY!"
INTRUDERS ATTACKING THE INN? THERE'S NOT A MINUTE TO LOSE, YOUNG MOUSEKINS!
HASTINGS, TELL THE POLICE IMMEDIATELY! DR. LIVESEY AND I WILL HEAD TO THE ADMIRAL BENBOW AHEAD OF THE LAW ENFORCEMENT!
HAVE MY HORSE SADDLED!
RIGHT AWAY, SIR!
MUNCH! CHOMP!
ZOMP
?
FLOP
!
PLONK
UFFFF!

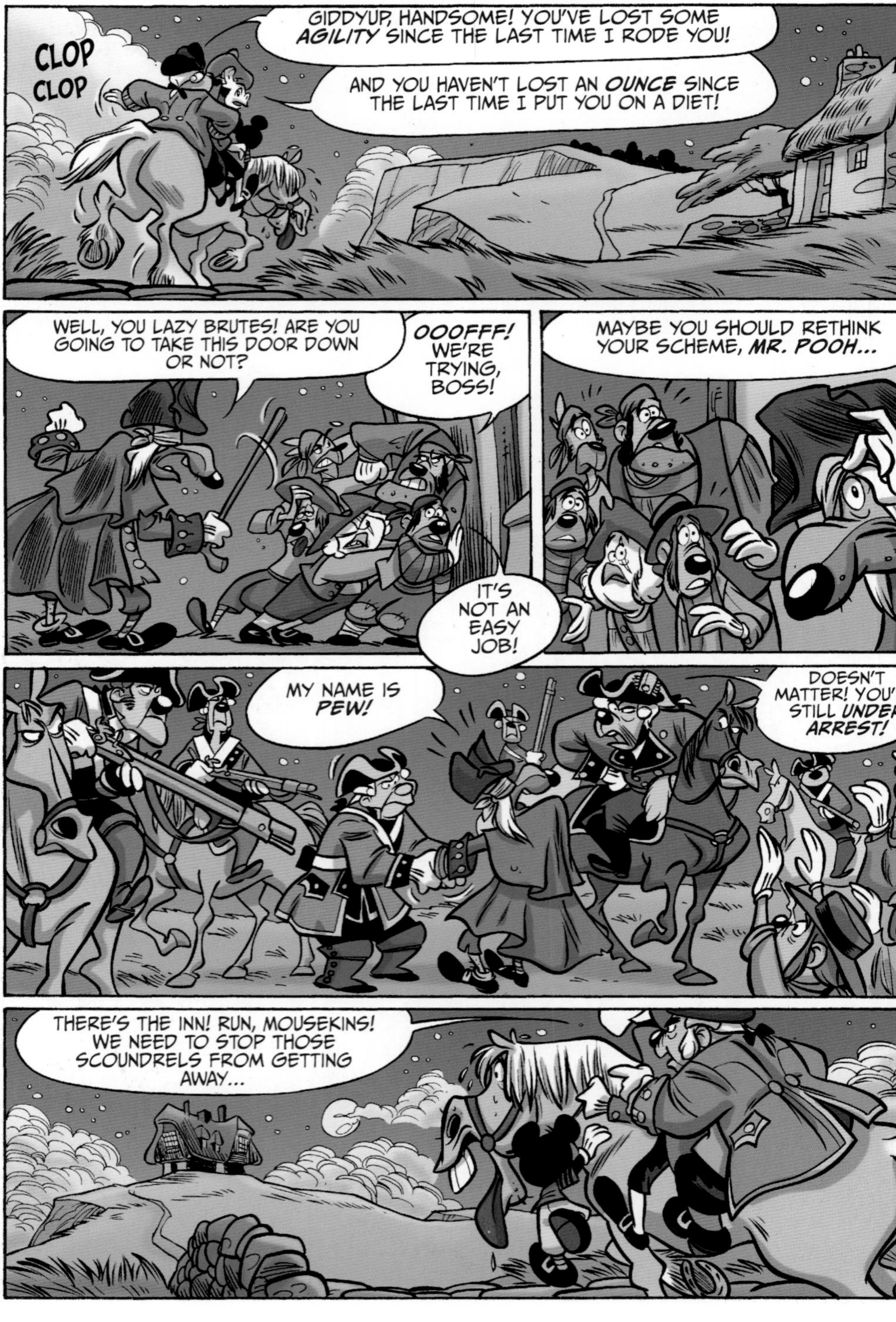
CLOP
CLOP
GIDDYUP, HANDSOME! YOU'VE LOST SOME AGILITY SINCE THE LAST TIME I RODE YOU!
AND YOU HAVEN'T LOST AN OUNCE SINCE THE LAST TIME I PUT YOU ON A DIET!
WELL, YOU LAZY BRUTES! ARE YOU GOING TO TAKE THIS DOOR DOWN OR NOT?
OOOFFF! WE'RE TRYING, BOSS!
IT'S NOT AN EASY JOB!
MAYBE YOU SHOULD RETHINK YOUR SCHEME, MR. POOH...
MY NAME IS PEW!
DOESN'T MATTER! YOU'RE STILL UNDER ARREST!
THERE'S THE INN! RUN, MOUSEKINS! WE NEED TO STOP THOSE SCOUNDRELS FROM GETTING AWAY...

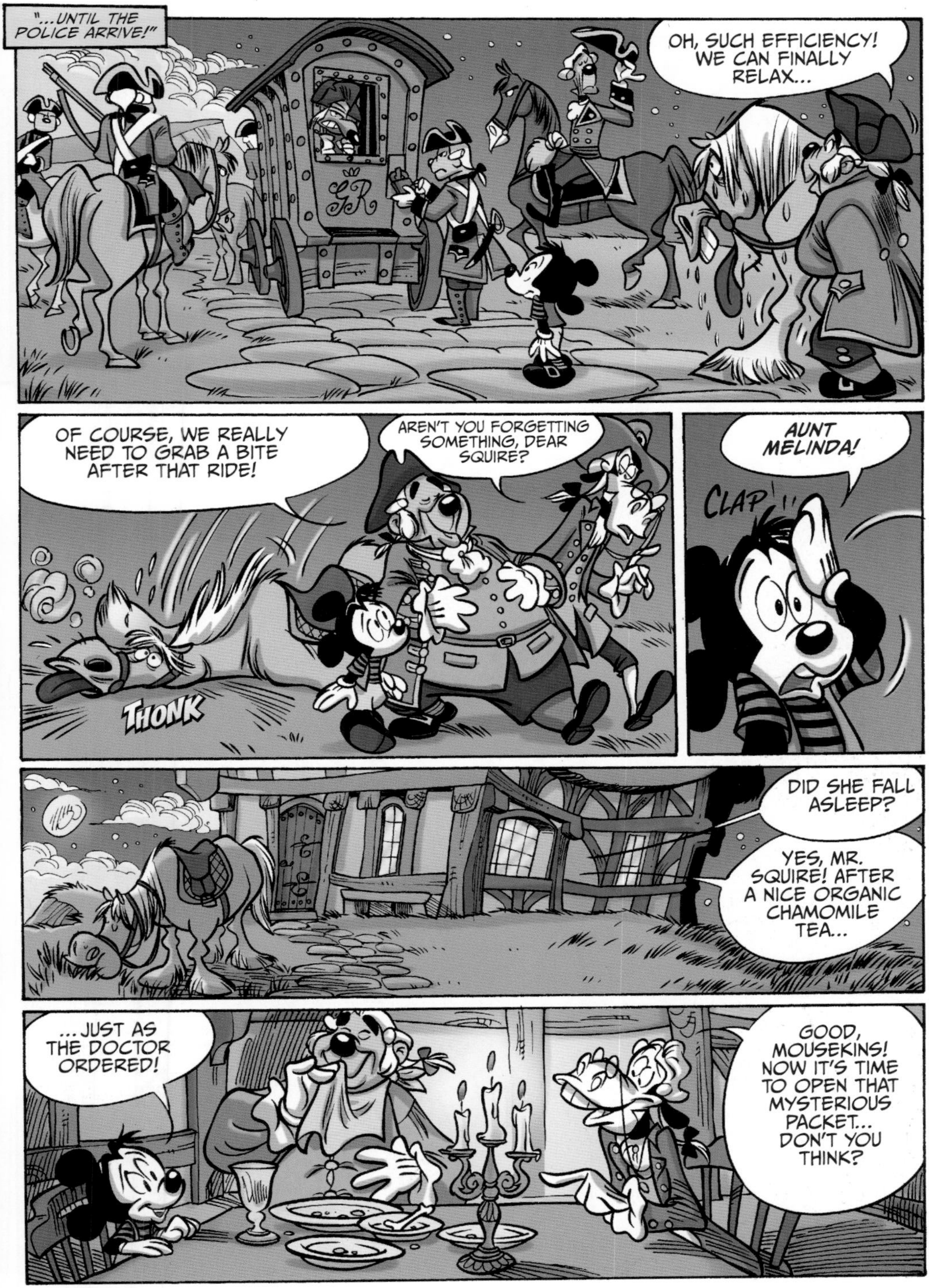
"...UNTIL THE POLICE ARRIVE!"
OH, SUCH EFFICIENCY! WE CAN FINALLY RELAX...
OF COURSE, WE REALLY NEED TO GRAB A BITE AFTER THAT RIDE!
AREN'T YOU FORGETTING SOMETHING, DEAR SQUIRE?
THONK
AUNT MELINDA!
CLAP
DID SHE FALL ASLEEP?
YES, MR. SQUIRE! AFTER A NICE ORGANIC CHAMOMILE TEA...
...JUST AS THE DOCTOR ORDERED!
GOOD, MOUSEKINS! NOW IT'S TIME TO OPEN THAT MYSTERIOUS PACKET... DON'T YOU THINK?

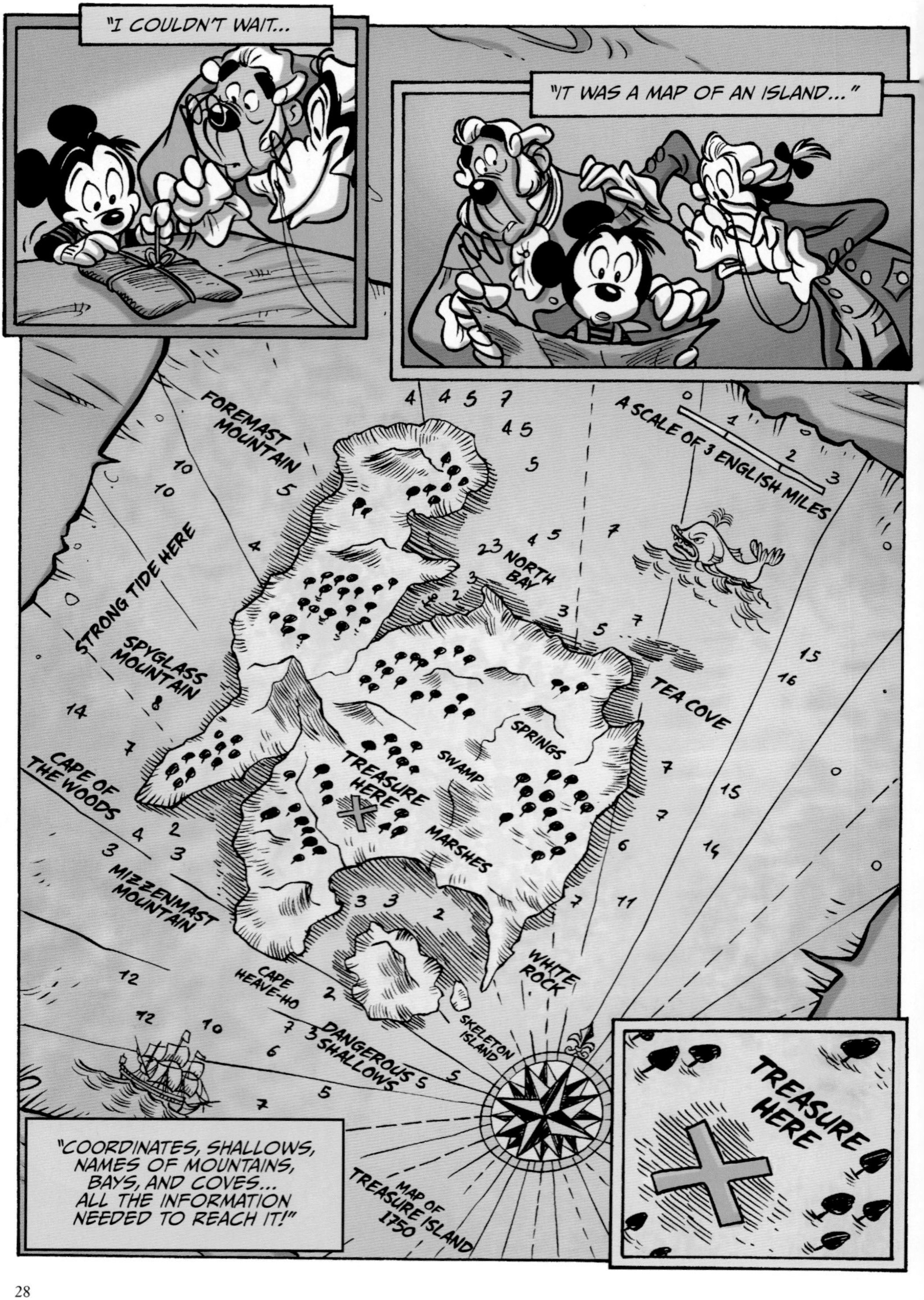
"I COULDN'T WAIT...
"IT WAS A MAP OF AN ISLAND..."
FOREMAST MOUNTAIN
A SCALE OF 3 ENGLISH MILES
STRONG TIDE HERE
NORTH BAY
SPYGLASS MOUNTAIN
TEA COVE
SPRINGS
SWAMP
TREASURE HERE
CAPE OF THE WOODS
MARSHES
MIZZENMAST MOUNTAIN
WHITE ROCK
CAPE HEAVE-HO
SKELETON ISLAND
DANGEROUS SHALLOWS
"COORDINATES, SHALLOWS, NAMES OF MOUNTAINS, BAYS, AND COVES... ALL THE INFORMATION NEEDED TO REACH IT!"
MAP OF TREASURE ISLAND 1750
TREASURE HERE

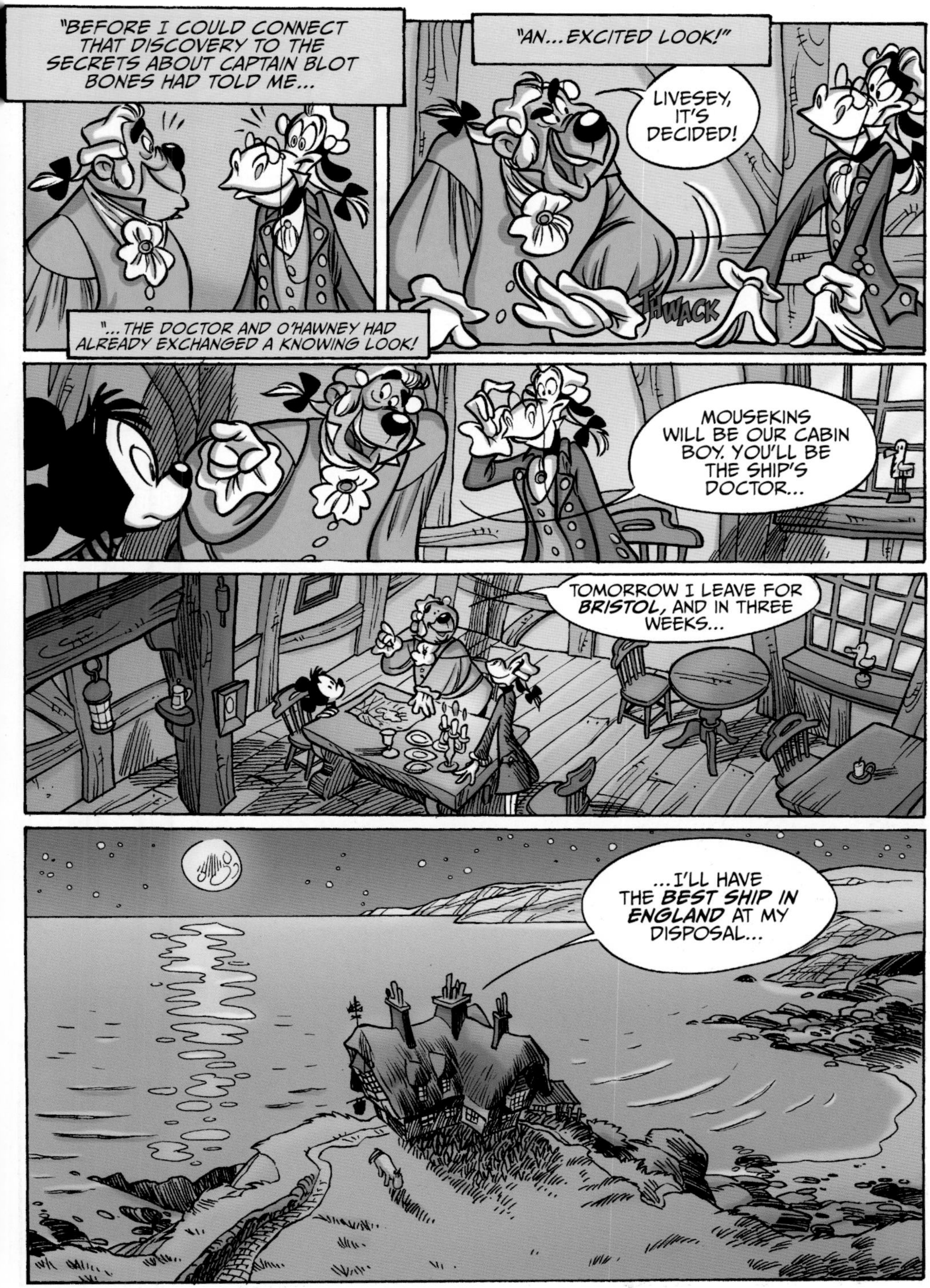
"BEFORE I COULD CONNECT THAT DISCOVERY TO THE SECRETS ABOUT CAPTAIN BLOT BONES HAD TOLD ME...
"...THE DOCTOR AND O'HAWNEY HAD ALREADY EXCHANGED A KNOWING LOOK!
"AN...EXCITED LOOK!"
LIVESEY, IT'S DECIDED!
THWACK
MOUSEKINS WILL BE OUR CABIN BOY. YOU'LL BE THE SHIP'S DOCTOR...
TOMORROW I LEAVE FOR **BRISTOL,** AND IN THREE WEEKS...
...I'LL HAVE THE **BEST SHIP IN ENGLAND** AT MY DISPOSAL...

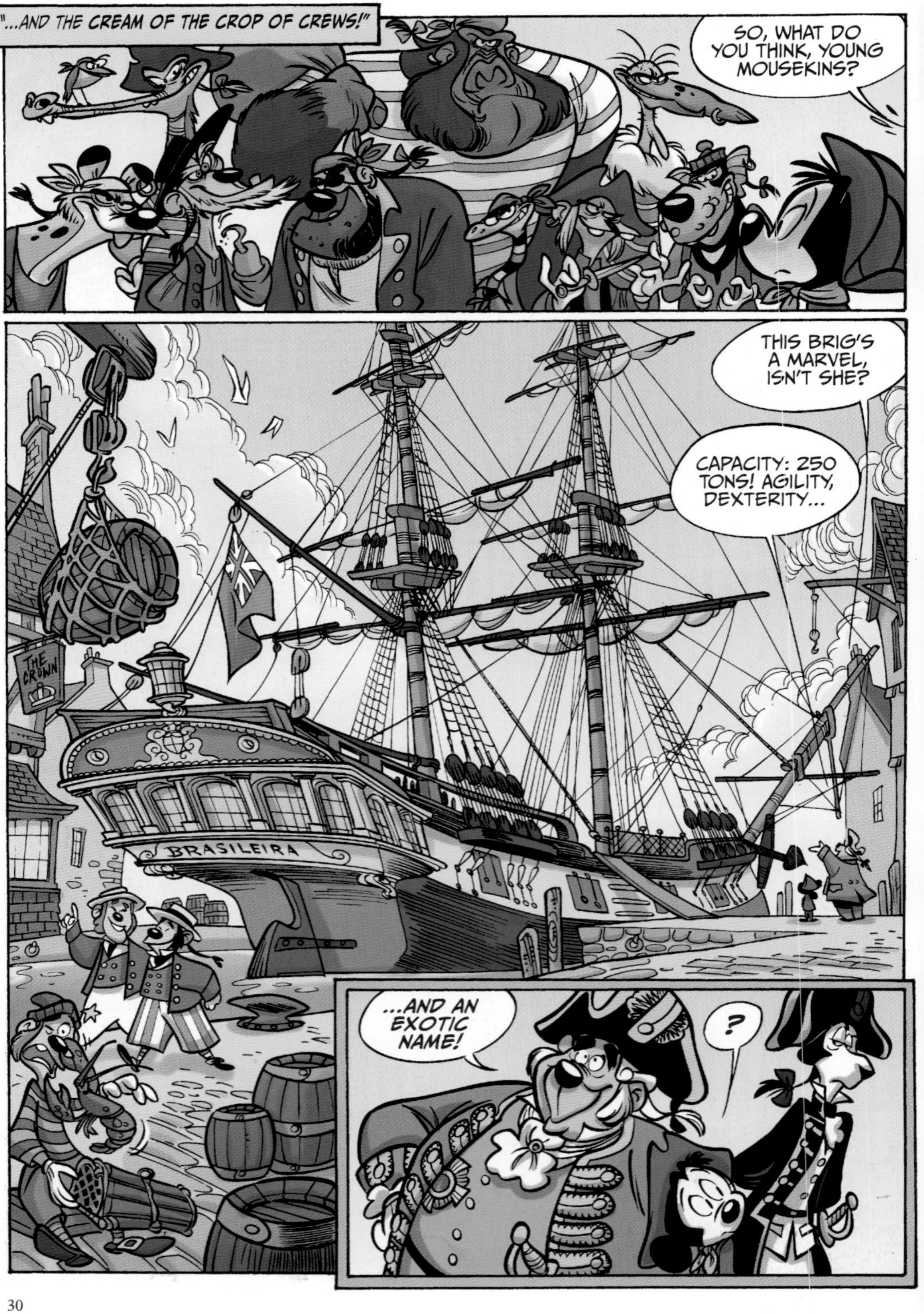
"...AND THE CREAM OF THE CROP OF CREWS!"
SO, WHAT DO YOU THINK, YOUNG MOUSEKINS?
THIS BRIG'S A MARVEL, ISN'T SHE?
CAPACITY: 250 TONS! AGILITY, DEXTERITY...
THE CROWN
BRASILEIRA
...AND AN EXOTIC NAME!
?

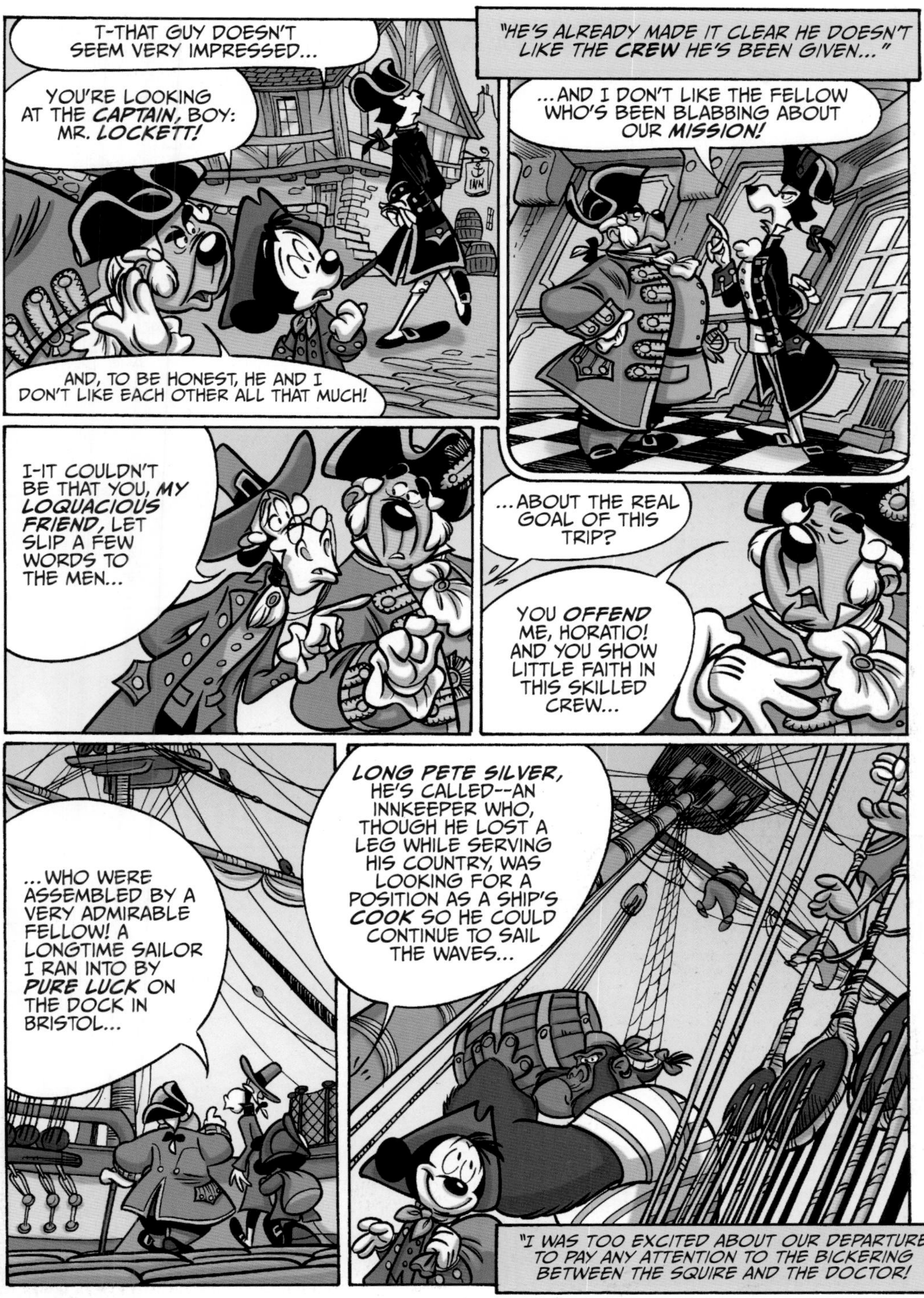
T-THAT GUY DOESN'T SEEM VERY IMPRESSED...
YOU'RE LOOKING AT THE *CAPTAIN,* BOY: MR. *LOCKETT!*
AND, TO BE HONEST, HE AND I DON'T LIKE EACH OTHER ALL THAT MUCH!
"HE'S ALREADY MADE IT CLEAR HE DOESN'T LIKE THE *CREW* HE'S BEEN GIVEN..."
...AND I DON'T LIKE THE FELLOW WHO'S BEEN BLABBING ABOUT OUR *MISSION!*
INN
I-IT COULDN'T BE THAT YOU, *MY LOQUACIOUS FRIEND,* LET SLIP A FEW WORDS TO THE MEN...
...ABOUT THE REAL GOAL OF THIS TRIP?
YOU *OFFEND* ME, HORATIO! AND YOU SHOW LITTLE FAITH IN THIS SKILLED CREW...
...WHO WERE ASSEMBLED BY A VERY ADMIRABLE FELLOW! A LONGTIME SAILOR I RAN INTO BY *PURE LUCK* ON THE DOCK IN BRISTOL...
LONG PETE SILVER, HE'S CALLED--AN INNKEEPER WHO, THOUGH HE LOST A LEG WHILE SERVING HIS COUNTRY, WAS LOOKING FOR A POSITION AS A SHIP'S *COOK* SO HE COULD CONTINUE TO SAIL THE WAVES...
"I WAS TOO EXCITED ABOUT OUR DEPARTURE TO PAY ANY ATTENTION TO THE BICKERING BETWEEN THE SQUIRE AND THE DOCTOR!

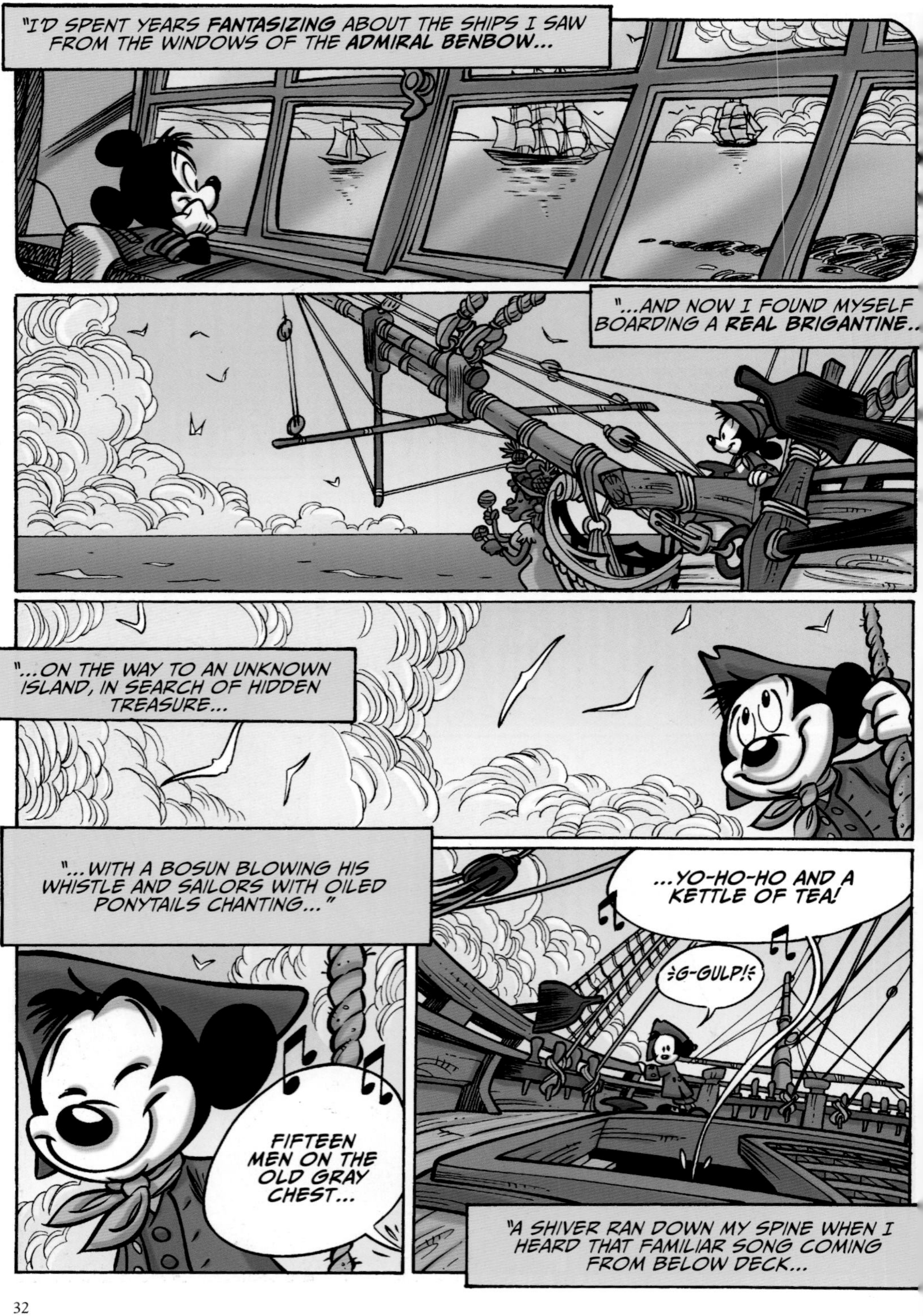
"I'D SPENT YEARS FANTASIZING ABOUT THE SHIPS I SAW FROM THE WINDOWS OF THE ADMIRAL BENBOW...
"...AND NOW I FOUND MYSELF BOARDING A REAL BRIGANTINE...
"...ON THE WAY TO AN UNKNOWN ISLAND, IN SEARCH OF HIDDEN TREASURE...
"...WITH A BOSUN BLOWING HIS WHISTLE AND SAILORS WITH OILED PONYTAILS CHANTING..."
FIFTEEN MEN ON THE OLD GRAY CHEST...
...YO-HO-HO AND A KETTLE OF TEA!
G-GULP!
"A SHIVER RAN DOWN MY SPINE WHEN I HEARD THAT FAMILIAR SONG COMING FROM BELOW DECK...

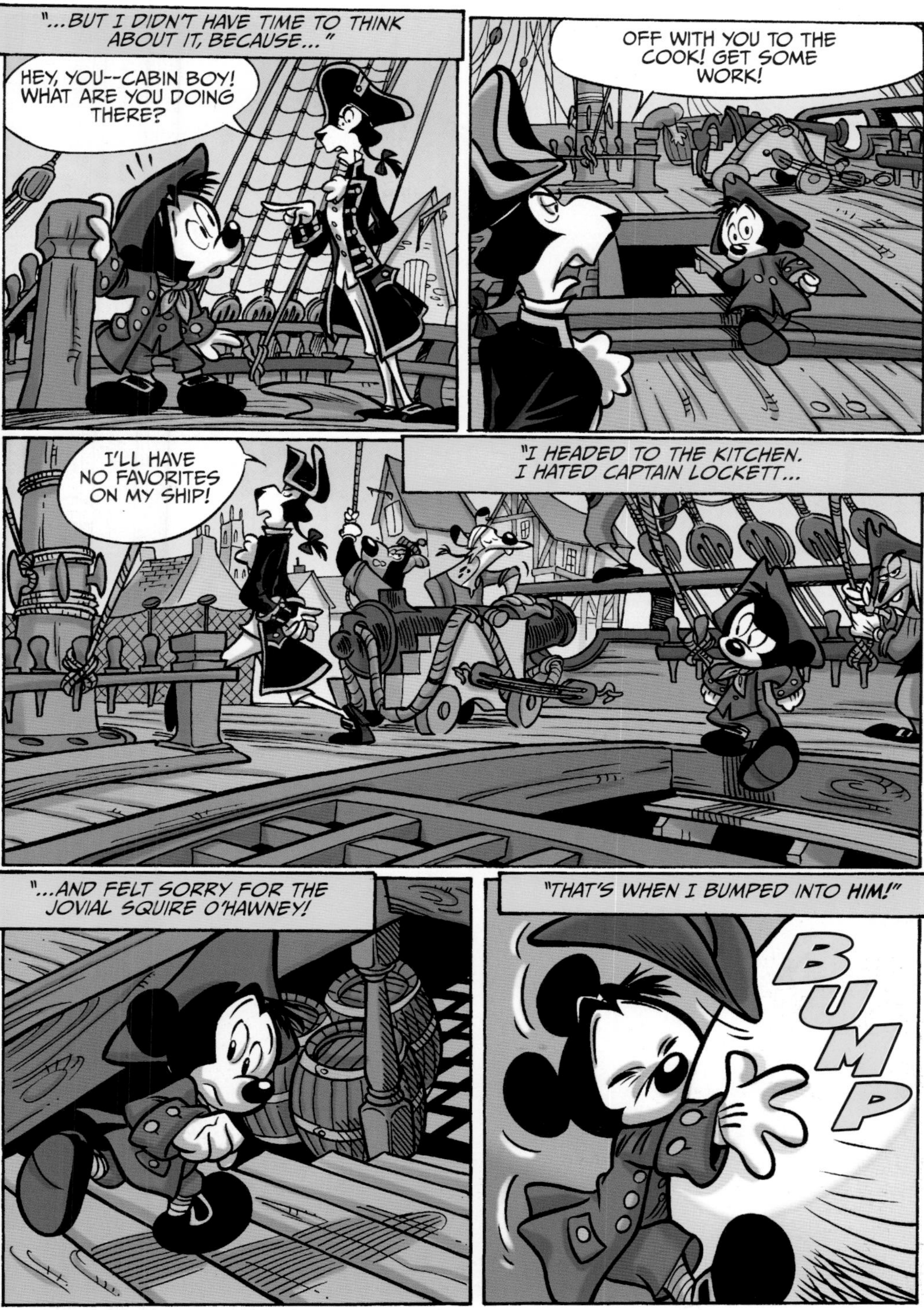
"...BUT I DIDN'T HAVE TIME TO THINK ABOUT IT, BECAUSE..."
HEY, YOU--CABIN BOY! WHAT ARE YOU DOING THERE?
OFF WITH YOU TO THE COOK! GET SOME WORK!
I'LL HAVE NO FAVORITES ON MY SHIP!
"I HEADED TO THE KITCHEN. I HATED CAPTAIN LOCKETT...
"...AND FELT SORRY FOR THE JOVIAL SQUIRE O'HAWNEY!
"THAT'S WHEN I BUMPED INTO HIM!"
BUMP

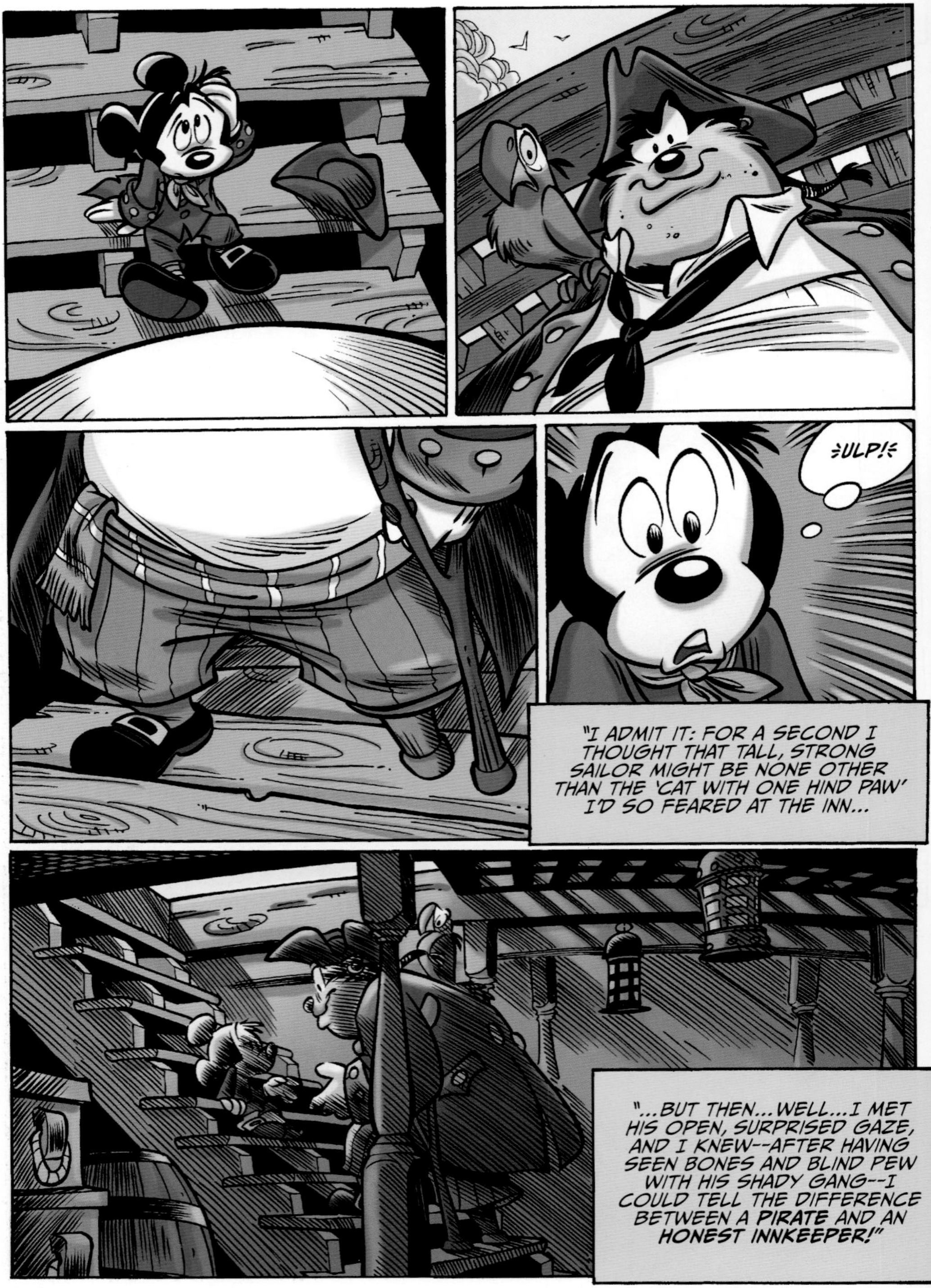

ULP!
"I ADMIT IT: FOR A SECOND I THOUGHT THAT TALL, STRONG SAILOR MIGHT BE NONE OTHER THAN THE 'CAT WITH ONE HIND PAW' I'D SO FEARED AT THE INN...
"...BUT THEN...WELL...I MET HIS OPEN, SURPRISED GAZE, AND I KNEW--AFTER HAVING SEEN BONES AND BLIND PEW WITH HIS SHADY GANG--I COULD TELL THE DIFFERENCE BETWEEN A PIRATE AND AN HONEST INNKEEPER!"

Y-YOU'RE *MR. SILVER*?

THAT'S ME, LITTLE ONE!

AND WHO MIGHT YOU BE?

JIM! JIM MOUSEKINS, SIR...

AT YOUR SERVICE!

HO HO HO! DID YOU HEAR THAT, OLD FRIEND?

WE'VE GOT A REAL RESPECTABLE LITTLE GUY 'ERE!

PIECES OF EIGHT! PIECES OF EIGHT!

ALL RIGHT, ALL RIGHT! I'LL INTRODUCE YOU...

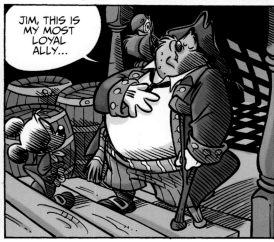

JIM, THIS IS MY MOST LOYAL ALLY...

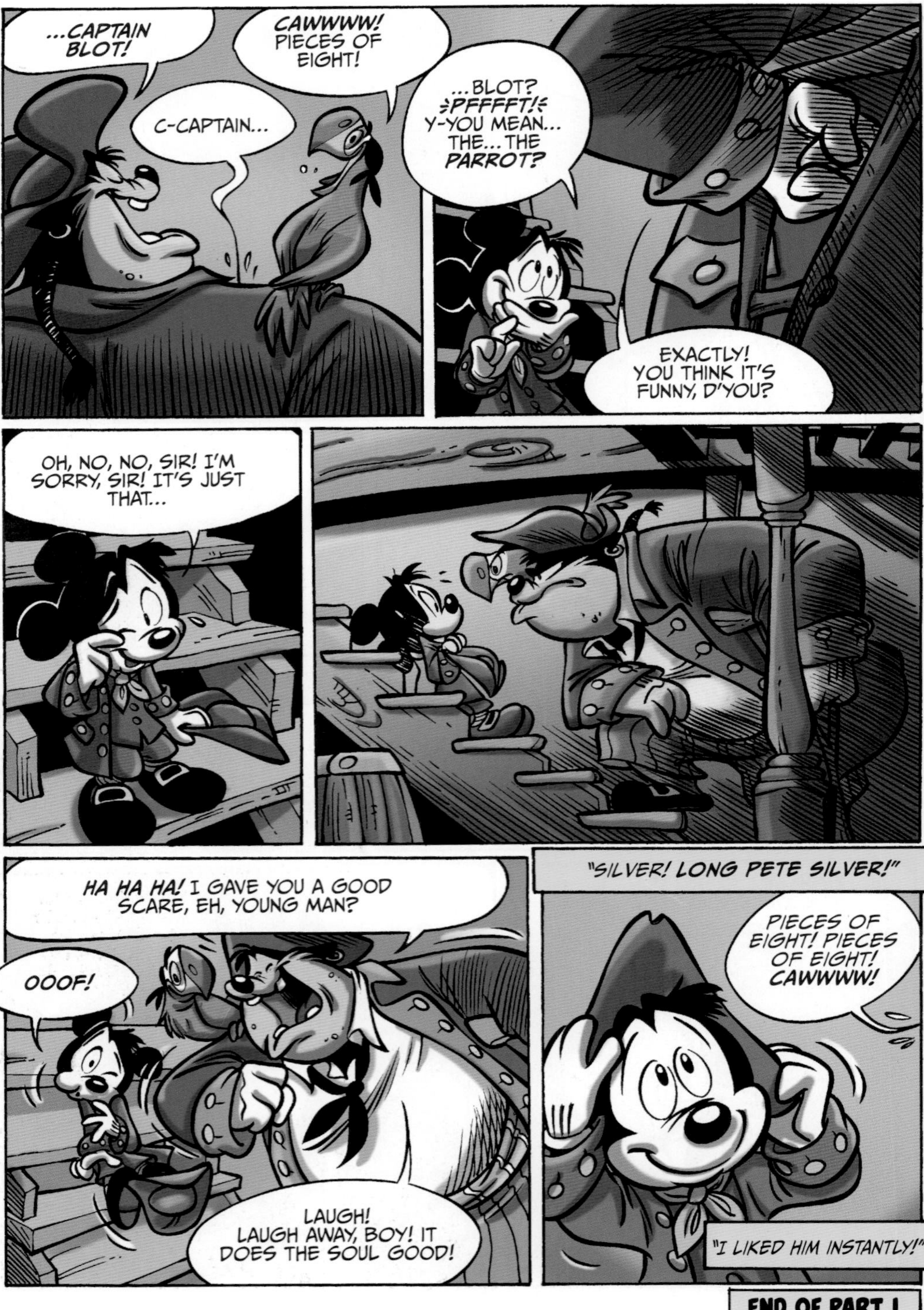
...CAPTAIN BLOT!
CAWWWW! PIECES OF EIGHT!
C-CAPTAIN...
...BLOT? PFFFFT! Y-YOU MEAN... THE... THE PARROT?
EXACTLY! YOU THINK IT'S FUNNY, D'YOU?
OH, NO, NO, SIR! I'M SORRY, SIR! IT'S JUST THAT...
HA HA HA! I GAVE YOU A GOOD SCARE, EH, YOUNG MAN?
OOOF!
LAUGH! LAUGH AWAY, BOY! IT DOES THE SOUL GOOD!
"SILVER! LONG PETE SILVER!"
PIECES OF EIGHT! PIECES OF EIGHT! CAWWWW!
"I LIKED HIM INSTANTLY!"

END OF PART I

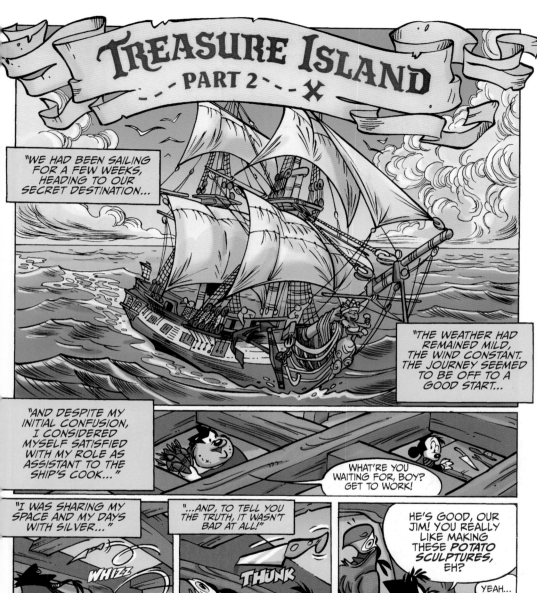

TREASURE ISLAND
PART 2

"WE HAD BEEN SAILING FOR A FEW WEEKS, HEADING TO OUR SECRET DESTINATION..."

"THE WEATHER HAD REMAINED MILD, THE WIND CONSTANT. THE JOURNEY SEEMED TO BE OFF TO A GOOD START..."

"AND DESPITE MY INITIAL CONFUSION, I CONSIDERED MYSELF SATISFIED WITH MY ROLE AS ASSISTANT TO THE SHIP'S COOK..."

WHAT'RE YOU WAITING FOR, BOY? GET TO WORK!

"I WAS SHARING MY SPACE AND MY DAYS WITH SILVER..."

"...AND, TO TELL YOU THE TRUTH, IT WASN'T BAD AT ALL!"

WHIZZ

THUNK

HE'S GOOD, OUR JIM! YOU REALLY LIKE MAKING THESE *POTATO SCULPTURES*, EH?

YEAH...

PIECES OF EIGHT! PIECES OF EIGHT!

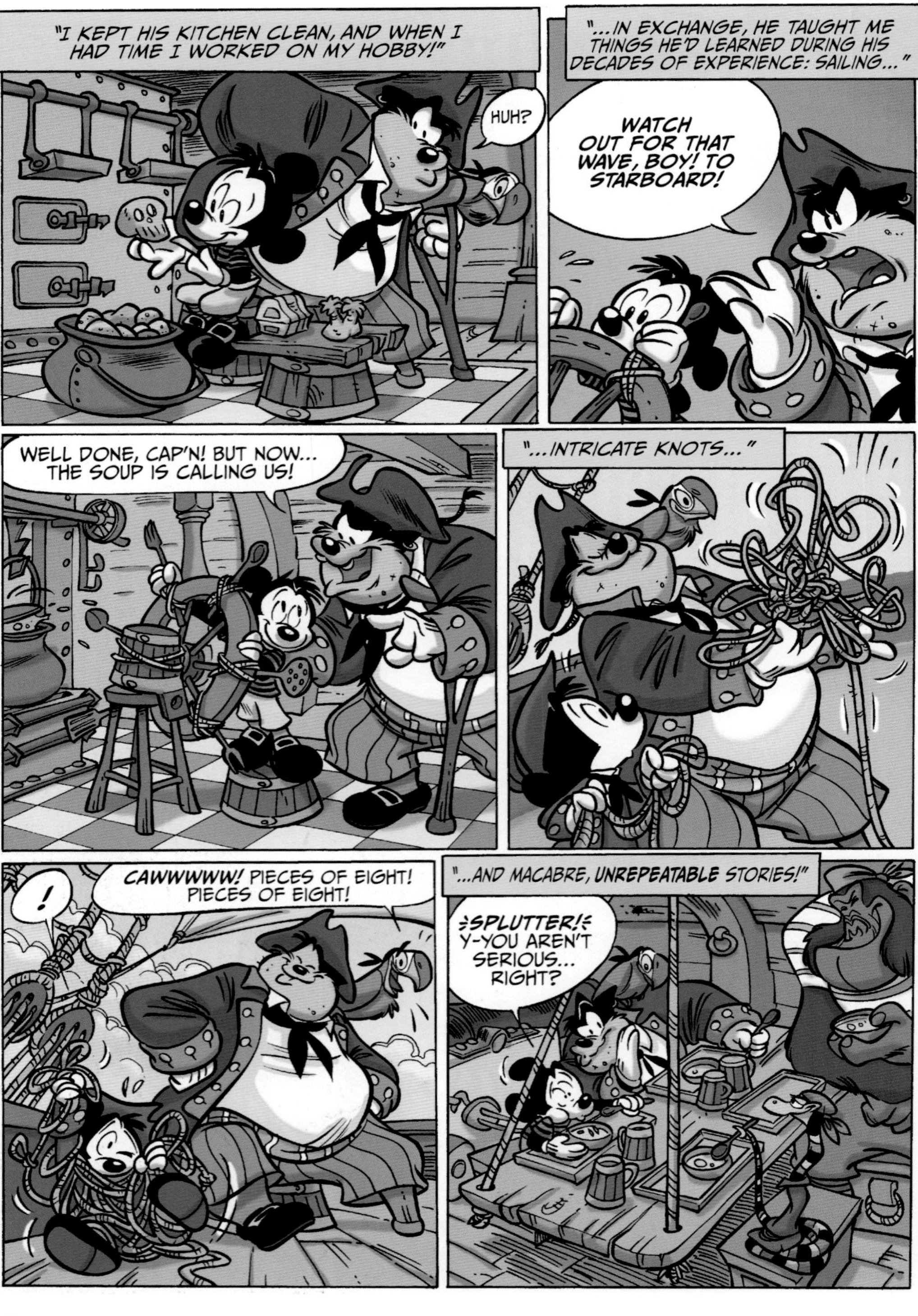
"I KEPT HIS KITCHEN CLEAN, AND WHEN I HAD TIME I WORKED ON MY HOBBY!"
HUH?
"...IN EXCHANGE, HE TAUGHT ME THINGS HE'D LEARNED DURING HIS DECADES OF EXPERIENCE: SAILING..."
WATCH OUT FOR THAT WAVE, BOY! TO STARBOARD!
WELL DONE, CAP'N! BUT NOW... THE SOUP IS CALLING US!
"...INTRICATE KNOTS..."
!
CAWWWWW! PIECES OF EIGHT! PIECES OF EIGHT!
"...AND MACABRE, UNREPEATABLE STORIES!"
SPLUTTER! Y-YOU AREN'T SERIOUS... RIGHT?

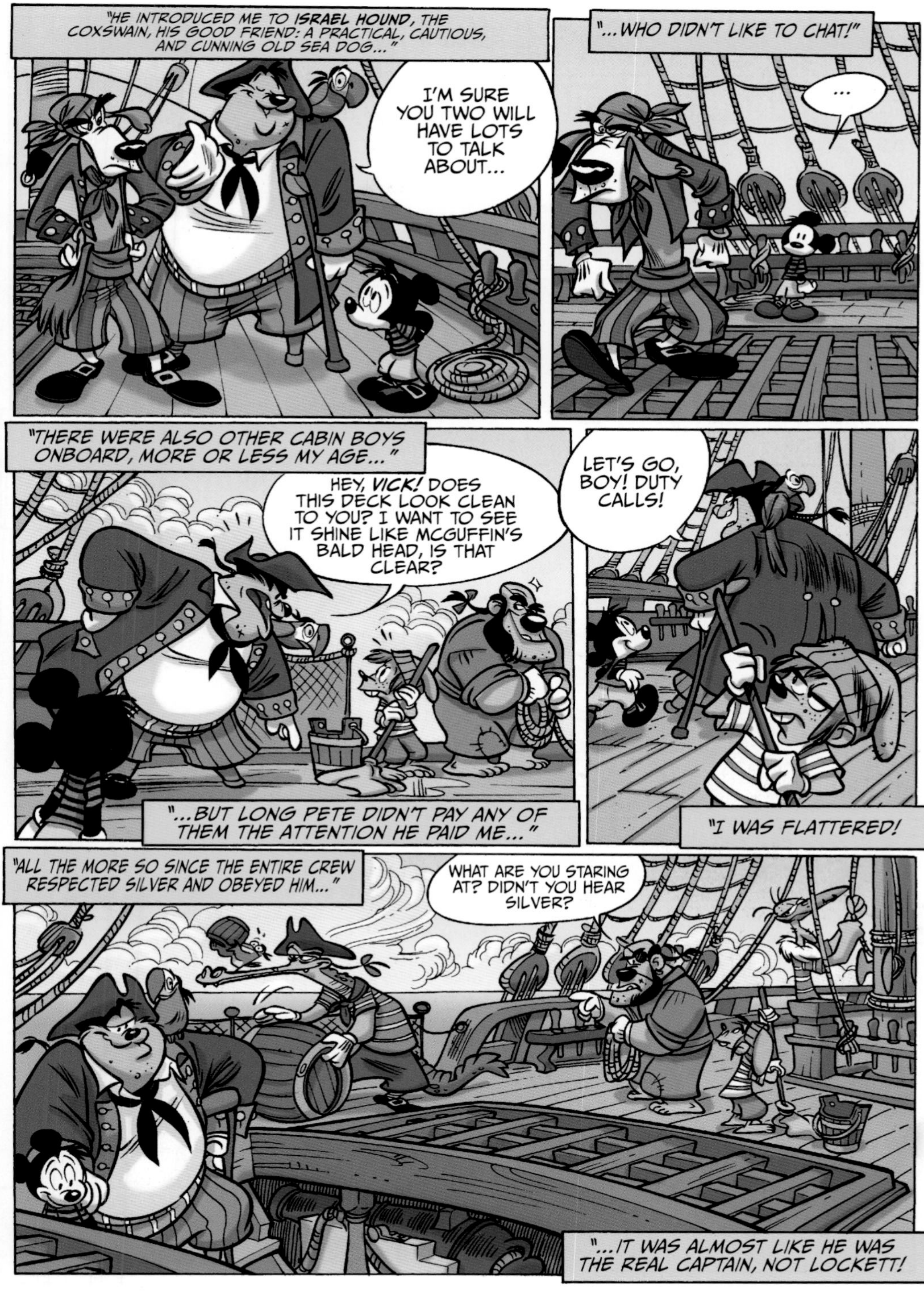
"HE INTRODUCED ME TO ISRAEL HOUND, THE COXSWAIN, HIS GOOD FRIEND: A PRACTICAL, CAUTIOUS, AND CUNNING OLD SEA DOG..."
I'M SURE YOU TWO WILL HAVE LOTS TO TALK ABOUT...
"...WHO DIDN'T LIKE TO CHAT!"
...
"THERE WERE ALSO OTHER CABIN BOYS ONBOARD, MORE OR LESS MY AGE..."
HEY, VICK! DOES THIS DECK LOOK CLEAN TO YOU? I WANT TO SEE IT SHINE LIKE MCGUFFIN'S BALD HEAD, IS THAT CLEAR?
"...BUT LONG PETE DIDN'T PAY ANY OF THEM THE ATTENTION HE PAID ME..."
LET'S GO, BOY! DUTY CALLS!
"I WAS FLATTERED!
"ALL THE MORE SO SINCE THE ENTIRE CREW RESPECTED SILVER AND OBEYED HIM..."
WHAT ARE YOU STARING AT? DIDN'T YOU HEAR SILVER?
"...IT WAS ALMOST LIKE HE WAS THE REAL CAPTAIN, NOT LOCKETT!

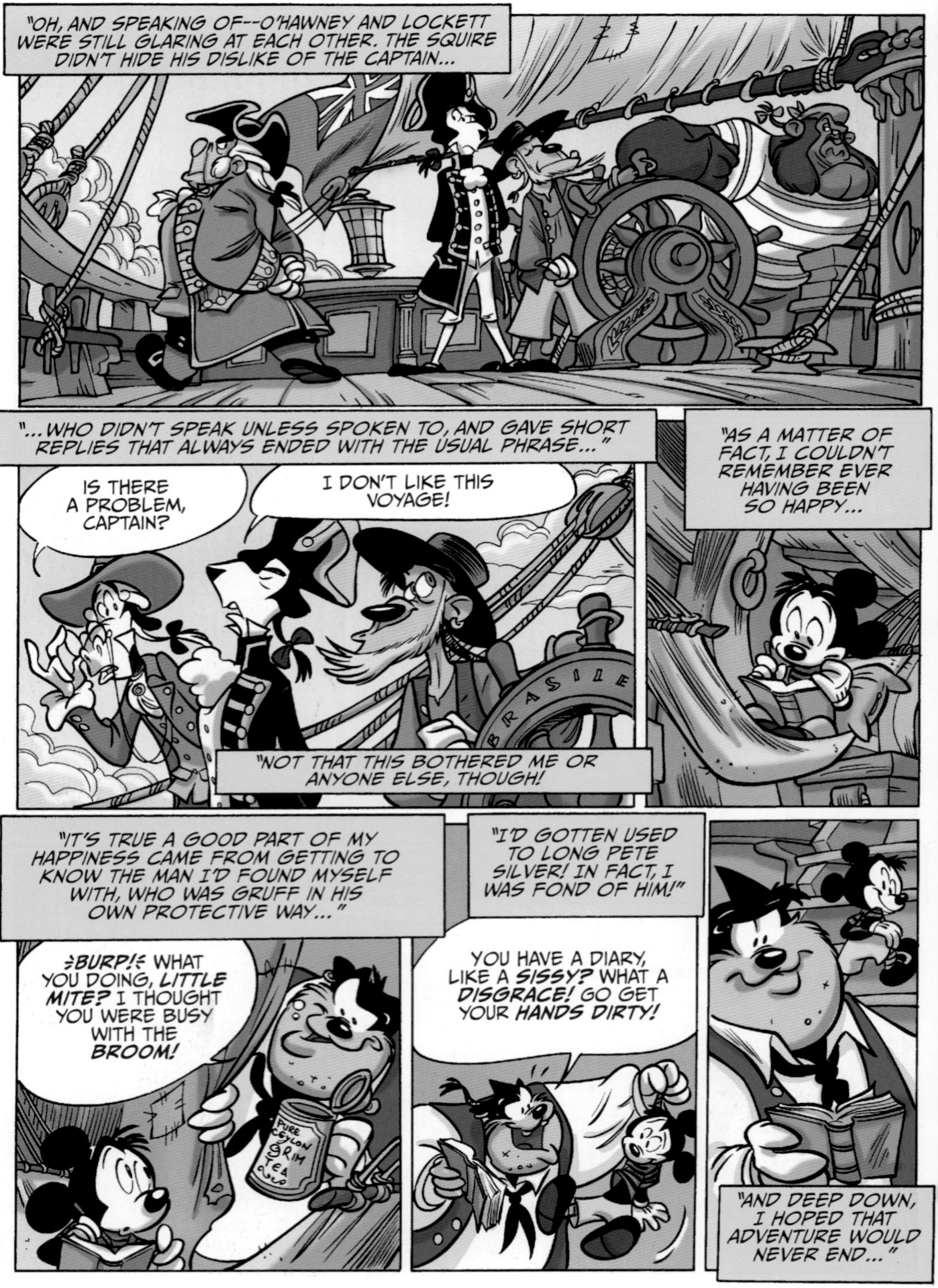
"OH, AND SPEAKING OF--O'HAWNEY AND LOCKETT WERE STILL GLARING AT EACH OTHER. THE SQUIRE DIDN'T HIDE HIS DISLIKE OF THE CAPTAIN...
"...WHO DIDN'T SPEAK UNLESS SPOKEN TO, AND GAVE SHORT REPLIES THAT ALWAYS ENDED WITH THE USUAL PHRASE..."
IS THERE A PROBLEM, CAPTAIN?
I DON'T LIKE THIS VOYAGE!
BRASILE
"NOT THAT THIS BOTHERED ME OR ANYONE ELSE, THOUGH!
"AS A MATTER OF FACT, I COULDN'T REMEMBER EVER HAVING BEEN SO HAPPY...
"IT'S TRUE A GOOD PART OF MY HAPPINESS CAME FROM GETTING TO KNOW THE MAN I'D FOUND MYSELF WITH, WHO WAS GRUFF IN HIS OWN PROTECTIVE WAY..."
BURP! WHAT YOU DOING, LITTLE MITE? I THOUGHT YOU WERE BUSY WITH THE BROOM!
PURE CEYLON GRIM TEA
"I'D GOTTEN USED TO LONG PETE SILVER! IN FACT, I WAS FOND OF HIM!"
YOU HAVE A DIARY, LIKE A SISSY? WHAT A DISGRACE! GO GET YOUR HANDS DIRTY!
"AND DEEP DOWN, I HOPED THAT ADVENTURE WOULD NEVER END..."

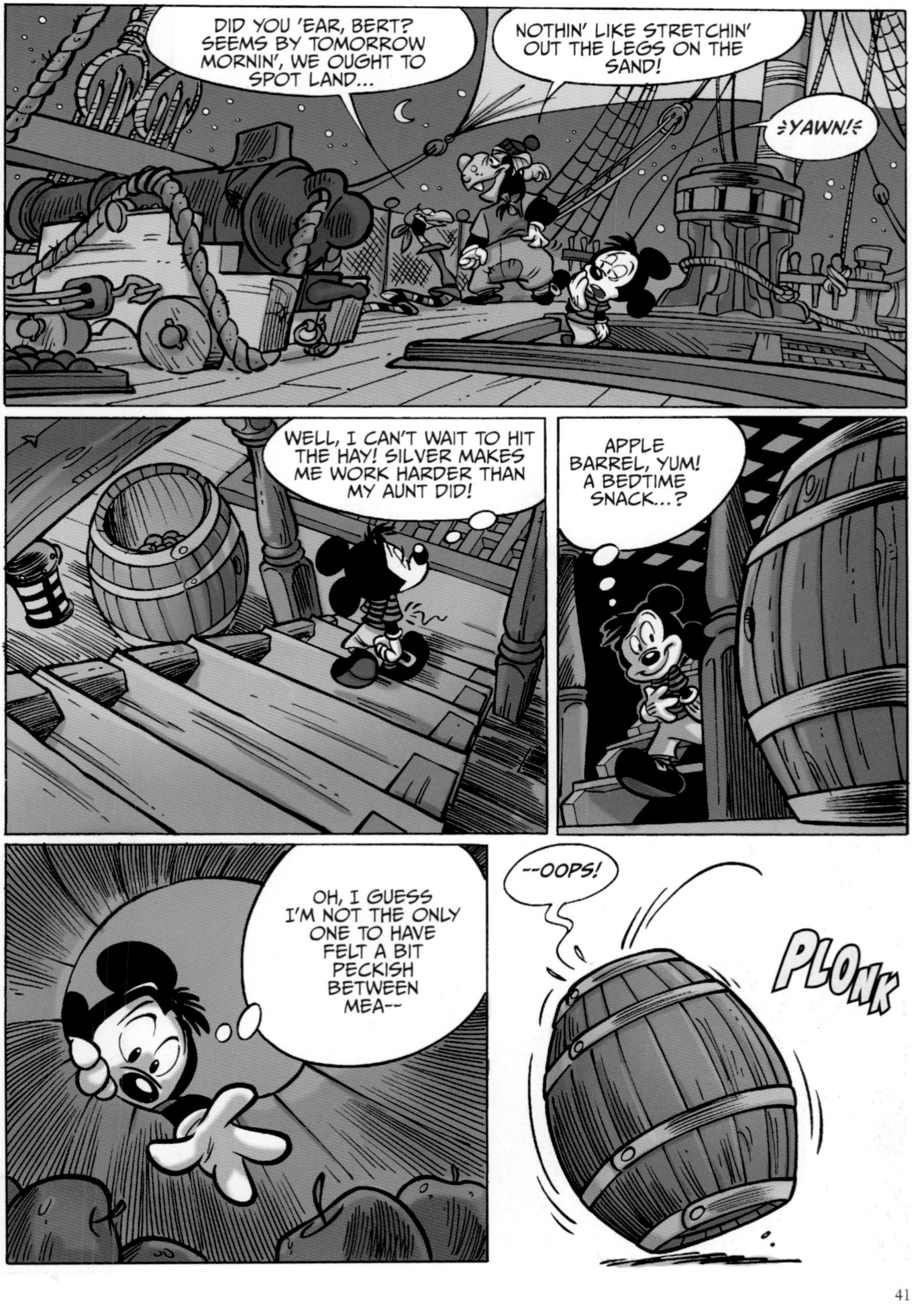
DID YOU 'EAR, BERT? SEEMS BY TOMORROW MORNIN', WE OUGHT TO SPOT LAND...
NOTHIN' LIKE STRETCHIN' OUT THE LEGS ON THE SAND!
YAWN!
WELL, I CAN'T WAIT TO HIT THE HAY! SILVER MAKES ME WORK HARDER THAN MY AUNT DID!
APPLE BARREL, YUM! A BEDTIME SNACK...?
OH, I GUESS I'M NOT THE ONLY ONE TO HAVE FELT A BIT PECKISH BETWEEN MEA--
--OOPS!
PLONK

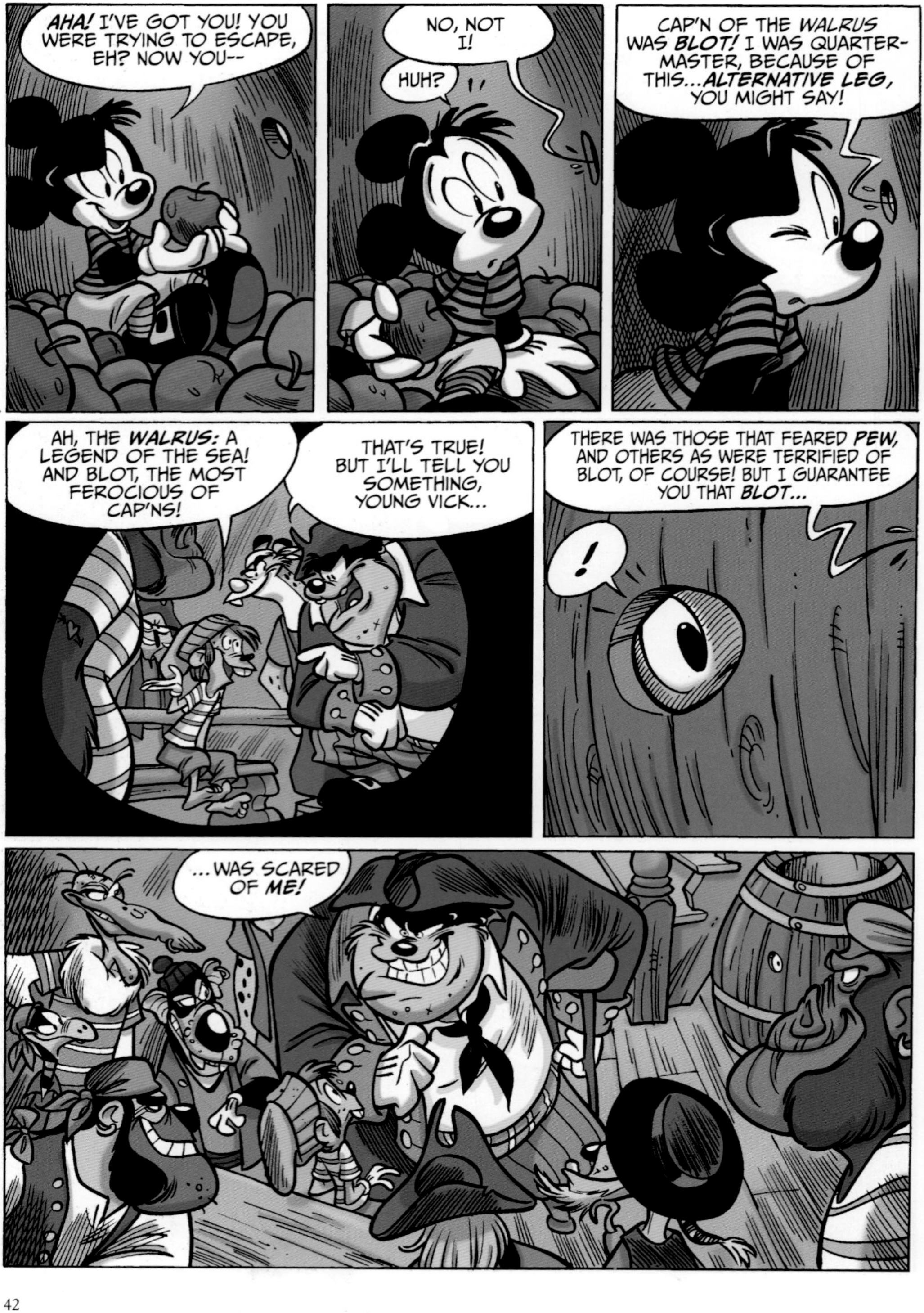

AHA! I'VE GOT YOU! YOU WERE TRYING TO ESCAPE, EH? NOW YOU--
NO, NOT I!
HUH?
CAP'N OF THE WALRUS WAS BLOT! I WAS QUARTER-MASTER, BECAUSE OF THIS...ALTERNATIVE LEG, YOU MIGHT SAY!
AH, THE WALRUS: A LEGEND OF THE SEA! AND BLOT, THE MOST FEROCIOUS OF CAP'NS!
THAT'S TRUE! BUT I'LL TELL YOU SOMETHING, YOUNG VICK...
THERE WAS THOSE THAT FEARED PEW, AND OTHERS AS WERE TERRIFIED OF BLOT, OF COURSE! BUT I GUARANTEE YOU THAT BLOT...
!
...WAS SCARED OF ME!

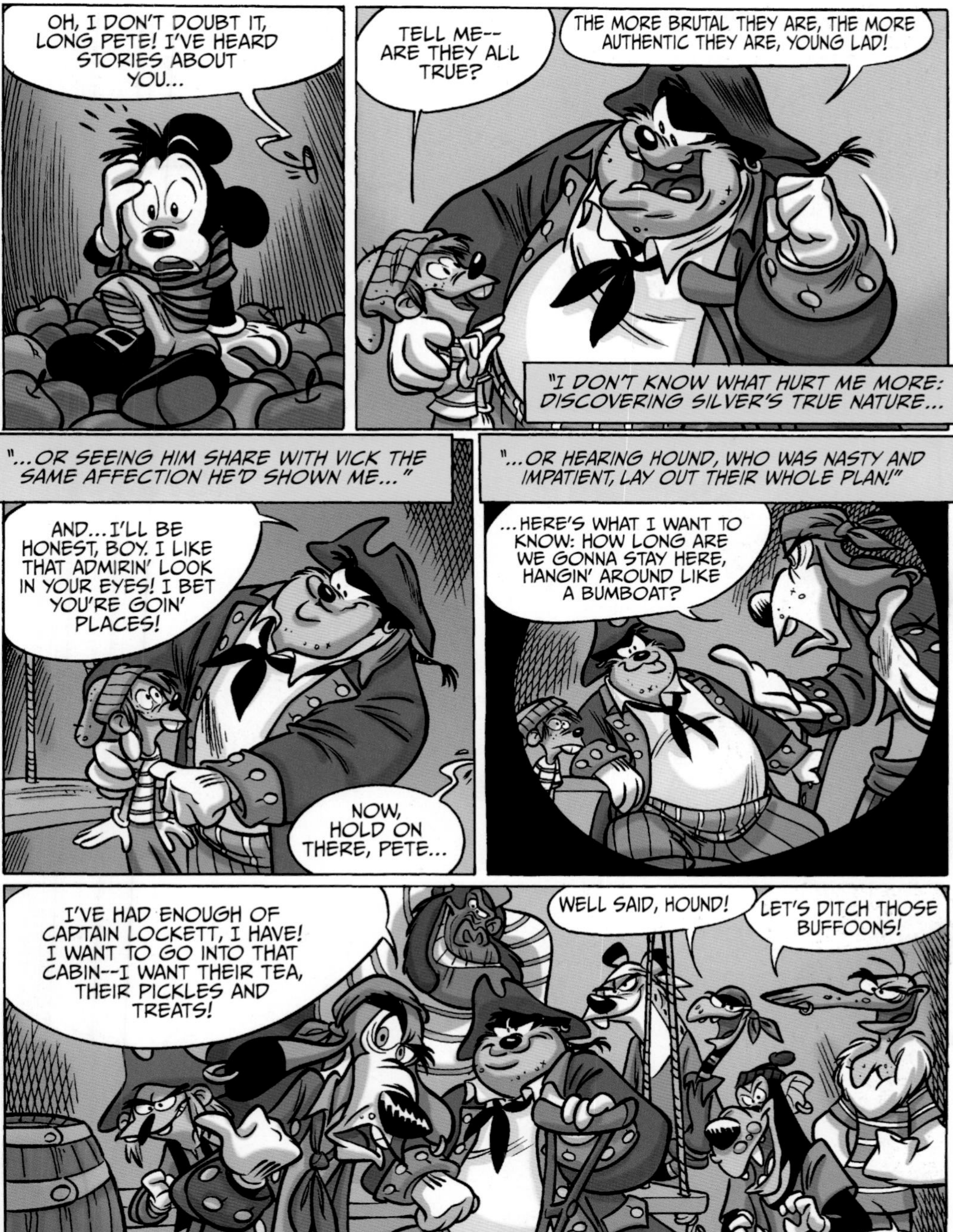
OH, I DON'T DOUBT IT, LONG PETE! I'VE HEARD STORIES ABOUT YOU...
TELL ME-- ARE THEY ALL TRUE?
THE MORE BRUTAL THEY ARE, THE MORE AUTHENTIC THEY ARE, YOUNG LAD!
"I DON'T KNOW WHAT HURT ME MORE: DISCOVERING SILVER'S TRUE NATURE...
"...OR SEEING HIM SHARE WITH VICK THE SAME AFFECTION HE'D SHOWN ME..."
AND... I'LL BE HONEST, BOY. I LIKE THAT ADMIRIN' LOOK IN YOUR EYES! I BET YOU'RE GOIN' PLACES!
NOW, HOLD ON THERE, PETE...
"...OR HEARING HOUND, WHO WAS NASTY AND IMPATIENT, LAY OUT THEIR WHOLE PLAN!"
...HERE'S WHAT I WANT TO KNOW: HOW LONG ARE WE GONNA STAY HERE, HANGIN' AROUND LIKE A BUMBOAT?
I'VE HAD ENOUGH OF CAPTAIN LOCKETT, I HAVE! I WANT TO GO INTO THAT CABIN--I WANT THEIR TEA, THEIR PICKLES AND TREATS!
WELL SAID, HOUND!
LET'S DITCH THOSE BUFFOONS!
WHAT ARE WE WAITING FOR?

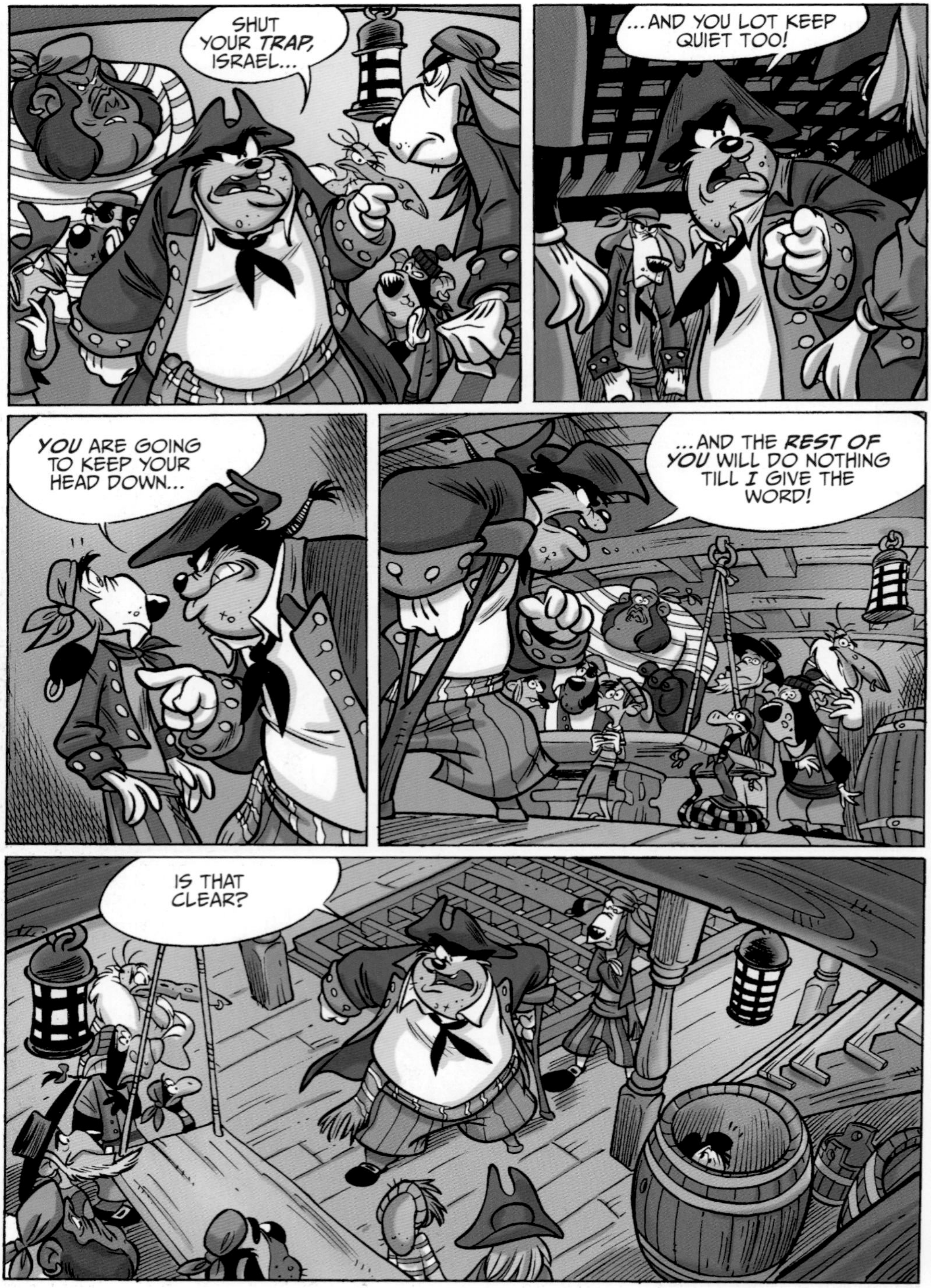
SHUT YOUR TRAP, ISRAEL...
...AND YOU LOT KEEP QUIET TOO!
YOU ARE GOING TO KEEP YOUR HEAD DOWN...
...AND THE REST OF YOU WILL DO NOTHING TILL I GIVE THE WORD!
IS THAT CLEAR?

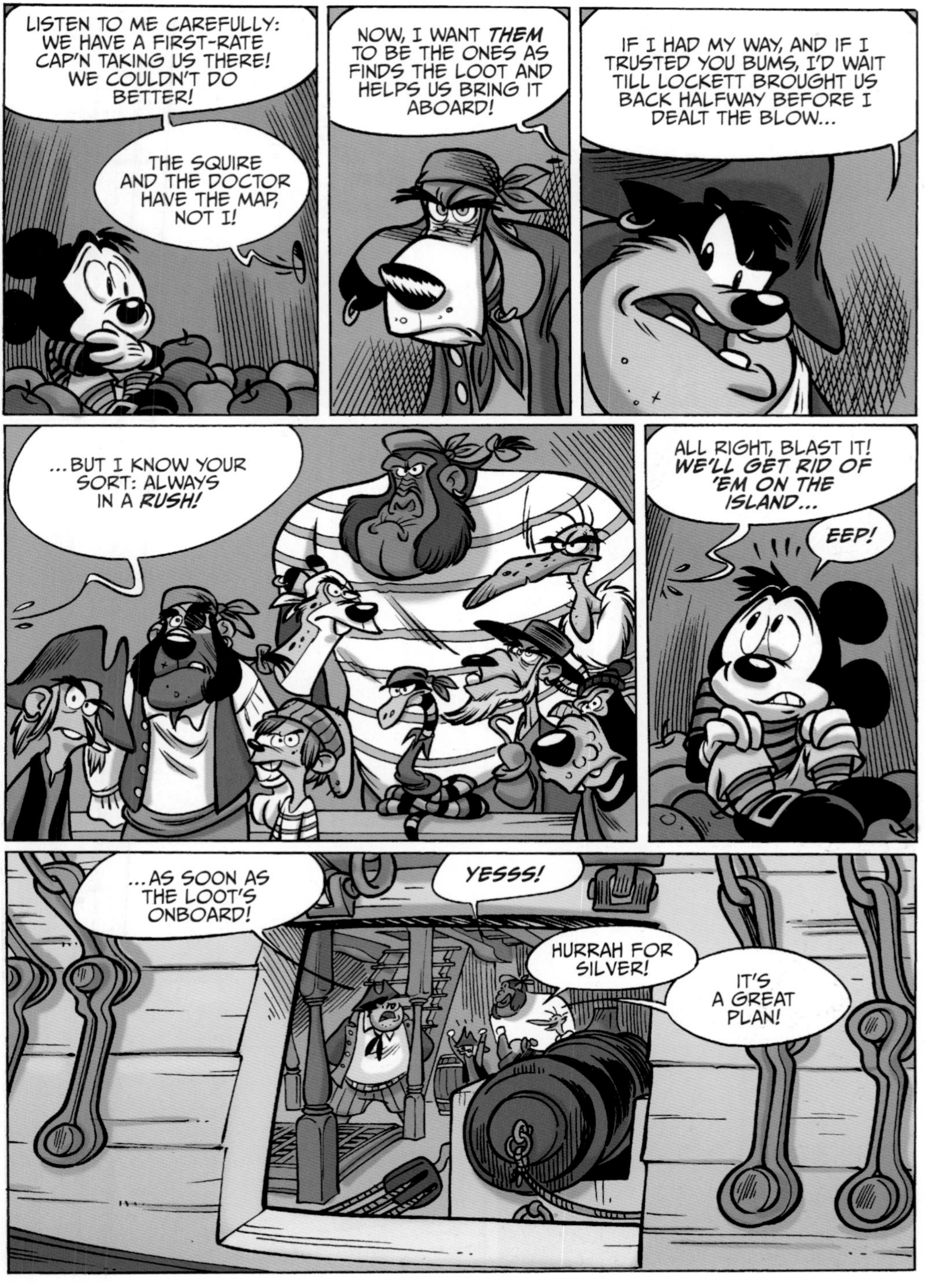
LISTEN TO ME CAREFULLY: WE HAVE A FIRST-RATE CAP'N TAKING US THERE! WE COULDN'T DO BETTER!
THE SQUIRE AND THE DOCTOR HAVE THE MAP, NOT I!
NOW, I WANT *THEM* TO BE THE ONES AS FINDS THE LOOT AND HELPS US BRING IT ABOARD!
IF I HAD MY WAY, AND IF I TRUSTED YOU BUMS, I'D WAIT TILL LOCKETT BROUGHT US BACK HALFWAY BEFORE I DEALT THE BLOW...
...BUT I KNOW YOUR SORT: ALWAYS IN A *RUSH!*
ALL RIGHT, BLAST IT! *WE'LL GET RID OF 'EM ON THE ISLAND...*
EEP!
...AS SOON AS THE LOOT'S ONBOARD!
YESSS!
HURRAH FOR SILVER!
IT'S A GREAT PLAN!

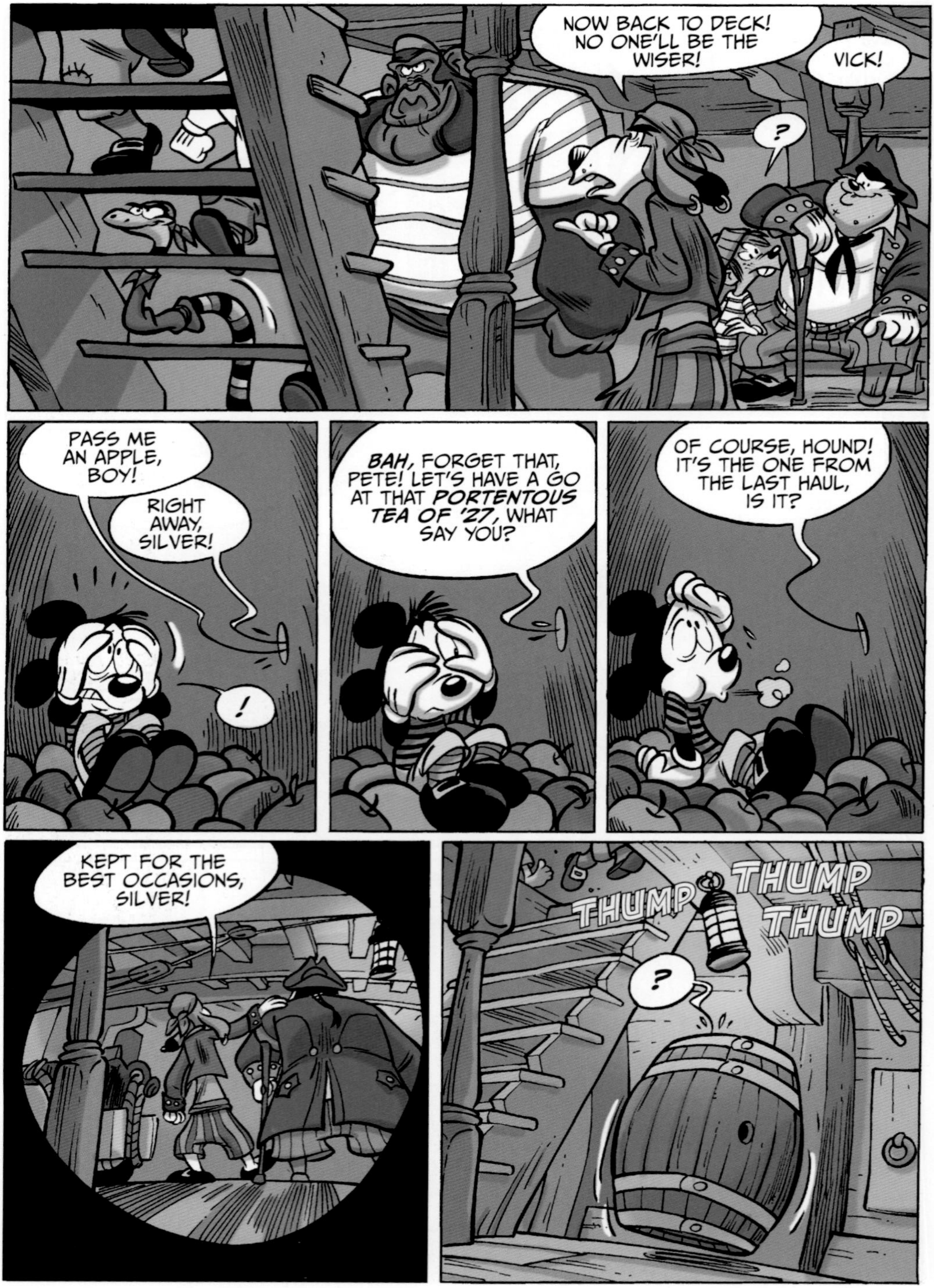

NOW BACK TO DECK! NO ONE'LL BE THE WISER!
VICK!
?
PASS ME AN APPLE, BOY!
RIGHT AWAY, SILVER!
!
BAH, FORGET THAT, PETE! LET'S HAVE A GO AT THAT PORTENTOUS TEA OF '27, WHAT SAY YOU?
OF COURSE, HOUND! IT'S THE ONE FROM THE LAST HAUL, IS IT?
KEPT FOR THE BEST OCCASIONS, SILVER!
THUMP THUMP
THUMP THUMP
?

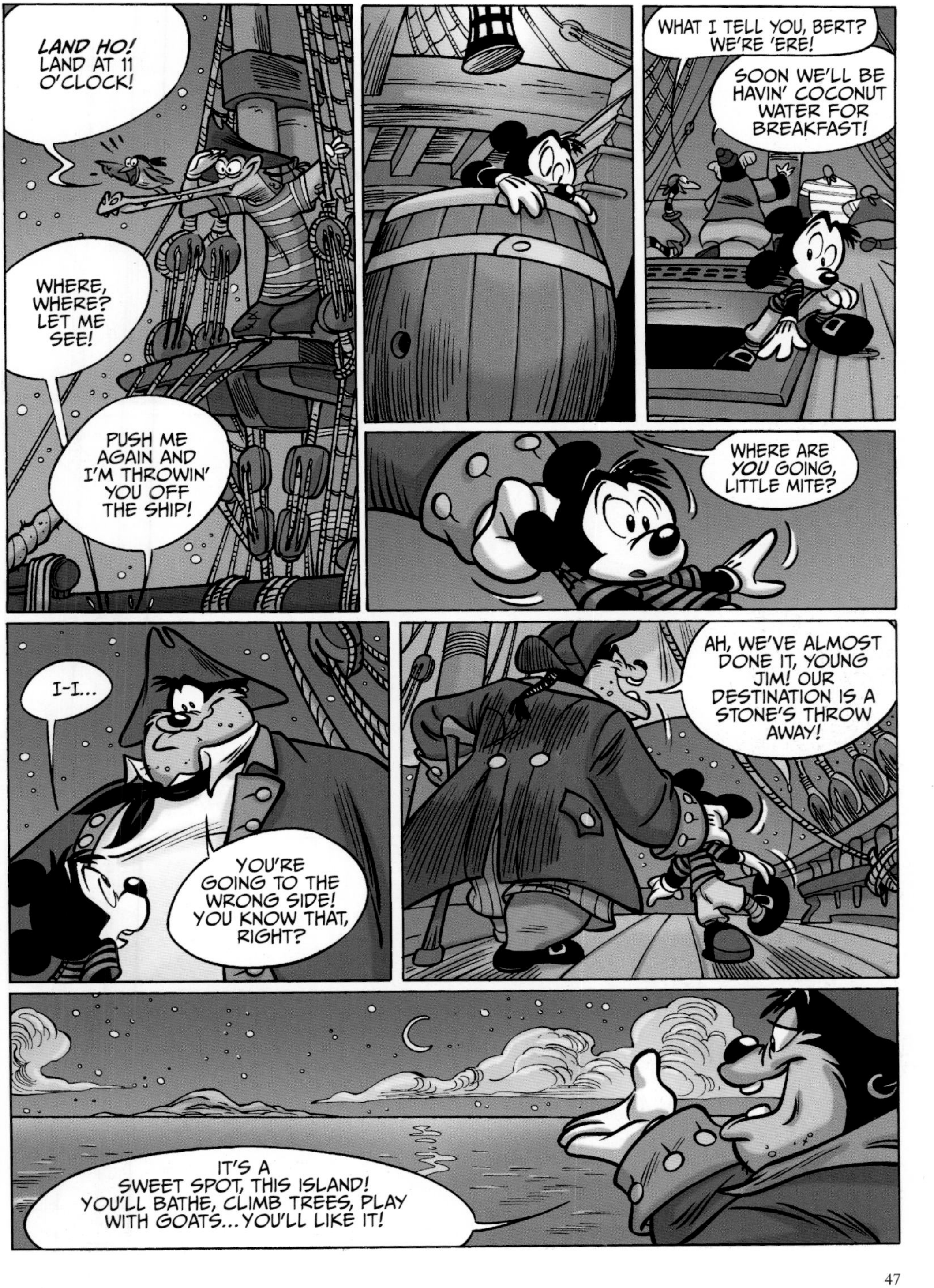

LAND HO! LAND AT 11 O'CLOCK!
WHERE, WHERE? LET ME SEE!
PUSH ME AGAIN AND I'M THROWIN' YOU OFF THE SHIP!
WHAT I TELL YOU, BERT? WE'RE 'ERE!
SOON WE'LL BE HAVIN' COCONUT WATER FOR BREAKFAST!
WHERE ARE YOU GOING, LITTLE MITE?
I-I...
YOU'RE GOING TO THE WRONG SIDE! YOU KNOW THAT, RIGHT?
AH, WE'VE ALMOST DONE IT, YOUNG JIM! OUR DESTINATION IS A STONE'S THROW AWAY!
IT'S A SWEET SPOT, THIS ISLAND! YOU'LL BATHE, CLIMB TREES, PLAY WITH GOATS... YOU'LL LIKE IT!

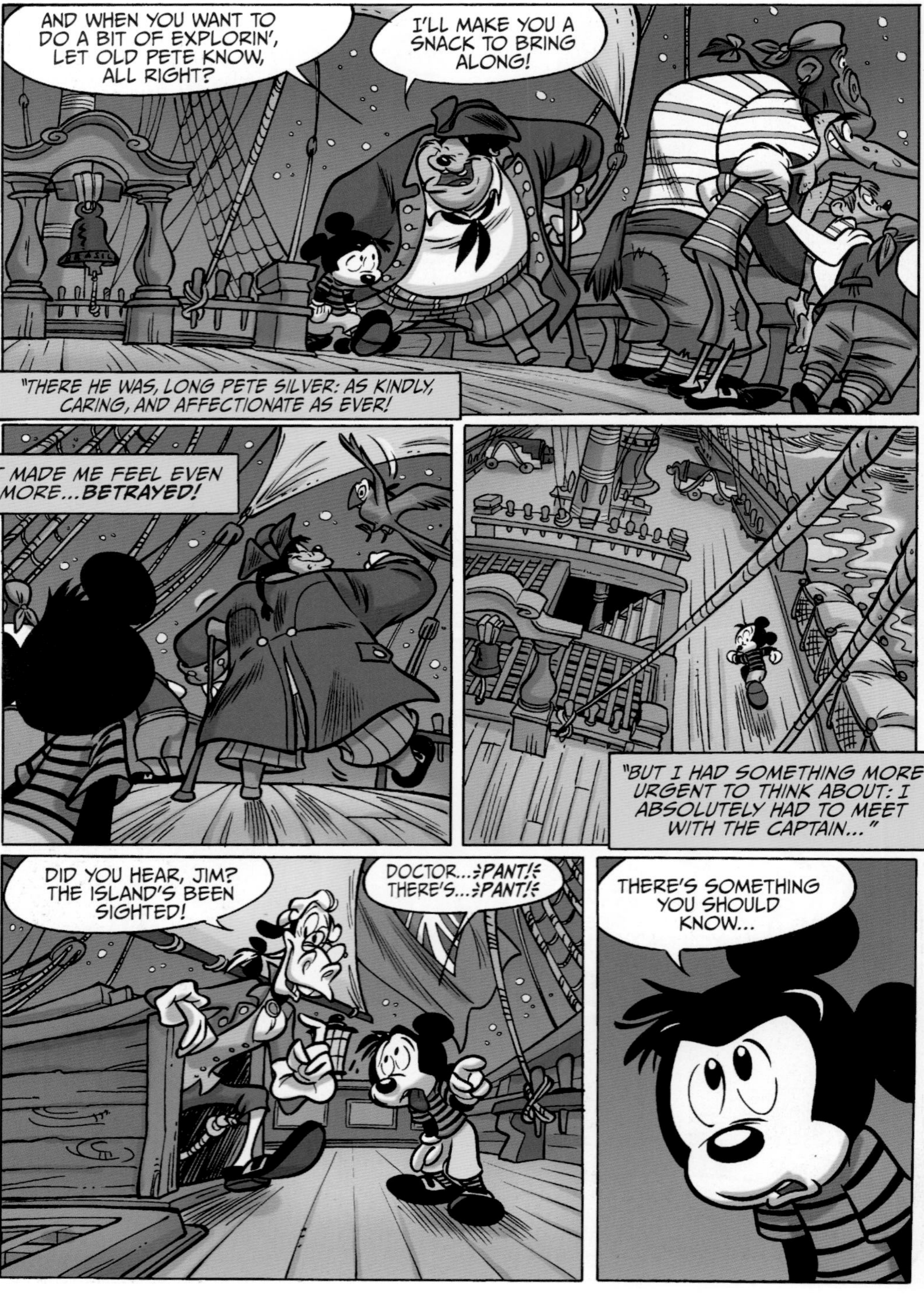

AND WHEN YOU WANT TO DO A BIT OF EXPLORIN', LET OLD PETE KNOW, ALL RIGHT?
I'LL MAKE YOU A SNACK TO BRING ALONG!
"THERE HE WAS, LONG PETE SILVER: AS KINDLY, CARING, AND AFFECTIONATE AS EVER!
"IT MADE ME FEEL EVEN MORE... BETRAYED!
"BUT I HAD SOMETHING MORE URGENT TO THINK ABOUT: I ABSOLUTELY HAD TO MEET WITH THE CAPTAIN..."
DID YOU HEAR, JIM? THE ISLAND'S BEEN SIGHTED!
DOCTOR... PANT! THERE'S... PANT!
THERE'S SOMETHING YOU SHOULD KNOW...

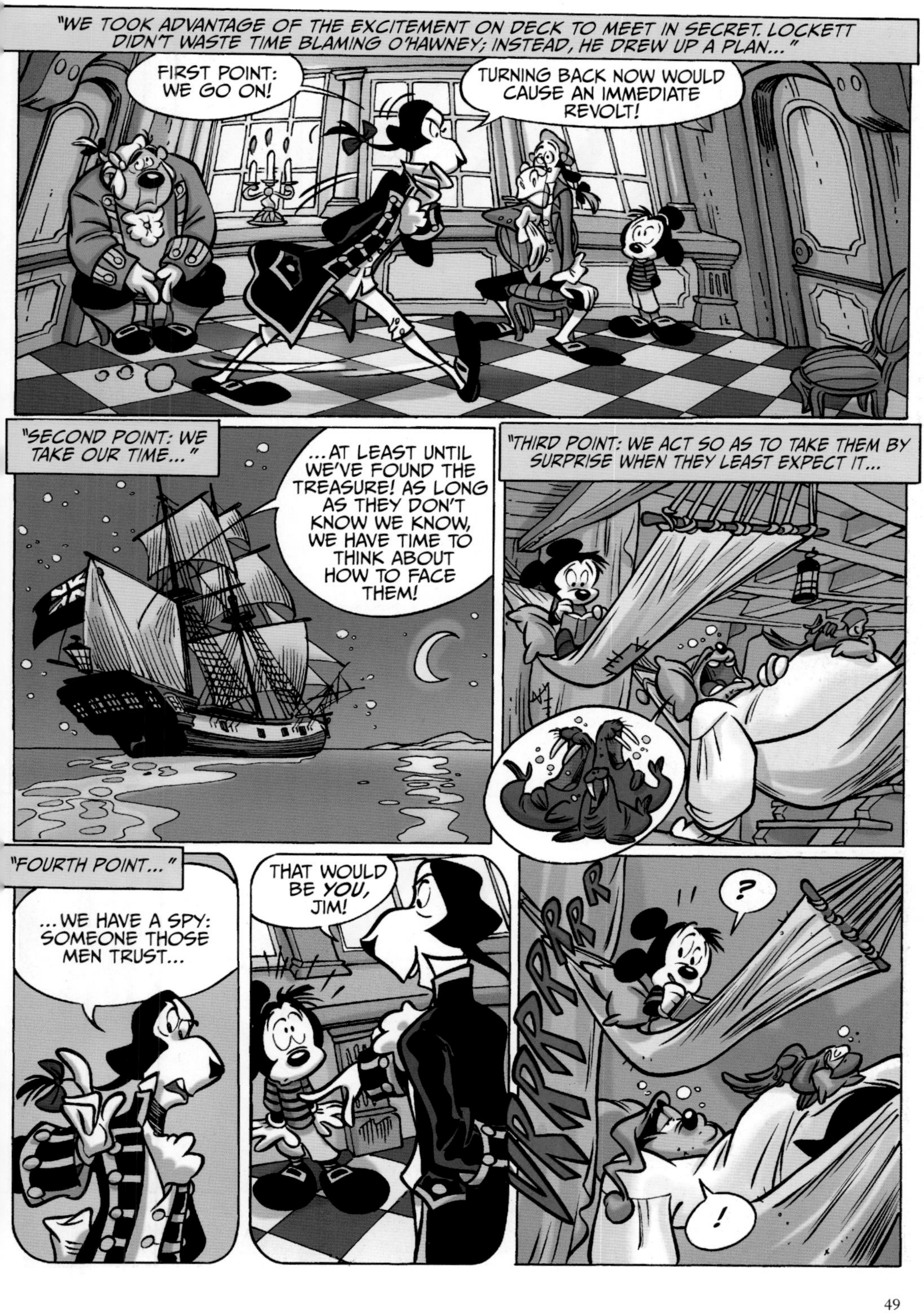
"WE TOOK ADVANTAGE OF THE EXCITEMENT ON DECK TO MEET IN SECRET. LOCKETT DIDN'T WASTE TIME BLAMING O'HAWNEY; INSTEAD, HE DREW UP A PLAN..."
FIRST POINT: WE GO ON!
TURNING BACK NOW WOULD CAUSE AN IMMEDIATE REVOLT!
"SECOND POINT: WE TAKE OUR TIME..."
...AT LEAST UNTIL WE'VE FOUND THE TREASURE! AS LONG AS THEY DON'T KNOW WE KNOW, WE HAVE TIME TO THINK ABOUT HOW TO FACE THEM!
"THIRD POINT: WE ACT SO AS TO TAKE THEM BY SURPRISE WHEN THEY LEAST EXPECT IT...
"FOURTH POINT..."
...WE HAVE A SPY: SOMEONE THOSE MEN TRUST...
THAT WOULD BE YOU, JIM!
?
WRRRRRRR
!

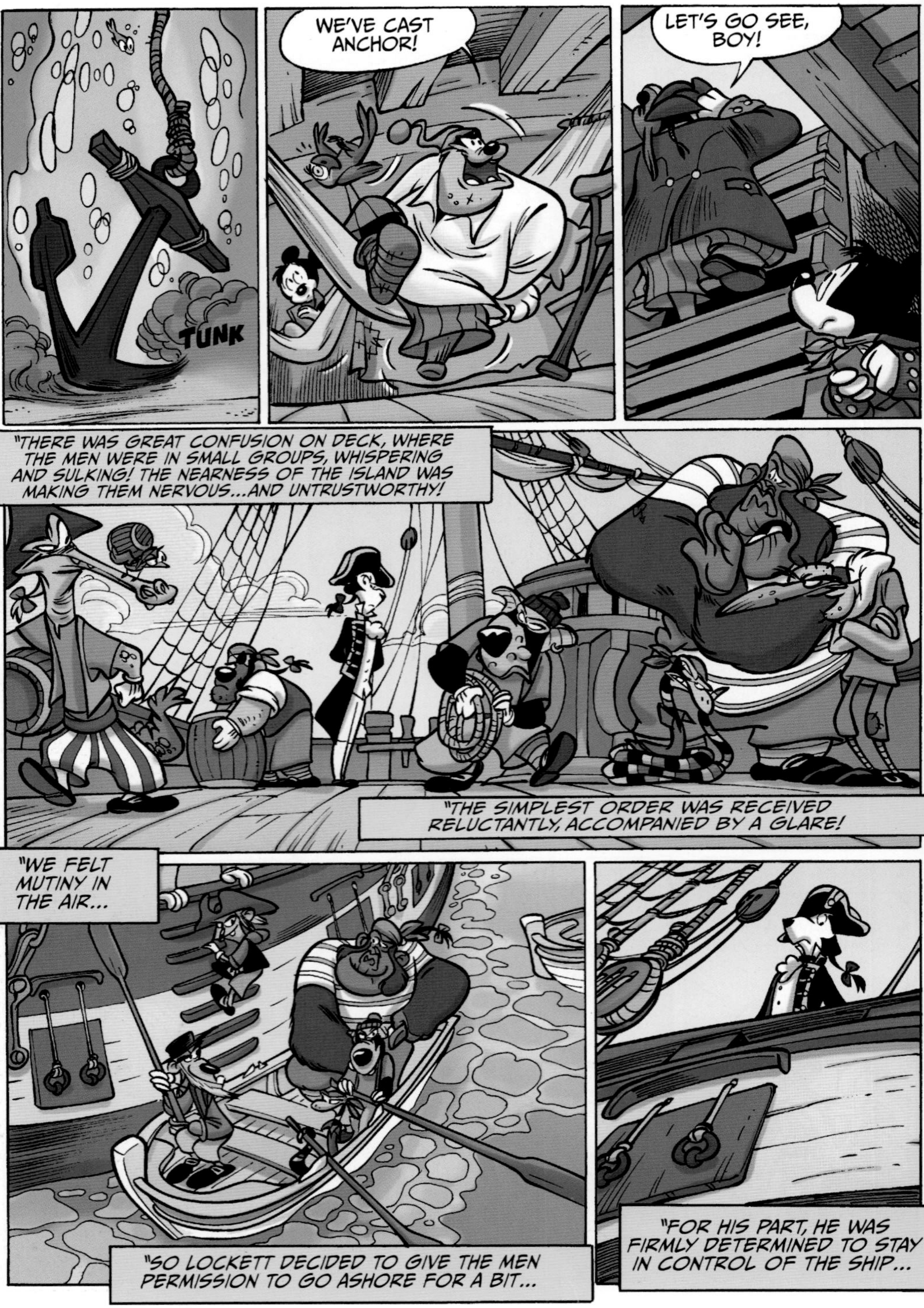
TUNK
WE'VE CAST ANCHOR!
LET'S GO SEE, BOY!
"THERE WAS GREAT CONFUSION ON DECK, WHERE THE MEN WERE IN SMALL GROUPS, WHISPERING AND SULKING! THE NEARNESS OF THE ISLAND WAS MAKING THEM NERVOUS...AND UNTRUSTWORTHY!
"THE SIMPLEST ORDER WAS RECEIVED RELUCTANTLY, ACCOMPANIED BY A GLARE!
"WE FELT MUTINY IN THE AIR...
"SO LOCKETT DECIDED TO GIVE THE MEN PERMISSION TO GO ASHORE FOR A BIT...
"FOR HIS PART, HE WAS FIRMLY DETERMINED TO STAY IN CONTROL OF THE SHIP...

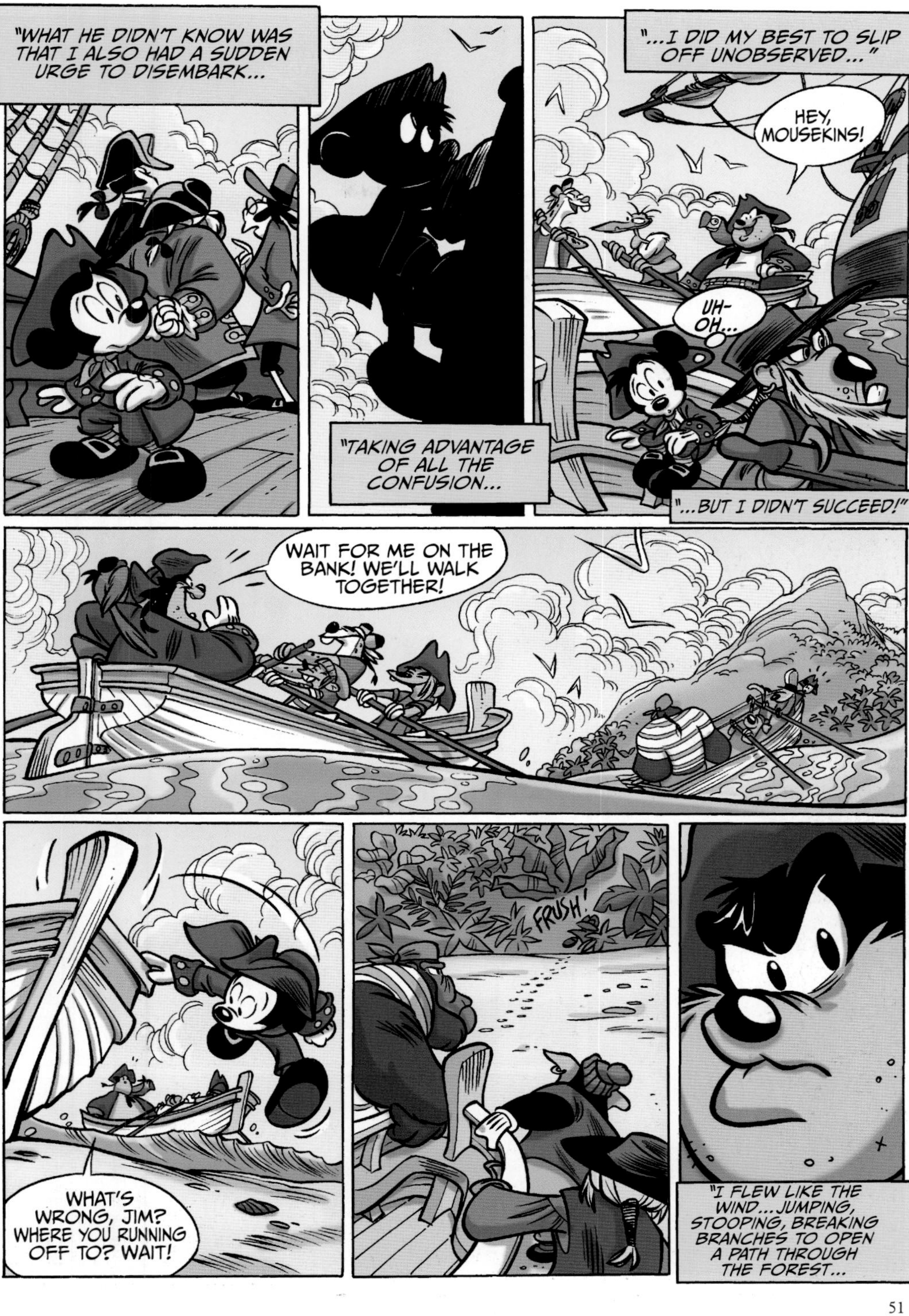
"WHAT HE DIDN'T KNOW WAS THAT I ALSO HAD A SUDDEN URGE TO DISEMBARK...
"TAKING ADVANTAGE OF ALL THE CONFUSION...
"...I DID MY BEST TO SLIP OFF UNOBSERVED..."
HEY, MOUSEKINS!
UH-OH...
"...BUT I DIDN'T SUCCEED!"
WAIT FOR ME ON THE BANK! WE'LL WALK TOGETHER!
WHAT'S WRONG, JIM? WHERE YOU RUNNING OFF TO? WAIT!
FRUSH!
"I FLEW LIKE THE WIND... JUMPING, STOOPING, BREAKING BRANCHES TO OPEN A PATH THROUGH THE FOREST...

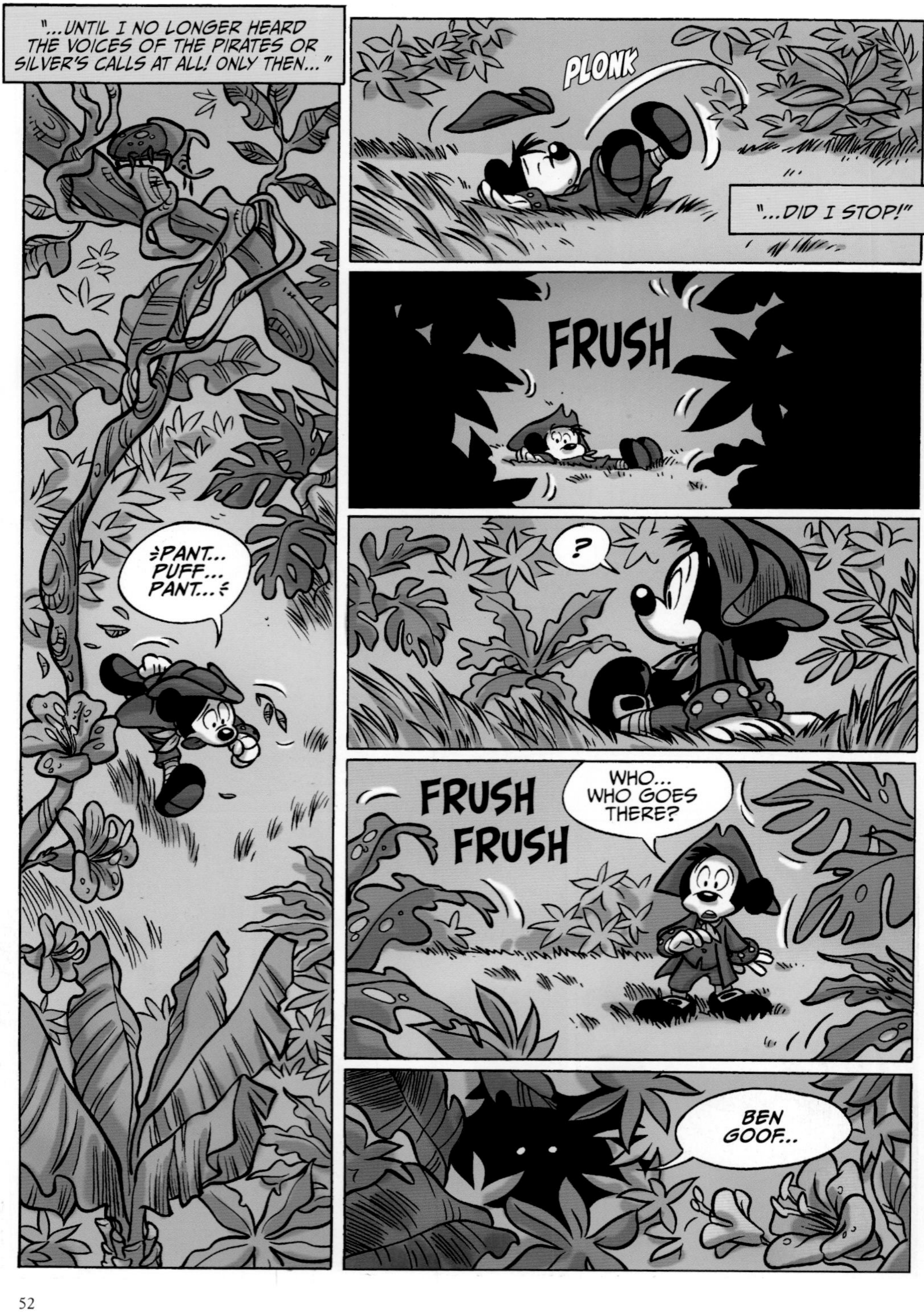
"...UNTIL I NO LONGER HEARD THE VOICES OF THE PIRATES OR SILVER'S CALLS AT ALL! ONLY THEN..."
PANT... PUFF... PANT...
PLONK
"...DID I STOP!"
FRUSH
?
FRUSH FRUSH
WHO... WHO GOES THERE?
BEN GOOF...

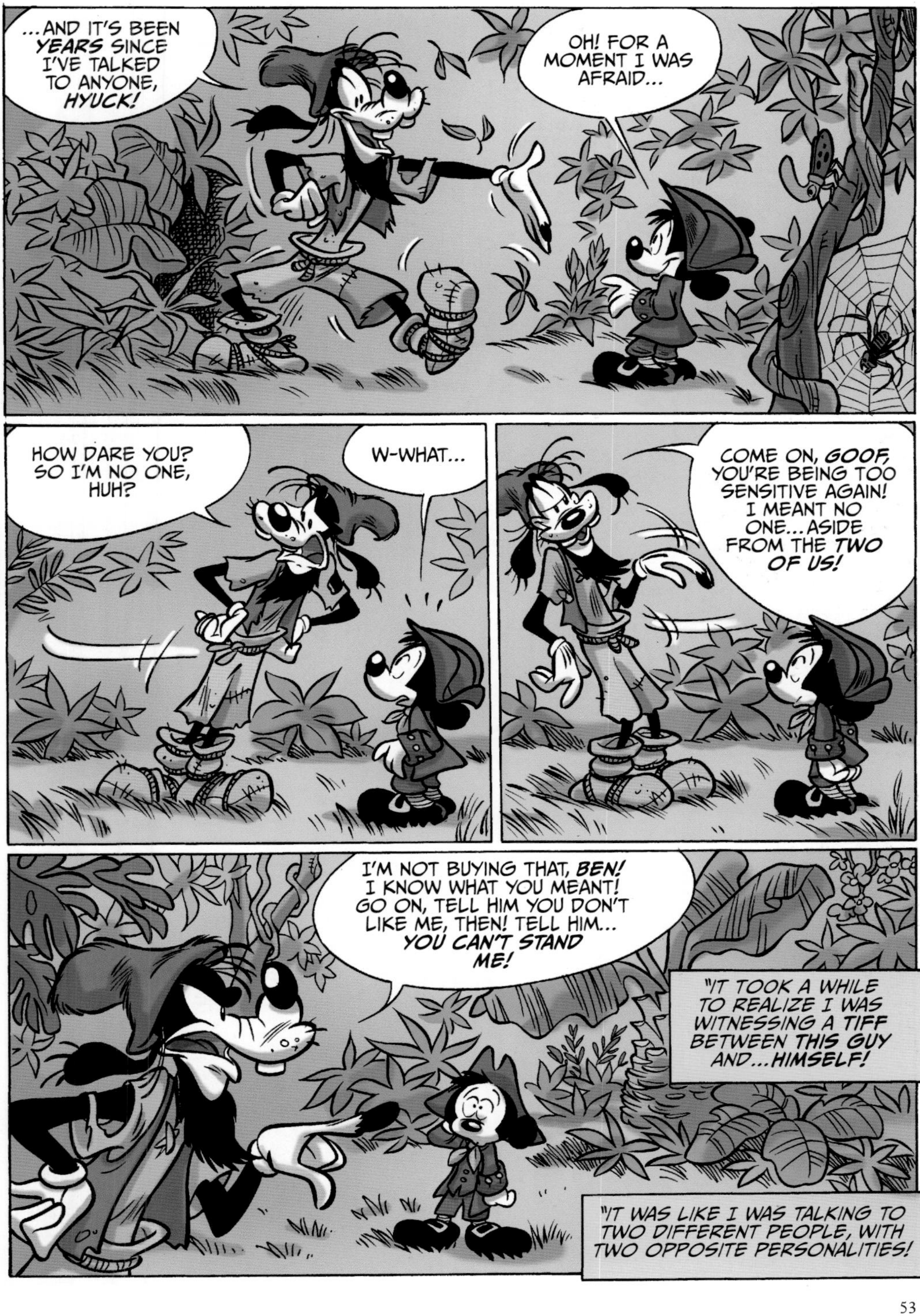

...AND IT'S BEEN *YEARS* SINCE I'VE TALKED TO ANYONE, *HYUCK!*
OH! FOR A MOMENT I WAS AFRAID...
HOW DARE YOU? SO I'M NO ONE, HUH?
W-WHAT...
COME ON, *GOOF*, YOU'RE BEING TOO SENSITIVE AGAIN! I MEANT NO ONE... ASIDE FROM THE *TWO OF US!*
I'M NOT BUYING THAT, *BEN!* I KNOW WHAT YOU MEANT! GO ON, TELL HIM YOU DON'T LIKE ME, THEN! TELL HIM... *YOU CAN'T STAND ME!*
"IT TOOK A WHILE TO REALIZE I WAS WITNESSING A *TIFF* BETWEEN *THIS GUY* AND... *HIMSELF!*
"IT WAS LIKE I WAS TALKING TO TWO DIFFERENT PEOPLE, WITH TWO OPPOSITE PERSONALITIES!

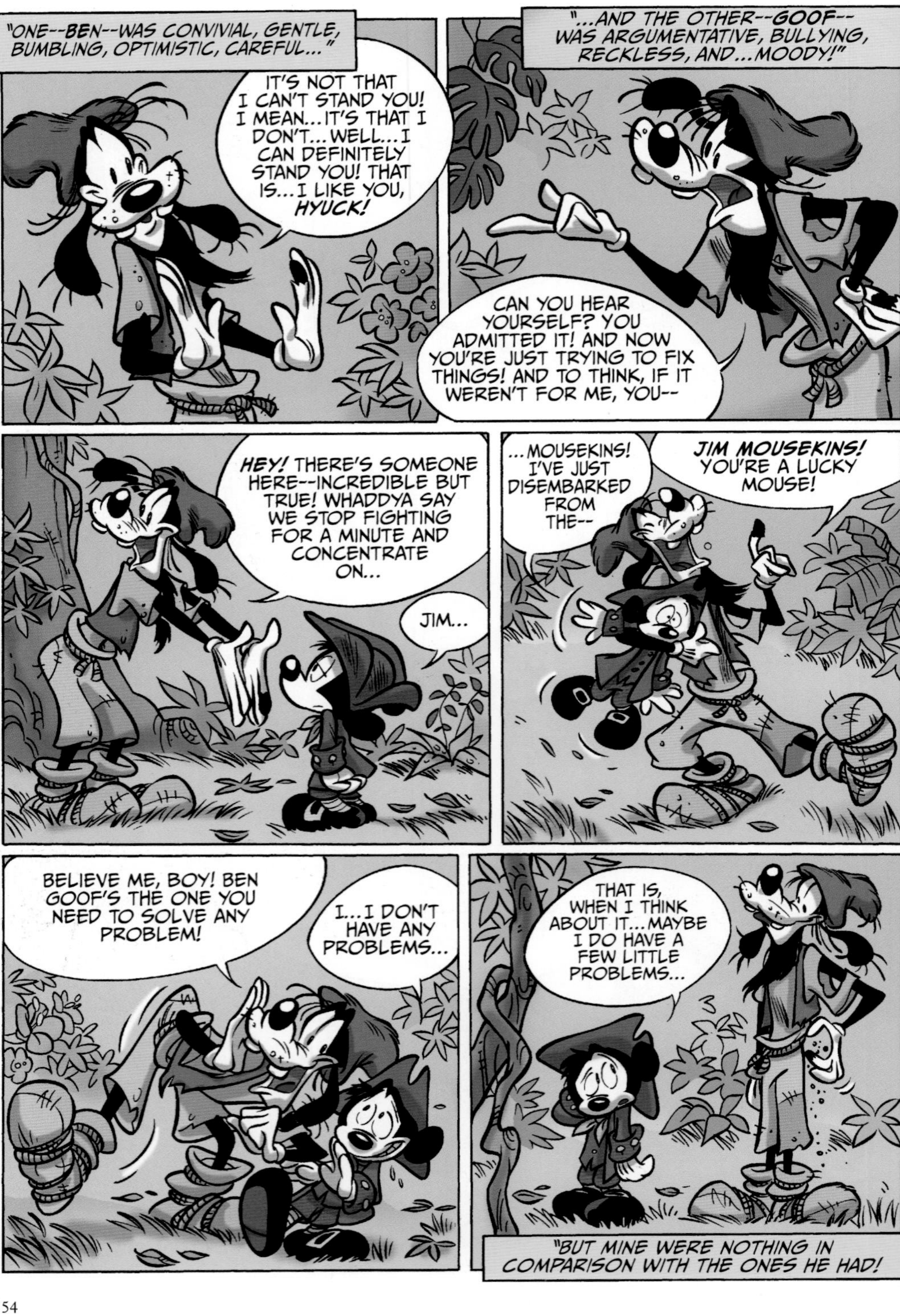
"ONE--BEN--WAS CONVIVIAL, GENTLE, BUMBLING, OPTIMISTIC, CAREFUL..."
IT'S NOT THAT I CAN'T STAND YOU! I MEAN...IT'S THAT I DON'T...WELL...I CAN DEFINITELY STAND YOU! THAT IS...I LIKE YOU, HYUCK!
"...AND THE OTHER--GOOF--WAS ARGUMENTATIVE, BULLYING, RECKLESS, AND...MOODY!"
CAN YOU HEAR YOURSELF? YOU ADMITTED IT! AND NOW YOU'RE JUST TRYING TO FIX THINGS! AND TO THINK, IF IT WEREN'T FOR ME, YOU--
HEY! THERE'S SOMEONE HERE--INCREDIBLE BUT TRUE! WHADDYA SAY WE STOP FIGHTING FOR A MINUTE AND CONCENTRATE ON...
JIM...
...MOUSEKINS! I'VE JUST DISEMBARKED FROM THE--
JIM MOUSEKINS! YOU'RE A LUCKY MOUSE!
BELIEVE ME, BOY! BEN GOOF'S THE ONE YOU NEED TO SOLVE ANY PROBLEM!
I...I DON'T HAVE ANY PROBLEMS...
THAT IS, WHEN I THINK ABOUT IT...MAYBE I DO HAVE A FEW LITTLE PROBLEMS...
"BUT MINE WERE NOTHING IN COMPARISON WITH THE ONES HE HAD!

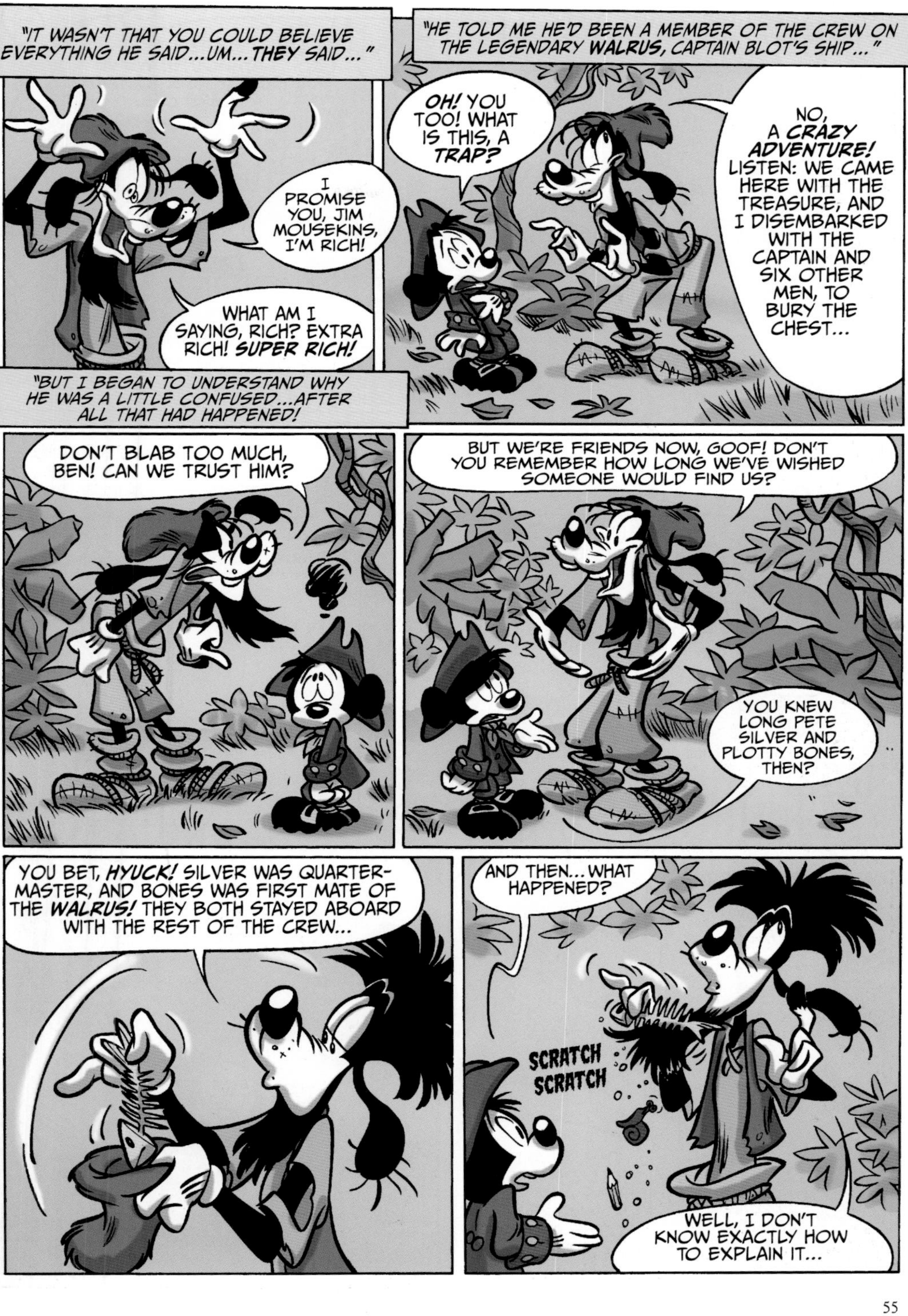
"IT WASN'T THAT YOU COULD BELIEVE EVERYTHING HE SAID...UM...THEY SAID..."
I PROMISE YOU, JIM MOUSEKINS, I'M RICH!
WHAT AM I SAYING, RICH? EXTRA RICH! SUPER RICH!
"BUT I BEGAN TO UNDERSTAND WHY HE WAS A LITTLE CONFUSED...AFTER ALL THAT HAD HAPPENED!
"HE TOLD ME HE'D BEEN A MEMBER OF THE CREW ON THE LEGENDARY WALRUS, CAPTAIN BLOT'S SHIP..."
OH! YOU TOO! WHAT IS THIS, A TRAP?
NO, A CRAZY ADVENTURE! LISTEN: WE CAME HERE WITH THE TREASURE, AND I DISEMBARKED WITH THE CAPTAIN AND SIX OTHER MEN, TO BURY THE CHEST...
DON'T BLAB TOO MUCH, BEN! CAN WE TRUST HIM?
BUT WE'RE FRIENDS NOW, GOOF! DON'T YOU REMEMBER HOW LONG WE'VE WISHED SOMEONE WOULD FIND US?
YOU KNEW LONG PETE SILVER AND PLOTTY BONES, THEN?
YOU BET, HYUCK! SILVER WAS QUARTER-MASTER, AND BONES WAS FIRST MATE OF THE WALRUS! THEY BOTH STAYED ABOARD WITH THE REST OF THE CREW...
AND THEN...WHAT HAPPENED?
SCRATCH SCRATCH
WELL, I DON'T KNOW EXACTLY HOW TO EXPLAIN IT...

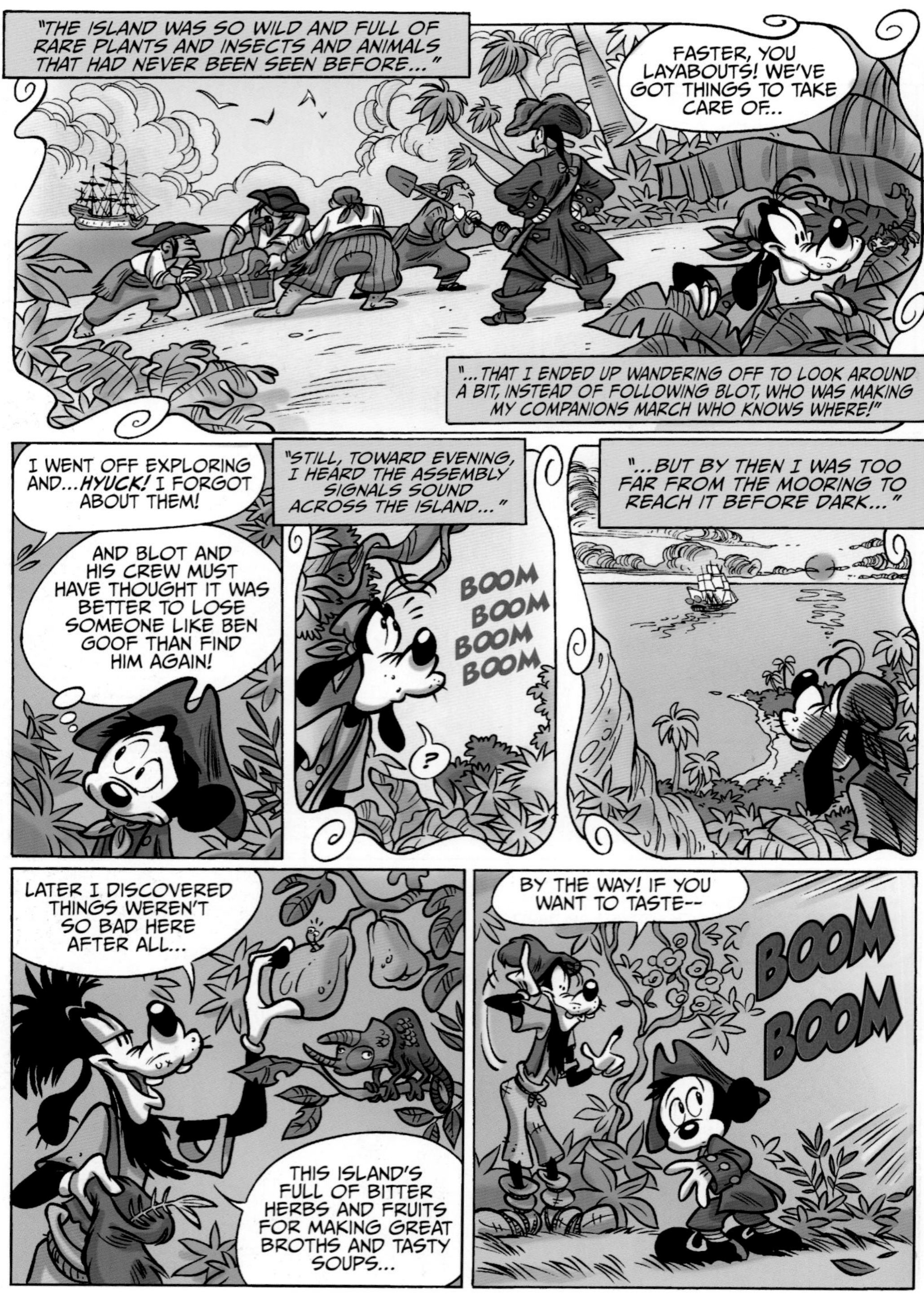
"THE ISLAND WAS SO WILD AND FULL OF RARE PLANTS AND INSECTS AND ANIMALS THAT HAD NEVER BEEN SEEN BEFORE..."
FASTER, YOU LAYABOUTS! WE'VE GOT THINGS TO TAKE CARE OF...
"...THAT I ENDED UP WANDERING OFF TO LOOK AROUND A BIT, INSTEAD OF FOLLOWING BLOT, WHO WAS MAKING MY COMPANIONS MARCH WHO KNOWS WHERE!"
I WENT OFF EXPLORING AND...HYUCK! I FORGOT ABOUT THEM!
AND BLOT AND HIS CREW MUST HAVE THOUGHT IT WAS BETTER TO LOSE SOMEONE LIKE BEN GOOF THAN FIND HIM AGAIN!
"STILL, TOWARD EVENING, I HEARD THE ASSEMBLY SIGNALS SOUND ACROSS THE ISLAND..."
BOOM BOOM BOOM BOOM
?
"...BUT BY THEN I WAS TOO FAR FROM THE MOORING TO REACH IT BEFORE DARK..."
LATER I DISCOVERED THINGS WEREN'T SO BAD HERE AFTER ALL...
THIS ISLAND'S FULL OF BITTER HERBS AND FRUITS FOR MAKING GREAT BROTHS AND TASTY SOUPS...
BY THE WAY! IF YOU WANT TO TASTE--
BOOM BOOM

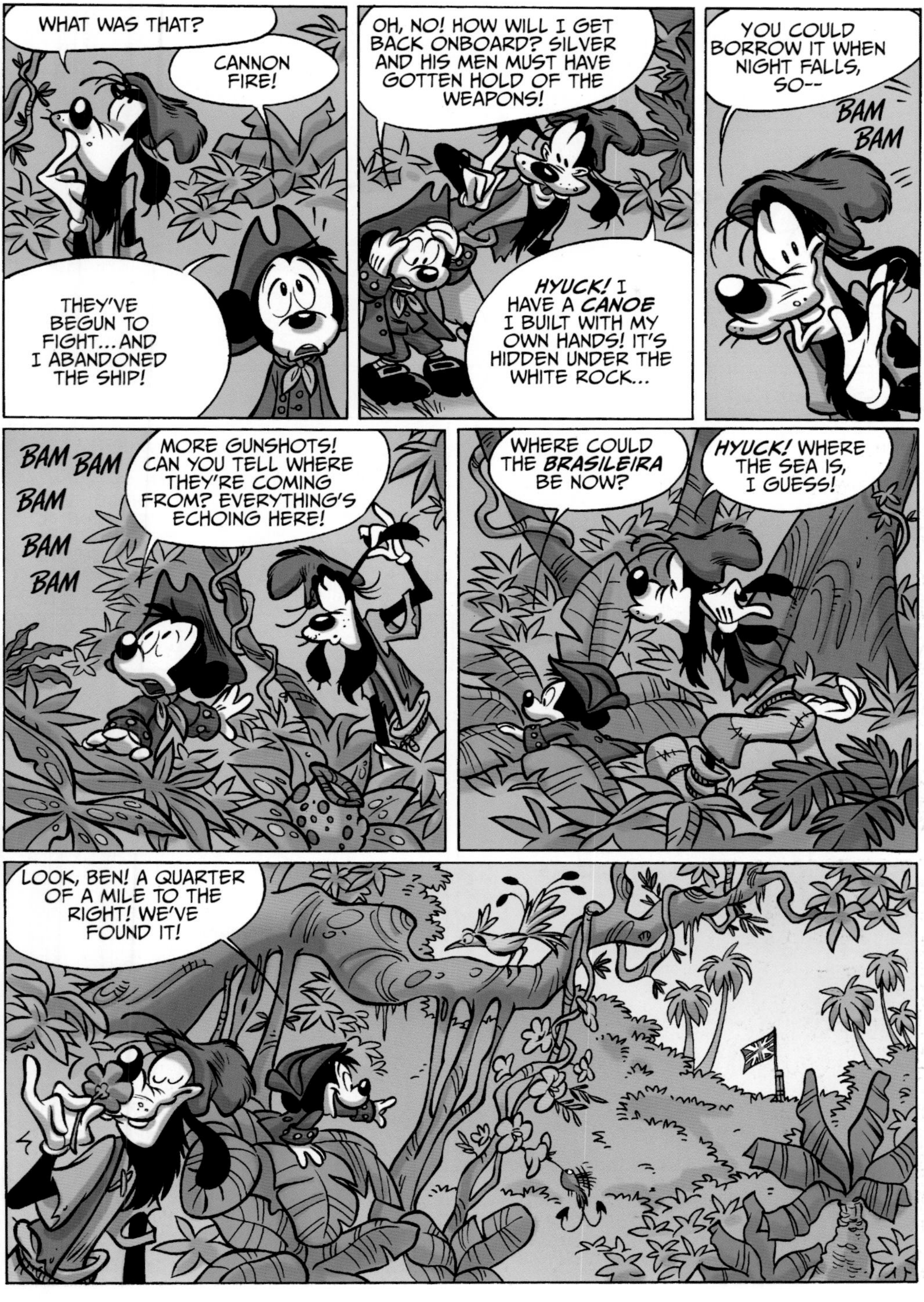
WHAT WAS THAT?
CANNON FIRE!
THEY'VE BEGUN TO FIGHT... AND I ABANDONED THE SHIP!
OH, NO! HOW WILL I GET BACK ONBOARD? SILVER AND HIS MEN MUST HAVE GOTTEN HOLD OF THE WEAPONS!
HYUCK! I HAVE A CANOE I BUILT WITH MY OWN HANDS! IT'S HIDDEN UNDER THE WHITE ROCK...
YOU COULD BORROW IT WHEN NIGHT FALLS, SO--
BAM BAM
BAM BAM BAM BAM BAM
MORE GUNSHOTS! CAN YOU TELL WHERE THEY'RE COMING FROM? EVERYTHING'S ECHOING HERE!
WHERE COULD THE BRASILEIRA BE NOW?
HYUCK! WHERE THE SEA IS, I GUESS!
LOOK, BEN! A QUARTER OF A MILE TO THE RIGHT! WE'VE FOUND IT!

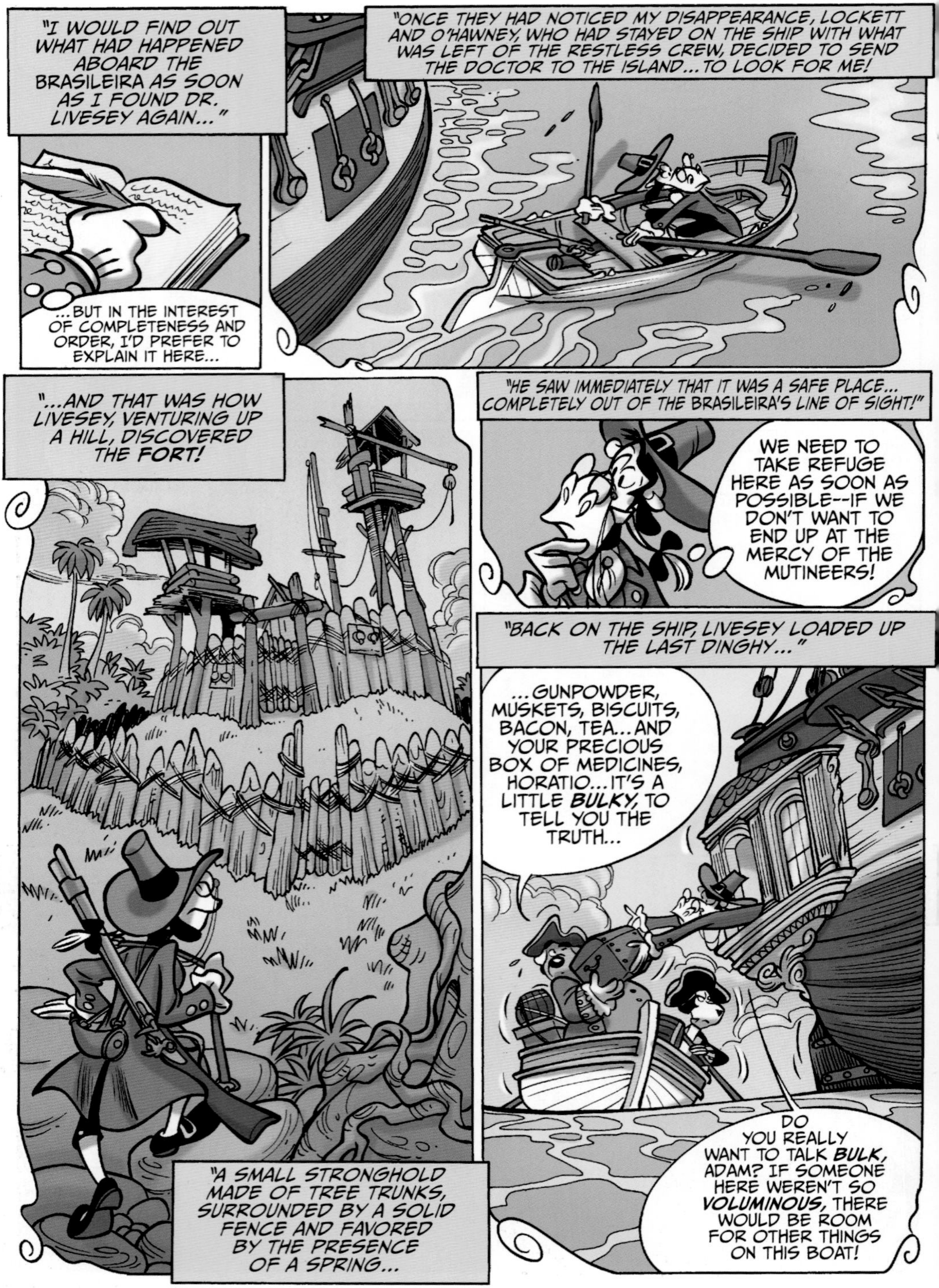
"I WOULD FIND OUT WHAT HAD HAPPENED ABOARD THE BRASILEIRA AS SOON AS I FOUND DR. LIVESEY AGAIN..."
...BUT IN THE INTEREST OF COMPLETENESS AND ORDER, I'D PREFER TO EXPLAIN IT HERE...
"ONCE THEY HAD NOTICED MY DISAPPEARANCE, LOCKETT AND O'HAWNEY, WHO HAD STAYED ON THE SHIP WITH WHAT WAS LEFT OF THE RESTLESS CREW, DECIDED TO SEND THE DOCTOR TO THE ISLAND... TO LOOK FOR ME!
"...AND THAT WAS HOW LIVESEY, VENTURING UP A HILL, DISCOVERED THE FORT!
"A SMALL STRONGHOLD MADE OF TREE TRUNKS, SURROUNDED BY A SOLID FENCE AND FAVORED BY THE PRESENCE OF A SPRING...
"HE SAW IMMEDIATELY THAT IT WAS A SAFE PLACE... COMPLETELY OUT OF THE BRASILEIRA'S LINE OF SIGHT!"
WE NEED TO TAKE REFUGE HERE AS SOON AS POSSIBLE--IF WE DON'T WANT TO END UP AT THE MERCY OF THE MUTINEERS!
"BACK ON THE SHIP, LIVESEY LOADED UP THE LAST DINGHY..."
...GUNPOWDER, MUSKETS, BISCUITS, BACON, TEA... AND YOUR PRECIOUS BOX OF MEDICINES, HORATIO... IT'S A LITTLE BULKY, TO TELL YOU THE TRUTH...
DO YOU REALLY WANT TO TALK BULK, ADAM? IF SOMEONE HERE WEREN'T SO VOLUMINOUS, THERE WOULD BE ROOM FOR OTHER THINGS ON THIS BOAT!

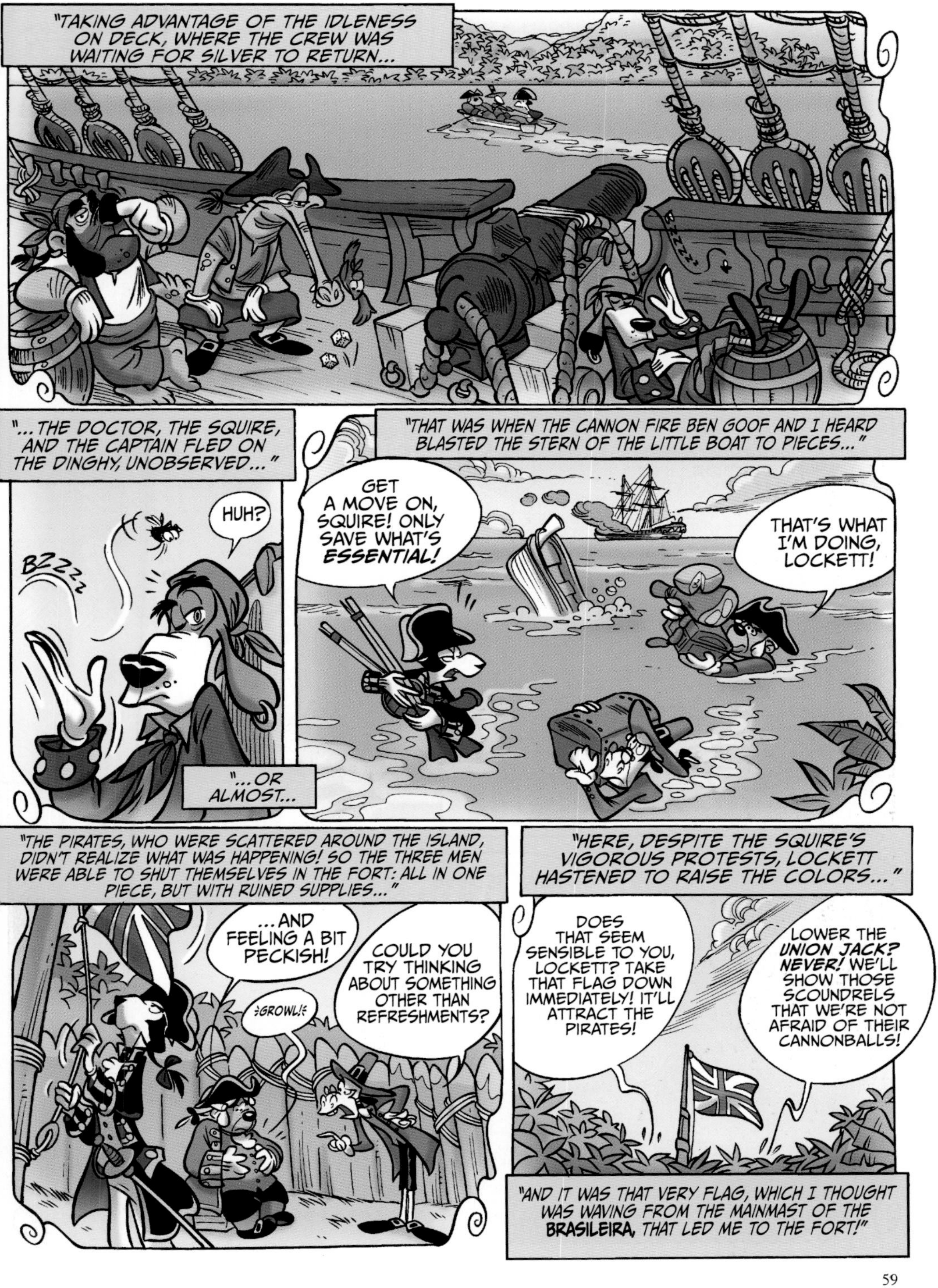

"TAKING ADVANTAGE OF THE IDLENESS ON DECK, WHERE THE CREW WAS WAITING FOR SILVER TO RETURN...
"...THE DOCTOR, THE SQUIRE, AND THE CAPTAIN FLED ON THE DINGHY, UNOBSERVED..."
BZZzzz
HUH?
"...OR ALMOST...
"THAT WAS WHEN THE CANNON FIRE BEN GOOF AND I HEARD BLASTED THE STERN OF THE LITTLE BOAT TO PIECES..."
GET A MOVE ON, SQUIRE! ONLY SAVE WHAT'S ESSENTIAL!
THAT'S WHAT I'M DOING, LOCKETT!
"THE PIRATES, WHO WERE SCATTERED AROUND THE ISLAND, DIDN'T REALIZE WHAT WAS HAPPENING! SO THE THREE MEN WERE ABLE TO SHUT THEMSELVES IN THE FORT: ALL IN ONE PIECE, BUT WITH RUINED SUPPLIES..."
...AND FEELING A BIT PECKISH!
GROWL!
COULD YOU TRY THINKING ABOUT SOMETHING OTHER THAN REFRESHMENTS?
"HERE, DESPITE THE SQUIRE'S VIGOROUS PROTESTS, LOCKETT HASTENED TO RAISE THE COLORS..."
DOES THAT SEEM SENSIBLE TO YOU, LOCKETT? TAKE THAT FLAG DOWN IMMEDIATELY! IT'LL ATTRACT THE PIRATES!
LOWER THE UNION JACK? NEVER! WE'LL SHOW THOSE SCOUNDRELS THAT WE'RE NOT AFRAID OF THEIR CANNONBALLS!
"AND IT WAS THAT VERY FLAG, WHICH I THOUGHT WAS WAVING FROM THE MAINMAST OF THE BRASILEIRA, THAT LED ME TO THE FORT!"

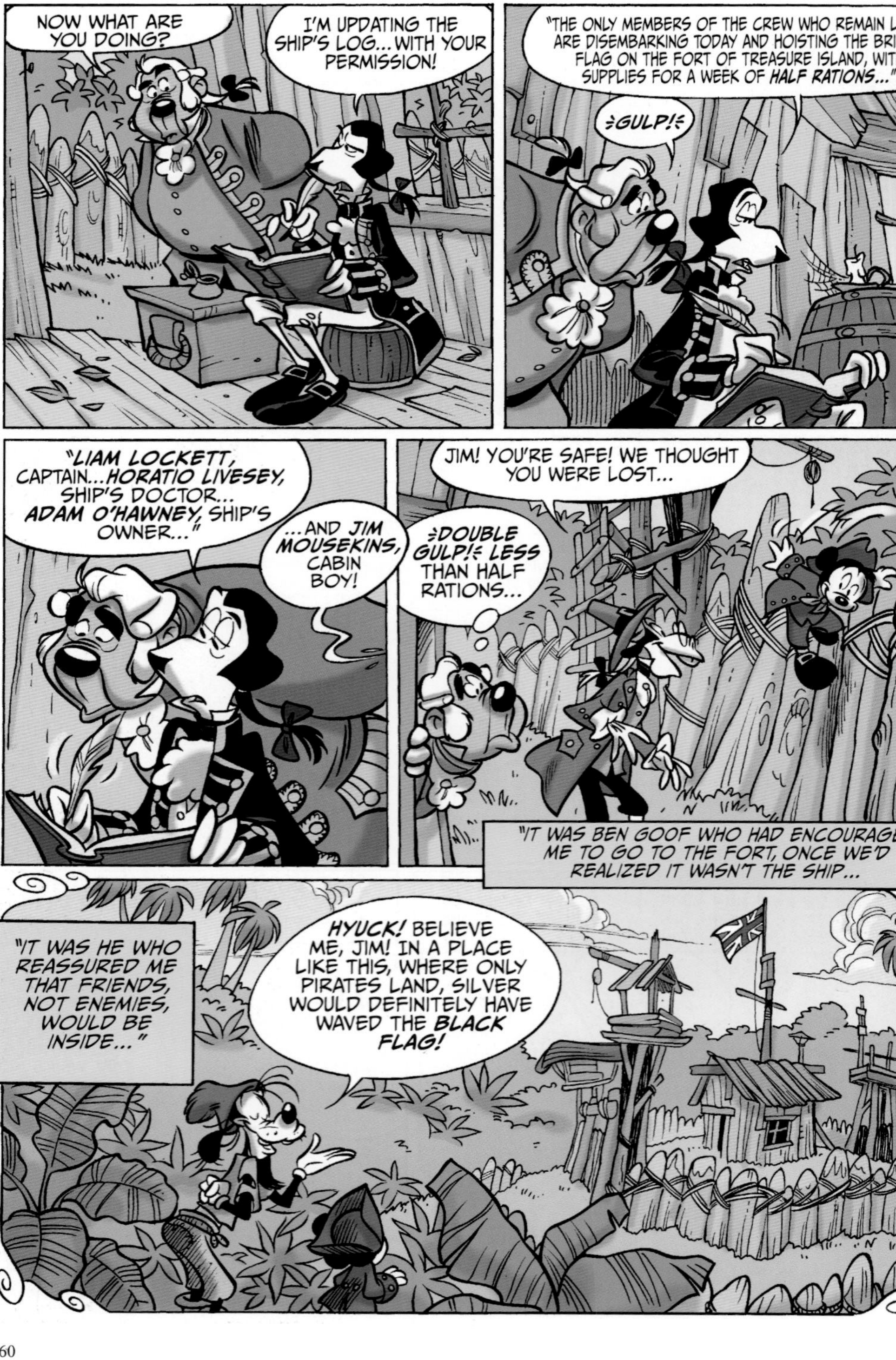
NOW WHAT ARE YOU DOING?
I'M UPDATING THE SHIP'S LOG... WITH YOUR PERMISSION!
"THE ONLY MEMBERS OF THE CREW WHO REMAIN LOYAL ARE DISEMBARKING TODAY AND HOISTING THE BRITISH FLAG ON THE FORT OF TREASURE ISLAND, WITH SUPPLIES FOR A WEEK OF HALF RATIONS..."
GULP!
"LIAM LOCKETT, CAPTAIN... HORATIO LIVESEY, SHIP'S DOCTOR... ADAM O'HAWNEY, SHIP'S OWNER..."
...AND JIM MOUSEKINS, CABIN BOY!
JIM! YOU'RE SAFE! WE THOUGHT YOU WERE LOST...
DOUBLE GULP! LESS THAN HALF RATIONS...
"IT WAS BEN GOOF WHO HAD ENCOURAGED ME TO GO TO THE FORT, ONCE WE'D REALIZED IT WASN'T THE SHIP...
"IT WAS HE WHO REASSURED ME THAT FRIENDS, NOT ENEMIES, WOULD BE INSIDE..."
HYUCK! BELIEVE ME, JIM! IN A PLACE LIKE THIS, WHERE ONLY PIRATES LAND, SILVER WOULD DEFINITELY HAVE WAVED THE BLACK FLAG!

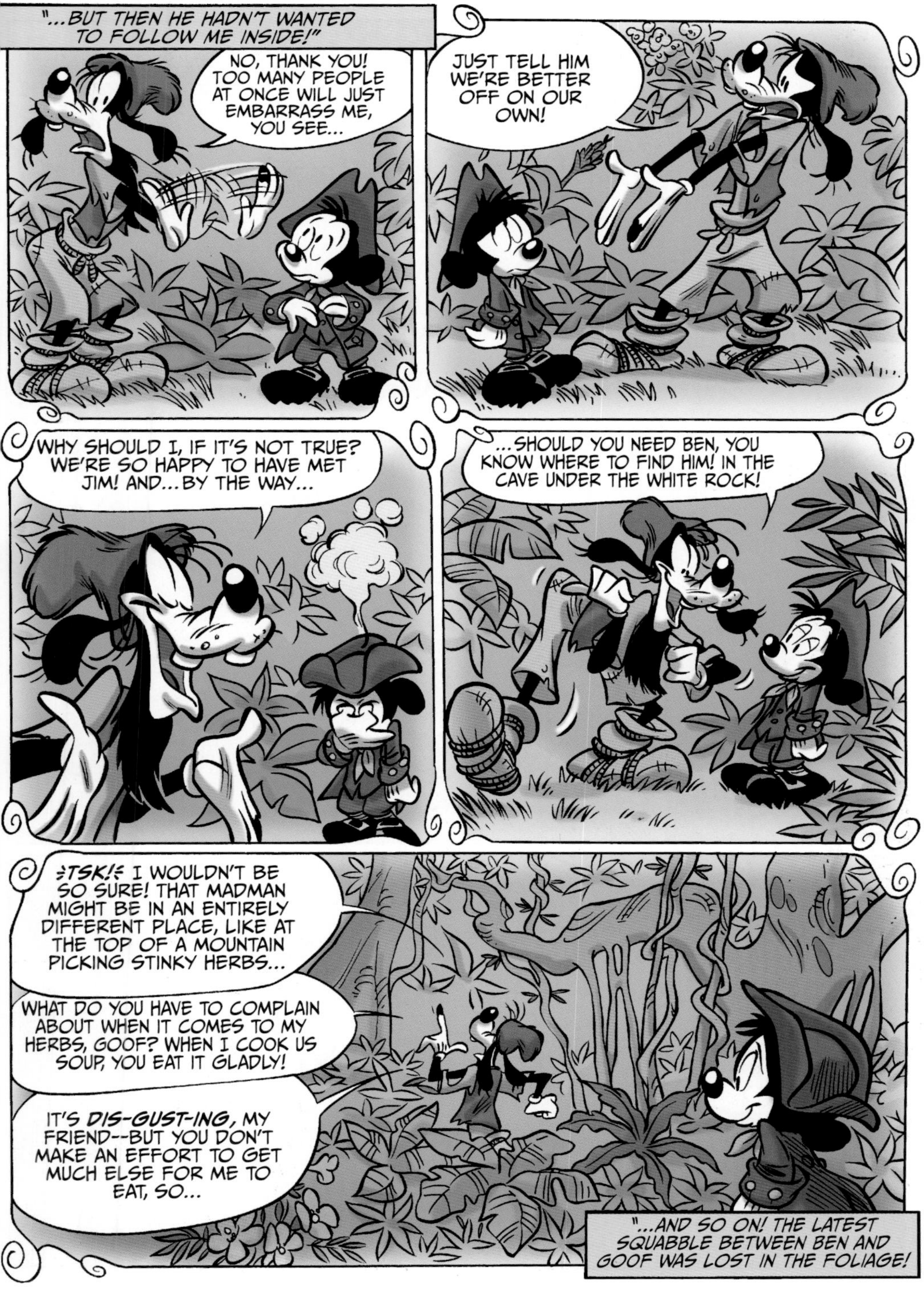
"...BUT THEN HE HADN'T WANTED TO FOLLOW ME INSIDE!"
NO, THANK YOU! TOO MANY PEOPLE AT ONCE WILL JUST EMBARRASS ME, YOU SEE...
JUST TELL HIM WE'RE BETTER OFF ON OUR OWN!
WHY SHOULD I, IF IT'S NOT TRUE? WE'RE SO HAPPY TO HAVE MET JIM! AND... BY THE WAY...
...SHOULD YOU NEED BEN, YOU KNOW WHERE TO FIND HIM! IN THE CAVE UNDER THE WHITE ROCK!
TSK! I WOULDN'T BE SO SURE! THAT MADMAN MIGHT BE IN AN ENTIRELY DIFFERENT PLACE, LIKE AT THE TOP OF A MOUNTAIN PICKING STINKY HERBS...
WHAT DO YOU HAVE TO COMPLAIN ABOUT WHEN IT COMES TO MY HERBS, GOOF? WHEN I COOK US SOUP, YOU EAT IT GLADLY!
IT'S DIS-GUST-ING, MY FRIEND--BUT YOU DON'T MAKE AN EFFORT TO GET MUCH ELSE FOR ME TO EAT, SO...
"...AND SO ON! THE LATEST SQUABBLE BETWEEN BEN AND GOOF WAS LOST IN THE FOLIAGE!

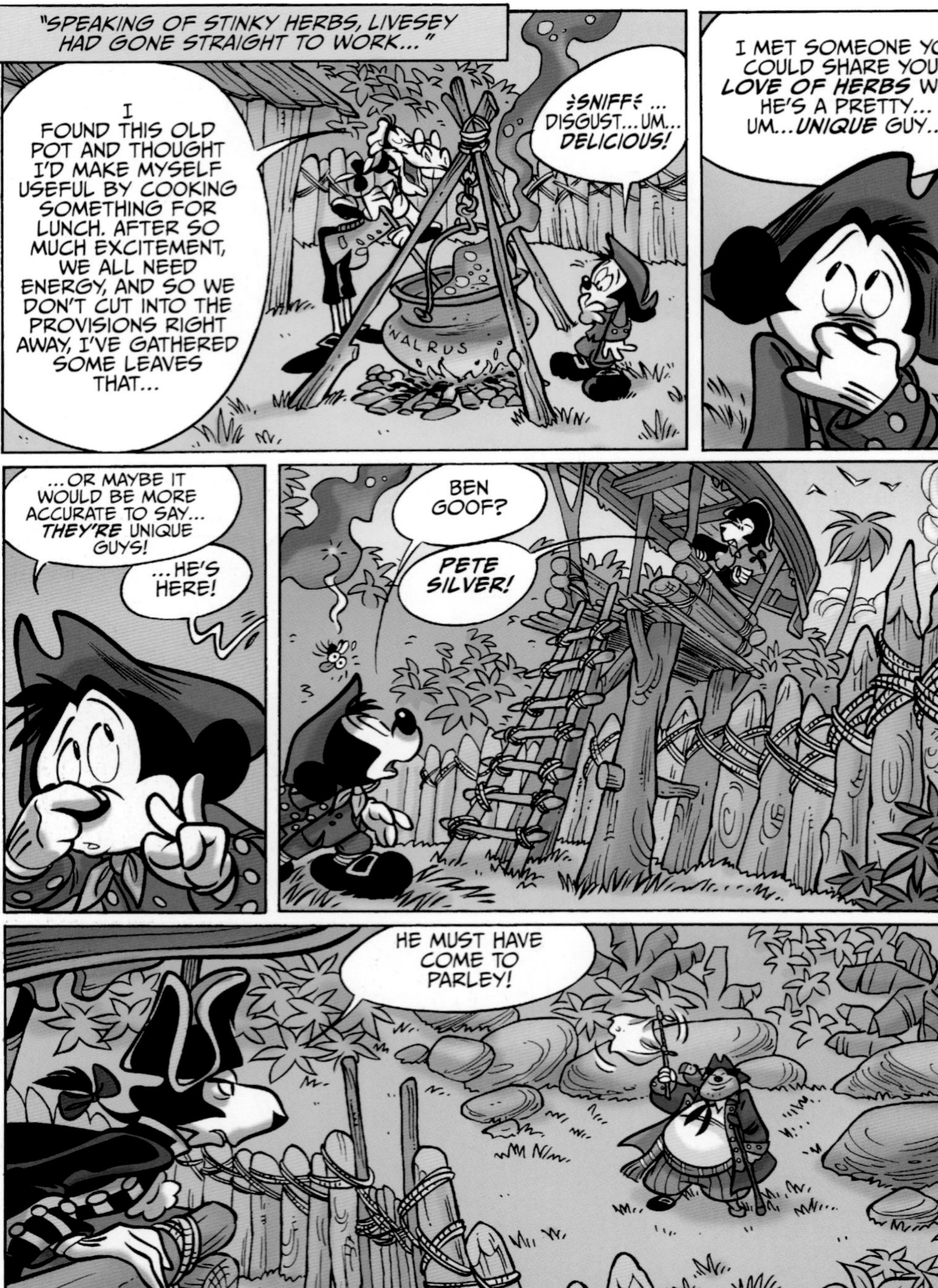

"SPEAKING OF STINKY HERBS, LIVESEY HAD GONE STRAIGHT TO WORK..."
I FOUND THIS OLD POT AND THOUGHT I'D MAKE MYSELF USEFUL BY COOKING SOMETHING FOR LUNCH. AFTER SO MUCH EXCITEMENT, WE ALL NEED ENERGY, AND SO WE DON'T CUT INTO THE PROVISIONS RIGHT AWAY, I'VE GATHERED SOME LEAVES THAT...
SNIFF ... DISGUST...UM... DELICIOUS!
WALRUS
I MET SOMEONE YOU COULD SHARE YOUR LOVE OF HERBS WITH! HE'S A PRETTY... UM...UNIQUE GUY...
...OR MAYBE IT WOULD BE MORE ACCURATE TO SAY... THEY'RE UNIQUE GUYS!
...HE'S HERE!
BEN GOOF?
PETE SILVER!
HE MUST HAVE COME TO PARLEY!

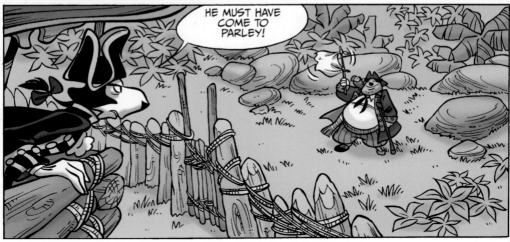

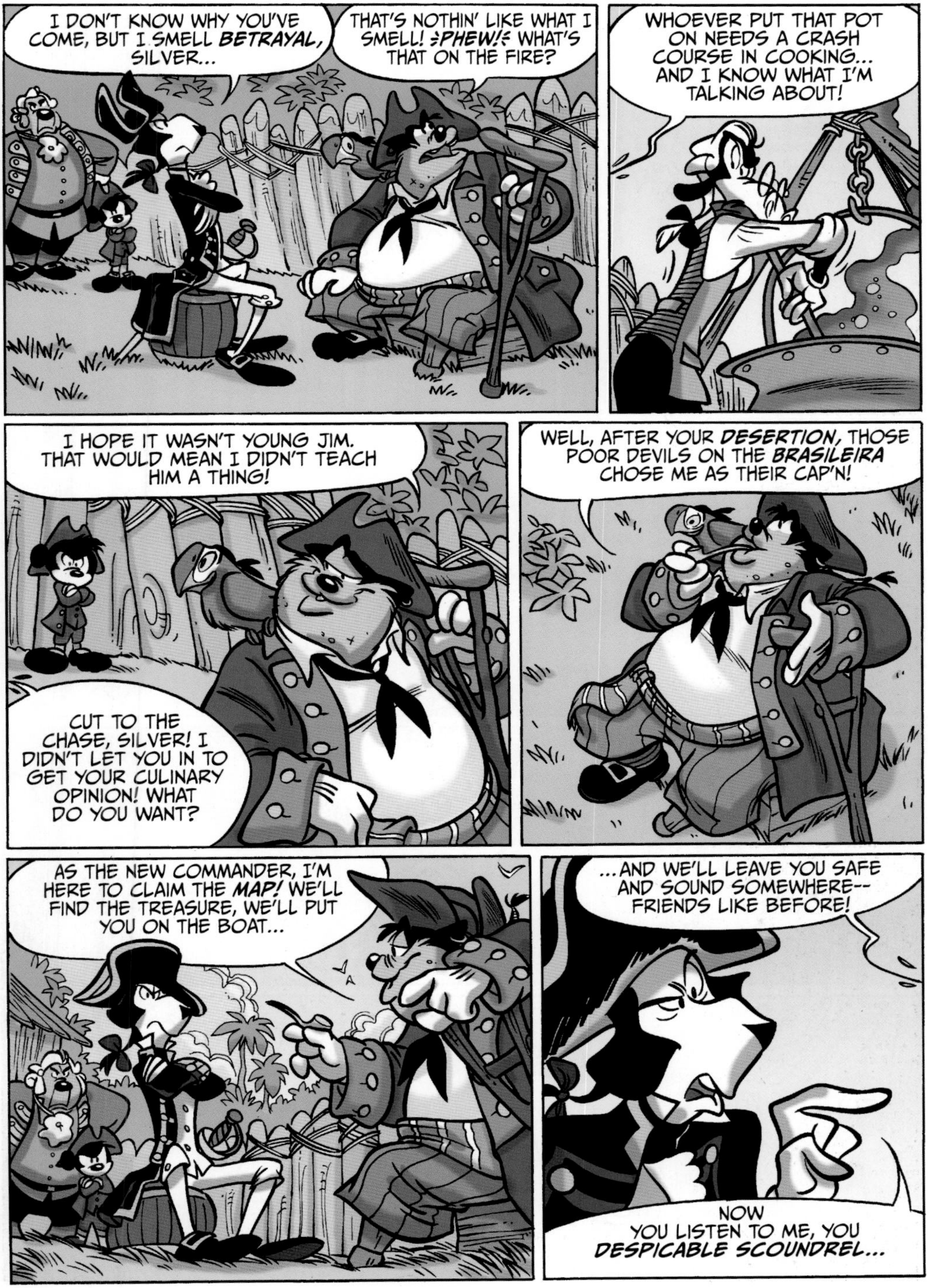
I DON'T KNOW WHY YOU'VE COME, BUT I SMELL BETRAYAL, SILVER...
THAT'S NOTHIN' LIKE WHAT I SMELL! PHEW! WHAT'S THAT ON THE FIRE?
WHOEVER PUT THAT POT ON NEEDS A CRASH COURSE IN COOKING... AND I KNOW WHAT I'M TALKING ABOUT!
I HOPE IT WASN'T YOUNG JIM. THAT WOULD MEAN I DIDN'T TEACH HIM A THING!
CUT TO THE CHASE, SILVER! I DIDN'T LET YOU IN TO GET YOUR CULINARY OPINION! WHAT DO YOU WANT?
WELL, AFTER YOUR DESERTION, THOSE POOR DEVILS ON THE BRASILEIRA CHOSE ME AS THEIR CAP'N!
AS THE NEW COMMANDER, I'M HERE TO CLAIM THE MAP! WE'LL FIND THE TREASURE, WE'LL PUT YOU ON THE BOAT...
...AND WE'LL LEAVE YOU SAFE AND SOUND SOMEWHERE-- FRIENDS LIKE BEFORE!
NOW YOU LISTEN TO ME, YOU DESPICABLE SCOUNDREL...

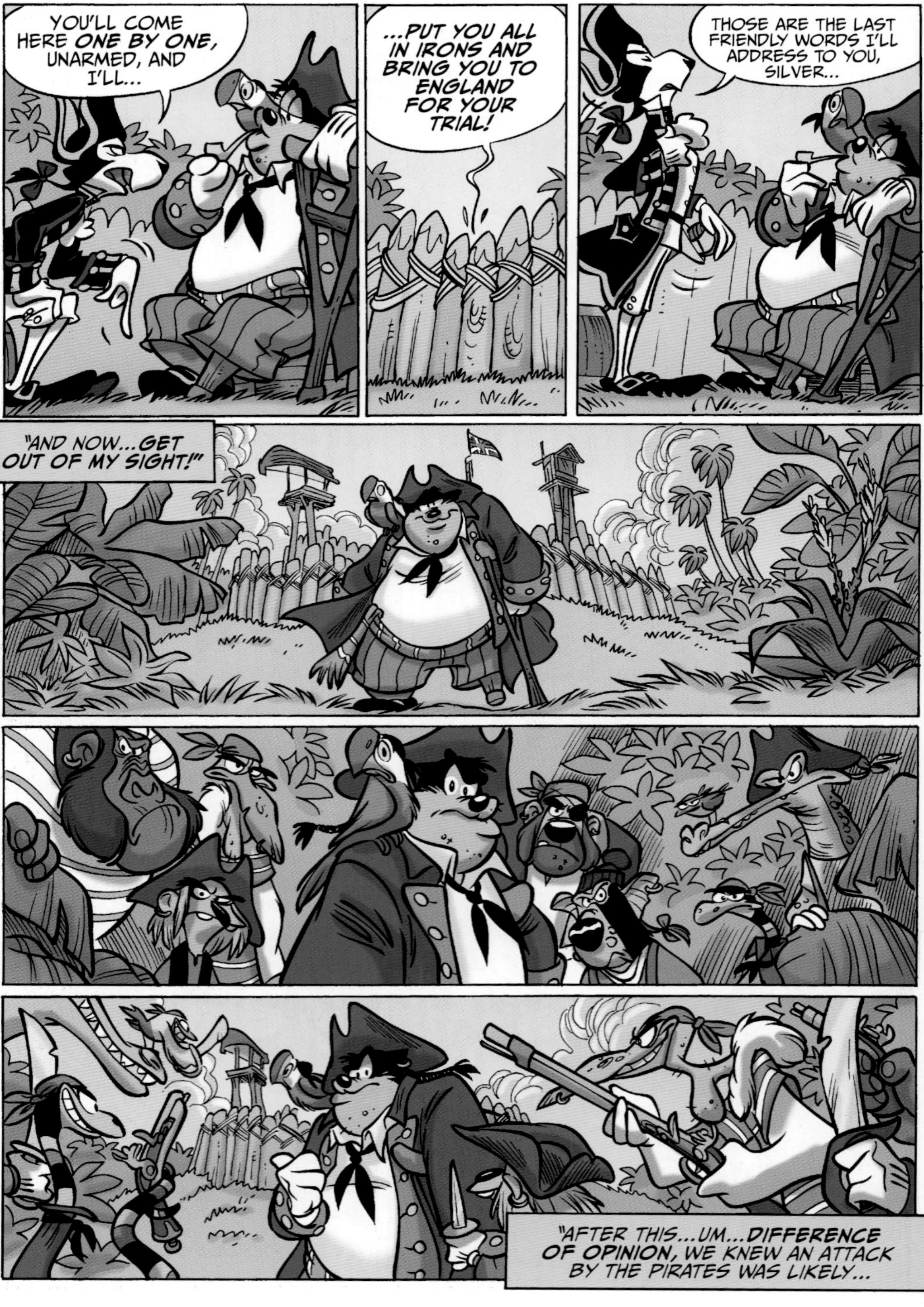
YOU'LL COME HERE ONE BY ONE, UNARMED, AND I'LL...
...PUT YOU ALL IN IRONS AND BRING YOU TO ENGLAND FOR YOUR TRIAL!
THOSE ARE THE LAST FRIENDLY WORDS I'LL ADDRESS TO YOU, SILVER...
"AND NOW...GET OUT OF MY SIGHT!"
"AFTER THIS...UM...DIFFERENCE OF OPINION, WE KNEW AN ATTACK BY THE PIRATES WAS LIKELY...

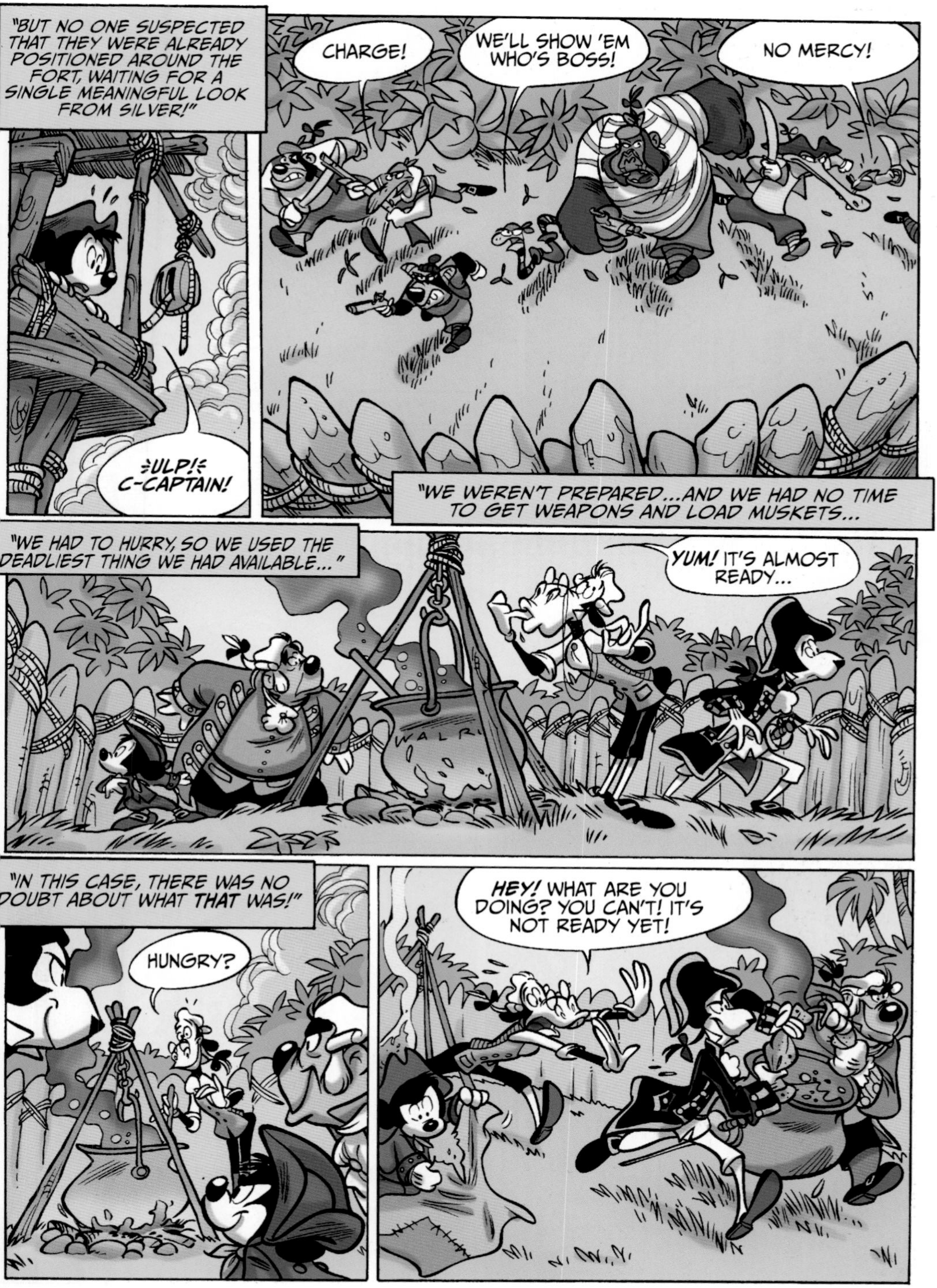
"BUT NO ONE SUSPECTED THAT THEY WERE ALREADY POSITIONED AROUND THE FORT, WAITING FOR A SINGLE MEANINGFUL LOOK FROM SILVER!"
CHARGE!
WE'LL SHOW 'EM WHO'S BOSS!
NO MERCY!
ULP! C-CAPTAIN!
"WE WEREN'T PREPARED...AND WE HAD NO TIME TO GET WEAPONS AND LOAD MUSKETS...
"WE HAD TO HURRY, SO WE USED THE DEADLIEST THING WE HAD AVAILABLE..."
YUM! IT'S ALMOST READY...
"IN THIS CASE, THERE WAS NO DOUBT ABOUT WHAT THAT WAS!"
HUNGRY?
HEY! WHAT ARE YOU DOING? YOU CAN'T! IT'S NOT READY YET!

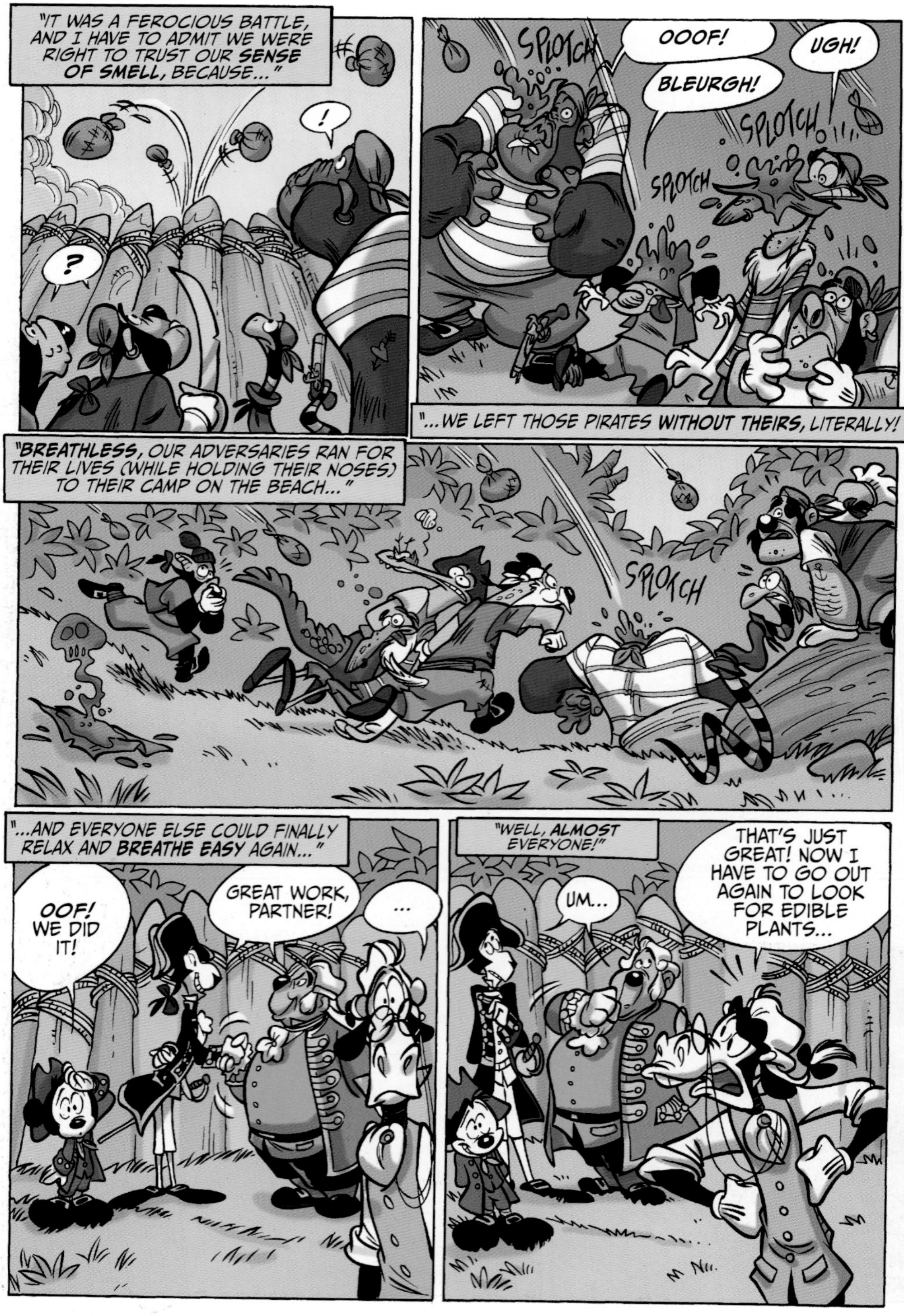
"IT WAS A FEROCIOUS BATTLE, AND I HAVE TO ADMIT WE WERE RIGHT TO TRUST OUR SENSE OF SMELL, BECAUSE..."
?
!
SPLOTCH
OOOF!
BLEURGH!
UGH!
SPLOTCH
SPLOTCH
"...WE LEFT THOSE PIRATES WITHOUT THEIRS, LITERALLY!
"BREATHLESS, OUR ADVERSARIES RAN FOR THEIR LIVES (WHILE HOLDING THEIR NOSES) TO THEIR CAMP ON THE BEACH..."
SPLOTCH
"...AND EVERYONE ELSE COULD FINALLY RELAX AND BREATHE EASY AGAIN..."
OOF! WE DID IT!
GREAT WORK, PARTNER!
...
"WELL, ALMOST EVERYONE!"
UM...
THAT'S JUST GREAT! NOW I HAVE TO GO OUT AGAIN TO LOOK FOR EDIBLE PLANTS...

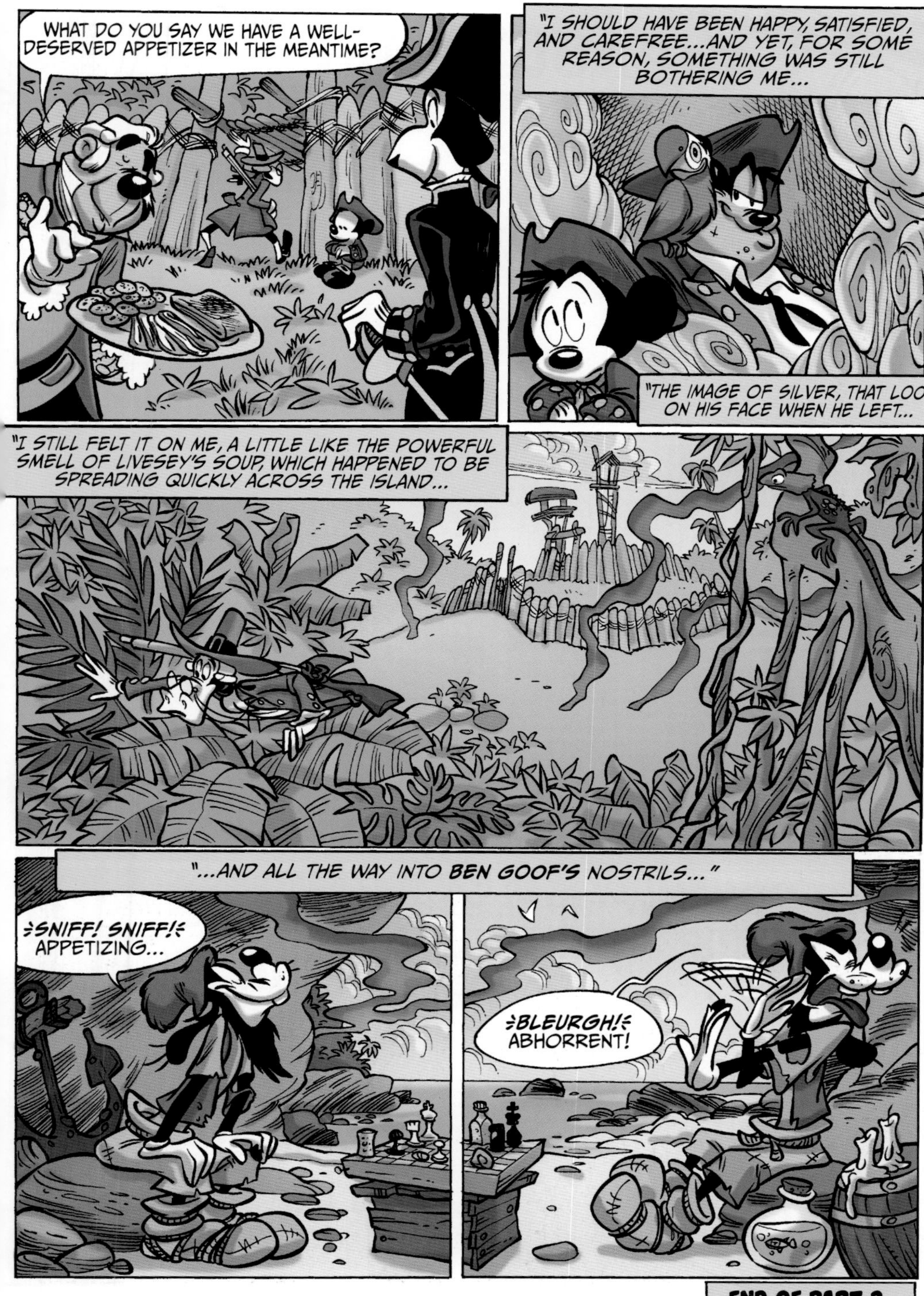
WHAT DO YOU SAY WE HAVE A WELL-DESERVED APPETIZER IN THE MEANTIME?
"I SHOULD HAVE BEEN HAPPY, SATISFIED, AND CAREFREE...AND YET, FOR SOME REASON, SOMETHING WAS STILL BOTHERING ME...
"THE IMAGE OF SILVER, THAT LOOK ON HIS FACE WHEN HE LEFT...
"I STILL FELT IT ON ME, A LITTLE LIKE THE POWERFUL SMELL OF LIVESEY'S SOUP, WHICH HAPPENED TO BE SPREADING QUICKLY ACROSS THE ISLAND...
"...AND ALL THE WAY INTO BEN GOOF'S NOSTRILS..."
SNIFF! SNIFF! APPETIZING...
BLEURGH! ABHORRENT!
END OF PART 2

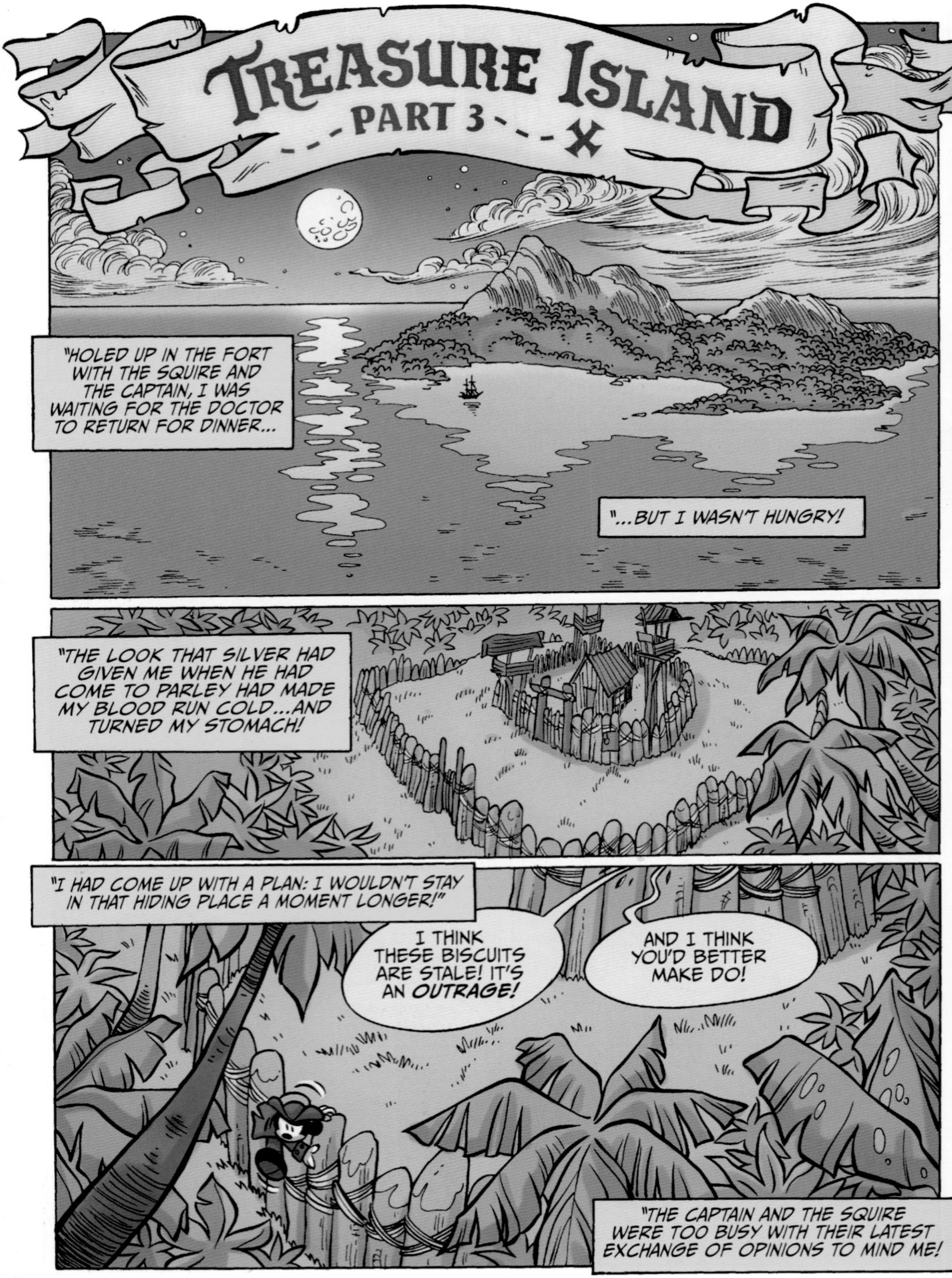
TREASURE ISLAND
PART 3
"HOLED UP IN THE FORT WITH THE SQUIRE AND THE CAPTAIN, I WAS WAITING FOR THE DOCTOR TO RETURN FOR DINNER...
"...BUT I WASN'T HUNGRY!
"THE LOOK THAT SILVER HAD GIVEN ME WHEN HE HAD COME TO PARLEY HAD MADE MY BLOOD RUN COLD...AND TURNED MY STOMACH!
"I HAD COME UP WITH A PLAN: I WOULDN'T STAY IN THAT HIDING PLACE A MOMENT LONGER!"
I THINK THESE BISCUITS ARE STALE! IT'S AN OUTRAGE!
AND I THINK YOU'D BETTER MAKE DO!
"THE CAPTAIN AND THE SQUIRE WERE TOO BUSY WITH THEIR LATEST EXCHANGE OF OPINIONS TO MIND ME!

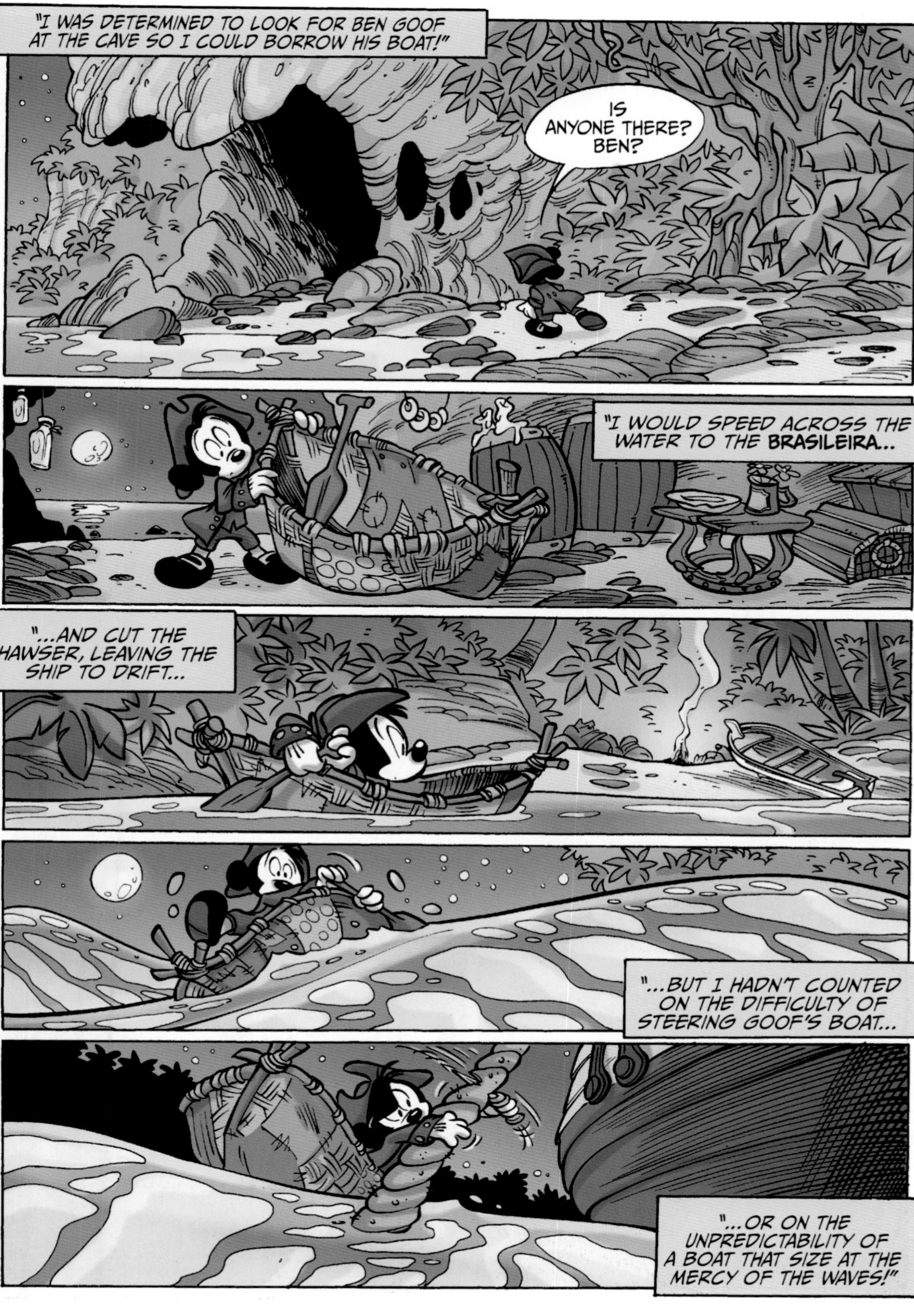
"I WAS DETERMINED TO LOOK FOR BEN GOOF AT THE CAVE SO I COULD BORROW HIS BOAT!"
IS ANYONE THERE? BEN?
"I WOULD SPEED ACROSS THE WATER TO THE BRASILEIRA...
"...AND CUT THE HAWSER, LEAVING THE SHIP TO DRIFT...
"...BUT I HADN'T COUNTED ON THE DIFFICULTY OF STEERING GOOF'S BOAT...
"...OR ON THE UNPREDICTABILITY OF A BOAT THAT SIZE AT THE MERCY OF THE WAVES!"

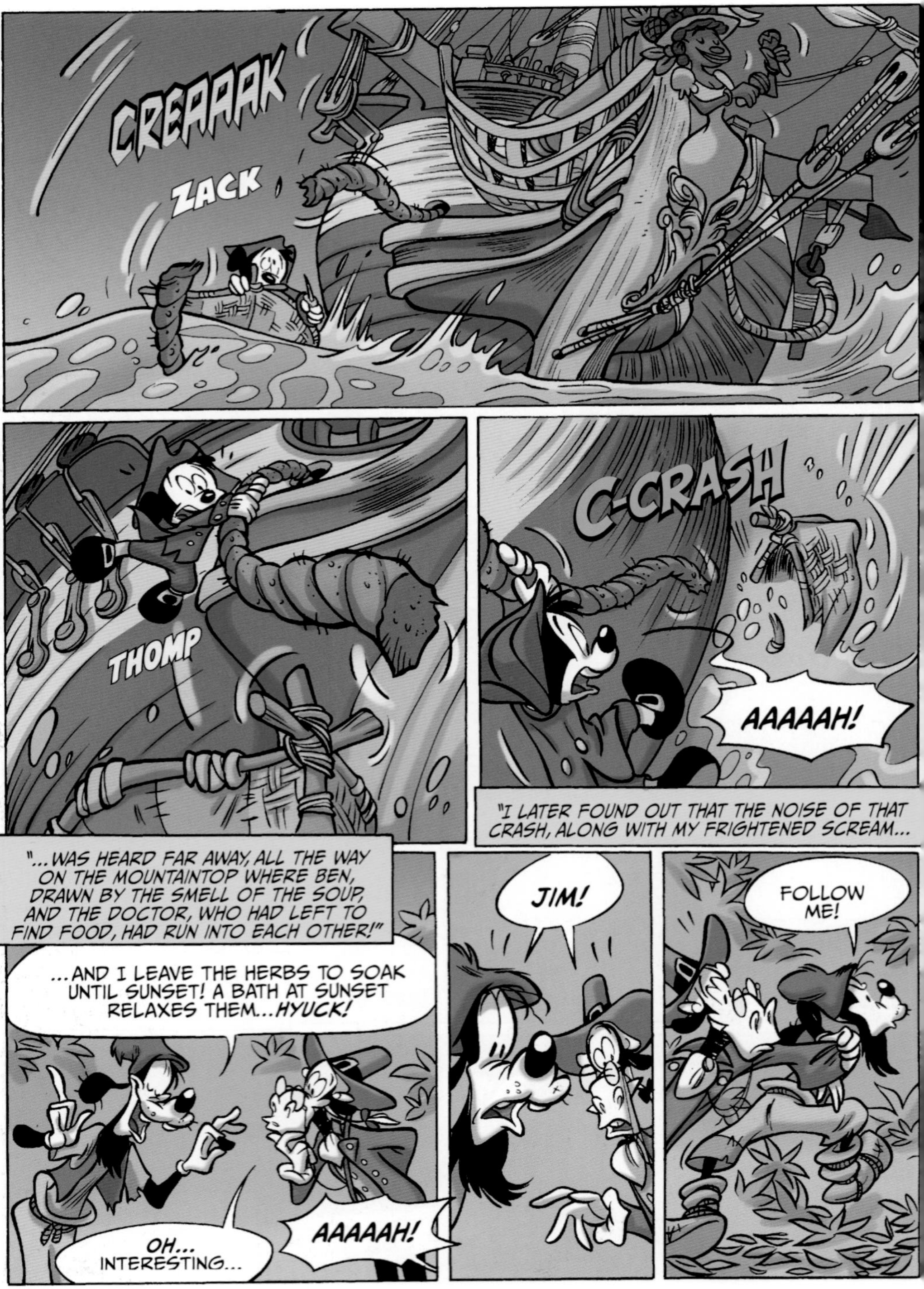
CREAAAK
ZACK
THOMP
C-CRASH
AAAAAH!
"I LATER FOUND OUT THAT THE NOISE OF THAT CRASH, ALONG WITH MY FRIGHTENED SCREAM...
"...WAS HEARD FAR AWAY, ALL THE WAY ON THE MOUNTAINTOP WHERE BEN, DRAWN BY THE SMELL OF THE SOUP, AND THE DOCTOR, WHO HAD LEFT TO FIND FOOD, HAD RUN INTO EACH OTHER!"
...AND I LEAVE THE HERBS TO SOAK UNTIL SUNSET! A BATH AT SUNSET RELAXES THEM...*HYUCK!*
OH... INTERESTING...
AAAAAH!
JIM!
FOLLOW ME!

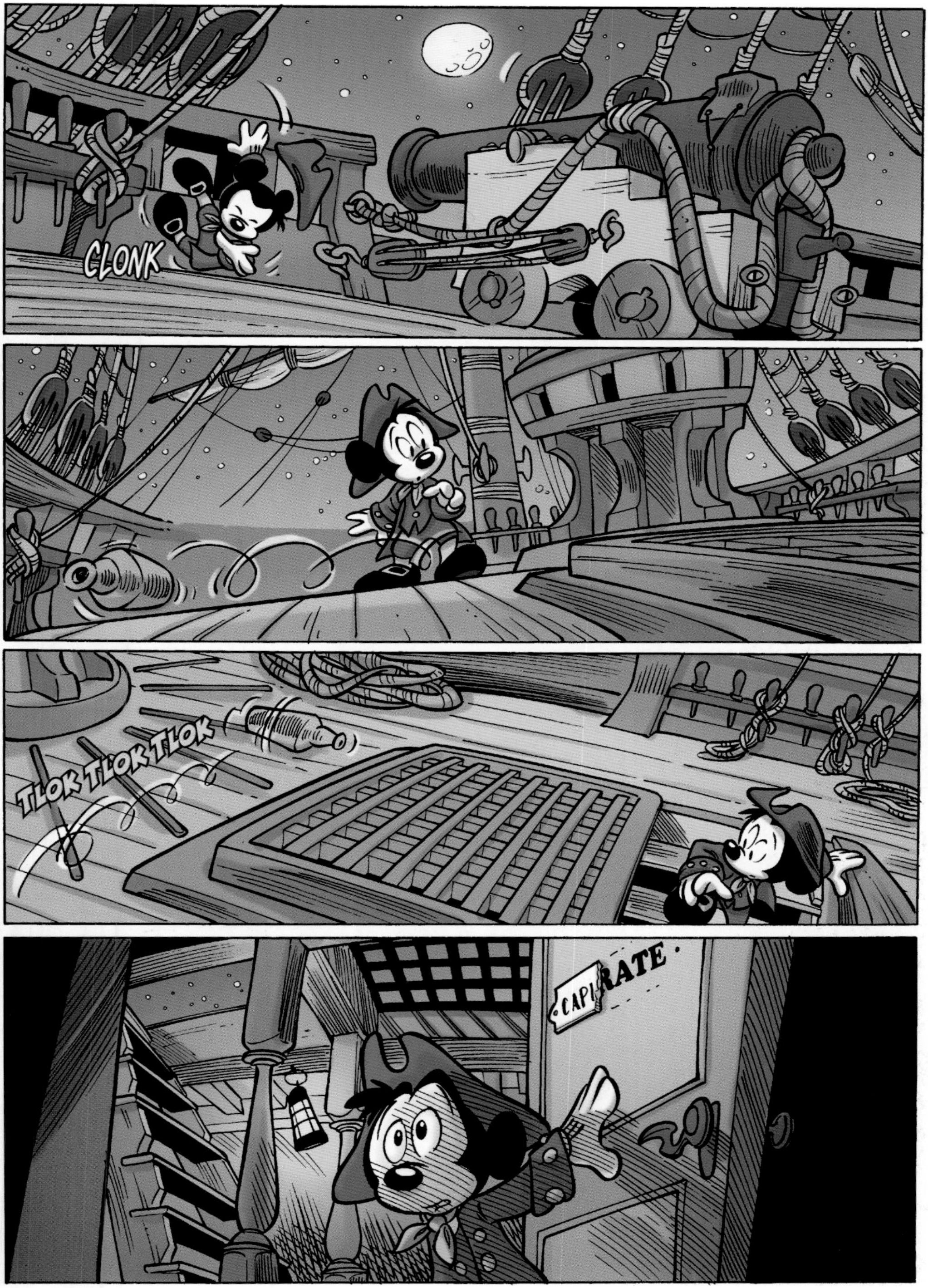
CLONK
TLOK TLOK TLOK
CAPI
RATE

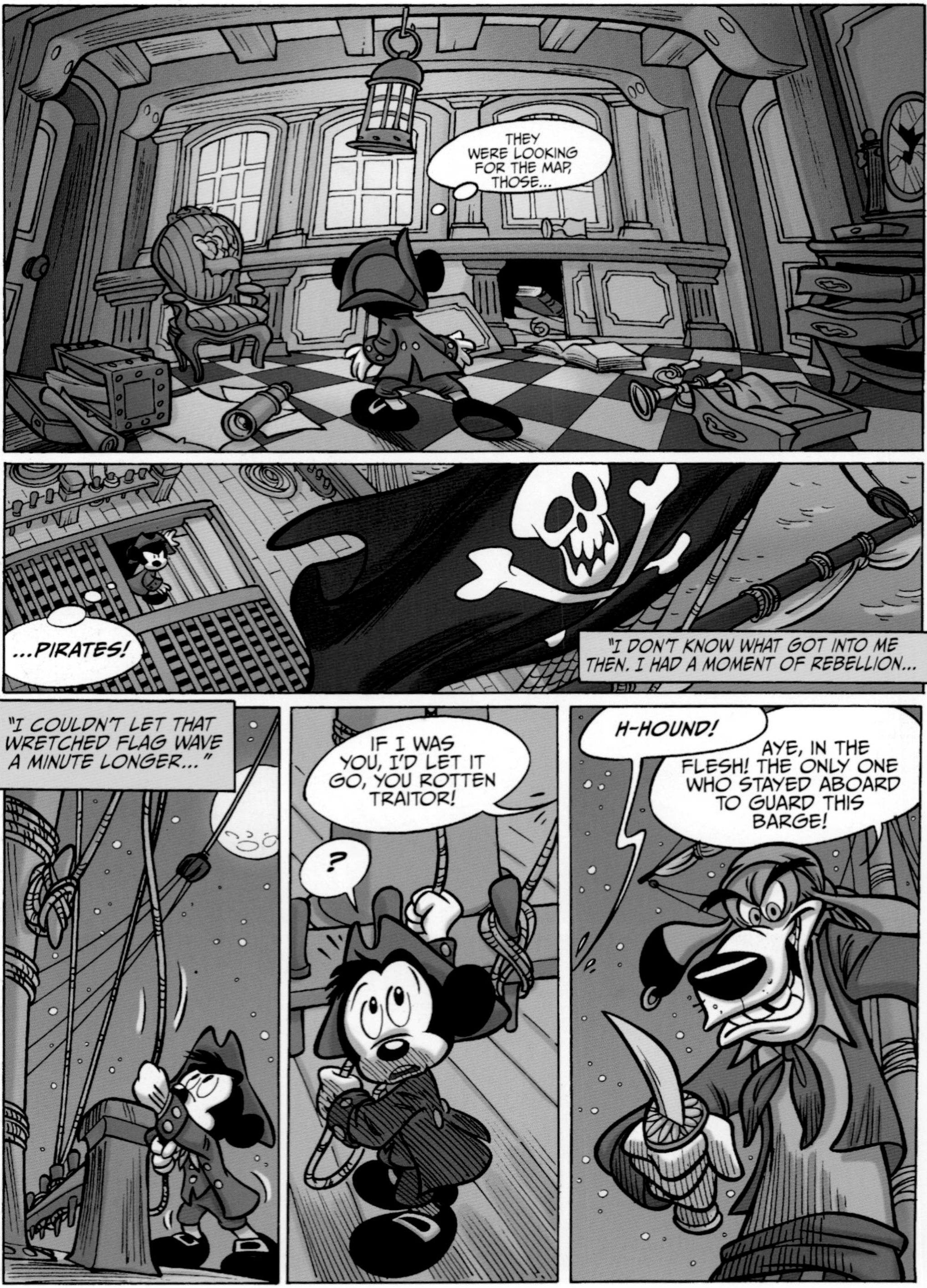
THEY WERE LOOKING FOR THE MAP, THOSE...
...PIRATES!
"I DON'T KNOW WHAT GOT INTO ME THEN. I HAD A MOMENT OF REBELLION...
"I COULDN'T LET THAT WRETCHED FLAG WAVE A MINUTE LONGER..."
IF I WAS YOU, I'D LET IT GO, YOU ROTTEN TRAITOR!
?
H-HOUND!
AYE, IN THE FLESH! THE ONLY ONE WHO STAYED ABOARD TO GUARD THIS BARGE!

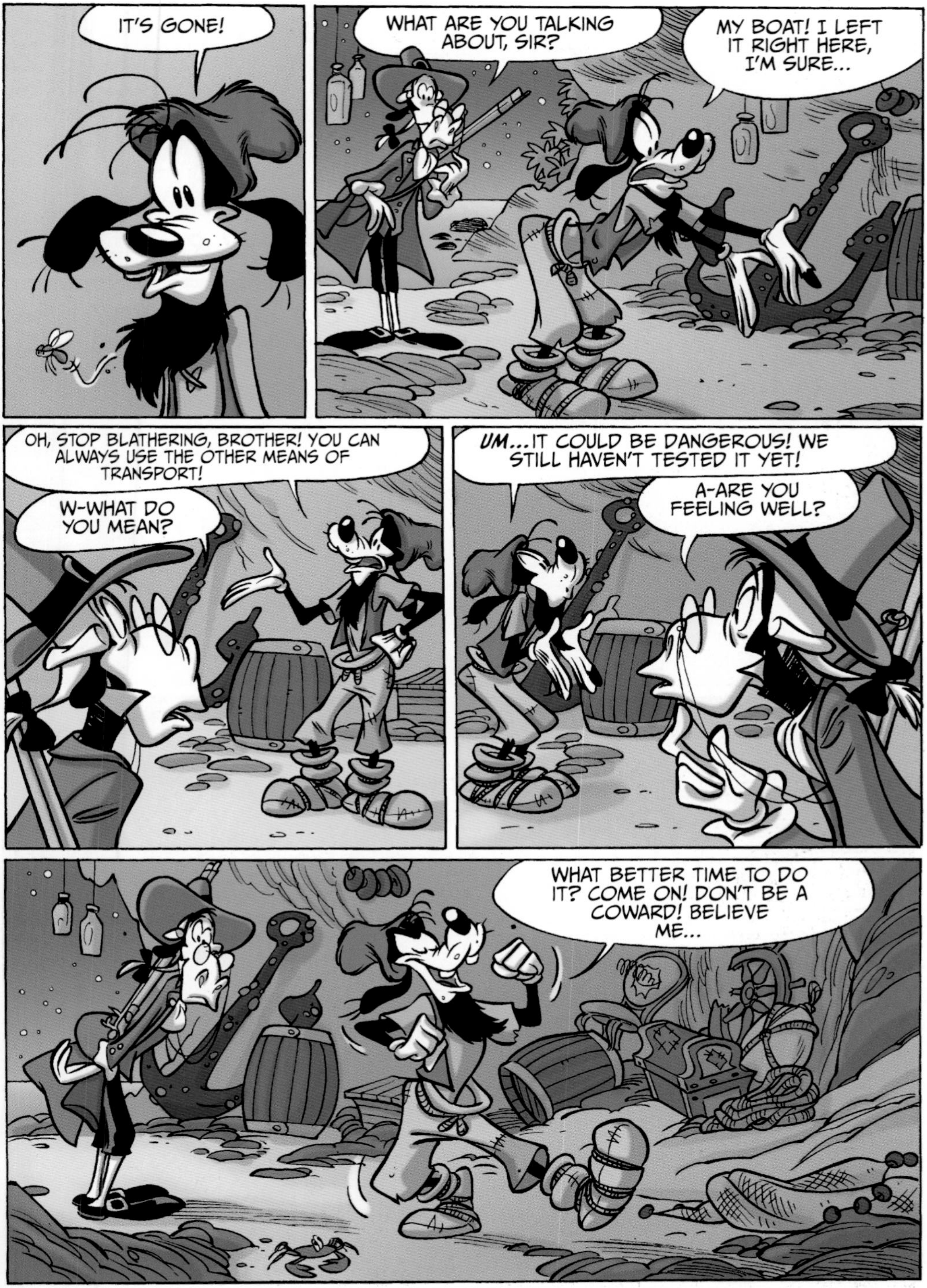

IT'S GONE!
WHAT ARE YOU TALKING ABOUT, SIR?
MY BOAT! I LEFT IT RIGHT HERE, I'M SURE...
OH, STOP BLATHERING, BROTHER! YOU CAN ALWAYS USE THE OTHER MEANS OF TRANSPORT!
W-WHAT DO YOU MEAN?
UM... IT COULD BE DANGEROUS! WE STILL HAVEN'T TESTED IT YET!
A-ARE YOU FEELING WELL?
WHAT BETTER TIME TO DO IT? COME ON! DON'T BE A COWARD! BELIEVE ME...

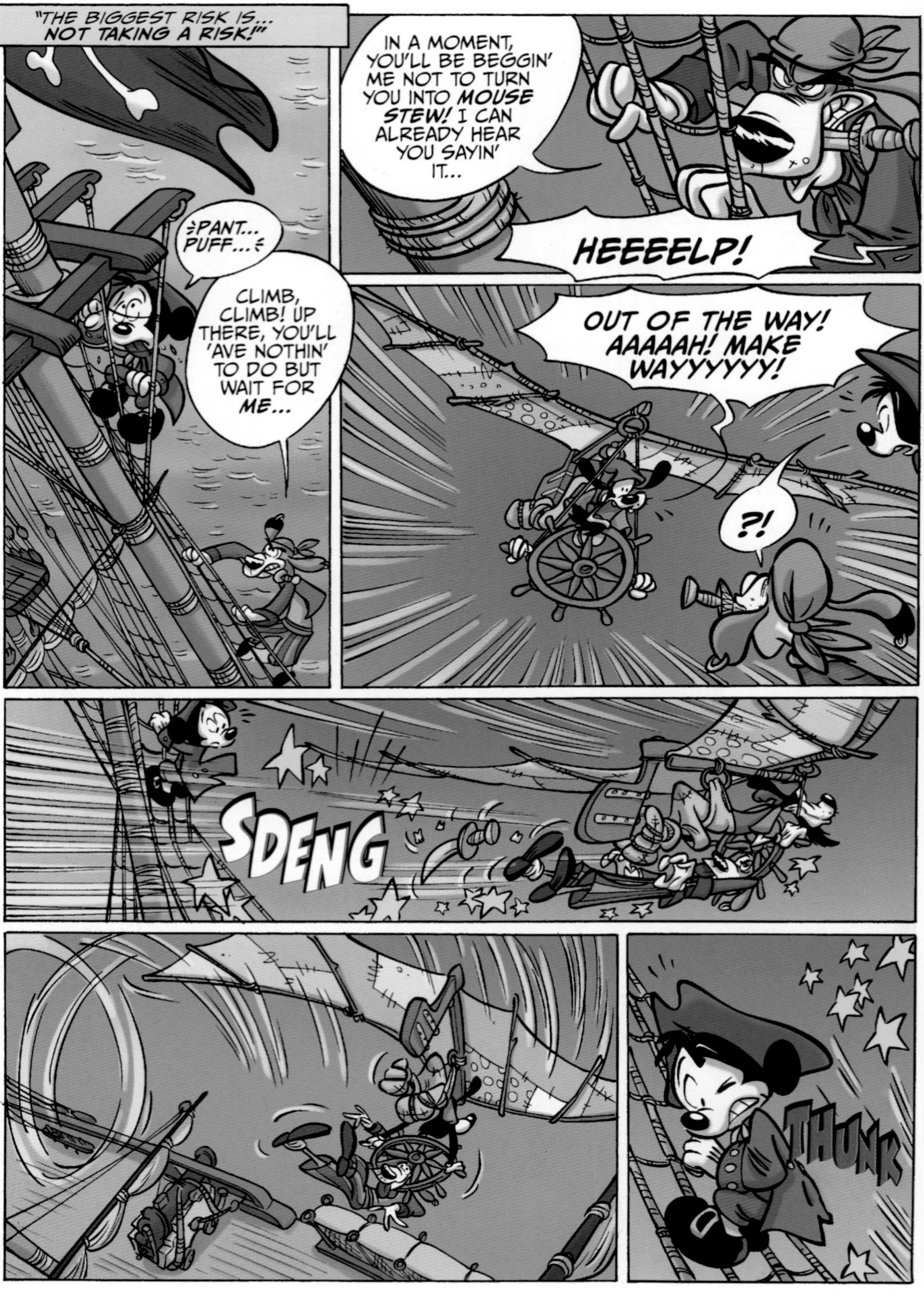
"THE BIGGEST RISK IS... NOT TAKING A RISK!"
IN A MOMENT, YOU'LL BE BEGGIN' ME NOT TO TURN YOU INTO MOUSE STEW! I CAN ALREADY HEAR YOU SAYIN' IT...
HEEEEELP!
PANT... PUFF...
CLIMB, CLIMB! UP THERE, YOU'LL 'AVE NOTHIN' TO DO BUT WAIT FOR ME...
OUT OF THE WAY! AAAAAH! MAKE WAYYYYYY!
?!
SDENG
THUNK

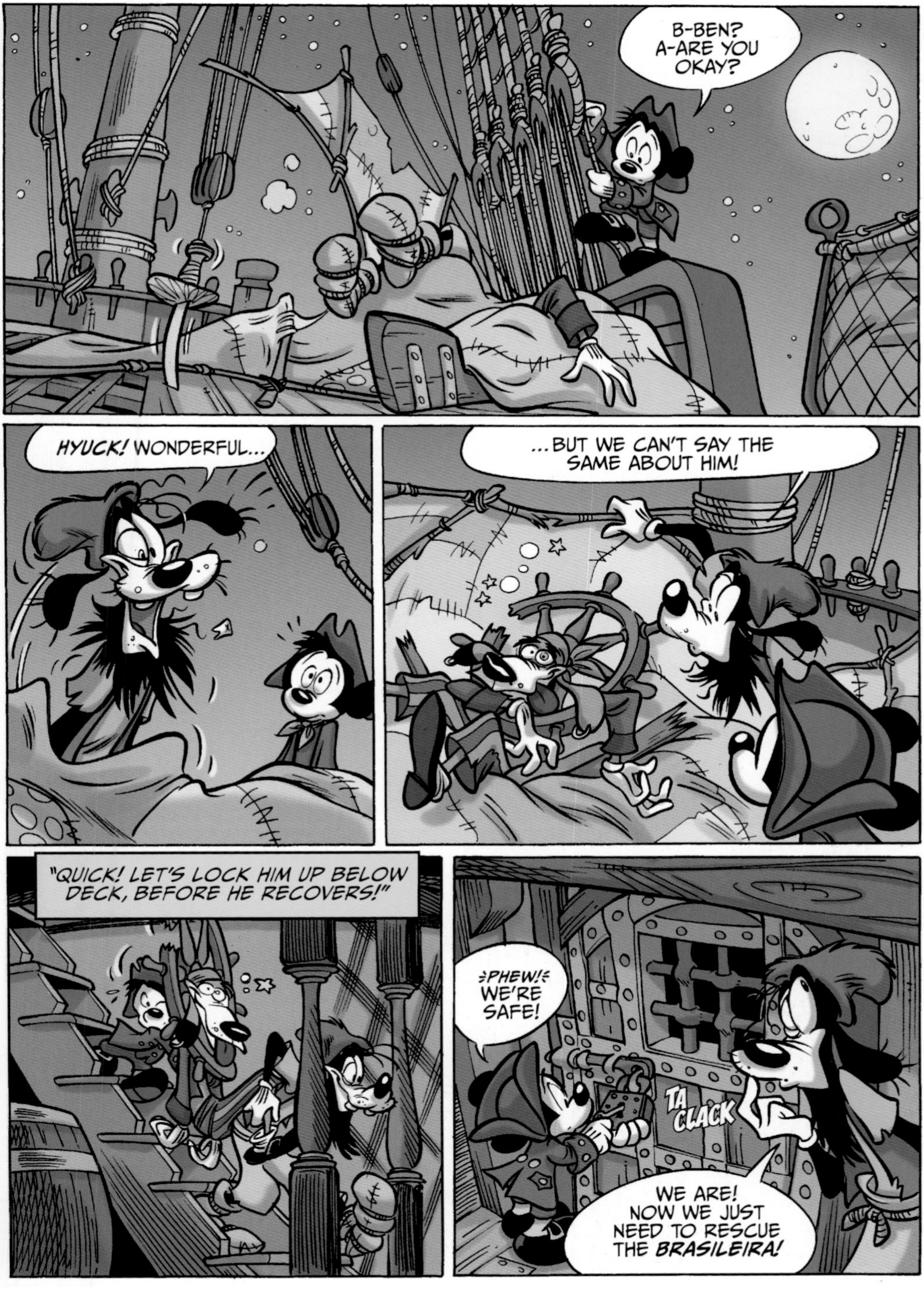
B-BEN? A-ARE YOU OKAY?
HYUCK! WONDERFUL...
...BUT WE CAN'T SAY THE SAME ABOUT HIM!
"QUICK! LET'S LOCK HIM UP BELOW DECK, BEFORE HE RECOVERS!"
PHEW! WE'RE SAFE!
TA CLACK
WE ARE! NOW WE JUST NEED TO RESCUE THE BRASILEIRA!

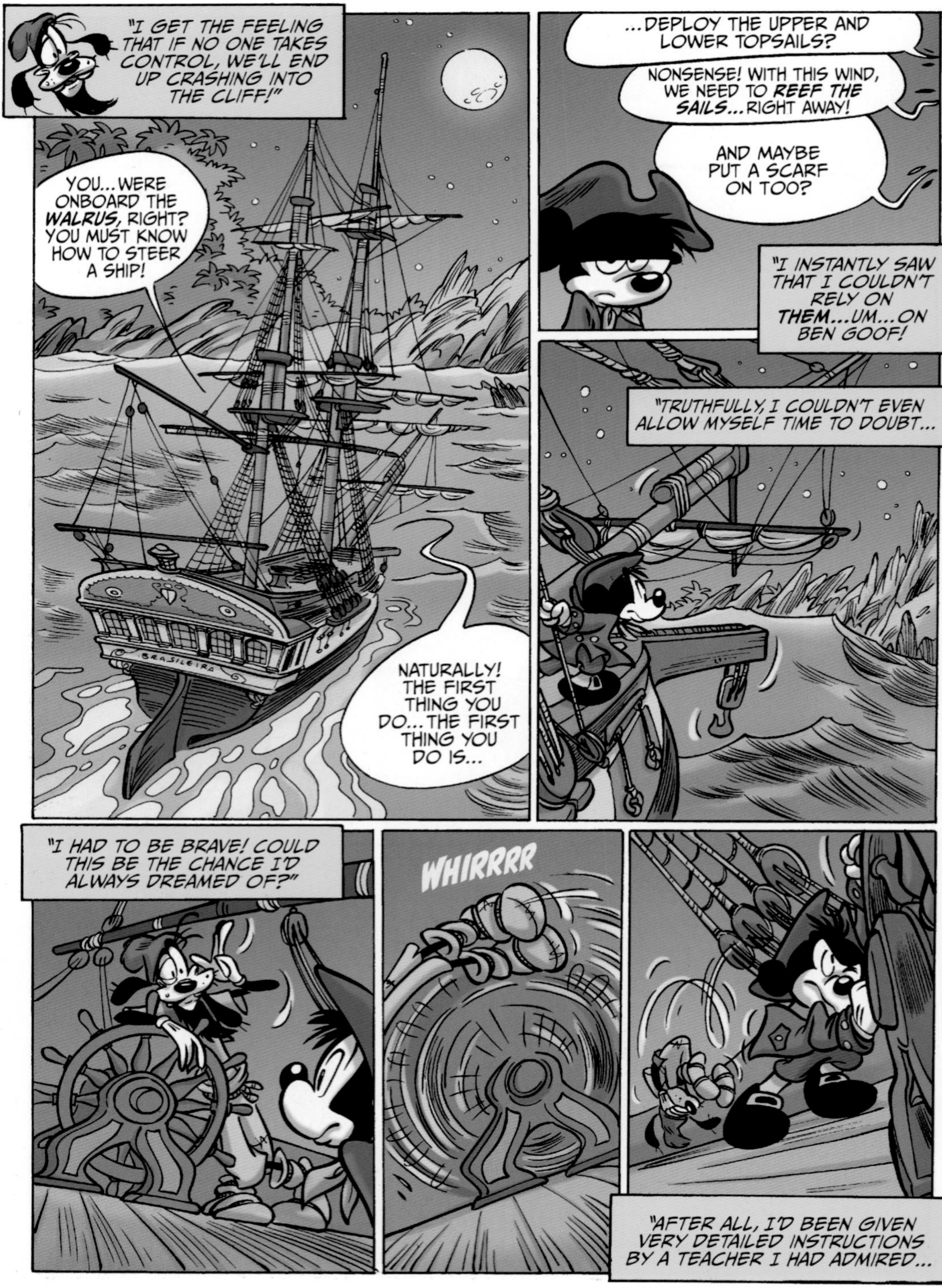
"I GET THE FEELING THAT IF NO ONE TAKES CONTROL, WE'LL END UP CRASHING INTO THE CLIFF!"
YOU...WERE ONBOARD THE WALRUS, RIGHT? YOU MUST KNOW HOW TO STEER A SHIP!
BRASILEIRA
NATURALLY! THE FIRST THING YOU DO...THE FIRST THING YOU DO IS...
...DEPLOY THE UPPER AND LOWER TOPSAILS?
NONSENSE! WITH THIS WIND, WE NEED TO REEF THE SAILS...RIGHT AWAY!
AND MAYBE PUT A SCARF ON TOO?
"I INSTANTLY SAW THAT I COULDN'T RELY ON THEM...UM...ON BEN GOOF!
"TRUTHFULLY, I COULDN'T EVEN ALLOW MYSELF TIME TO DOUBT...
"I HAD TO BE BRAVE! COULD THIS BE THE CHANCE I'D ALWAYS DREAMED OF?"
WHIRRRR
"AFTER ALL, I'D BEEN GIVEN VERY DETAILED INSTRUCTIONS BY A TEACHER I HAD ADMIRED...

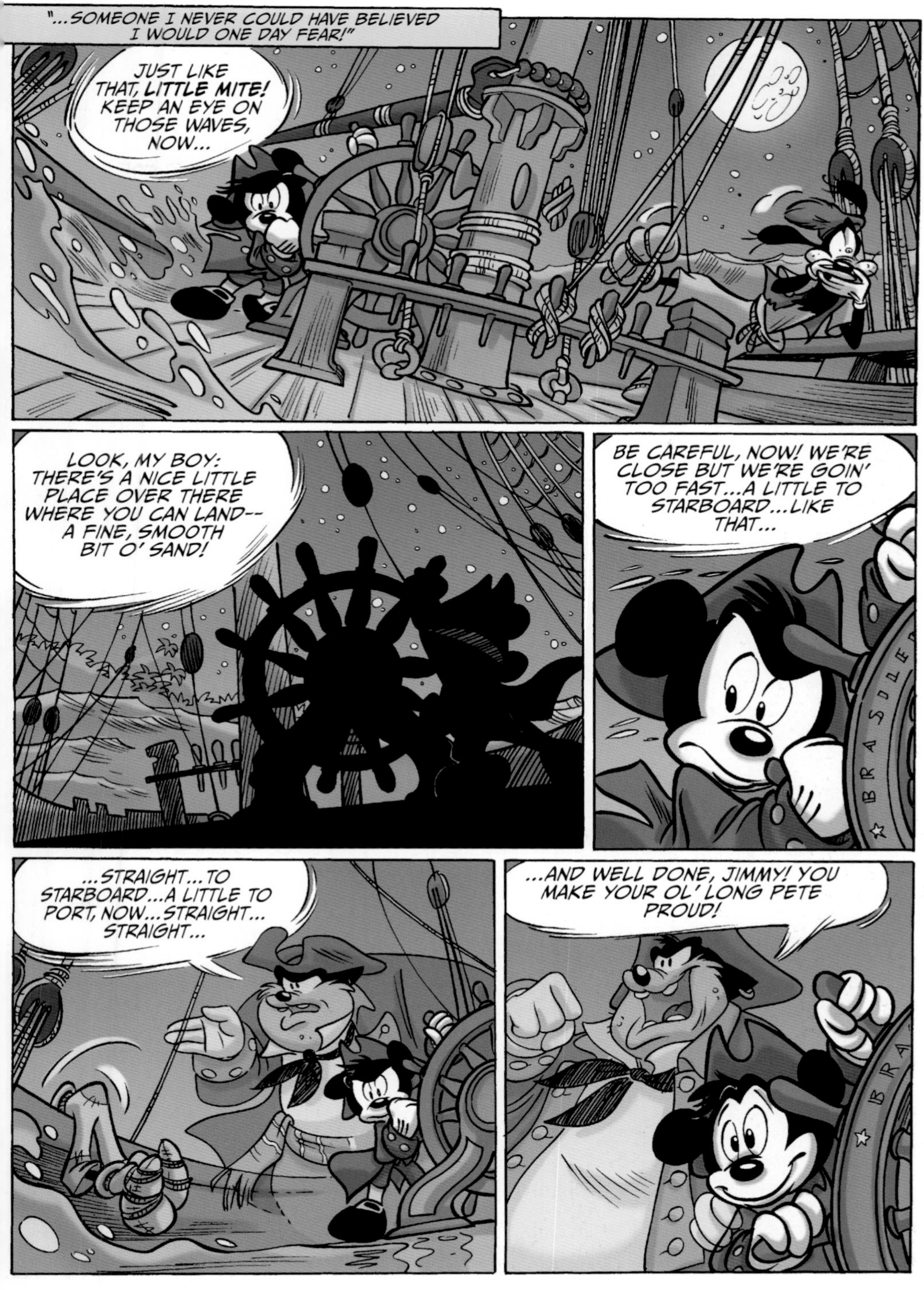
"...SOMEONE I NEVER COULD HAVE BELIEVED I WOULD ONE DAY FEAR!"
JUST LIKE THAT, LITTLE MITE! KEEP AN EYE ON THOSE WAVES, NOW...
LOOK, MY BOY: THERE'S A NICE LITTLE PLACE OVER THERE WHERE YOU CAN LAND-- A FINE, SMOOTH BIT O' SAND!
BE CAREFUL, NOW! WE'RE CLOSE BUT WE'RE GOIN' TOO FAST...A LITTLE TO STARBOARD...LIKE THAT...
...STRAIGHT...TO STARBOARD...A LITTLE TO PORT, NOW...STRAIGHT... STRAIGHT...
...AND WELL DONE, JIMMY! YOU MAKE YOUR OL' LONG PETE PROUD!

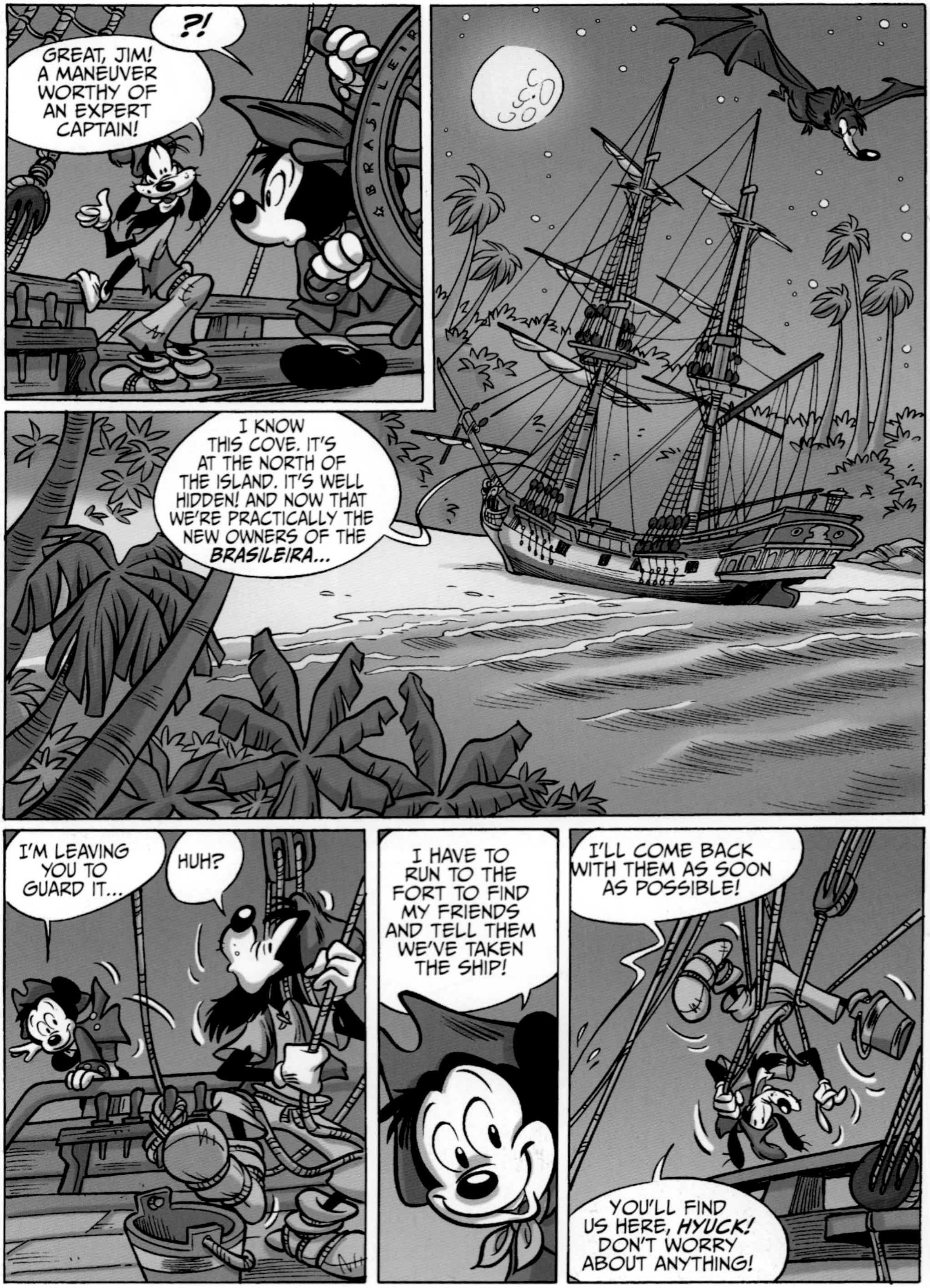
?!
GREAT, JIM! A MANEUVER WORTHY OF AN EXPERT CAPTAIN!
I KNOW THIS COVE. IT'S AT THE NORTH OF THE ISLAND. IT'S WELL HIDDEN! AND NOW THAT WE'RE PRACTICALLY THE NEW OWNERS OF THE *BRASILEIRA*...
I'M LEAVING YOU TO GUARD IT...
HUH?
I HAVE TO RUN TO THE FORT TO FIND MY FRIENDS AND TELL THEM WE'VE TAKEN THE SHIP!
I'LL COME BACK WITH THEM AS SOON AS POSSIBLE!
YOU'LL FIND US HERE, *HYUCK!* DON'T WORRY ABOUT ANYTHING!

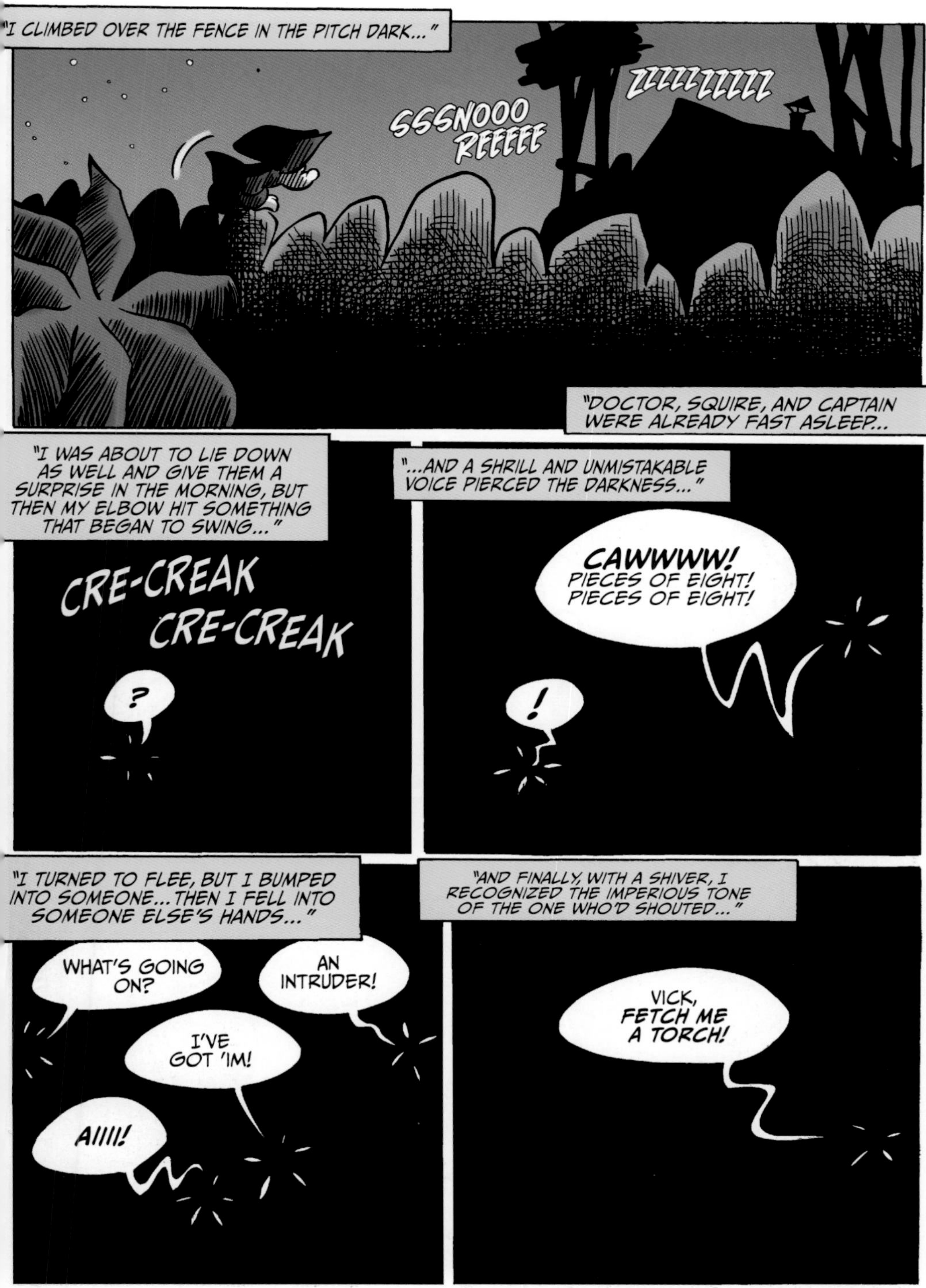
"I CLIMBED OVER THE FENCE IN THE PITCH DARK..."
SSSNOOO REEEEE
ZZZZZZZZZZ
"DOCTOR, SQUIRE, AND CAPTAIN WERE ALREADY FAST ASLEEP...
"I WAS ABOUT TO LIE DOWN AS WELL AND GIVE THEM A SURPRISE IN THE MORNING, BUT THEN MY ELBOW HIT SOMETHING THAT BEGAN TO SWING..."
CRE-CREAK CRE-CREAK
?
"...AND A SHRILL AND UNMISTAKABLE VOICE PIERCED THE DARKNESS..."
CAWWWW! PIECES OF EIGHT! PIECES OF EIGHT!
!
"I TURNED TO FLEE, BUT I BUMPED INTO SOMEONE... THEN I FELL INTO SOMEONE ELSE'S HANDS..."
WHAT'S GOING ON?
AN INTRUDER!
I'VE GOT 'IM!
AIIII!
"AND FINALLY, WITH A SHIVER, I RECOGNIZED THE IMPERIOUS TONE OF THE ONE WHO'D SHOUTED..."
VICK, FETCH ME A TORCH!

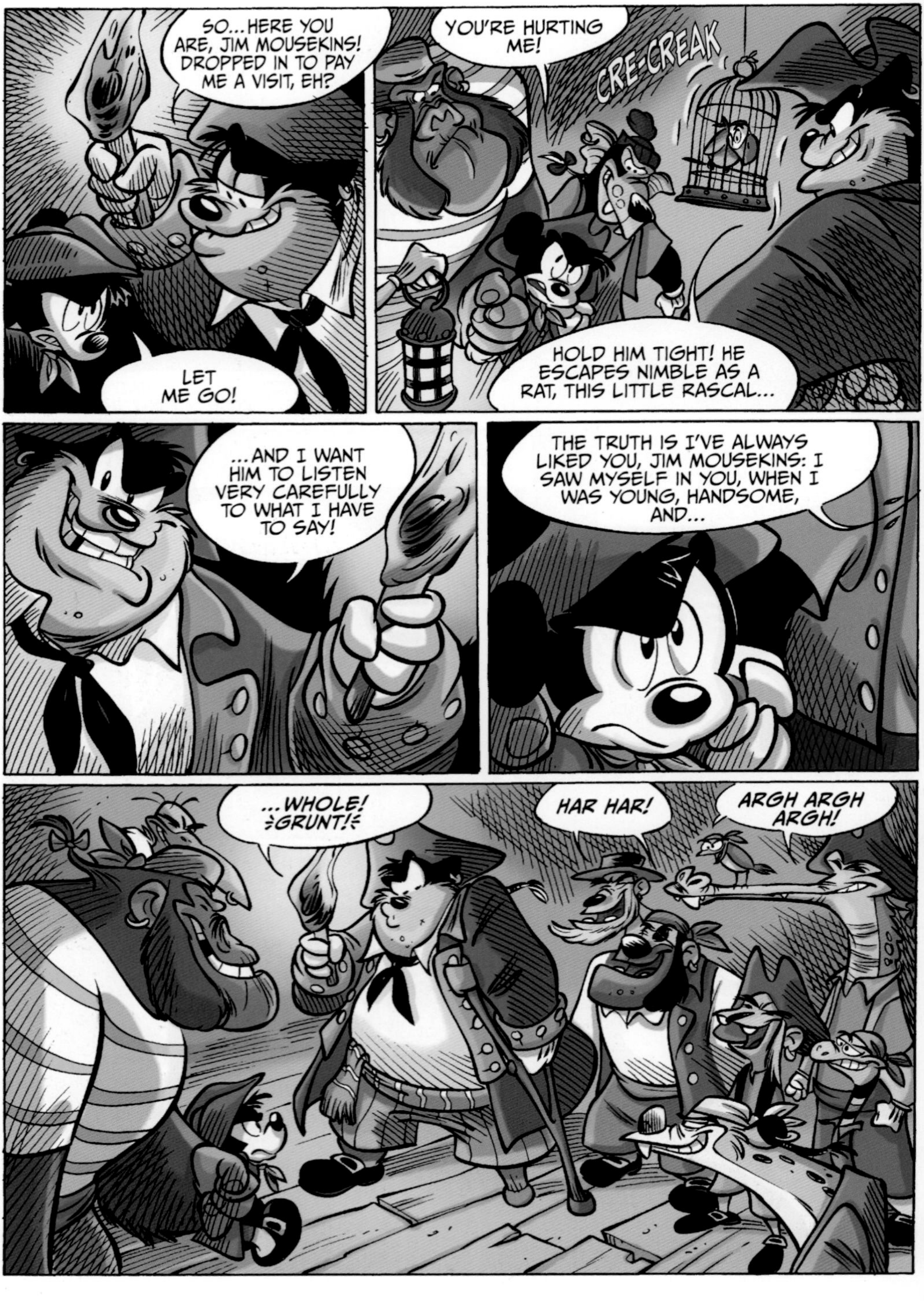
SO...HERE YOU ARE, JIM MOUSEKINS! DROPPED IN TO PAY ME A VISIT, EH?
LET ME GO!
YOU'RE HURTING ME!
CRE-CREAK
HOLD HIM TIGHT! HE ESCAPES NIMBLE AS A RAT, THIS LITTLE RASCAL...
...AND I WANT HIM TO LISTEN VERY CAREFULLY TO WHAT I HAVE TO SAY!
THE TRUTH IS I'VE ALWAYS LIKED YOU, JIM MOUSEKINS: I SAW MYSELF IN YOU, WHEN I WAS YOUNG, HANDSOME, AND...
...WHOLE! GRUNT!
HAR HAR!
ARGH ARGH ARGH!

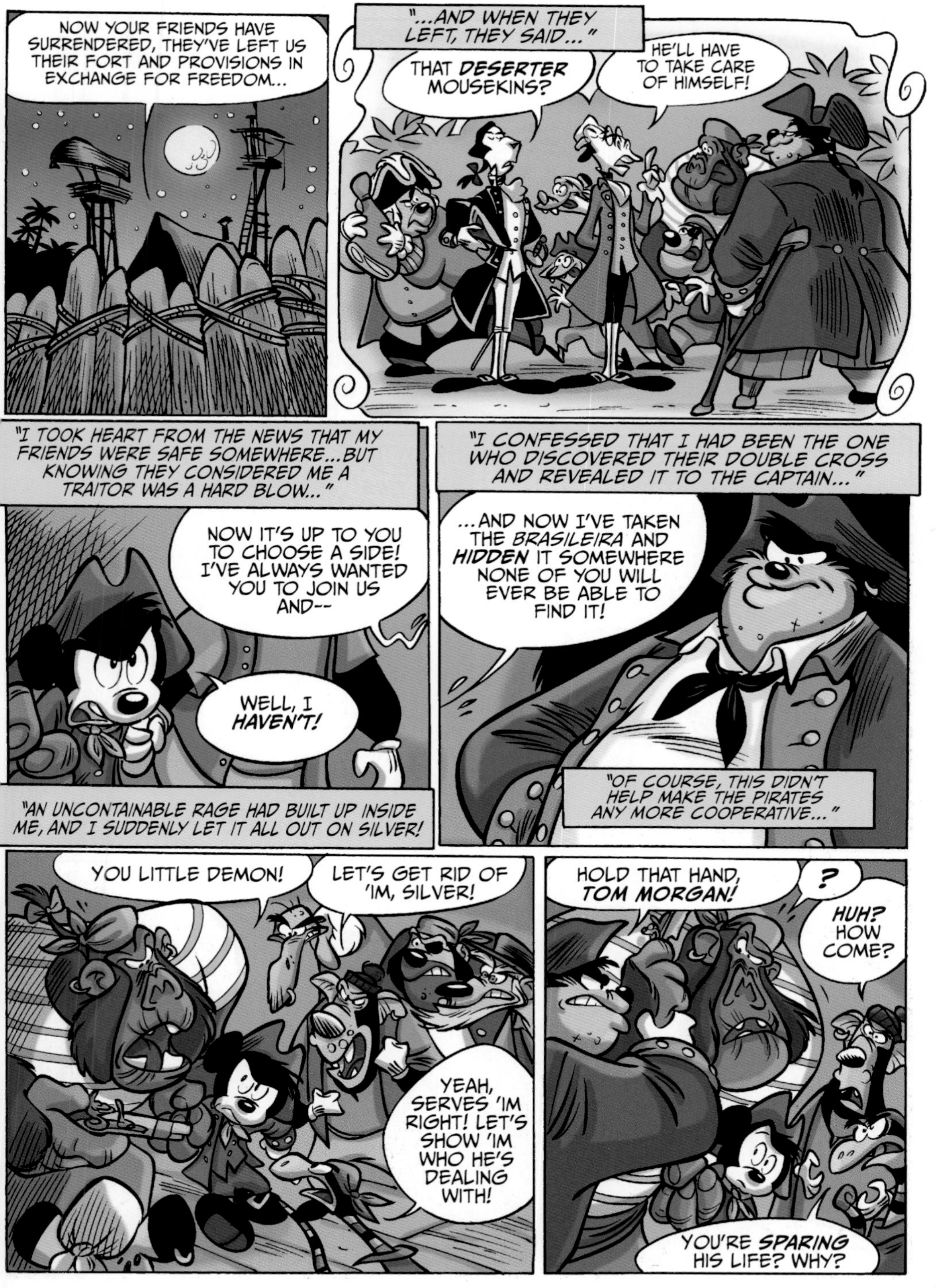

NOW YOUR FRIENDS HAVE SURRENDERED, THEY'VE LEFT US THEIR FORT AND PROVISIONS IN EXCHANGE FOR FREEDOM...
"...AND WHEN THEY LEFT, THEY SAID..."
THAT DESERTER MOUSEKINS?
HE'LL HAVE TO TAKE CARE OF HIMSELF!
"I TOOK HEART FROM THE NEWS THAT MY FRIENDS WERE SAFE SOMEWHERE...BUT KNOWING THEY CONSIDERED ME A TRAITOR WAS A HARD BLOW..."
NOW IT'S UP TO YOU TO CHOOSE A SIDE! I'VE ALWAYS WANTED YOU TO JOIN US AND--
WELL, I HAVEN'T!
"I CONFESSED THAT I HAD BEEN THE ONE WHO DISCOVERED THEIR DOUBLE CROSS AND REVEALED IT TO THE CAPTAIN..."
...AND NOW I'VE TAKEN THE BRASILEIRA AND HIDDEN IT SOMEWHERE NONE OF YOU WILL EVER BE ABLE TO FIND IT!
"OF COURSE, THIS DIDN'T HELP MAKE THE PIRATES ANY MORE COOPERATIVE..."
"AN UNCONTAINABLE RAGE HAD BUILT UP INSIDE ME, AND I SUDDENLY LET IT ALL OUT ON SILVER!
YOU LITTLE DEMON!
LET'S GET RID OF 'IM, SILVER!
YEAH, SERVES 'IM RIGHT! LET'S SHOW 'IM WHO HE'S DEALING WITH!
HOLD THAT HAND, TOM MORGAN!
?
HUH? HOW COME?
YOU'RE SPARING HIS LIFE? WHY?

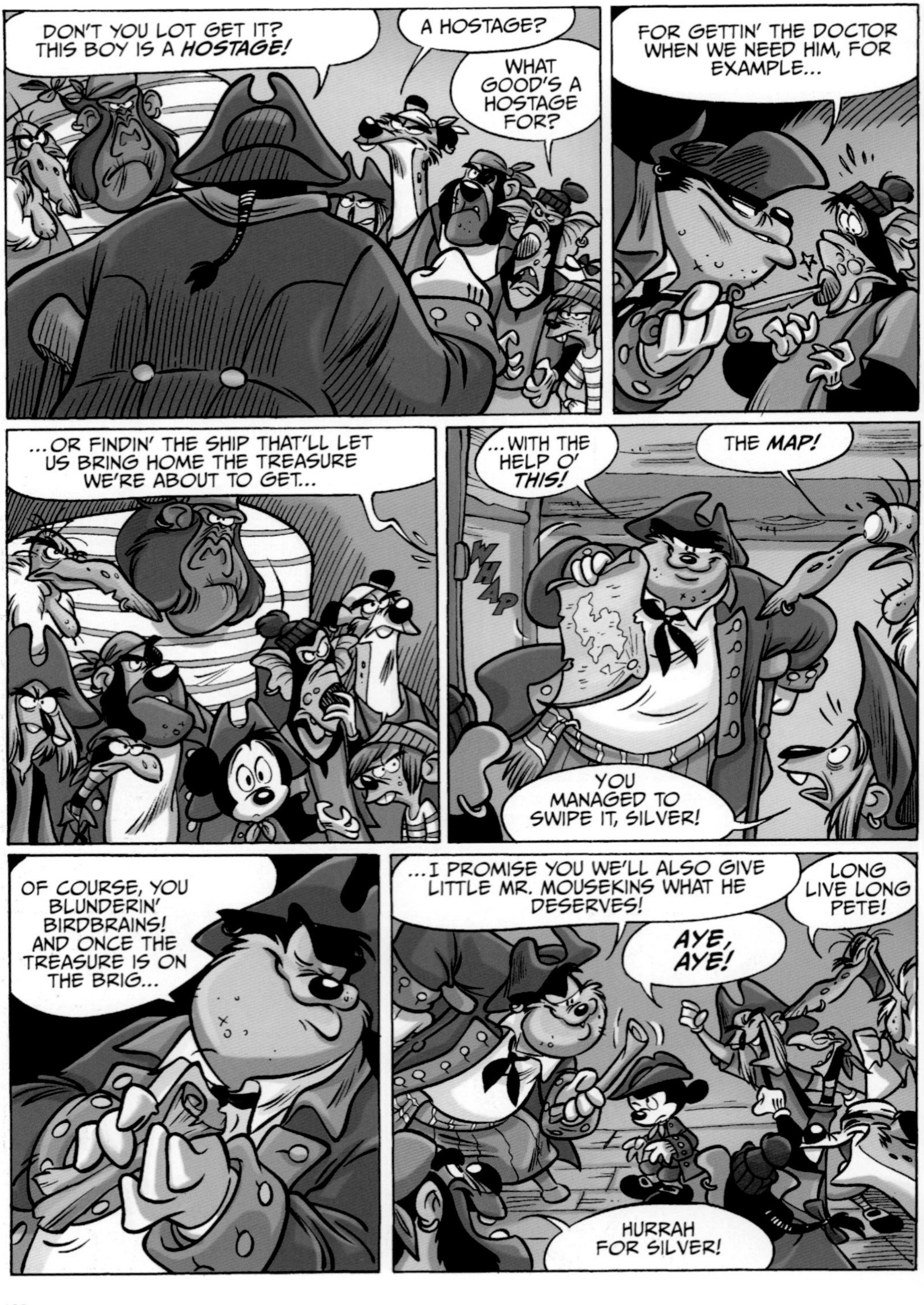

DON'T YOU LOT GET IT? THIS BOY IS A HOSTAGE!
A HOSTAGE?
WHAT GOOD'S A HOSTAGE FOR?
FOR GETTIN' THE DOCTOR WHEN WE NEED HIM, FOR EXAMPLE...
...OR FINDIN' THE SHIP THAT'LL LET US BRING HOME THE TREASURE WE'RE ABOUT TO GET...
...WITH THE HELP O' THIS!
WHAP
THE MAP!
YOU MANAGED TO SWIPE IT, SILVER!
OF COURSE, YOU BLUNDERIN' BIRDBRAINS! AND ONCE THE TREASURE IS ON THE BRIG...
...I PROMISE YOU WE'LL ALSO GIVE LITTLE MR. MOUSEKINS WHAT HE DESERVES!
LONG LIVE LONG PETE!
AYE, AYE!
HURRAH FOR SILVER!

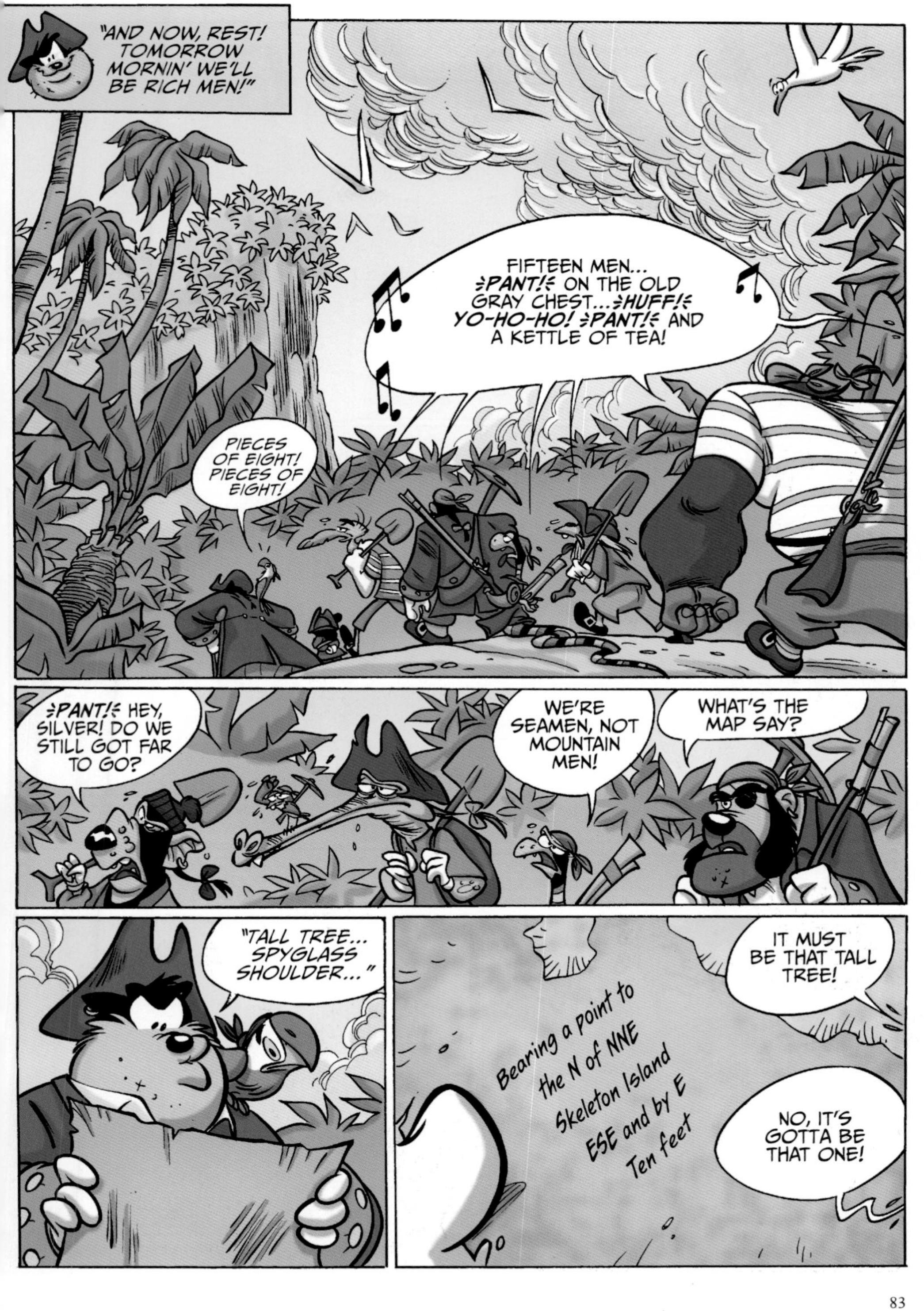

"AND NOW, REST! TOMORROW MORNIN' WE'LL BE RICH MEN!"
FIFTEEN MEN... PANT! ON THE OLD GRAY CHEST... HUFF! YO-HO-HO! PANT! AND A KETTLE OF TEA!
PIECES OF EIGHT! PIECES OF EIGHT!
PANT! HEY, SILVER! DO WE STILL GOT FAR TO GO?
WE'RE SEAMEN, NOT MOUNTAIN MEN!
WHAT'S THE MAP SAY?
"TALL TREE... SPYGLASS SHOULDER..."
Bearing a point to the N of NNE Skeleton Island ESE and by E Ten feet
IT MUST BE THAT TALL TREE!
NO, IT'S GOTTA BE THAT ONE!

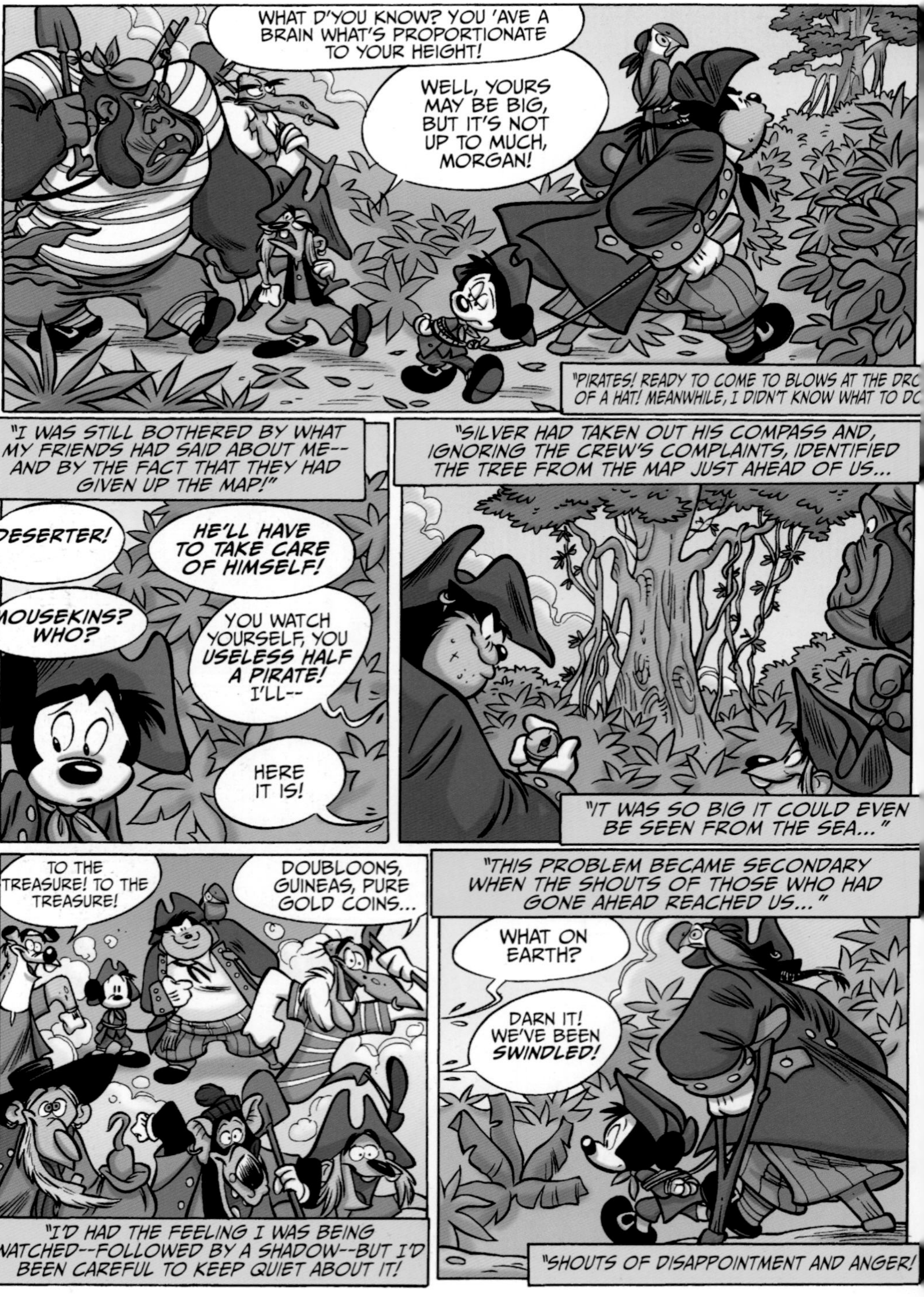
WHAT D'YOU KNOW? YOU 'AVE A BRAIN WHAT'S PROPORTIONATE TO YOUR HEIGHT!
WELL, YOURS MAY BE BIG, BUT IT'S NOT UP TO MUCH, MORGAN!
"PIRATES! READY TO COME TO BLOWS AT THE DRO OF A HAT! MEANWHILE, I DIDN'T KNOW WHAT TO DO
"I WAS STILL BOTHERED BY WHAT MY FRIENDS HAD SAID ABOUT ME--AND BY THE FACT THAT THEY HAD GIVEN UP THE MAP!"
DESERTER!
HE'LL HAVE TO TAKE CARE OF HIMSELF!
MOUSEKINS? WHO?
YOU WATCH YOURSELF, YOU USELESS HALF A PIRATE! I'LL--
HERE IT IS!
"SILVER HAD TAKEN OUT HIS COMPASS AND, IGNORING THE CREW'S COMPLAINTS, IDENTIFIED THE TREE FROM THE MAP JUST AHEAD OF US...
"IT WAS SO BIG IT COULD EVEN BE SEEN FROM THE SEA..."
TO THE TREASURE! TO THE TREASURE!
DOUBLOONS, GUINEAS, PURE GOLD COINS...
"I'D HAD THE FEELING I WAS BEING WATCHED--FOLLOWED BY A SHADOW--BUT I'D BEEN CAREFUL TO KEEP QUIET ABOUT IT!
"THIS PROBLEM BECAME SECONDARY WHEN THE SHOUTS OF THOSE WHO HAD GONE AHEAD REACHED US..."
WHAT ON EARTH?
DARN IT! WE'VE BEEN SWINDLED!
"SHOUTS OF DISAPPOINTMENT AND ANGER!

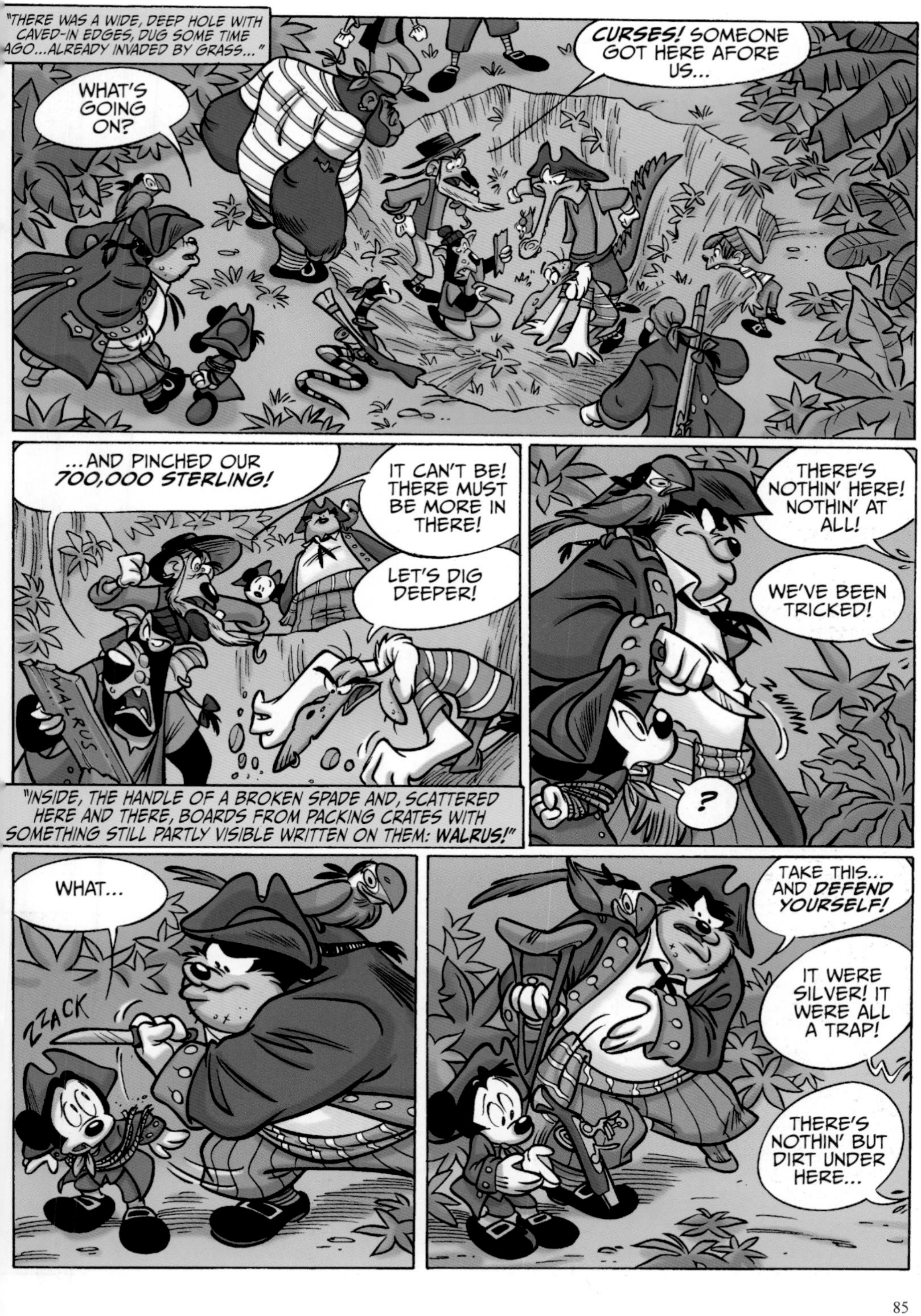
"THERE WAS A WIDE, DEEP HOLE WITH CAVED-IN EDGES, DUG SOME TIME AGO...ALREADY INVADED BY GRASS..."
WHAT'S GOING ON?
CURSES! SOMEONE GOT HERE AFORE US...
...AND PINCHED OUR 700,000 STERLING!
IT CAN'T BE! THERE MUST BE MORE IN THERE!
LET'S DIG DEEPER!
WALRUS
"INSIDE, THE HANDLE OF A BROKEN SPADE AND, SCATTERED HERE AND THERE, BOARDS FROM PACKING CRATES WITH SOMETHING STILL PARTLY VISIBLE WRITTEN ON THEM: WALRUS!"
THERE'S NOTHIN' HERE! NOTHIN' AT ALL!
WE'VE BEEN TRICKED!
ZWINN
?
WHAT...
ZZACK
TAKE THIS... AND DEFEND YOURSELF!
IT WERE SILVER! IT WERE ALL A TRAP!
THERE'S NOTHIN' BUT DIRT UNDER HERE...

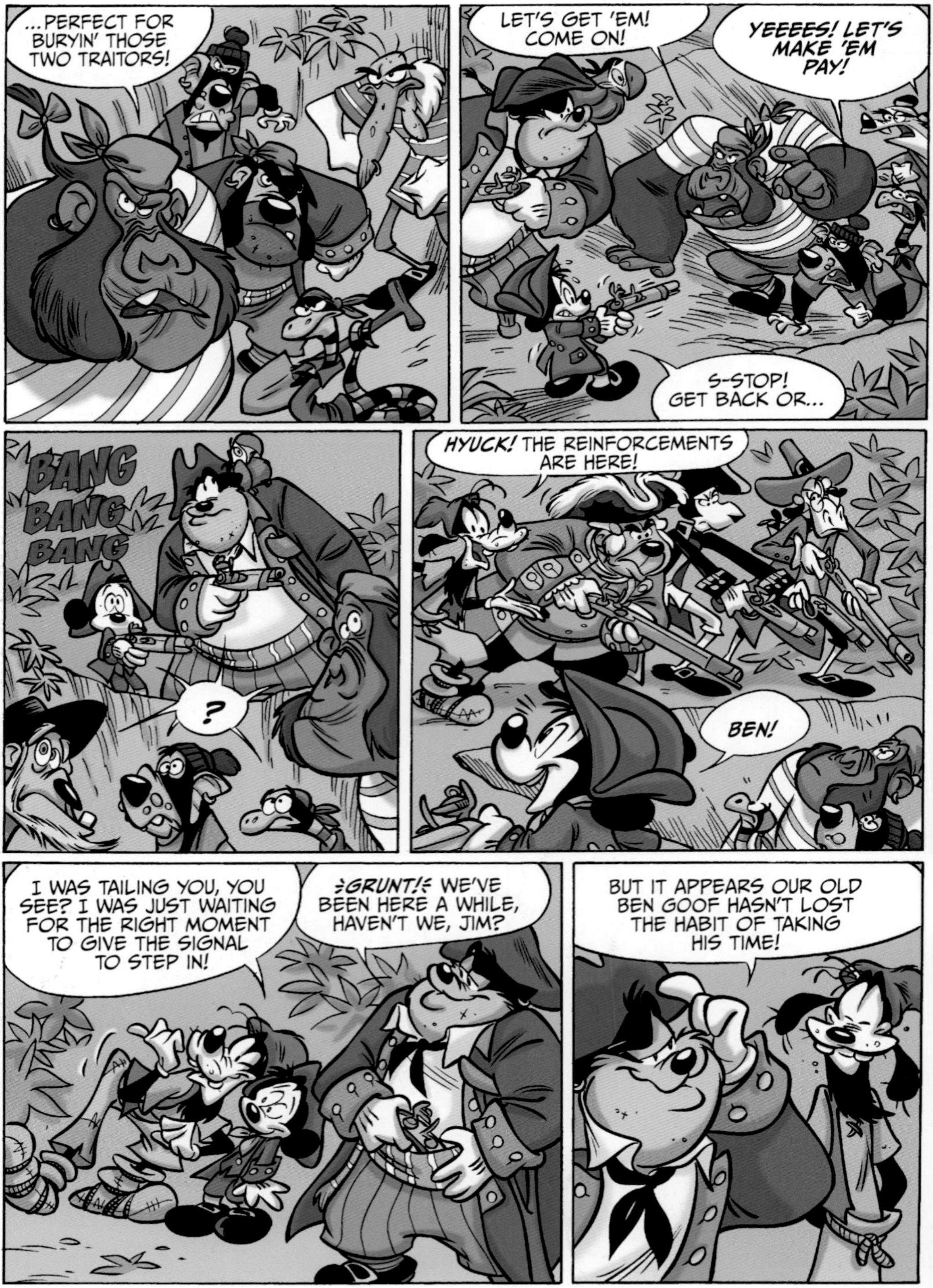
...PERFECT FOR BURYIN' THOSE TWO TRAITORS!
LET'S GET 'EM! COME ON!
YEEEES! LET'S MAKE 'EM PAY!
S-STOP! GET BACK OR...
BANG
BANG
BANG
?
HYUCK! THE REINFORCEMENTS ARE HERE!
BEN!
I WAS TAILING YOU, YOU SEE? I WAS JUST WAITING FOR THE RIGHT MOMENT TO GIVE THE SIGNAL TO STEP IN!
GRUNT! WE'VE BEEN HERE A WHILE, HAVEN'T WE, JIM?
BUT IT APPEARS OUR OLD BEN GOOF HASN'T LOST THE HABIT OF TAKING HIS TIME!

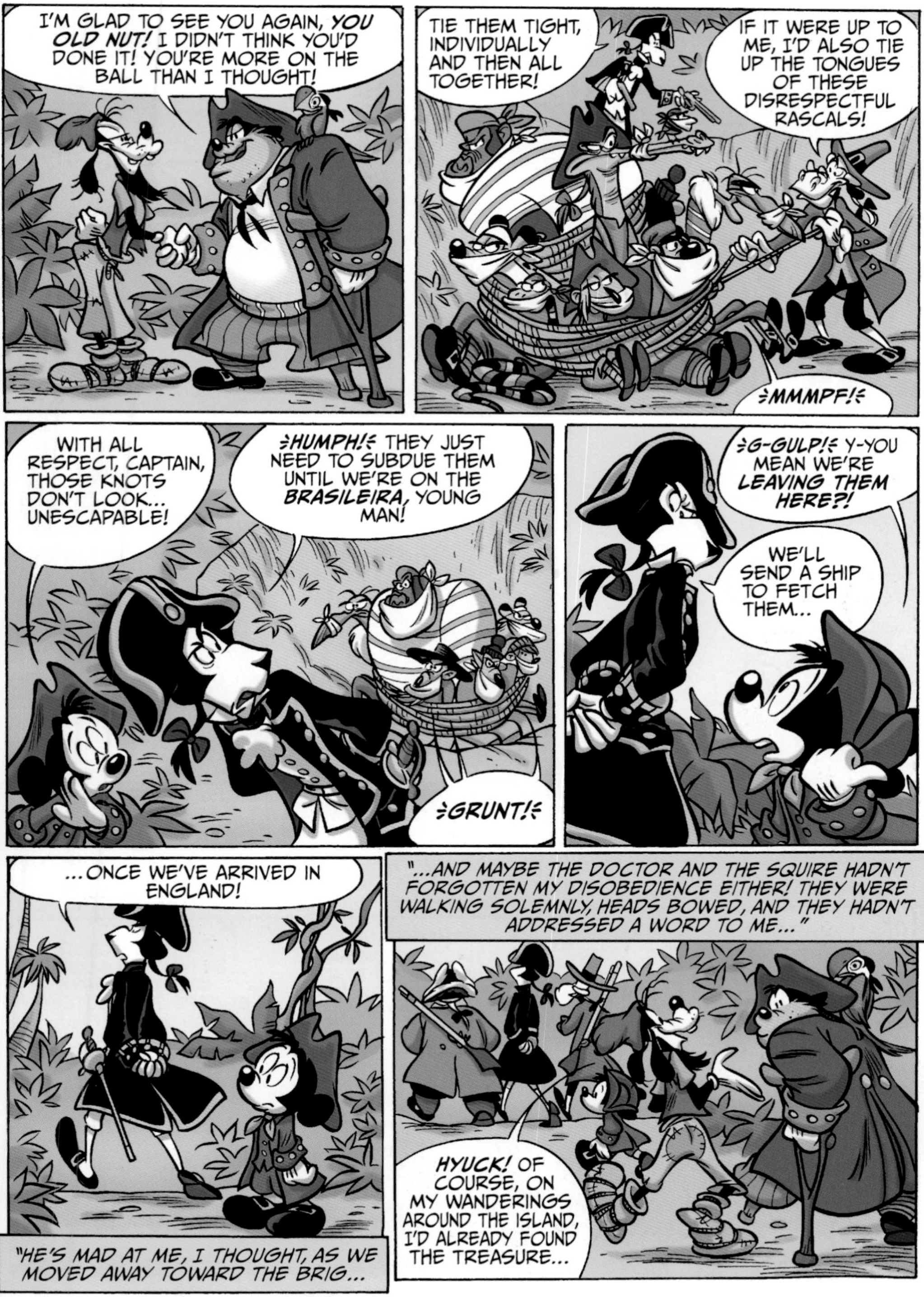
I'M GLAD TO SEE YOU AGAIN, YOU OLD NUT! I DIDN'T THINK YOU'D DONE IT! YOU'RE MORE ON THE BALL THAN I THOUGHT!
TIE THEM TIGHT, INDIVIDUALLY AND THEN ALL TOGETHER!
IF IT WERE UP TO ME, I'D ALSO TIE UP THE TONGUES OF THESE DISRESPECTFUL RASCALS!
MMMPF!
WITH ALL RESPECT, CAPTAIN, THOSE KNOTS DON'T LOOK... UNESCAPABLE!
HUMPH! THEY JUST NEED TO SUBDUE THEM UNTIL WE'RE ON THE BRASILEIRA, YOUNG MAN!
GRUNT!
G-GULP! Y-YOU MEAN WE'RE LEAVING THEM HERE?!
WE'LL SEND A SHIP TO FETCH THEM...
...ONCE WE'VE ARRIVED IN ENGLAND!
"HE'S MAD AT ME, I THOUGHT, AS WE MOVED AWAY TOWARD THE BRIG...
"...AND MAYBE THE DOCTOR AND THE SQUIRE HADN'T FORGOTTEN MY DISOBEDIENCE EITHER! THEY WERE WALKING SOLEMNLY, HEADS BOWED, AND THEY HADN'T ADDRESSED A WORD TO ME..."
HYUCK! OF COURSE, ON MY WANDERINGS AROUND THE ISLAND, I'D ALREADY FOUND THE TREASURE...

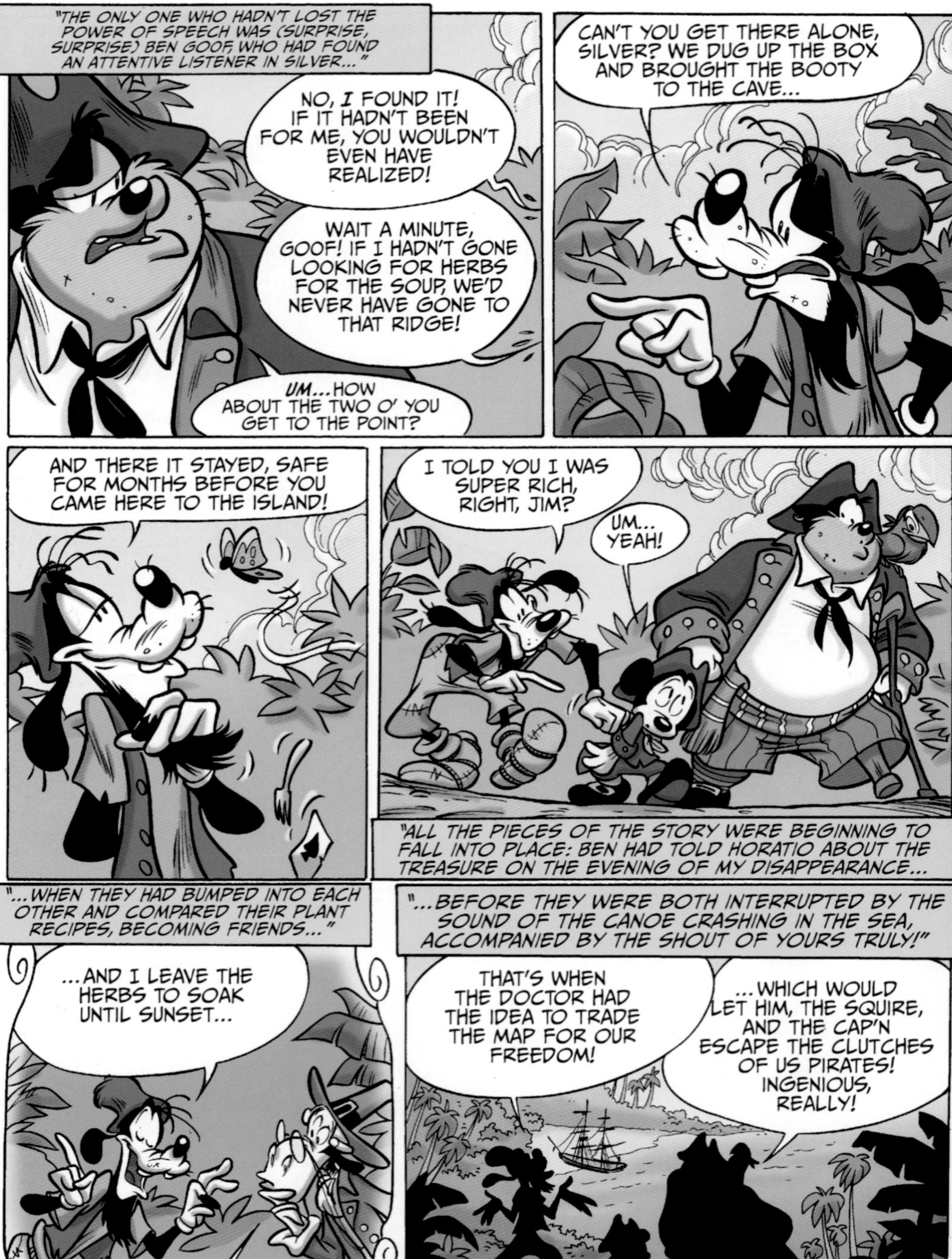
"THE ONLY ONE WHO HADN'T LOST THE POWER OF SPEECH WAS (SURPRISE, SURPRISE) BEN GOOF, WHO HAD FOUND AN ATTENTIVE LISTENER IN SILVER..."
NO, I FOUND IT! IF IT HADN'T BEEN FOR ME, YOU WOULDN'T EVEN HAVE REALIZED!
WAIT A MINUTE, GOOF! IF I HADN'T GONE LOOKING FOR HERBS FOR THE SOUP, WE'D NEVER HAVE GONE TO THAT RIDGE!
UM...HOW ABOUT THE TWO O' YOU GET TO THE POINT?
CAN'T YOU GET THERE ALONE, SILVER? WE DUG UP THE BOX AND BROUGHT THE BOOTY TO THE CAVE...
AND THERE IT STAYED, SAFE FOR MONTHS BEFORE YOU CAME HERE TO THE ISLAND!
I TOLD YOU I WAS SUPER RICH, RIGHT, JIM?
UM... YEAH!
"ALL THE PIECES OF THE STORY WERE BEGINNING TO FALL INTO PLACE: BEN HAD TOLD HORATIO ABOUT THE TREASURE ON THE EVENING OF MY DISAPPEARANCE...
"...WHEN THEY HAD BUMPED INTO EACH OTHER AND COMPARED THEIR PLANT RECIPES, BECOMING FRIENDS..."
...AND I LEAVE THE HERBS TO SOAK UNTIL SUNSET...
OH, INTERESTING!
"...BEFORE THEY WERE BOTH INTERRUPTED BY THE SOUND OF THE CANOE CRASHING IN THE SEA, ACCOMPANIED BY THE SHOUT OF YOURS TRULY!"
THAT'S WHEN THE DOCTOR HAD THE IDEA TO TRADE THE MAP FOR OUR FREEDOM!
...WHICH WOULD LET HIM, THE SQUIRE, AND THE CAP'N ESCAPE THE CLUTCHES OF US PIRATES! INGENIOUS, REALLY!

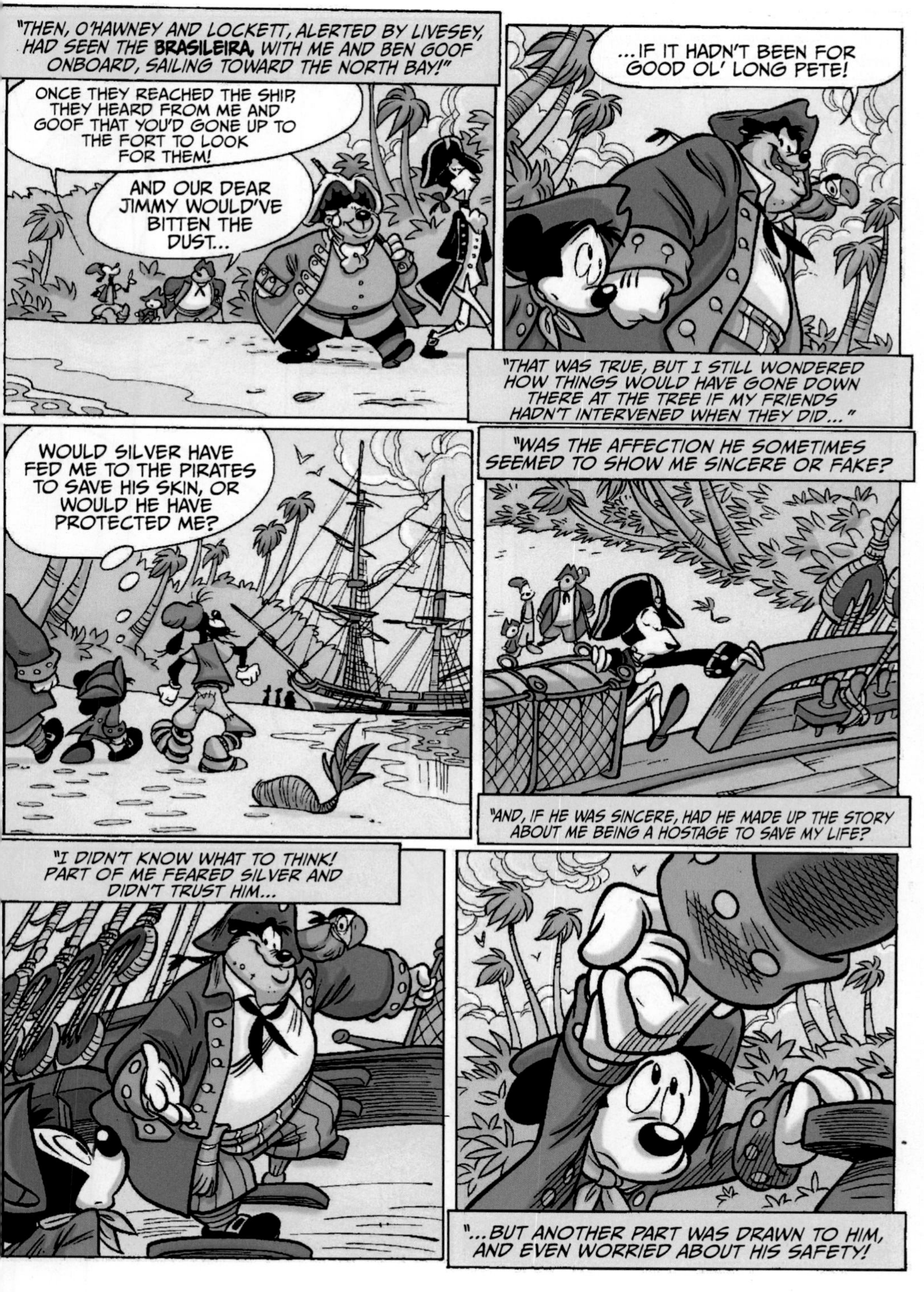
"THEN, O'HAWNEY AND LOCKETT, ALERTED BY LIVESEY, HAD SEEN THE BRASILEIRA, WITH ME AND BEN GOOF ONBOARD, SAILING TOWARD THE NORTH BAY!"
ONCE THEY REACHED THE SHIP, THEY HEARD FROM ME AND GOOF THAT YOU'D GONE UP TO THE FORT TO LOOK FOR THEM!
AND OUR DEAR JIMMY WOULD'VE BITTEN THE DUST...
...IF IT HADN'T BEEN FOR GOOD OL' LONG PETE!
"THAT WAS TRUE, BUT I STILL WONDERED HOW THINGS WOULD HAVE GONE DOWN THERE AT THE TREE IF MY FRIENDS HADN'T INTERVENED WHEN THEY DID..."
WOULD SILVER HAVE FED ME TO THE PIRATES TO SAVE HIS SKIN, OR WOULD HE HAVE PROTECTED ME?
"WAS THE AFFECTION HE SOMETIMES SEEMED TO SHOW ME SINCERE OR FAKE?
"AND, IF HE WAS SINCERE, HAD HE MADE UP THE STORY ABOUT ME BEING A HOSTAGE TO SAVE MY LIFE?
"I DIDN'T KNOW WHAT TO THINK! PART OF ME FEARED SILVER AND DIDN'T TRUST HIM...
"...BUT ANOTHER PART WAS DRAWN TO HIM, AND EVEN WORRIED ABOUT HIS SAFETY!

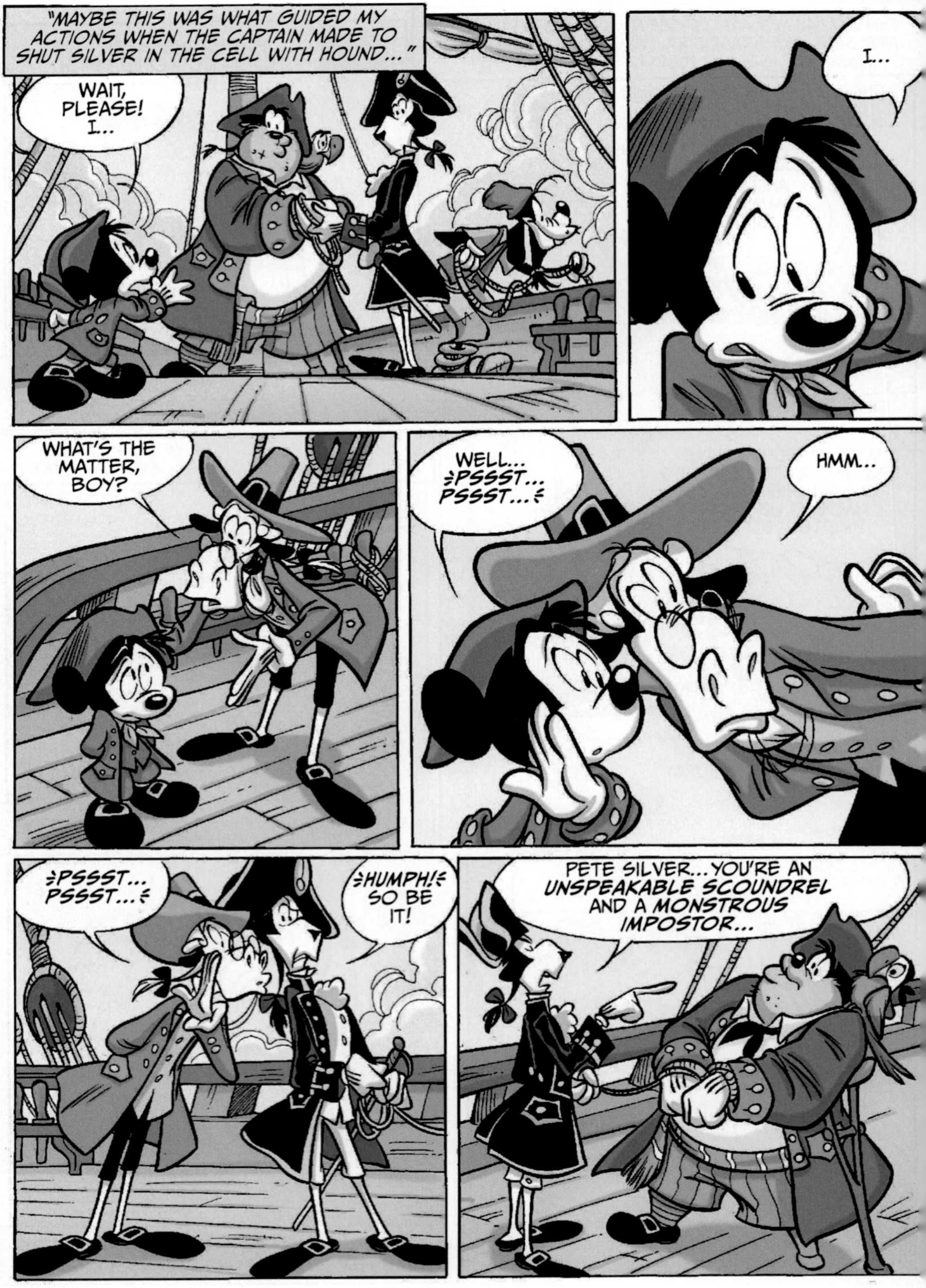
"MAYBE THIS WAS WHAT GUIDED MY ACTIONS WHEN THE CAPTAIN MADE TO SHUT SILVER IN THE CELL WITH HOUND..."
WAIT, PLEASE! I...
I...
WHAT'S THE MATTER, BOY?
WELL... PSSST... PSSST...
HMM...
PSSST... PSSST...
HUMPH! SO BE IT!
PETE SILVER... YOU'RE AN UNSPEAKABLE SCOUNDREL AND A MONSTROUS IMPOSTOR...

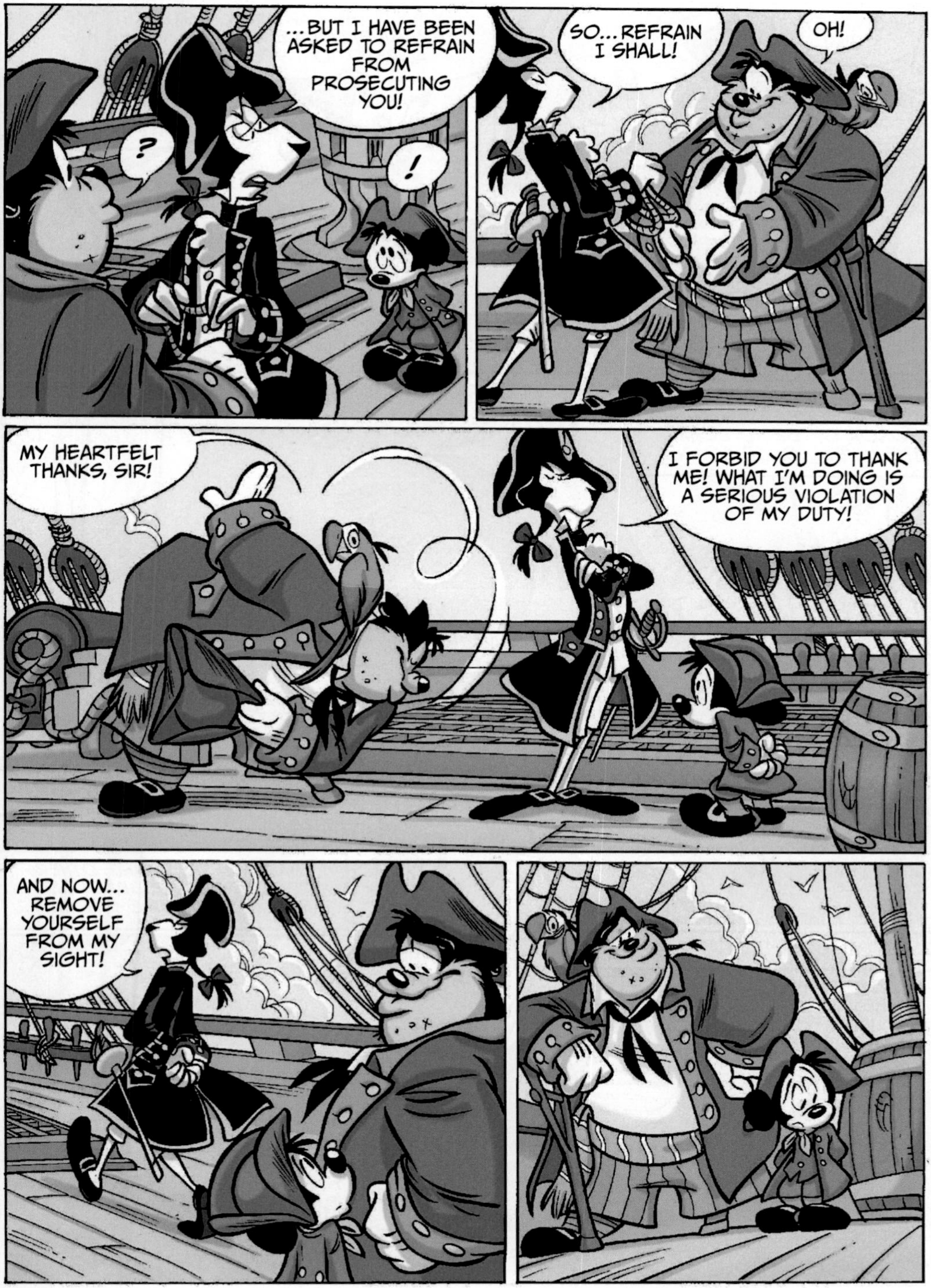

...BUT I HAVE BEEN ASKED TO REFRAIN FROM PROSECUTING YOU!
?
!
SO...REFRAIN I SHALL!
OH!
MY HEARTFELT THANKS, SIR!
I FORBID YOU TO THANK ME! WHAT I'M DOING IS A SERIOUS VIOLATION OF MY DUTY!
AND NOW... REMOVE YOURSELF FROM MY SIGHT!

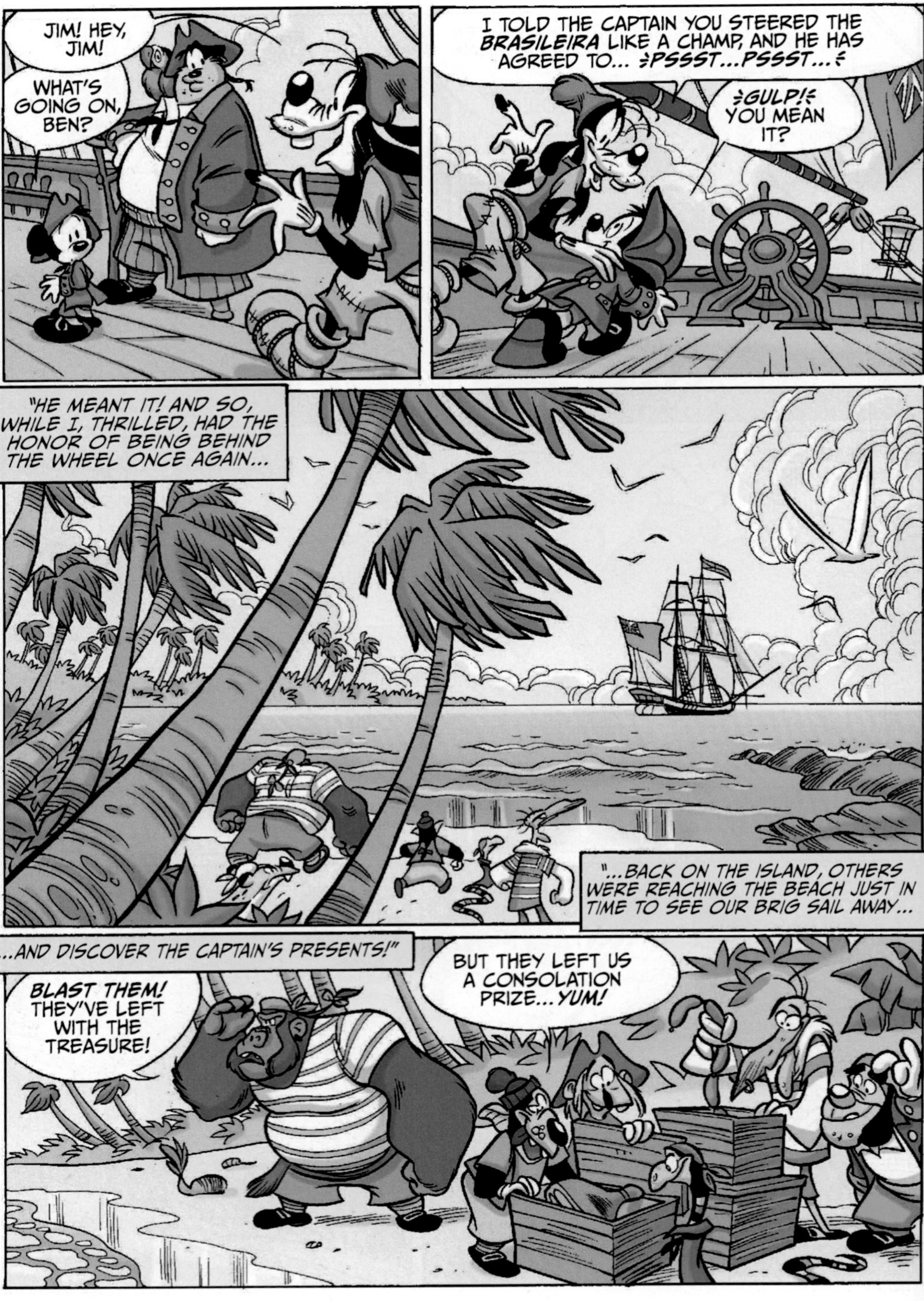

JIM! HEY, JIM!
WHAT'S GOING ON, BEN?
I TOLD THE CAPTAIN YOU STEERED THE BRASILEIRA LIKE A CHAMP, AND HE HAS AGREED TO... PSSST...PSSST...
GULP! YOU MEAN IT?
"HE MEANT IT! AND SO, WHILE I, THRILLED, HAD THE HONOR OF BEING BEHIND THE WHEEL ONCE AGAIN...
"...BACK ON THE ISLAND, OTHERS WERE REACHING THE BEACH JUST IN TIME TO SEE OUR BRIG SAIL AWAY...
"...AND DISCOVER THE CAPTAIN'S PRESENTS!"
BLAST THEM! THEY'VE LEFT WITH THE TREASURE!
BUT THEY LEFT US A CONSOLATION PRIZE... YUM!

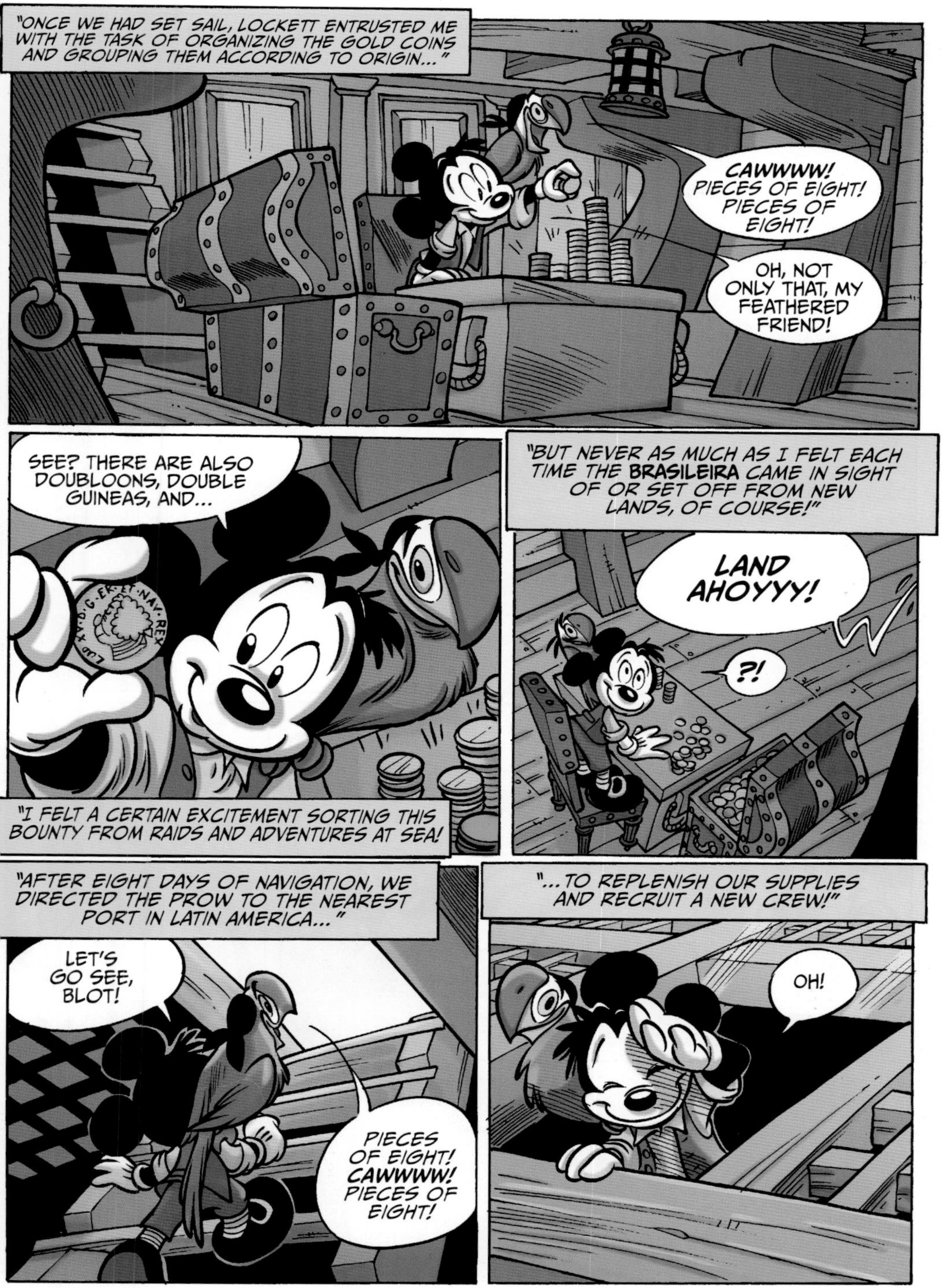
"ONCE WE HAD SET SAIL, LOCKETT ENTRUSTED ME WITH THE TASK OF ORGANIZING THE GOLD COINS AND GROUPING THEM ACCORDING TO ORIGIN..."
CAWWWW! PIECES OF EIGHT! PIECES OF EIGHT!
OH, NOT ONLY THAT, MY FEATHERED FRIEND!
SEE? THERE ARE ALSO DOUBLOONS, DOUBLE GUINEAS, AND...
"I FELT A CERTAIN EXCITEMENT SORTING THIS BOUNTY FROM RAIDS AND ADVENTURES AT SEA!
"BUT NEVER AS MUCH AS I FELT EACH TIME THE BRASILEIRA CAME IN SIGHT OF OR SET OFF FROM NEW LANDS, OF COURSE!"
LAND AHOYYY!
?!
"AFTER EIGHT DAYS OF NAVIGATION, WE DIRECTED THE PROW TO THE NEAREST PORT IN LATIN AMERICA..."
LET'S GO SEE, BLOT!
PIECES OF EIGHT! CAWWWW! PIECES OF EIGHT!
"...TO REPLENISH OUR SUPPLIES AND RECRUIT A NEW CREW!"
OH!

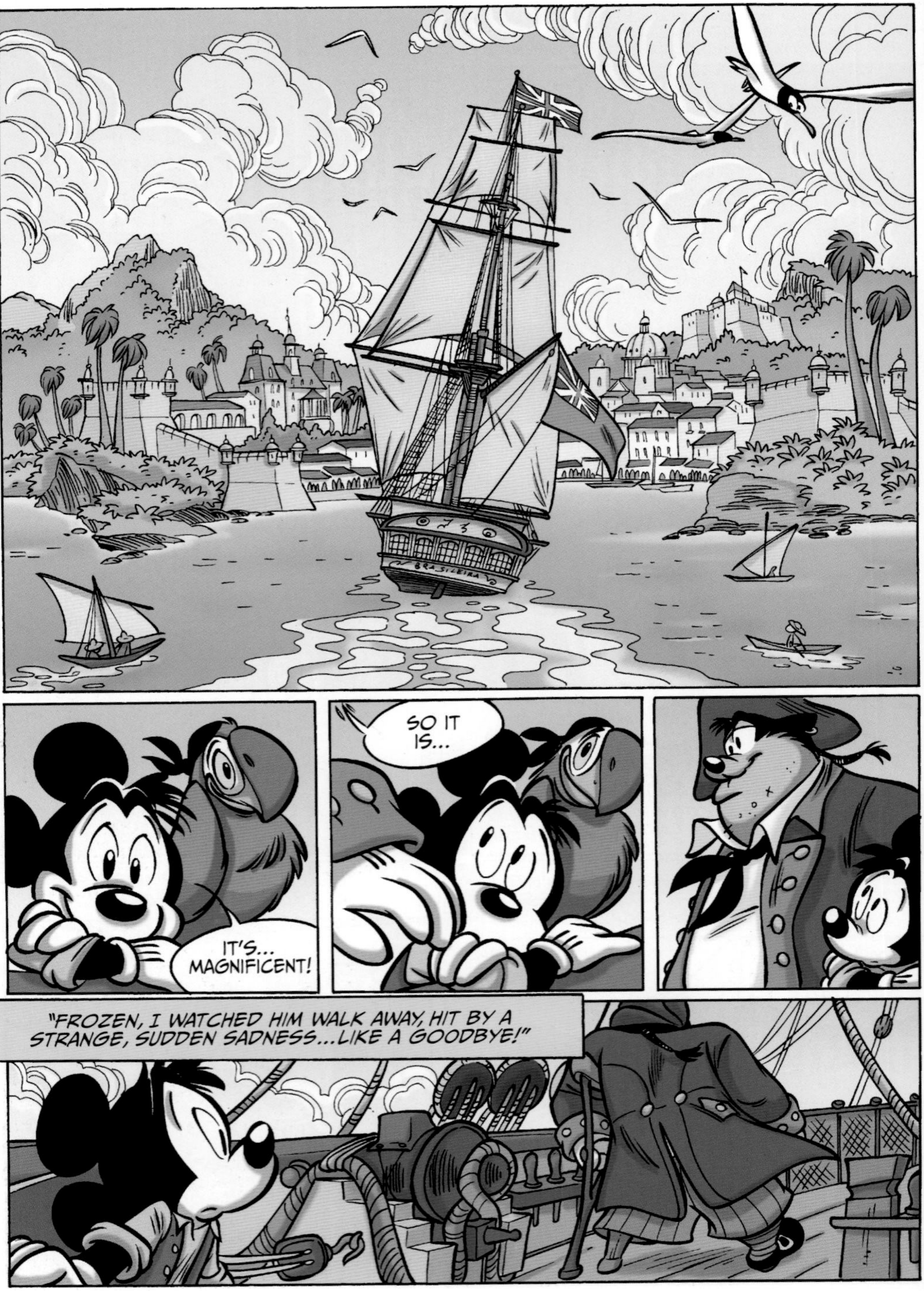
BRASILEIRA
IT'S... MAGNIFICENT!
SO IT IS...
"FROZEN, I WATCHED HIM WALK AWAY, HIT BY A STRANGE, SUDDEN SADNESS...LIKE A GOODBYE!"

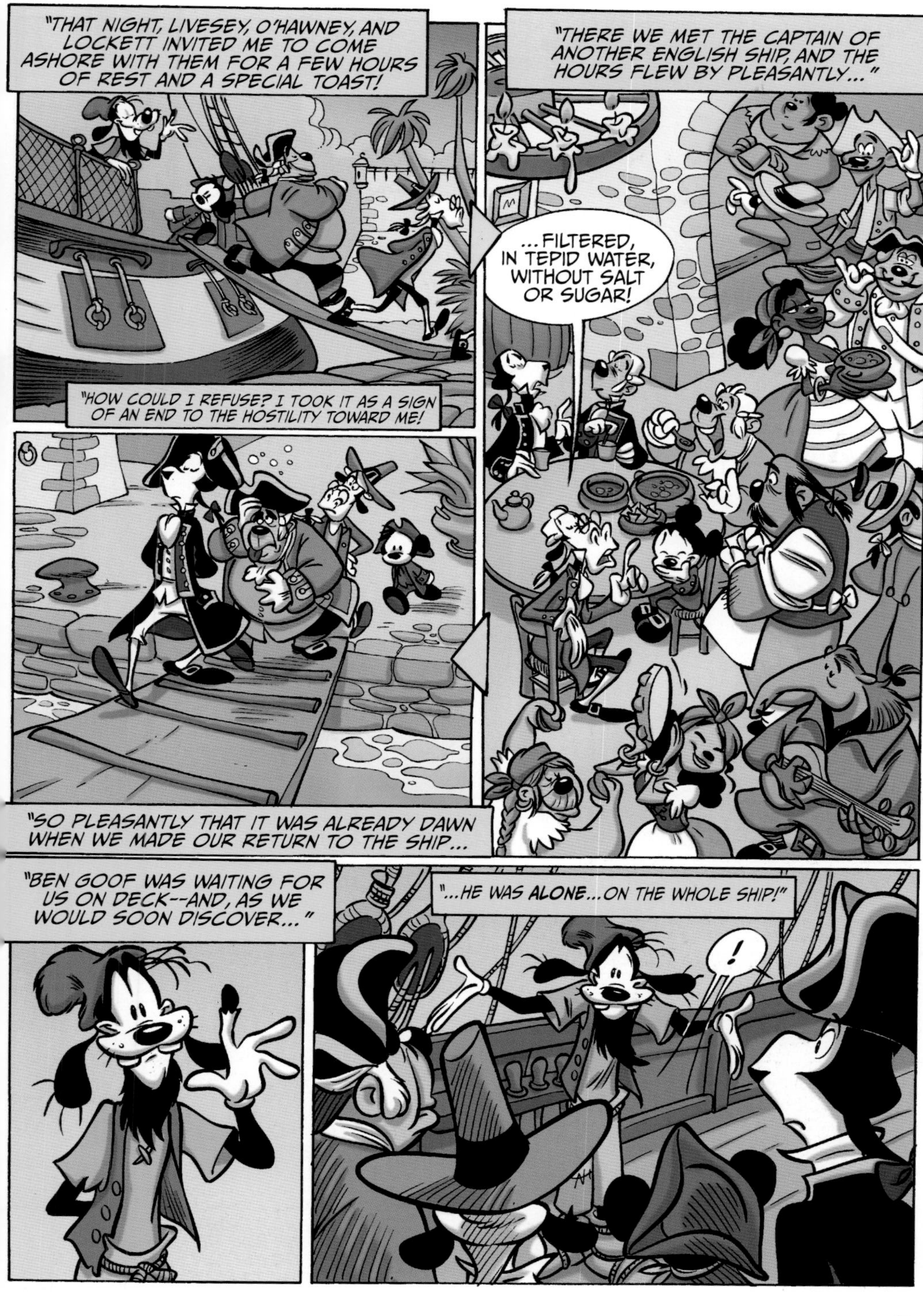
"THAT NIGHT, LIVESEY, O'HAWNEY, AND LOCKETT INVITED ME TO COME ASHORE WITH THEM FOR A FEW HOURS OF REST AND A SPECIAL TOAST!
"HOW COULD I REFUSE? I TOOK IT AS A SIGN OF AN END TO THE HOSTILITY TOWARD ME!
"THERE WE MET THE CAPTAIN OF ANOTHER ENGLISH SHIP, AND THE HOURS FLEW BY PLEASANTLY..."
...FILTERED, IN TEPID WATER, WITHOUT SALT OR SUGAR!
"SO PLEASANTLY THAT IT WAS ALREADY DAWN WHEN WE MADE OUR RETURN TO THE SHIP...
"BEN GOOF WAS WAITING FOR US ON DECK--AND, AS WE WOULD SOON DISCOVER..."
"...HE WAS ALONE...ON THE WHOLE SHIP!"
!

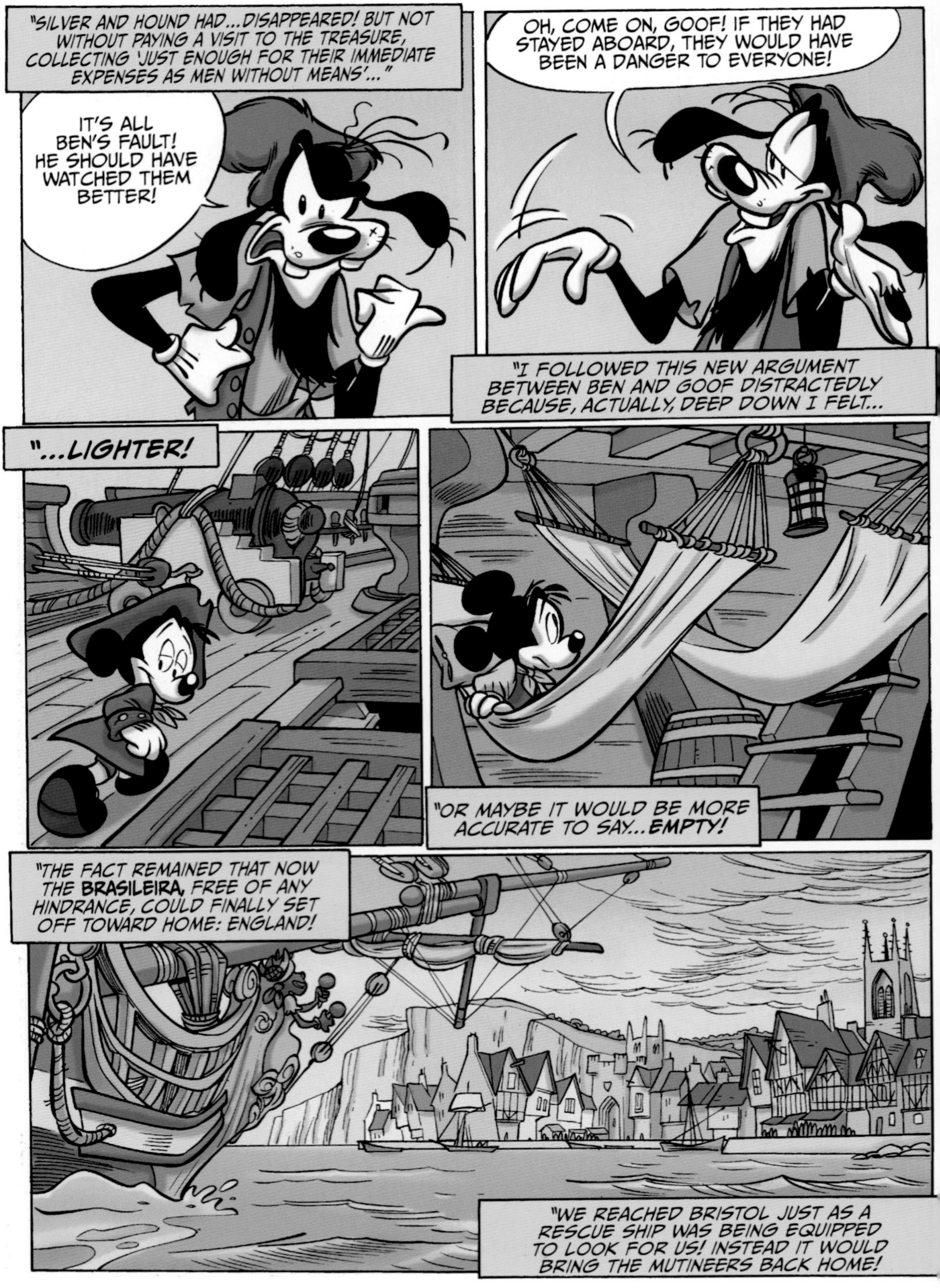
"SILVER AND HOUND HAD...DISAPPEARED! BUT NOT WITHOUT PAYING A VISIT TO THE TREASURE, COLLECTING 'JUST ENOUGH FOR THEIR IMMEDIATE EXPENSES AS MEN WITHOUT MEANS'..."
IT'S ALL BEN'S FAULT! HE SHOULD HAVE WATCHED THEM BETTER!
OH, COME ON, GOOF! IF THEY HAD STAYED ABOARD, THEY WOULD HAVE BEEN A DANGER TO EVERYONE!
"I FOLLOWED THIS NEW ARGUMENT BETWEEN BEN AND GOOF DISTRACTEDLY BECAUSE, ACTUALLY, DEEP DOWN I FELT...
"...LIGHTER!
"OR MAYBE IT WOULD BE MORE ACCURATE TO SAY...EMPTY!
"THE FACT REMAINED THAT NOW THE BRASILEIRA, FREE OF ANY HINDRANCE, COULD FINALLY SET OFF TOWARD HOME: ENGLAND!
"WE REACHED BRISTOL JUST AS A RESCUE SHIP WAS BEING EQUIPPED TO LOOK FOR US! INSTEAD IT WOULD BRING THE MUTINEERS BACK HOME!

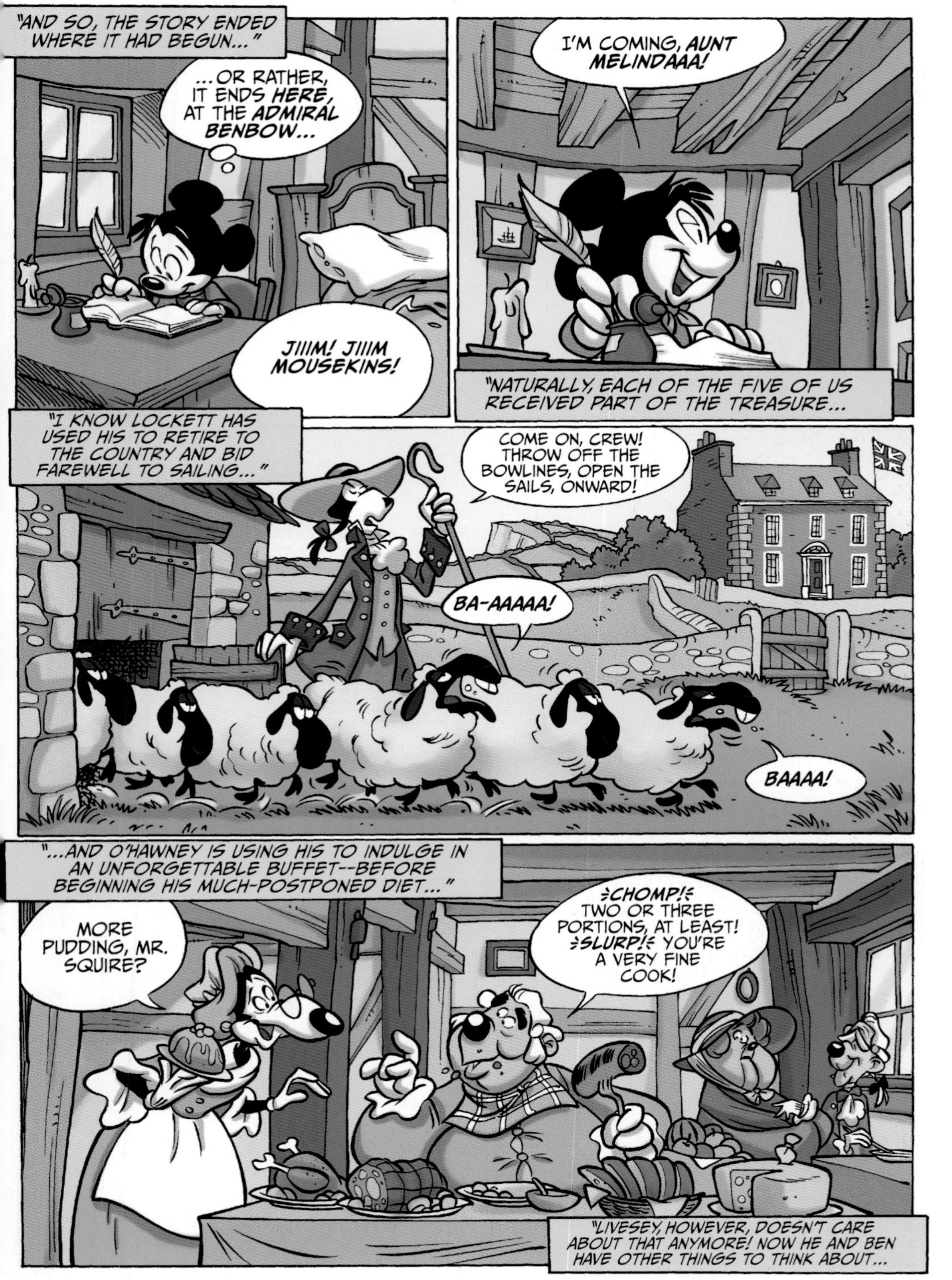
"AND SO, THE STORY ENDED WHERE IT HAD BEGUN..."
...OR RATHER, IT ENDS HERE, AT THE ADMIRAL BENBOW...
JIIIM! JIIIM MOUSEKINS!
I'M COMING, AUNT MELINDAAA!
"NATURALLY, EACH OF THE FIVE OF US RECEIVED PART OF THE TREASURE...
"I KNOW LOCKETT HAS USED HIS TO RETIRE TO THE COUNTRY AND BID FAREWELL TO SAILING..."
COME ON, CREW! THROW OFF THE BOWLINES, OPEN THE SAILS, ONWARD!
BA-AAAAA!
BAAAA!
"...AND O'HAWNEY IS USING HIS TO INDULGE IN AN UNFORGETTABLE BUFFET--BEFORE BEGINNING HIS MUCH-POSTPONED DIET..."
MORE PUDDING, MR. SQUIRE?
CHOMP! TWO OR THREE PORTIONS, AT LEAST! SLURP! YOU'RE A VERY FINE COOK!
"LIVESEY, HOWEVER, DOESN'T CARE ABOUT THAT ANYMORE! NOW HE AND BEN HAVE OTHER THINGS TO THINK ABOUT...

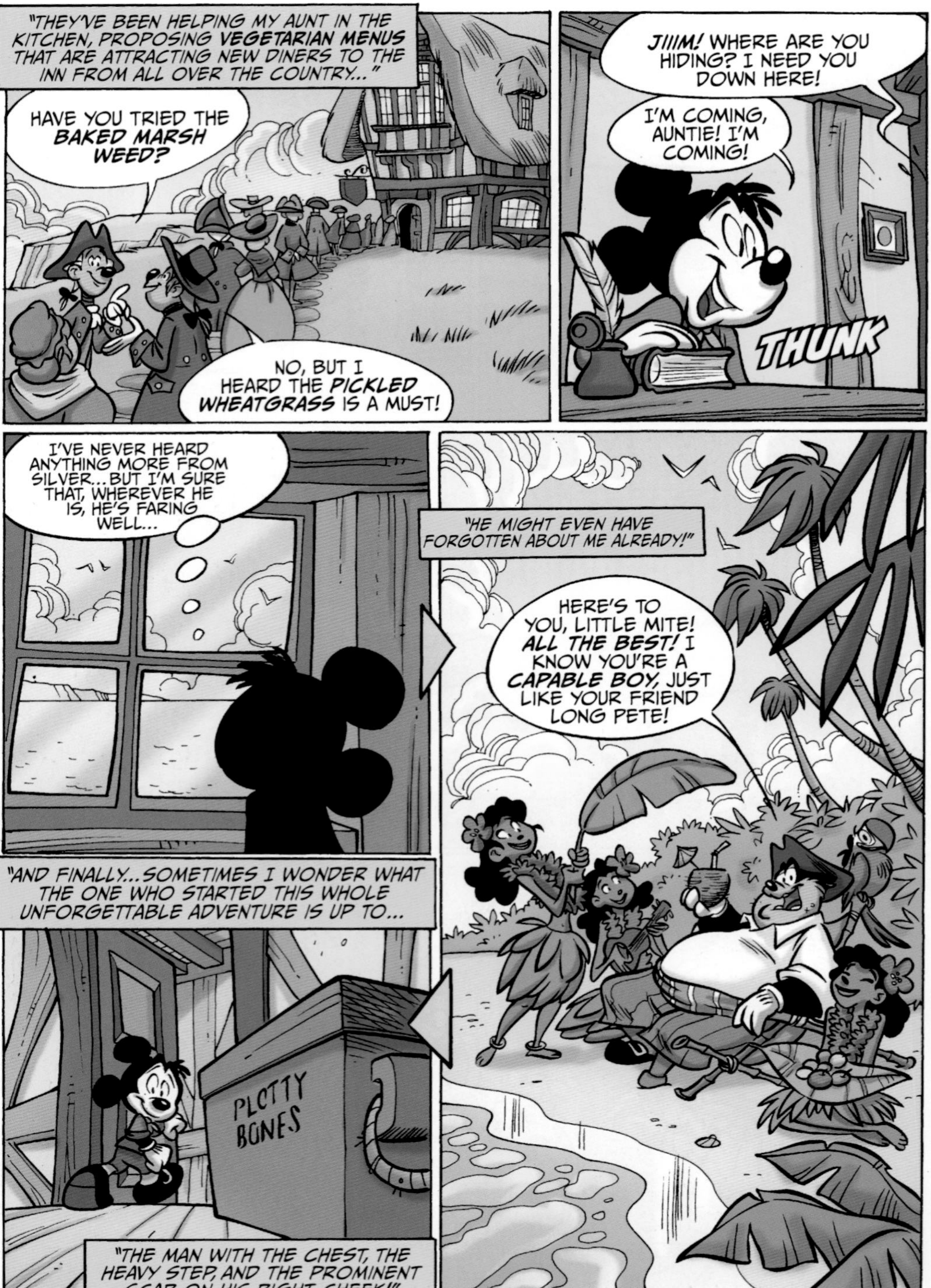
"THEY'VE BEEN HELPING MY AUNT IN THE KITCHEN, PROPOSING VEGETARIAN MENUS THAT ARE ATTRACTING NEW DINERS TO THE INN FROM ALL OVER THE COUNTRY..."
HAVE YOU TRIED THE BAKED MARSH WEED?
NO, BUT I HEARD THE PICKLED WHEATGRASS IS A MUST!
JIIIM! WHERE ARE YOU HIDING? I NEED YOU DOWN HERE!
I'M COMING, AUNTIE! I'M COMING!
THUNK
I'VE NEVER HEARD ANYTHING MORE FROM SILVER... BUT I'M SURE THAT, WHEREVER HE IS, HE'S FARING WELL...
"HE MIGHT EVEN HAVE FORGOTTEN ABOUT ME ALREADY!"
HERE'S TO YOU, LITTLE MITE! ALL THE BEST! I KNOW YOU'RE A CAPABLE BOY, JUST LIKE YOUR FRIEND LONG PETE!
"AND FINALLY... SOMETIMES I WONDER WHAT THE ONE WHO STARTED THIS WHOLE UNFORGETTABLE ADVENTURE IS UP TO...
PLOTTY BONES
"THE MAN WITH THE CHEST, THE HEAVY STEP, AND THE PROMINENT SCAR ON HIS RIGHT CHEEK!"

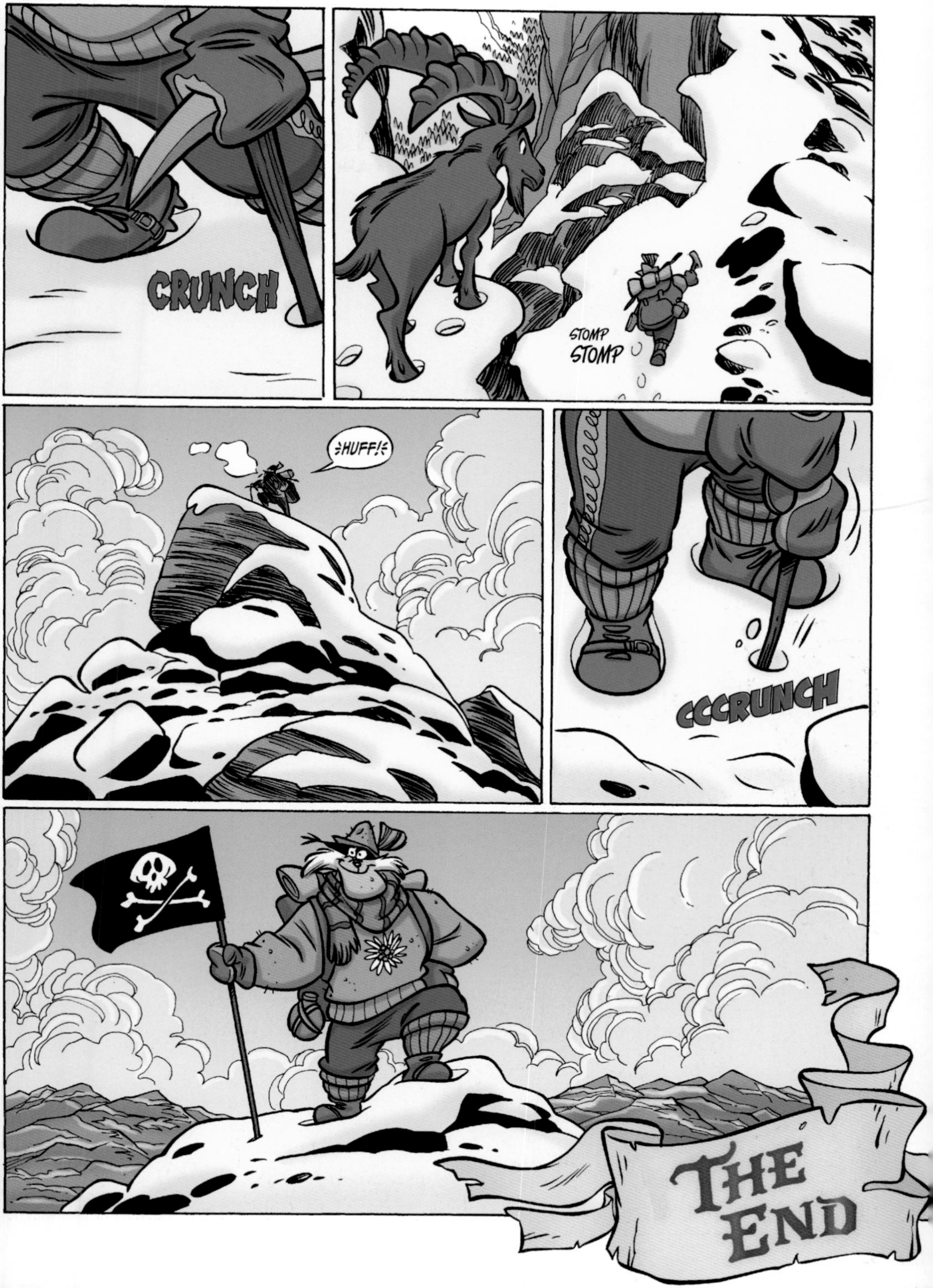
CRUNCH
STOMP
STOMP
HUFF!
CCCRUNCH
THE END

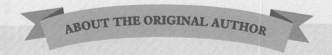

ABOUT THE ORIGINAL AUTHOR

ROBERT LOUIS STEVENSON

(1850–1894)

Robert Louis Stevenson was a Scottish writer in the nineteenth century. He is most well-known for his novels, such as *Treasure Island*, *Kidnapped*, and *Strange Case of Dr. Jekyll and Mr. Hyde*. Many of his works are now considered classics of literature and have been translated for the whole world to enjoy.

Stevenson was born on November 13, 1850, in Edinburgh, Scotland. He was the only son of Margaret Isabella Balfour and Thomas Stevenson, a civil engineer. He always had an interest in writing and knew from an early age that he wanted to become a writer. At the age of twenty-eight, Stevenson published his first book.

Treasure Island, Stevenson's most popular novel, was written in 1883. His idea for the story began with a map he had drawn for his stepson; he decided to create a pirate adventure based on the map, and *Treasure Island* was born.

Most of Stevenson's life was spent travelling and his writing drew much inspiration from the places he visited. Early in his life, he had traveled the European mainland, where he connected with other artists and writers. He spent the later years of his life in the South Seas and finally settled down in Samoa. During his time in the South Sea islands, he learned about the local cultures and the inhabitants, and he became very familiar with the landscapes and atmosphere. All of this experience helped him to create stories, poems, essays, and other works throughout his career.

Stevenson's stories often explored the human condition, while weaving in adventure, romance, irony, horror, and suspense. To this day, his stories are admired all over the world.

Donald, Scrooge, and the whole crew face the monsters of the deep!

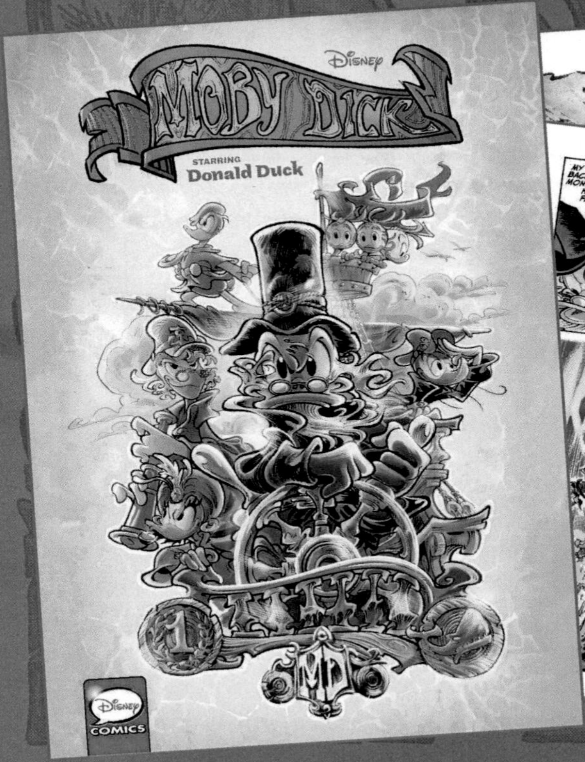
DISNEY
MOBY DICK
STARRING
Donald Duck

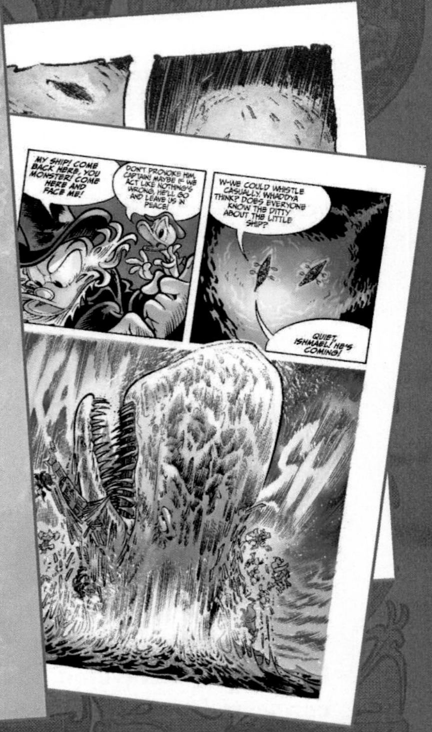
MY SHIP! COME BACK HERE, YOU MONSTER! COME HERE AND FACE ME!
DON'T PROVOKE HIM, CAPTAIN! MAYBE IF WE ACT LIKE NOTHING'S WRONG, HE'LL GO AND LEAVE US IN PEACE!
W-WE COULD WHISTLE CASUALLY. WHADD'YA THINK? DOES EVERYONE KNOW THE DITTY ABOUT THE LITTLE SHIP?
QUIET, ISHMAEL! HE'S COMING!

Disney Moby Dick, starring Donald Duck

In an adaptation of Herman Melville's classic, Scrooge McDuck, Donald, and nephews venture out on the high seas in pursuit of the white whale Moby Dick who stole Captain Quackhab's lucky dime. As Quackhab scours the ocean in pursuit of his nemesis, facing other dangers of the sea, the crew begin to wonder: how far will their captain go for revenge?

ISBN 978-1-50671-157-7 ❁ $10.99

DARK HORSE BOOKS

AVAILABLE AT YOUR LOCAL COMICS SHOP OR BOOKSTORE! To find a comics shop in your area, visit comicshoplocator.com. For more information or to order direct: On the web: DarkHorse.com Email: mailorder@darkhorse.com Phone: 1-800-862-0052 Mon.–Fri. 9 AM to 5 PM Pacific Time

DISNEY COMICS

Books that Middle Readers will Love!

Glister | Andi Watson

Strange things happen around Glister Butterworth. A young girl living on her family's English estate, Glister has unusual adventures every day, like the arrival of a teapot haunted by a demanding ghost, a crop of new relatives blooming on the family tree, a stubborn house that walks off its land in a huff, and a trip to Faerieland to find her missing mother.

ISBN 978-1-50670-319-0 $14.99

Tree Mail | Mike Raicht, Brian Smith

Rudy—a determined frog—hopes to overcome the odds and land his dream job delivering mail to the other animals on Popomoko Island! Rudy always hops forward, no matter what obstacle seems to be in the way of his dreams!

ISBN 978-1-50670-096-0 $12.99

Poppy! and the Lost Lagoon | Matt Kindt, Brian Hurtt

At the age of ten, Poppy Pepperton is the greatest explorer since her grandfather Pappy! When a shrunken mummy head speaks, adventure calls Poppy and her sidekick/guardian, Colt Winchester, across the globe in search of an exotic fish—along the way discovering clues to what happened to Pappy all those years ago!

ISBN 978-1-61655-943-4 $14.99

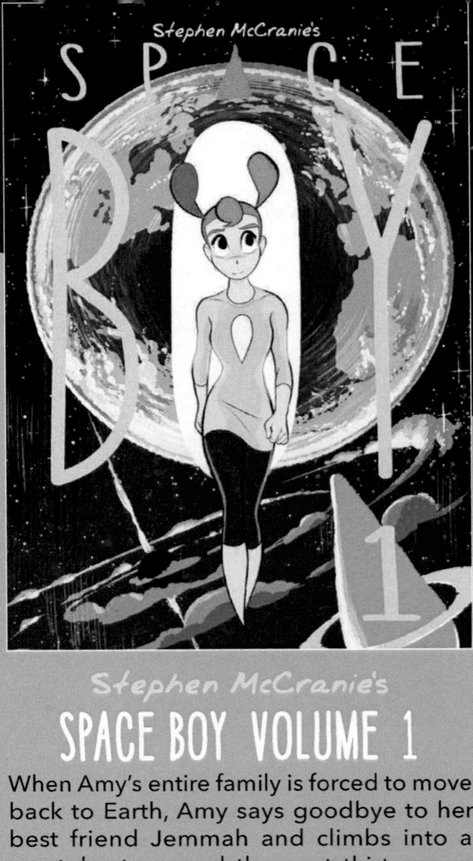
Stephen McCranie's
SPACE
BOY
1

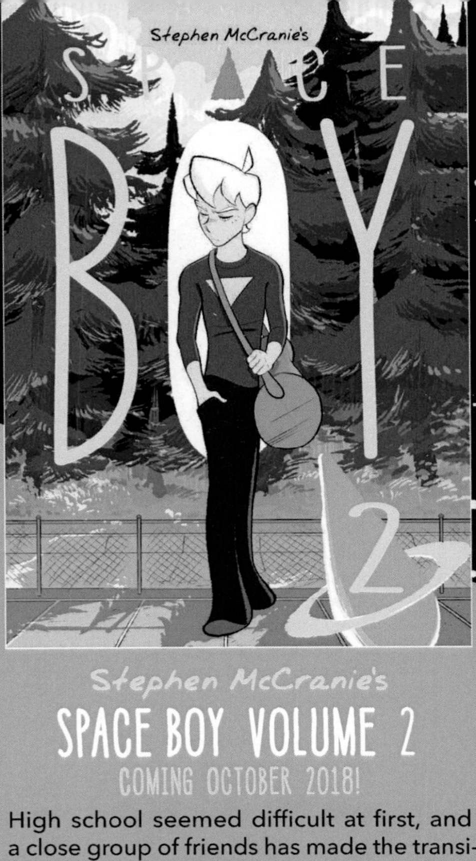
Stephen McCranie's
SPACE
BOY
2

Stephen McCranie's

SPACE BOY VOLUME 1

When Amy's entire family is forced to move back to Earth, Amy says goodbye to her best friend Jemmah and climbs into a cryotube to spend the next thirty years frozen in suspended animation, heading toward her new home. Her life will never be the same . . . and Jemmah is going to grow up without her.

ISBN 978-1-50670-648-1 $10.99

Stephen McCranie's

SPACE BOY VOLUME 2

COMING OCTOBER 2018!

High school seemed difficult at first, and a close group of friends has made the transition to Earth easier for Amy, but now she finds herself falling down a rabbit hole in her relationship with Oliver—the boy with no flavor.

ISBN 978-1-50670-680-1 $10.99

Available at your local comics shop or bookstore! To find a comics shop in your area, visit comicshoplocator.com

"TRULY ONE OF THE MOST THOUGHTFUL EXAMPLES I'VE EVER SEEN OF A TEENAGED GIRL IN FICTION."

—NARRATIVE INVESTIGATIONS

For more information or to order direct:
on the web DarkHorse.com
email mailorder@darkhorse.com
phone 1-800-862-0052
Mon.–Fri. 9 AM to 5 PM Pacific Time